W9-ALK-138

PRAISE FOR *THE PRACTICE HOUSE*

"A stunning, pitch-perfect tale of a star-crossed, Depression-era love triangle. National Book Award finalist Laura McNeal is a magnificent writer."

—Lily King, author of *Euphoria*

THE
PRACTICE HOUSE

THE
PRACTICE HOUSE

A NOVEL

LAURA McNEAL

Published by Little A, New York

www.apub.com

Amazon, the Amazon logo, and Little A are trademarks of Amazon.com, Inc., or its affiliates.

ISBN-10 (hardcover): 1477817905
ISBN-13 (hardcover): 9781477817902

ISBN-10 (paperback): 1503937259
ISBN-13 (paperback): 9781503937253

Cover design by Rachel Adam Rogers

Printed in the United States of America

For Tom
Meum et Tuum

PART ONE

1

On the April day when the Americans mounted the stone steps and pushed the door buzzer, rain had fallen for eleven of the last eleven days, and Aldine McKenna was waiting, metaphorically speaking, for her Japanese man. She and her sister, Eileen, were stuck as usual in Aunt Sedge's house on Bellevue Crescent. The house was bigger than their father's had been, and much closer to the shops in Ayr, but Aunt Sedge watched over them more—"As I promised your poor father," she would say until Aldine thought she might scream. Even when Sedge went to visit a friend, she left a list of chores a mile long and told the neighbors to keep an eye out, which really meant *spy*, didn't it?

Aunt Sedge was Charity Sedgewick McKenna, their father's sister, older by nine years and his opposite in every way. When going out, she always wore a fascinator or a small rakish hat, gloves, and whichever animal-shaped brooch matched the fascinator. She had no children of her own and had tried to host the girls weekly when they were little, planning a different cultural outing every Saturday, but her ideas of fun were confining and dull: when they were four and five, she wanted them to go with her to hear chamber music, but they kicked their legs and sighed too often. Their mother told Aunt Sedge—no one ever called her Charity—that perhaps she should just try to have fun with the girls, so Sedge planned a tea party with all of her old bears and dolls sitting around a child's antique table. Although it was a delicious tea, with three different kinds of flower-topped bakery cakes, including orange spice with four layers of the creamiest white frosting Aldine had ever tasted, Aldine and Leenie felt silly and self-conscious, because those bears and dolls belonged to a grown person and thus couldn't possibly be alive. Adding to the awkwardness was the fact that a Japanese man sat in the corner the whole time, smiling grimly, never saying a word, just nodding now and then. Later, their father said the Japanese man was Aunt Sedge's true love and he had come to see if she would marry him and go live in Japan, but Sedge had said no, for some reason. Perhaps it was too late for her, their father said. This had made a deep impression on both girls, and the efforts of Charity Sedgewick to keep Aldine and Leenie, now nineteen and twenty, from falling in love at the wrong time with the wrong person and their fear of waiting until it was too late made for a combustible situation.

Leenie was the most childlike but also the most dutiful. She had cut up beef for the pie and hung wash over the Aga, two things on Sedge's chore list, and now she was knitting, which had a calming effect on some souls, but not Leenie's. It made her peevish, complaining that Aldine had not even started her share, which was true. Aldine was drinking, as she always drank, overly sweetened Fortnum's tea. It was 4:30. "Half past nothing," their father used to joke, "half till nothing more."

No man had come close to courting Aldine in a year at least unless you counted old Dr. O'Malley. She'd expected to be quizzed about her mathematical skills when she went in for the job but the doctor didn't follow this line at all. "You're the one who sang Mendelssohn in church, are you not?" he'd asked, a surprising question because it had been a while, months, perhaps even a year. "'Wings of a Dove,' wasn't it?" She said aye, she'd been the one, and he'd asked no other questions, but just nodded and said, "Right then," and left the room. She wasn't sure she'd been hired until his nurse, Mrs. Terlip, told her so. Aldine liked the work. The sums weren't difficult to add and sort, and Dr. O'Malley liked to keep the rooms warm. He talked pleasantly to everyone, old, young, rich, poor, and when no one was near, he hummed tunelessly with a funny little smile on his face, his way of thinking, or so she supposed.

In his office late one winter's afternoon, when the clients were gone, and Mrs. Terlip, too (to Leenie, Aldine referred to the woman as *Mrs. Turnip*), and already the light was seeping away, the doctor had taken her arm and run his ancient fingers along the underside of her wrist and said in a low, gentle voice, "The smooth-skinned girl," which made her draw her arm away, though she smiled so as not to offend him. When the following day he gave her a set of Bakelite bracelets and said he hoped she "took no offense," she'd presumed he was talking about his earlier remark and said, "No offense taken at all, I'm sure," and, having slipped the bracelets over her hand, she was surprised by the small but actual thrill that passed through her when she presented her wrist for him to admire. The old doctor was alone, after all, and she understood the wretchedness of that.

Aldine stared at Aunt Sedge's Japanese lithograph of a huge white-fingered wave about to crush a fishing boat and thought of the Japanese man. Was he still pining for Charity Sedgewick? Did her aunt think of him when she went to bed every night alone? Is that why she had this tragic picture on her wall, where the water seemed to reach down like claws to destroy the tiny bareheaded men bowed down in the boat?

She was down to the last swallow of her second cup, the dregs of which she would sometimes, if she were alone, touch with the tip of her tongue like an anteater, when she heard the door buzzer. God, it was an irritating sound—like you were treating someone to electric shocks—but through the side window she saw two men in three-piece suits and homburgs and that seemed like fun beginning.

"It's men," she told Leenie.

Leenie was studying the knitting chart so she hardly looked up. "What men?" She had George Prendergast, anyway. Such as he was. Sedge had never met him and Leenie always insisted he was just a passing thing, not a type strong enough to imprint—*imprint* being the word Sedgewick sometimes used for seduction, as if they were baby geese.

"Strange men," Aldine said. She checked her hair in the hall mirror and thought that even if they were selling something it would be a change.

"Pretend we're not home."

But of course Aldine went to the door.

The men were, as she'd hoped, young. One was homely and the other was starkly not. The tall one had very arresting sea-gray eyes, dark hair that curled in spite of how short it was cut, and a very kissable forehead. "I'm Elder Cooper," he said in an American voice, "and this is Elder Lance."

"Charmed," Aldine said, but she didn't shake hands because a tradesman was waiting on Mrs. Nith's front step and looking over now and then, tilting his black umbrella.

Elder Lance had an upturned nose, which leaked in the cold, and his teeth, what he showed of them when he tried to smile, were faintly gingery like his hair and freckles. Both men were wearing cloth gloves and holding books within the shelter of their umbrellas, and their coats were clean but of poor fit and quality.

"And what would you be elders of?" Aldine asked just as Leenie said, from the parlor, "Oh, you wooly piece of shit!"

Elder Cooper colored slightly. "We're not selling anything," he said, "if that's what's worrying your . . ."

"That's just my sister," Aldine said, "and she doesn't mean you."

Leenie came up behind her. "This here's Elder Cooper," Aldine said. "And that one's Elder Lance."

Aldine knew that now she was the one being compared. Since earliest childhood Aldine had drawn pictures of herself with straight lines—her straight brown hair, her too-long legs, her too-long neck and arms, and she had very little bosom besides—whereas pictures of her sister, had she drawn them, would've flown from pleasing sweeps to curves. Leenie had gotten her full share of buxomness and Aldine's besides, and if that were not enough, Leenie's hair got all the curl.

Aldine could feel Leenie's irritation, so she added, "Not sure what the elder part means yet."

"We're from the Church of Jesus Christ of Latter-day Saints," Elder Forehead said in a rush, as if he expected them to step back and shut the door. His umbrella was too large to fit next to his companion's, so the other man stood a step behind, and rain flowed down the metal tips of their umbrella spokes and splashed on pink stones that were so wet the men might have been statues standing in a fountain. "We have a message to share with you."

Leenie gave out a laugh that sounded frisky, to Aldine's surprise. "Did you not announce you weren't selling anything?"

The ginger one held his umbrella tightly and said, "We're *not* selling anything," and Elder Forehead jumped in with, "We're here because we have something to give."

Aldine almost laughed at that. What, she would later wonder while smoking cigarettes in a poorly insulated Kansas schoolhouse, would have happened to her and Leenie if the men had not seemed so comically earnest, like a pair of stray dogs? Was Elder Cooper the right man or the wrong man if you applied the Allegory of the Japanese Man?

Aldine checked the street (no one was passing and Mrs. Nith's visitor had gone in) and said, "It's Baltic out. Would you care for tea?"

2

Leenie thought Aldine would send them packing, so she was as shocked as the men were when Aldine asked them in.

"Are you alone here?" the good-looking one asked.

"Oh, no," Leenie said, because she didn't want them to think they were defenseless. "We live with our aunt."

"Shall we introduce ourselves?" Elder Forehead asked.

"She's very reclusive," Aldine said, and Leenie almost laughed.

There were open jars of Silver and Golden Shred on the tray in the living room—lemon marmalade for Aldine, orange for Leenie. Empty cups and crumbs making it obvious tea was already over, and that only two of them had been drinking it, but no one brought up the aunt again.

The ginger boy tugged off his gloves, laid them on the sofa, then must have seen—as Leenie had—the dark spot where he'd been touching the glove to his runny nose, because at once he turned them over. Leenie decided it was Aldine's monkey pile—Aldine asked them in; she could entertain them—so she settled herself on the pink velvet sofa beneath the stilled curl of the Japanese wave and picked up the chart for the sweater that was driving her insane. Aldine took the hint and carried the teapot to the kitchen to refill.

"Knitting?" the ginger one asked.

Leenie nodded. *Obviously,* she refrained from adding. But then the other one, Cooper, started talking, and he had a way about him.

"Are you twins?" Cooper asked her. He leaned forward, elbows on knees. "Leenie, right?" Later she would learn that he often sat that way when talking to people, giving them his full attention.

"Yes, as in Eileen. We're not twins, though. I'm the eldest. Can't you tell?"

He shook his head. "Do you have any other brothers and sisters?"

"Nay."

A slight pause, not at all awkward. The rain running down the window glass and thudding on the roof. The room warmer because he was in it.

"What are you knitting?"

"A jumper. It's for myself because it'd be cruel to make anyone wear a thing that I knitted."

"I think it looks nice. I'd wear it." His smile was large and unforced. He had such unspoiled teeth and a small, humble-seeming crinkle around the eyes when he grinned.

"Oh, I doubt that, but thanks. What about you? Do you have brothers and sisters?"

"Yes," he said. "Four. A brother that's fifteen and three younger sisters."

"How lucky!" Leenie said. "I love big families." She realized she hadn't asked the ginger one anything and he was just staring around the room. "And you? Do you have a giant family also?"

"I have two younger brothers," he said.

"And where are they?"

"Kansas. That's where my family lives."

"What's that like? Kansas?"

"A lot drier than this," he said.

Before Aldine even came back with a fresh pot and scones and butter and smoked venison sandwiches, Leenie had decided she liked them both, but especially Cooper. He was so boyish and clean seeming, as if he'd been carved from a bar of soap and brought to life. It was hard going, though, when the preaching started. Leenie tried not to look horrified when Cooper stopped grinning and became very serious and said he wanted to tell them about a fifteen-year-old boy who saw two angel-people hovering above him in the woods.

As Cooper spoke—Joseph Smith this, Joseph Smith that—Leenie hoped he couldn't tell that she was pondering his forehead and his sea-water eyes and that she was wishing he would stop preaching and start talking about home or anything at all besides revelations. When Cooper said Joseph Smith prayed for wisdom, Leenie nodded stiffly. He then told quite a long story about how God appeared to Joseph in what Cooper seemed to be calling a pillow of light.

To avoid commenting on something so outlandish, Leenie asked, "More tea?" even though their cups were still full.

"I'm sorry. We can't," Cooper said.

"What do you mean, you *can't*?" Leenie asked.

"We don't drink tea or coffee. It's part of our faith," Lance said. "No alcohol, either. And we don't smoke."

"No tea? Ever?"

"Ever."

Well, that was bizarre. Better that they had come into the house and said, Would you care to join our church? We don't breathe oxygen! Or drink water! Or eat food!

The men accepted scones, at least. Aldine held up the jar of Silver Shred, but Cooper shook his head a little more vigorously than seemed polite, so Leenie laughed and said she agreed completely. Too perfumy, the Silver was, like something you'd rather wash with than eat. Only Aldine had ever liked it.

A gate clanged on the street and Leenie wondered if her aunt could possibly have taken an earlier bus back from Troon.

"It probably sounds strange," Cooper said. "Well, it must. I've been in your country one year, eight months, two weeks, and one day and not one person has believed me yet." He swallowed and summoned a voice from somewhere in his chest. "But I testify," he said, his eyes on Aldine's, then Leenie's, pleading with them, "that it's the truth."

Aldine swallowed a sip of tea and looked at the carpet, as if not sure how to greet such an exposure of the soul. She was embarrassed, Leenie saw.

After a pause, Aldine looked at both men in turn and asked, "Are you sure it's not due to the tea business?"

"What?"

"The not drinking tea. Maybe people think, *Oh, I could never.*"

"I don't see how it could be that," Cooper said. He walked to the window and gazed at the wet glass and the wet street, the soaking wet stones of the conjoined houses, and something about him tugged at Leenie's being.

"Do you ever hear from your family at all?" she asked.

He drew something from his pocket and unfolded a picture that was unremarkable: a sun with lines sticking out of it, two figures, small and big, holding hands, the word *lov*, some squarish shapes. Each week, he said, his youngest sister, Sarah, who was three, drew him a picture, and his mother sent it to him, and he carried one with him at all times in case he got discouraged, which happened a fair amount.

He said that when he was eighteen he'd been fed up because there were so few Mormons where they lived in New York, and he was tired of the rules his mother and father imposed on him—no drinking, no smoking, scripture study every single evening around the table—and their irrational disapproval of a Catholic girl who was achingly good in every way except that she was not Mormon. They wanted him to go on a mission, too, but he didn't want to go. He was planning to leave them all—the church, his family—when one day Sarah was sick and he had to stay home with her while his parents went to a funeral. She was hungry, so he put a plate of food before her, went to get something, a magazine, and when he returned, her face was bright red. "She choked for the longest time. I didn't know what to do. I really had no idea." He prayed that if God would let him save her, he would do it. He would go on a mission like his parents wanted.

Leenie waited.

"I pressed on the right part of her chest somehow. It came out—it was a clump of bread."

"Ah," Aldine said.

"I made an effort to believe after that. And more and more I found that I did believe, that it was all true, and I could keep my promise."

Aldine sat very stiffly in her chair, the thick Bakelite bracelets gleaming on her arm as she held the teacup unnaturally still.

"Could we—would you mind—if we come again next Saturday?" Elder Cooper asked.

"Certainly," Leenie said, not giving Aldine a second to interject, her whole being calm and steady. "For tea," she added, and then remembered the men didn't drink it, and that she and Aldine would have to ask Aunt Sedge for permission to entertain two unmarried missionaries from America, and of course Aunt Sedge would say absolutely not. "We'll have more sandwiches next time," Leenie said hopelessly, "and cakes."

"Could we say a prayer before we leave?" Cooper asked, a question no one had ever asked Leenie before, but the situation had no precedent from start to finish, so she just nodded.

"Our Eternal Father," he began.

Aldine ducked her head but kept her eyes open, staring hard at Leenie. Probably she was wondering if this was how people got into cults and such.

Leenie, for her part, went on feeling a stillness inside herself as she listened to Elder Cooper's deep, sure American voice. A change was beginning, she felt.

3

O ur *Aunt is not well please meet us 2 o'clock Monday, The Cream Pot, High Street.*

That was the dishonest note they had to send Cooper and Lance. It gave things an illicit thrill, in Aldine's opinion, though Aldine was more than a little alarmed to read the inscription Elder Cooper had written in the blue hardback copy of the Book of Mormon he gave them:

For Aldine and Eileen McKenna, Ayr, Scotland, April 13, 1929

We believe all things, we hope all things, we have endured many things, and hope to be able to endure all things.

Endure? That was the new church's promise? What more might they have to endure beyond their father's death, their mother's death, and the possibility of living to middle age without a single interesting thing happening to them? Had it not been for Cooper's adorability, which seemed to have destroyed Leenie's limited common sense, Aldine would have mislaid the Bible-ish book on a seawall.

"Why are you going on with this?" Aldine asked.

"I don't know."

"You loved that story about his sister and the bread lump."

"You didn't? You don't like a person who prays to save his little sister?"

"I don't *dis*like it. I wouldn't join a religion for him, though."

Leenie took to reading the Bible-ish book, which looked more like a Jane Austen novel than a holy testament, in their bedroom every night. "Try reading it aloud with me," Leenie said. "See if you get the calm feeling."

"I never get calm feelings," Aldine said. Religious talk made her qualmish.

"Oh, just read a bit. How do you know?"

"*I, Nephi,*" Aldine said, annoyed already at the unfamiliar names. "*Having been born of goodly parents.* Is it 'Nee-fie' or 'Neffy?'"

Leenie smoked while she listened. "'Neffy,' is how I say it. Go on."

"*Therefore I was taught somewhat in all the learning of my father; and having seen many afflictions in the course of my days, nevertheless, having been highly favored of the Lord . . .*"

After a whole page of that business, Leenie asked if she felt it. The Calm Feeling. Aldine said only if the calm feeling was a wish to off herself. Leenie was still smoking, and as usual she looked like a child playing a role, and that's why she liked it. She thought a tarry matured her. "I'll bet we'd feel it more," Leenie said, sighing, "if Elder Cooper were reading it."

"*You* would, anyway."

"I love the way his voice goes all rich and chocolatey."

Aldine eyed her. "What about George? Where's he in all this?"

"I told you he wasn't my Japanese man. Anyway, I told him not to come round for a while."

Aldine knew she should feel a bit sorry for George at this moment, but she didn't. He worked at a motor shop, played darts, and drank but wasn't the one to lead in anything, even a lark, and he'd once said Aldine reminded him of Buster Keaton.

Leenie said there was a church meeting they could attend a week later in Glasgow, where no one would know them (the Cream Pot having proved overly public), and she wanted to be able to say they'd read the whole book by then. "Let's keep going. It'll get more thrilling, maybe."

It did not, not even when they skipped. Somewhere in the second book of Neffy, Aldine said she was pretty sure it was all blether.

Leenie lay flat on her back, eyes on the sloped wallpapered ceiling that was pink rose after pink rose. "Why?"

"Well, for starters, God and Jesus appearing to a runt of a farmer boy in the woods," Aldine said, snorting a little.

"No," Leenie said decisively. "That I believe dead certain, like Elder Cooper does. Think on it, Deenie. It's no more peculiar than Jesus rolling back the stone of his tomb after he died, and look how many loads of people believe that."

"No," Aldine said. "It's not the same at all."

"It's *less* peculiar, the fact is. Haven't you ever been somewhere alone," Leenie said, "like the hill above the Doon when there's a low fog, and you see sun poke through in a column, like? I think that's what it was for Joseph, only he saw God." Leenie stopped to pick something off the tip of her tongue; then she inhaled again.

"You mean he saw the sun and it was *like* God or it *was* God?"

"Oh, *was*. Why not?"

Leenie always did fancy herself a mystic. "Why doesn't God step through the sun for everybody then?" she asked. "And save all the babies that choke on lumps of bread."

"I don't know about the babies. Nobody does. But most people don't pray for wisdom," she said. "And they don't listen, either."

"Did you?"

"Sort of."

"What do you mean, *sort of*?"

Leenie shook her head and stubbed out her cigarette in the ceramic dish that had been painted, inexpertly, with a picture of Castle Culzean. "I prayed to ask if it was true."

"And what?"

"The answer was yes."

Aldine was astounded. "I think the answer was that you love Elder William Cooper's forehead and you want to lie with him in the biblical manner."

Leenie took the book back from Aldine and said, "You've never believed in God. That's why you can't stop thinking everything's lust."

"Look me in the eye and tell me you don't dream of him ravishing you nightly."

"He's a *missionary*. It's like asking if I'm gone on the reverend."

"I can't believe it. Sedge is going to die ten thousand deaths when you tell her," Aldine said. "*He's* your Japanese man."

"Maybe he is and maybe he isn't. In any case, I'm not going to stop believing something that makes me feel right inside."

"Are you going to marry him and leave me here on Bellevue Crescent with Aunt Sedge?"

"Don't be silly. Missionaries can't go around with girls or talk about love with their converts."

"How do you know?"

"I just do. He's never said an improper word and neither have I."

"Don't move to America."

"All right," Leenie said. "I'm going to sleep now." As usual, Leenie was asleep in two seconds, and Aldine lay awake wondering what would happen when Elder Cooper took his soul-winning forehead home.

4

Three Saturdays later, the four of them knelt down in an empty park, grass soaking their knees, and prayed for the Spirit to tell them the church was true. What Aldine saw while her knees were soaking was Elder Cooper's focused eyes, the concentrated force of his passion—it looked like faith but it could have been love—every time he looked at Leenie.

"Are you ready to be baptized?" Elder Cooper asked.

"Yes," Leenie said.

"But the *tea*," Aldine said to Leenie. "She can't live without it," she said to Cooper.

"I'm not worried," Leenie said.

Aldine wanted to ask was she worried about giving up tarries, but she didn't.

"How about you," Cooper asked Aldine. He did the thing with his eyes.

"I'll think on it," Aldine said.

The Saturday after that, Leenie told Aunt Sedge she was going to the Cream Pot, but where she really meant to go was the mouth of the Doon for baptism, which it turned out was not a sprinkling on the forehead but a full dunking. She would need to wear all white ("Like a *bride*?" Aldine said) and go all the way underwater.

"No," Aldine said. "You're not doing that."

"You can't stop me."

"I could tell Sedge."

"You wouldn't."

"I might."

"I don't care. She can't stop me, either. People have always done what their faith told them to do."

"You're not Joan of Arc."

"I didn't say I was."

"You're going to become a Mormon and then you're going to go to America and marry him."

"I told you he hasn't said a word about love."

Leenie started to put on her graduation dress: white pongee in a sailor style.

"That's what you're wearing to meet John the Baptist?"

Leenie pressed on the pleats of the skirt. "Don't worry," she said. "If I go to America, I'll go to the temple place for you and Mum and Dad someday."

Cooper had shown them a picture of a cathedral-type building in Salt Lake City. He said you could go there and do a thing (Aldine couldn't recall what), say some words, and it was a spell, kind of, and you'd be joined to your family even if they were dead already.

Leenie kissed her and covered her white graduation getup with a coat, and she must have gotten by Aunt Sedge all right because Aldine saw her walking swiftly down the sidewalk to High Street. She found her again on the bank where the Doon met the Irish Sea, a beautiful spot for anything but going swimming in your clothes. Elder Cooper and Elder Lance were standing there looking a little ridiculous because they, too, were wearing white. As Aldine stood behind a tree, Leenie scuffled down the steep, muddy bank into the cold, brown water. She felt dishonest hiding from them all, so she stepped out, called hello, and waved.

Leenie waved back.

"How's the water?" Aldine called to her. She had that curious detachment that comes of not taking a thing seriously that she did not feel deeply herself. It was like when a boy said he was mad for you and you just felt impatient. His love could not be deep or real if you felt nothing at all.

They'd been to this spot with their father loads of times before he died. Wild swans floated out to sea and collected in a white wedge on what was, in summer, a beautiful cream-blue stretch of tide. On sunny days, the river glittered and the willow trees trailed their leaves in the shallows, all of it sparkling and benign. Today the clouds were particulate and unyielding, the air dreary white, and not even the ducks seemed to enjoy the water.

Lance waded in after Cooper and Leenie.

"It's positively Baltic!" Leenie squealed, lagging behind Cooper now, hanging back as the current soaked her thighs.

"Remember those hounds?" Aldine called.

Leenie barely nodded, but Aldine knew she did. It was something they'd recalled for each other every time their father brought them here, which was more often after their mother died. They used to eat vanilla tablet with him on the ruined stone wall, where you could see both the start of the ocean and the end of the river. He would sit without talking, which meant he was thinking about their mother, so they would go off and try to find fairy circles, a ring of wild mushrooms you could stand within to make a wish. They were still searching the time the red-eared man had come to the riverbank with a pair of big-eyed, long-nosed, jittery dogs. Knotted ropes noosed the dogs' necks, and the man held tightly to the dogs when he plunged into the water. The dogs reared like horses, but the man kept plunging, walking in circles waist-deep. The dogs kept their heads above the surface, twisting and lurching, always trying to find a means of escape from the cold and the rope, but this only forced them to swim like helpless motors beside the man, and this came to seem like the point.

"That's horrid!" Aldine said, not even bothering to lower her voice, and Leenie asked (more quietly) their father to save the dogs, but he just stayed on the rock wall and said, "They're racing hounds. He's training them up."

Aldine hoped one of the wild swans would fly up and beat the man on his big red ears, but nothing happened. After the dogs did their exercising, they were led, sopping and cold, to the riverbank, and the man walked them out of sight.

Aldine wished it were sunny, or at least one of those tormented afternoons when silvery clouds broke apart for dazzling sunshine in between the bursts of rain, but no. Aldine felt—she couldn't help it—that Leenie was letting herself be one of those trained dogs because she was in love with Elder Cooper. To the north, the beach curved like a shorn hoof for two or three miles, not a soul out for a walk or a swim. Leenie stood up to her waist in the river, and she waved nervously to Aldine, who waved back, and Aldine wondered if it was true that the dead hovered nearby, watching. Maybe their father was watching the missionaries from the stone wall, and watching Aldine, too. "Stay by her," he'd said. "You're the youngest but you have the older nature."

In the river, Elder Cooper lifted his right arm. He was wearing a white dress shirt with the sleeves rolled up, and underneath the dress shirt was a white undershirt, soaked through, and underneath that, a not unaffecting physique. He held his arm stiffly up and bent at the elbow, like someone about to say, *I do solemnly swear.* "Eileen Rose McKenna," he said. "In the name of the Father, the Son, and the Holy Ghost."

Leenie willingly buckled, as though to drown. For a second, she was a pale riven shape under the water. Then he rescued her and she stood again, the River Doon running off her face and hair. She sputtered and smiled at Elder Cooper, and then at Aldine.

"You now, Deenie?" Leenie said, wading out, already close enough to tug on Aldine's wrist.

"Can't," Aldine said. "I'm wearing black."

"It's not that important what you wear," Elder Cooper said.

"Maybe another day," Aldine said. "When it's hot out."

~

After Leenie left to marry Will, Aldine sometimes dreamed that she was in the river, slipping on the stones that lay on the bottom as she trudged out to be baptized. In the dream, it was Elder Lance who held Aldine and raised his right arm, and the cold sank into her bones as though the water were running through and not around her body. Elder Lance held out his wet, freckled arm to steady her, but when he ducked her under, he held her there and she struggled like the greyhounds until she thought she would drown, her eyes open the whole time and searching everywhere for Leenie and Will but not finding them, or her father, either, and then she was awake, and she was alone in the rose-papered room at the top of Aunt Sedgewick's silent house.

5

Come live with us, Leenie wrote. *There's a box factory that's owned by a member and you could get a better job than working for Old Malleyman, who can't be long for this world anyway to hear Aunt Sedge go on about him. I feel sure that your Japanese man is around here somewhere!*

Dr. O'Malley was housebound now. Aunt Sedge said he should have a proper nurse, not a young unmarried secretary who'd already stirred up talk.

"I counted up my savings," Aldine finally told her aunt. "With what Leenie says she'll send I have just enough for a third-class ticket."

It was not true. Leenie had no money to send. But Aldine had obtained the money another way.

"Oh, Aldine," Aunt Sedgewick said. She smoothed the cushion beside her with a small wrinkled hand. It was a sunny day, perfect for going out, but there they sat. "Living with a married couple so far from home," Sedgewick added. "It won't suit you."

"I want to go," Aldine said.

"There's someone here for you, dear. He'll come along."

Aldine had never asked Aunt Sedgewick about the Japanese man. "It isn't that," she said. After a long time she added, "I'll miss you mind and body."

Aunt Sedgewick nodded once and seemed about to speak, but her eyes were full of tears, and she stayed on the sofa in the sunny room until Aldine kissed her on the cheek and went out, trying very hard to keep her shoes from making any noise as she opened the front door and closed it behind her.

6

For the first six months in Brooklyn, Leenie was sympathetic to Aldine's dismissals of Mormon men who wanted to date her and convert her at the same time. "Too ancient," she agreed about Anton Buchreiter, who was at least fifty. "A bit dim," she admitted about Harold Coombs. But Floyd Gerg, to Leenie's mind, was perfect: young, good-looking, solid, kind. Floyd Gerg was, in fact, handsome in a stiff, Nordic way, though he seemed about as animated as a tree. He'd called Aldine Sister McKenna until she made him stop, reminding him that she was not strictly a sister, not yet (*nor ever*, she added in her mind). Leenie had several times pointed out that Brother Gerg had a good job at the Steinway factory and would soon have his own flat. Aldine pointed out that she had never heard him laugh.

"He wants to marry you," Leenie said.

"How could you possibly know that? He never speaks!"

"He told Will."

"I can't marry him."

"He's going to ask you. He's working up the courage."

"Tell Will to tell him I haven't made up my mind to be baptized."

"You're too picky, Deen. He'd be a good father."

No, she couldn't picture it. They were stiff as dead plants with one another. And yet Leenie had invited him to Sunday dinner again, probably after telling Will that Floyd needed to talk more and draw Aldine out.

By this point it was August and sweltering. Aldine sat on a bench in Fort Greene Park craving a cup of Fortnum's and a lick of Silver Shred on toast. Maybe she should quit boxes and try for a job in a shop, where at least she could look outside now and then. She stared crossly down at a newspaper someone had left on the bench. It was folded to the part that listed jobs and opportunities.

Culturally-inclined Country School in beautiful Loam County, Kansas, seeks forward-looking primary teacher with musical skills. Fair salary, room and board included. Apply to Ansel Price, Dorland, Kansas.

She was as forward-looking as the next girl. She could sing, play the piano, and fiddle. She had memorized every poem her father knew, and every poem in the eighth reader. She knew her times tables and wrote with what examiners (and Dr. O'Malley, too) called a "beautiful hand." Perhaps Kansas was not too far by train, and she could visit Leenie and the baby on weekends.

She folded the newspaper section until it would fit in her pocketbook and went looking for a stamp.

7

In a car parked on a side street of Dorland, Kansas, the wife and three children of Ansel Price sat waiting in heavy silence. The street was oiled; the town was hot and still. The car had been parked in the shade, but that was before shopping and banking and visiting with Mrs. Odekirk and Mrs. Eichely and Reverend Bakely's wife, and now the afternoon sun glared down on the old Ford. The heat was stifling and when Mrs. Price touched the edge of her finger to her upper lip, it came away moist. "Wait here," her husband had said. "I won't be ten seconds." And then had hurried across the deserted street for the post office.

She'd known it wouldn't be ten seconds, but she didn't expect it to be ten minutes, either. Ten minutes and counting. She turned to the backseat, where her three children sat squeezed sullenly together. Clare, fingering a recent outcropping of acne at his chin, seemed to anticipate her thoughts and said quietly, "He told us to wait here."

"I'll go!" Neva said. She was out the door before more could be said about it. She disappeared into the post office, a small brick cube featuring a sidewall of glass blocks near the entrance. Clare watched the liquid blur of Neva's small body as she dashed behind them. Once he'd seen a woman passing behind these glass blocks and for an enlivening second or two had imagined this woman would emerge naked, but she had not, of course. It was just Mrs. Rackham, wearing beige.

Another minute or two passed without anyone coming out. *That man,* Mrs. Price thought. Then, after looking up and down the street, she thought, *This town.* She closed her eyes, then opened them again and said, "Clare, go fetch Neva."

As he went, Charlotte called after him. "And tell His Highness that we're about to combust out here!"

"Don't call your father that," Mrs. Price said but Charlotte noticed she didn't put any starch into it. Charlotte stretched her legs onto the vacated backseat and hitched her skirt a few inches, not that it helped much. Another minute or two passed but it felt longer to Charlotte. Her father did not appear, nor did Neva or Clare. "God!" she said. "Is there a troll in there picking them off one by one?"

Her mother said nothing. But she was thinking things. Charlotte knew that much. In her journal she'd written of her mother: *She thought it all and said not a thing.*

Beyond the train station, Mr. Tanner's wagon turned onto Main Street pulled by two mules. Whenever her father saw Mr. Tanner in his wagon, he said, "He likes two good mules." That's what Mr. Tanner always said when neighbors advised him to invest in something motor driven. *I like two good mules.* As the wagon slowly approached, Mr. Tanner kept his gaze cast forward. Charlotte stared at him hard, willing him to turn his eyes toward her, but he didn't. He passed by looking like a statue of himself.

"Okay, that's it. I'm going in," she said, and waited for her mother to say something, almost daring it, but her mother stared straight ahead.

When she got inside the post office, Charlotte found Neva sitting on the counter with her toothpick legs dangling, Clare standing close to the opposite wall studying the wanted posters, and her father, pencil in hand, bent over the counter staring at a sheet of paper in front of him so intently that he didn't notice her approach. When she said, "What're you writing?" he jumped in a way that interested her. It almost seemed that she'd just glimpsed her father as he might be when his family was not around, as a grown man without wife and son and daughters attached.

"Oh," he said. "Just an advertisement. Terence Tidball said he'd put in a notice for us free of charge if I'd send him the text."

Terence Tidball, who worked worlds away at the *Herald Tribune* in New York City. A lunatic idea if ever there was one. But, still, she leaned forward to see what her father had written. He'd made a number of false starts and erasures; what remained was this: *Country School in Loam County, Kansas, seeks primary teacher. Salary, room and board included. Apply to Ansel Price, Dorland, Kansas.*

"Oh, that's sure to work," Charlotte said. "We'll probably need a wheelbarrow to carry all the responses."

Her father was a tall, stately man who could often see the funny side of things, but he didn't see the funny side of this.

"Huh," Clare murmured from his position some feet away, but only to himself, evidently in response to one of the posters he was reading. Neva, who had been tenderly but intently working her front teeth between thumb and forefinger—both teeth were loosening—withdrew her hand to say, "What, Clare?" but Clare was too intent on his poster reading to reply.

Charlotte felt peevish without knowing quite why. "What's so important about this teacher?" she asked her father and when he didn't answer, she said, "It's always just been one big crab apple after another in that pitiful little schoolhouse, anyway." Which wasn't exactly true. There had been Mrs. Groe for a while. But after her, it was crab apples, and nothing but.

Abruptly her father pulled out his wallet and slid from it a scrap of paper that he passed to her along with an envelope. "That's Terence

Tidball's box number and that's an envelope. If you're through plaguing me, maybe you could address it."

Though it was on a scrap of paper, her father had written the address in his beautiful cursive, the one he used when he took care with things. While she worked on the envelope, she couldn't help but notice that he was quickly scribbling additions to his advertisement before folding the paper in two.

"Want me to proofread?" she said, extending an open hand, but he took the envelope from her without a word, slipped the folded advertisement inside, sealed it, and with—this much she saw—just the barest moment of hesitation, dropped it into the slot for outgoing mail.

"Did you change it?" she asked, but whatever other man she'd glimpsed when she'd walked into the post office had now slipped away. What was left was her everyday father, who swept up Neva with one arm and said, "C'mon now, all of you, or we'll have the bride stewing in her juices."

The bride was what he called their mother, and Charlotte thought that if her own husband ever tried, eighteen years into the marriage, to refer to her as the bride, she would have to kill him.

In the car, moving down the highway, the air was streaming again but as soon as her father turned onto the country road, the dust fell on Charlotte's skin and mouth and tongue. Her underclothes stuck and clung and the heat seemed first to have rubberized the cups of her brassiere and then molded them to her breasts. When she slipped her hand inside her blouse to adjust the whole nightmarish apparatus, Clare stared at her openly until she said, "What are you looking at?"

Clare turned his head away from his sister and stared out his own window. He was wondering when he would ever see a girl completely naked and then he was wondering whether seeing his own sister naked would put him off wanting to see other girls naked, because if that was what would happen he would need to avoid it at all costs. He began diverting himself by remembering the names of every person on the wanted lists he had been looking at. Hillary Henderson, alias Bill Henderson, alias "2 Gun" Henderson, bank robbery. J. J. Comiskey, also known as "Peanuts" and "Dirty Neck," for stealing 478 cases of Cream of Kentucky whiskey consigned to but never reaching Chicago. Nicholas "Nick" Delmore, murder of prohibition agent. Gloria Lisa Carter, missing from home, fourteen years old but looks eighteen. Jack David Salter. Sally "Goodie" Fahrenstock. On and on, one after another, that was how good his memory was when he wanted it to be.

Neva sat between them, which she liked. She was happy again, now that they were moving. Part of the fun of going to town was in coming back home. She worked her loose teeth and wondered where she left her tin of box elder bugs. The stair closet, she decided. Or maybe the tack room. One or the other. But she would have to find them or they would perish like the last ones. That's what Charlotte had said when she'd shown them to her and asked what was wrong with them. *They have perished,* Charlotte told her. The car was moving and the engine was humming and she decided to fall asleep. She laid her head against Charlotte because Charlotte was softer, but Charlotte pushed her off and said, "Too hot, Nevie," so she laid her head against Clare's shoulder and of course Clare didn't mind.

Charlotte, sitting directly behind her father, was sullenly regarding his thick, wavy black hair. One night, after he had read aloud from *A Midsummer Night's Dream* for everybody in the front room, Charlotte and her friend Opal had walked outside to look at the sky and Opal had said that she thought Charlotte's father must have descended from nobility or at least somebody aristocratic. The effect of this remark on Charlotte was odd. Initially she felt a pleasant swelling of pride but that was immediately supplanted by the need to debunk the notion entirely. Soon after, therefore, she began to refer to her father as His Highness. In a way it fit him, the way he could just take himself out of the real world. She knew no one who stood taller or worked harder than he did, but he wasn't like the other hardworking farmers who continued the worrying when they were done with the working. He could look into a book or stare out a window and leave them all behind, and who knew what he was thinking then? His thoughts were some of the very few in the world that Charlotte actually wondered about. He made such odd decisions. What was he thinking, for example, when he thought Ellie Hoffman was the woman he should marry? What was he thinking when he brought her back here to Dorland? What was he thinking when he borrowed money to buy all that land on the wrong side of the hogback? And what was he thinking in advertising in New York City for someone to come here to teach unwashed farm kids in a pitiful one-room school-house? How did he imagine that anyone in her right mind would leave New York City for Dorland, Kansas? Why, in other words, couldn't he just come down out of the clouds and stick to the here and now, and do those things a grown man was supposed to do?

Almost lazily she announced, "His Highness is putting an ad in the *Herald Tribune*. He thinks an office girl in New York City will want to come teach in our horrid country school."

The stricken look on her mother's face as she turned toward her father was a reward in itself. Her mother didn't speak a word, but none was needed.

"And why not?" her father said, and—another reward—his tone was beyond doubt defensive. He then said something in a mumble that Charlotte couldn't make out.

"Pardon?" she said.

He jerked his head sideways and his voice was low and defiant. "I *said* a man can't catch a fish without bait in the water!"

She thought, *In that metaphor the teacher is a fish, the advertisement is the bait, and the water is murky,* but she said nothing. They rode on in silence, except for the *tink-tinking* of small rocks on the undercarriage. Neva slept. Charlotte set her finger into Neva's open hand and felt the hand close softly and wished now that she hadn't pushed the girl away.

After a long while, Clare turned from his window-staring and said, "What's a common-law wife, anyhow?"

Charlotte stifled a laugh. Her mother drew a quick breath but it was her father who explained. If there was one thing that you could count on from him, it was his ready explanation of other people's dire situations. It was his own dire circumstance that he wouldn't put under the magnifying glass.

When her father finished his explanation of common-law marriage, Clare considered it a few seconds and said, "So they just live together like a married couple until they sort of become one?"

Her father said that was correct, more or less. They had only to hold themselves out as man and wife.

This was too much for her mother, who straightened her back. "But without solemnizing the act," she said, "it is not a true marriage in the eyes of God."

"What kind of solemnizing did Adam and Eve do?" Charlotte wanted to know, but no one answered.

Her father said, "Why are you asking, Clare?"

"Oh," Clare said. "It was this man on a wanted poster named Kilian Smith. The poster said he stabbed his common-law wife. He's wanted for murder."

Kilian Smith wore a dapper hat and dapper bow tie. In the photograph he stared right back at Clare with eyes that seemed surprisingly mild. And yet a man with eyes that gentle had wound up stabbing to death the woman he loved, which was impossible to imagine and made you wonder about the strangeness of romance.

8

As a return address, Aldine wrote *General Delivery, Post Office Next to Woolworth Building, New York City*. Then she dropped her letter to Ansel Price in a post box as she might drop a bottled message into the sea. She made herself wait two weeks before checking for mail, and when she was handed a letter with a return address from Mr. Ansel Price, Loam County Schools, Dorland, Kansas, she was surprised at the wave of unease that rose within her. She felt almost ill from holding the unopened letter in her hands. She moved to a corner of the lobby. She suddenly realized just how keenly she wanted to escape Floyd's stillness as he sat beside her in church or in Leenie's flat, his body so inert that he seemed almost asexual, and yet his goodness was so irreproachable that she felt stifled. She had to escape the feeling she had when she watched Will and Leenie hold hands during prayer at the dinner table, their bond an electrical current that did not reach her even if Leenie took Aldine's hand. In their presence, she was a dark window.

Aldine drew in a great draft of air. She closed her eyes and kept them closed as she fingered open the envelope and unfolded the letter. When she opened them again and read, *Dear Miss McKenna, It is with pleasure that we offer you the position*, she felt an excitement she'd not felt since she decided to sail to New York. That decision had not turned out well, maybe, but it had led to this, and the job in Kansas would be all her own doing from start to finish.

Before she left the building, she had written back with her acceptance, and that night, well into dinner, she said, "I think I might go to Kansas and teach school."

They stared, of course, so she unfolded the letter from the school and showed them.

Will, who had been carefully spooning grape jelly, looked at her in a disbelieving way. "That's where Elder Lance is from. You remember."

She had not and was not pleased to remember it now.

"Do you know where Kansas is?" he asked.

"Yes," Aldine lied. There had been no prior need to memorize the position of American states. Perhaps it was farther than she thought.

"I just barely got you back with me!" Leenie said. "What if you don't like it? Besides, you can't go that far by yourself!"

Aldine stared at the dark jelly. So it was distant, the place called Kansas. "It's no farther than you went, Leen."

"But it's different. I had Wills. You had me. What'll you have?"

"A more thrilling job," Aldine said, wondering if it was more than a hundred miles. "My own life." She hated it when Leenie called him Wills. She'd decided she would have to pretend a little bit in order to get their approval. "Plus, they're Mormons," she added.

Will was again looking at the letter. "How do you know?"

"It said in the advertisement. It warned that anyone uncomfortable living with adherents of the Church of Latter-day Saints need not apply. Though it said applicants needn't be adherents themselves."

Will fell silent and Aldine pressed her advantage. "And besides, with a babe coming you'll soon need more room here. You've been kind not to say so, but it's the truth all the same."

"But the train," Leenie said. "That'll cost a packet because it's so far off."

Will shook his head. "Your aunt wouldn't forgive me," he said. He began smoothing his small measure of jelly onto his toast. "It's out of the question."

"I've already bought it," she said.

Leenie didn't like this, and gave Will a worried look before she said, "How do you have the money, Deen?"

"Dr. O'Malley," Aldine said carefully, "gave me a big raise after you left."

"You never said a thing before!"

"How do you think I got here?" Aldine said irritably.

Leenie shrugged. "Sedge, of course."

"No," Aldine said. "She didn't have it. Not after she paid for yours."

Leenie was kind enough to look guilty. "How much do you have?" she asked.

Aldine didn't want to tell her. If it wasn't more than she deserved, it was more than she deserved from a doctor whose accounts she'd kept for three years.

"I lost nearly all of it in the exchange rate."

"But how much?"

She had come this far. "I started with a thousand pounds."

The silence in the room expressed their astonishment. She spun her bracelets under the table, the smooth rings warm against her wrist.

"A thousand?" Leenie said. Will didn't speak, but the way he looked at her made her feel she'd been selfish in some way.

"It cost three hundred quid to buy a third-class bunk. And as you know, a pound is worth very little here."

"But you still had enough to buy a train ticket?"

"Yes. I've not touched it since I started working."

"I can't believe you want to leave me," Leenie said.

"I don't want to *leave* you. I need to find my own way, Leenie." She gave her sister a heartfelt look, wishing she could explain that she thought it would be nearby, no farther than Edinburgh was from Ayr. "I do."

The table fell silent then and remained silent until at last in a small voice, Leenie said, "When would you go then?"

~

Dr. O'Malley had wanted to look at her without her clothes on. He had said, in his reasonable voice, that it would be like the statue of Venus de Milo, like nudes in a painting. For perhaps the last time in his life, he would see beauty. She could give him that small gift, couldn't she? He wouldn't touch her. It was not a sin to be beautiful, or to be looked upon as a thing of beauty. He had explained it very well, and she had been sorry for him, to be what he was: old and alone, sick with some kind of cancer.

So in his sitting room with the high ceiling like a church, with the heavy velvet drapes and the small panes of icy glass through which light became more wistful, she had at last unbuttoned her dress and let it fall, removing then her slip, her brassiere, her garter belt, her stockings, and finally her drawers. She had not known what to do then, so she asked.

"What now?"

He said, "Nothing, just let me look at you a while," and that was what he did, his eyes lowered, his hands clasped. His admiration made her shivery-sick and she was careful not to look down, not to see what he saw. He cleared his throat.

"What?"

"Perhaps you would sing the Mendelssohn."

She closed her eyes, remembering the words. It seemed to her deeply irreverent, but she found having something to do diverting. She started in almost a murmur but her voice settled into itself. She no longer trembled as she stood, and only felt awkward again when she fell quiet and began putting everything back on, each step all fingers and thumbs because he was watching her and saying, "Shame to cover that. And that. And that." She felt naked inside her clothes walking back to Aunt Sedge's house. She wrote him a letter that night resigning her position as his secretary.

A day or two later he sent £1000 to her by messenger. Ten notes, one hundred quid each, new-looking and sharp, unsoiled. It was a startling sum, so immense that for a while she regarded the packet as though it were a genie's lamp. He had enclosed a brochure for the TSS *Transylvania*, a steamship of the Anchor Line. It departed, like the *Caledonia*, from Glasgow.

Go and be happy, he wrote. *As you have made me.*

Under the hard-bottomed davenport in Leenie's flat, in a suitcase, she kept the brochure for the *Transylvania*, which in turn held Dr. O'Malley's money and his note. When Leenie and Will had gone to bed, she quietly slid the case out and read the note again. *Go and be happy.* What remained of the money was £700 6s. 3d. Less than $200 once she handed it across the counter at the bureau of exchange. It might be enough for the train ticket to Kansas, she thought, if she added her wages to it. It would have to be.

9

Two days and nights Aldine sat on the train and stared at fields through her own reflection, and saw no water to speak of. She carried three blood-spotted handkerchiefs in her pocketbook when she stepped off the train in Dorland, touching the last one to her nose and wishing for a river to make everything wet and cool, as it had been in her imagination. But she saw no lochs, no rivers, not even a burn. She had to settle for a station bog where water trickled into a rust-bloomed sink near a ghastly commode. When she'd combed her dusty hair, washed her face without soap, and checked the chapped edges of her nose for blood, she changed her dress to the black one printed all over with shells and pinned once more to her hair the tan beret just like the one in *Vogue* that she'd knitted in Leenie's flat. Her skin looked ashy white against the rouge she rubbed into her lips.

None of this quite killed the pleasure of the letter of acceptance in her purse that said she was just what they were looking for. That was it exactly—*just what we are looking for*—and written in such a fine hand it might have come from a hotel menu. *Yours sincerely, Ansel Price.* She took the letter out and held it while she waited for this very man to appear and fetch her.

Dorland, Kansas, appeared to consist of plain pastel houses in a row, each one small and lonesome in its own dry yard, and a huge white building made of columns that looked like stone tubes. *FARMER'S CO-OP*, it said in painted black letters near the top. Beyond the lane where she stood, which was called Spruce Street, she could see leafy trees, bits of red brick buildings, and a gray structure that had an impressively tall hedge along one side. The street in front of those buildings was so straight she could see all the way to the end, and it wasn't a very long way before the trees and buildings stopped and the yellowish countryside began again. She wanted to walk into town and see if there was a hotel or pub where she could get something to drink, but she was afraid to leave the vicinity of the platform.

Minutes passed, and she ventured off the platform to the road, which was unpaved. She felt the sun heating her bare arms—scorching them, most likely—but the air felt clean and good after so many hours in the stuffy train. She walked, little stones rolling under her shoes, to the end of the block that contained the platform, then turned back. No one came, not by foot or by car. A bug leaped away from her foot, his body the color of dust. Another popped out every time she moved, so she bent down, curious, and saw one hiding in a clump of weeds: just a grasshopper like those at home but striped in alien colors, gold and black, with a big reptilian eye. She straightened up with a feeling that was part exhilaration, part unease. The road went on being empty, so finally she asked the man in the ticket booth if Mr. Ansel Price had already come to the station and left.

The man cocked his head. "Ansel Price, do you mean?" and when she nodded, the man said, "Nope. Haven't seen Ansel at all today."

She strode back into the glaring sun. What a disaster if she'd gotten it all wrong somehow. The man knew Ansel Price, so it was not the wrong town. Maybe he'd had car trouble. She was telling herself it would just be another minute when the man from the ticket booth came out and said, "You family of the Prices?"

Aldine shook her head and hid the blood-spotted handkerchief in her fist. "I came out to be the new teacher," she said.

"What?" he said, as if she were speaking Chinese.

She said it again, more slowly.

He seemed not only uncertain of her meaning, but irritated that he was made to feel uncertain. "Which school?" he asked.

"I think it's called Stony Bank."

"Stuny Bonk?" he said, echoing her.

"Stony," she repeated. "Stony Bank."

He still looked baffled. "Well, Mr. Tanner lives near the Prices," he said, gesturing toward a round bearded man reading something in front of the post office. "He'll take you if you want to go with him."

She did, she supposed. She certainly couldn't stay here.

"Thank you," she said, and the ticket booth man nodded and said she was lucky it was Saturday; folks come to town on Saturday.

Aldine thought she could not have understood him; other than themselves and the man across the street, there was not a soul to be seen. She said so, and he said what sounded like, "Cinema."

"What?"

"Might be they're all at the matinee," he said, and he introduced her to Mr. Tanner, who had not a car but a wagon with a team of black mules. She wondered in a hungry, hopeless way how far it was and climbed up beside him. She sat with folded hands already gritty from touching the wagon. Without even entering the shady town, they headed for the place in the distance that seemed exactly like the place they were, and she watched the furrows spoke by, one long row fanning slowly into another, until it began to seem that there was nothing else left in the world but hoof plods, furrows, creaking wheels, and the sweat glistening on the rumps of the animals made to pull them.

Mr. Tanner had not spoken, nor did he look at her. Occasionally he made a clucking sound and said something to the mules—"Edna,

Edna," it seemed to her—but otherwise he stared straight forward, almost as if the world had lost interest for him.

In front of them one of the mules shat casually. This, too, passed without laugh or joke or comment. It was too much. She had to speak.

"Where's the wheat?" she asked, not that she knew a thing about wheat. A salesman on the train had talked to her of wheat prices and thousands of new-tilled acres until his voice was just a drone. But the fields around her seemed nothing but dirt.

"Not up yet," Mr. Tanner said, and allowed himself a dull review of the landscape before staring forward again. "It's seeding time."

Her skin felt so dusty and the air was so dry that she wondered if dust covered the pupils that let her gaze out of her dusty head. Finally they passed a farmhouse. After a long time, another. She had seen many of the same kind from the train and could not get used to how frail and far apart they were. At home and in New York, the houses were made of stone. These were just wood.

She almost started when Mr. Tanner said, "I suppose it isn't what you expected."

When she turned, she saw that he had been following her gaze out to the countryside, and something in her went out to him then, this round man with his frayed cuffs and tattered boots, so she said, "I'll wager it has its own beauty, doesn't it, though—once you have the feel for it?"

A small rough laugh broke from behind his beard, but at what she wouldn't know, for he said nothing. After a while, he clucked and again said, "Edna, Edna."

"Who's Edna?"

Mr. Tanner seemed startled. "What's that now?"

She slowed down her voice. "Who is Edna?" she asked, and when this seemed only to boost his confusion, she said, "Is one of the beasts named Edna?"

The man's expression relaxed. "Oh," he said. "You thought I was saying Edna, but I wasn't. I was saying, 'Ed now.' That's the old fella on the left. The other one is Billy." A second or two passed. "You cannot beat a good mule." Another pause. "Their legs are all the same length, I think that's the main thing. So they ride smooth. Plus, they're smarter than horses." He allowed himself a glance at Aldine. "Both Ed and Billy can open a horse gate. They just have to see you do it twice and that's it."

After a few more fields passed by, Mr. Tanner said abruptly, "Another example is that a horse will just kick at you anywhere but a mule will wait and plan and aim above the waist, that's how smart they are." He was nodding to himself now. "These two mules here, I wouldn't trade them for six horses, or for love or money neither." The vehemence of this proclamation surprised her, so she let a little time pass before venturing with, "And when you say, 'Ed now,' what do you mean by it?"

"Say again?" he said, and she did and this time he understood her.

"Oh. Ed will drift left. He's blind in the right so he wants to drift left and Billy's been with him so long she just lets him do it."

That Billy was a girl was a small revelation Aldine decided not to pursue.

Minutes passed, a good many of them, it seemed to Aldine as she stared off, and then when she turned around, Mr. Tanner was regarding her.

"What did you say your name was?" he asked.

She said it and he repeated it so badly that she said it again and though he again gave it rough treatment, she nodded and said, "Yes, that's it. Aldine McKenna."

A long creaking minute passed. Then Mr. Tanner said, "And where're you from?"

"Scotland."

He made a sound like it stumped him, and then, to her surprise, he asked, "What's that like?"

"Wet," she said. "Burns wherever you look." She closed her eyes briefly to pretend she was there, moving slowly among dark green sheltering trees. When she opened her eyes, she caught him looking at her again. It seemed an odd look, neither friendly nor admiring.

"Burns," he said. "Wet burns."

"Aye."

More silence.

She said, "Will ye have children at the school then?"

He looked forward at the sweating mules and went on looking for so long that she wondered if he heard the question. Or perhaps it was her accent. Maybe, she thought, people in Kansas—including the children she taught—wouldn't understand a word she said.

"No," he said. "Not anymore. We have the one boy and he's done with school."

When he went no further, she said, "All grown then?"

"Yes," he said. "All done growing."

He fell silent then, and the wheels jounced and turned and she had nearly fallen into a doze when Mr. Tanner's voice, as if from some distance, said, "That'll be the Price place."

And so she saw it for the first time: the far-off tree in bright yellow leaf, the tall white house, the huge gray barn that you could tell, as you got closer, had once been red. The land surrounding was flat and dry, chunky and hard brown on the furrow tops and only barely darker in the crevices.

"The school?" she asked.

"That way," Mr. Tanner said, and pointed, but she couldn't see anything.

10

Aldine expected to climb down from the wagon when Mr. Tanner drew the mules to a stop near the yard gate, but Mr. Tanner just sat, so she sat, too. A sloshing, motor-spinning sound came from the back of the house, and Aldine guessed she'd arrived while someone was washing clothes.

"You in there, Ellie?" Mr. Tanner called out. "You got a visitor!"

After a moment or two, a woman in a blue apron dress stepped onto the porch. Her hair was mouse-brown and oily, held up from her neck with pins. She hadn't quite lost all of her looks. Her eyes were a pale blue, as if a stronger shade had been washed out of them, and they peered out with an expression that Aldine would later come to think of as suppressed disappointment. She shaded her eyes with her hand as Mr. Tanner said, "This is Alleen McCanna."

"Aldine McKenna," Aldine corrected, but her voice was a low rasp, and the woman on the porch looked at her as if she'd just made a gagging spasm and feared she might make one again. Even under the dowdy apron dress, the woman's figure was statuesque, her breasts so prominent as to seem bovine. That Aldine was here, in this place, among these people, out of her own self-determination, made her failure as an adult human being seem inarguable. She pressed her lips inward to keep from crying. Is this what had made her aunt choose the lonely house on Bellevue Crescent over life in Japan? The known world over this terrible conspicuous not-belonging?

"Alleen McCandless," Mr. Tanner said again, this time a bit louder. "The new schoolteacher your husband hired."

Mrs. Price looked at her with a confusion that had behind it a skeptical tint. "I didn't know Ansel had hired anyone," Mrs. Price said, and seemed to be studying Aldine. "It's nice to meet you."

Aldine still sat on the wagon under a beating sun. Mr. Tanner shifted and held the reins like he was anxious to turn his team around. The crazed sloshing, grinding noise kept on, hurling unseen clothes together in the drum on the back porch. An overgrown teenage girl, almost a woman, came strolling out the back door and reached down to rub her hands lovingly all over the head of the ribby black-faced dog that rose to her arrival and nosed her at every step. The girl was fleshier than Mrs. Price and unrestrained-looking, like a rampant hollyhock too big for the yard, and Aldine imagined the girl might be frolicsome with the boys, an idea that she would later reflect on because of its stark wrongness. When the greeting with the dog was finally done, she said, "So how're Ed and Billy?"

Mr. Tanner nodded and said, "Good as ever."

Then the girl looked at Aldine and said sunnily, "This your new hired hand, Mr. Tanner?"

The girl laughed at her own joke, though no one else did. In fact, Mr. Tanner didn't seem even to regard it as one. "I've brought her here for you folks," he said. "New teacher your father hired."

The whole party sank back into silence, and Aldine felt like a package no one wanted to pay for. She sat stiffly, back straight, as if posture was the answer. Finally she cleared her throat. "I have a letter," she said, and when she brought it out, she noticed that her hand trembled. "Did you not get mine then?"

Mrs. Price shielded her eyes again and reached up for the letter, studying first the envelope and then the contents. Aldine wanted a bath. She wanted dinner. She wanted to close her eyes and open them again on the rose-papered ceiling of the attic in Ayr, where she would hear Leenie's muffled breathing beside her and know they had not left home.

"Well, you better come in," Mrs. Price said when she had stuffed the letter back into the envelope. "Come in and we'll get this sorted out when Ansel gets back from planting."

"You came here from New York?" the older girl said, taking her turn with the letter, still rubbing the wriggly black-faced dog with her left hand.

"Not New York. Scotland," Mr. Tanner said, unbending stiffly and descending to offer his hand to Aldine. "It's why she talks the way she does."

There was nothing to be done now but climb out of his wagon.

"Scotland," Aldine said, accepting Mr. Tanner's hand, which was rough and rootlike. "Scotland, then New York."

"Can't think why you'd leave either of those places for here!" the girl said cheerfully, taking Aldine's suitcase for her. "But now you're here, so come on in. My name's Charlotte. And that's"—she nodded at the dog—"Artemis."

"The Goddess of the Hunt," Aldine said, but not very loudly, and no one seemed to hear.

Aldine called a thank-you to Mr. Tanner but he was already maneuvering his mules and gave no acknowledgment. Inside, the house was hot like the train compartment, but its neatness was undeniable. She hadn't been expected, yet every surface was clean, every object in perfect order. There was a front parlor with two floral-print chairs and a sofa set around a braided rug and a cathedral radio on legs (so they *did* have electricity), and there was a wooden telephone box on the wall as well. The man on the train said there might not be electricity or telephones or running water. Sheer curtains gave the room a yellowish color, not unpleasant, like it was already the jack-o'-lantern hour of dusk. A mahogany-framed photograph of a stiff, unfriendly man startled Aldine—what if that were Ansel Price? His clothes were old-fashioned, though, and he wore a monocle, so she hoped it was someone else.

"You came from New York City, you said?"

The question gave her a start, and she turned around to find Mrs. Price standing in the doorway. Aldine wondered how long she'd been standing like that. "Aye. New York City."

"Do you smoke cigarettes?"

"No." This was not quite the truth. "Well, I have naw for a long while. My sister would naw allow it."

Mrs. Price enunciated, "Your sister would *not* allow it?"

Aldine nodded.

Mrs. Price said, "Well we don't, either. Not inside or outside or anywhere. Our youngest one, it closes up her passages."

Aldine was nodding again. "That's fine then," she said.

"Also it's vulgar for a woman."

"Aye," Aldine said. She let her eyes drift away from Mrs. Price. The truth of it was that if ever she had loads of money her first purchase would be tarries and a good supply at that.

Charlotte came out of the kitchen with a little plate of pickled beets and carrots. She was already chewing one of them. "Mom doesn't think smoking is ladylike," she said, offering Aldine the platter. "She thinks only city vixens smoke."

Mrs. Price was looking at her stiffly but Charlotte kept smiling. Her lips were somehow moist, her hair somehow buoyant. Aldine declined the pickled vegetables—she did not want to pluck them up with her fingers as was evidently the custom. Charlotte slipped two more beet slices into her mouth, then took up Aldine's luggage and turned to her mother. "Attic room?"

Mrs. Price nodded.

Aldine was conscious of her heels on the hollow wood, of the plainness of the house's sounds. A lack of carpets, she supposed.

"Neva might be up there," Mrs. Price said. "I don't know why she didn't come running to see who was here."

"In the barn, is my guess. She said Krazy Kat had kittens."

Charlotte went clomping up the stairs with Aldine's suitcase, and Aldine followed, smelling Charlotte's talcum powder and her own gritty sweat soaked into the armpits of her best black dress. They reached the landing with its view of a hallway and three doors, then started to climb again. "It's a good thing you're so small," Charlotte said. "I barely fit in this room."

In fact, Aldine could only stand up in the center of the stifling hot attic, which was not papered or painted or, for that matter, clean. Dust lay on everything and in everything and formed a shifting, unsheddable skin. She could see particles on the windowsills, on the unpainted floorboards, hovering in the air by the dirty yellowed sheers that hung by the attic's small single window. Aldine stared at an iron bed that looked as if it had been sifted all over with flour.

"Ugh," Charlotte said, and reached a finger to the bed. She drew a line in the dust on the coverlet. "Sweet mother of God, if the Mother saw this, she'd throw a royal fit. *Tolerate no uncleanliness*, and all that."

"Excuse me?"

"It's one of Benjamin Franklin's slogans the Mother likes to tap you on the head with every chance you get. *Tolerate no uncleanliness in body, clothes, or habitation.* That's the full quotation."

Aldine nodded and wondered whether Mr. Franklin was a Mormon. It seemed quite possible.

"We just don't get up here much and the truth is, it's hard enough keeping up with the rest of the house," Charlotte said. "The wind isn't even supposed to blow in September. February, March, April—those are the regular blow months. That's when you have to turn the radio up or put the covers over your head or sing yourself silly to block out the noise. And you don't clean the dust till the wind stops, either. No point. I think it comes through glass. Through walls. But lately it's worse than ever. It's like you can't even eat without swallowing the neighbor's field. I keep hoping we'll go to California, where my aunt lives but my dad says it's just a couple of bad years."

She sighed and folded up the coverlet so the dust would remain inside it. "I'll get you a fresh one from the cupboard, and bring wet rags for wiping it all down. Then it'll be clean enough for a while."

"Thanks very much," Aldine said. She was sick with disappointment, half smothered by regret. *Beautiful Loam County, Kansas.* "I'm sorry I came."

Charlotte opened her eyes wide. They were a muddy sort of blue but enormous, like the rest of her. Her cheeks were cherry pink, her lashes black. She and her mother didn't look at all alike but Aldine could see what it would mean to them both to brush their hair and put them into other clothes and set them down anywhere but here. Which in turn made her wonder what Kansas would do for her own looks.

"You're sorry?" Charlotte asked. Her face was full of apology. "That's my fault. I shouldn't have said all that about the dust. It's not so bad really. You'll like it fine here."

"But to come noo," Aldine said, unable to remember how Americans said *now*. "When you're all thinking of leaving."

Charlotte used one of her big soft hands to wipe a strand of curly hair off her forehead. She laughed in a way that would have been nice to hear if Aldine hadn't been so sick with regret. "Oh, don't worry," Charlotte said. "My dad isn't thinking of leaving. He thinks we all ought to be proud to live on the same farm that his father got from his father that his father got from, I don't know, Tecumseh or somebody."

Who Tecumseh was, Aldine couldn't guess. She said, "Your mother didn't seem happy. To see me, I mean."

"*Didna,*" Charlotte said. "Is that how you said it? *Didna.*"

Aldine nodded, though it didn't sound at all the same.

"I told my dad it was silly to advertise the Stony Bank School in New York, of all places," Charlotte went on. "He's got this friend there from when he worked for the Harvey House—did you stop and eat at one?"

Aldine shook her head, trying to memorize how Charlotte had said Stony Bank.

"Well, my dad has this friend in the newspaper business named Terence Tidball who said he'd put in an ad for free—Dad is a big one for 'contacts'—and Dad said that he was taking Terence up on his offer because by God he would bring music and culture to the prairie or die trying. My dad would, I mean, not Terence Tidball."

Aldine didn't know what to say to this. The place was not at all what she'd imagined. Where were the rivers? Where were the clouds? Where were the green pastures?

"Are you hungry?" Charlotte asked.

"Aye," Aldine said, more fervently than she meant. "And clarty."

Charlotte gave Aldine a look of incomprehension.

"Dirty," Aldine said.

"Well, I'll go see if we have enough water for a bath. It's washday, though. I'll be back with a clean spread in a sec."

Aldine's legs felt unsteady, and she reached out to hold one of the bed knobs.

"Why don't you lie down? You look kind of faint."

Aldine lay down on the plain white sheet and closed her eyes until Charlotte had gone clomping away. When she opened them, she stood and pulled aside the sheers of the curved window, the glass of which was faintly blue. Through the blue lens she could see a bare field, a dark chicken, a running child in a smock. *That must be Neva*, Aldine thought, and closed her eyes to the room.

11

The footsteps on the stairs to the attic were too brisk and tappity to be Charlotte's. A round face, small and brown, peered in at Aldine from the doorway. The girl had eyes and skin the color of treacle. "I'm Geneva," she said, stepping past the threshold. "You can call me Neva, though." She'd caught sight of Aldine's bracelets and had to prize her eyes from them. "Are you Allene?"

"Aldine," Aldine said. It occurred to her that Neva's tiny body was perfectly proportioned to the room.

Neva put her small hand on Aldine's bracelets, the ones Dr. O'Malley had bought, or which had been his wife's, Aldine had never been sure. The girl rubbed her finger over the yellow one, then the black. "Are they wood?" Neva asked.

"No. Bakelite. Like the telephone."

"It's like you came from Montgomery Wards!" Neva said. "Dad sent away for a teacher and here you are."

Neva's two front teeth were gone and when she smiled the bare gums made her look like an impish vampire. "Come on!" she said, pulling on the bracelet arm, leading Aldine along, talking and talking. She said their radio came from Montgomery Wards, and that the Hintons on the next farm over had gotten their whole house from Montgomery Wards, but not the front, which Mrs. Hinton said she had to have or she wasn't staying another minute, so her father had built the porch but hadn't charged them because the Hintons were new and it was good to help the new people when so many others were leaving but it turned out that the Hintons left, anyway, and after only a year. She said there was bathwater downstairs and chicken pie pretty soon and that Krazy Kat had five kittens except one of them didn't look too good and did Aldine know how to nurse kittens?

Aldine said she didn't, and she followed Neva's ponytail and stream of chatter down to a tub that had been filled for her on the back porch. "You can bathe in there," Neva said. "We won't let Clare come in." She raised her eyebrows and smiled the wide pink-gum smile.

"You have another sister?" Aldine asked, as glad to see the full tub of water as she was dismayed to find herself in a place where, once again, she would not have a private bath in a scoured white bog. They didn't even have running water. Yet how could this be?

"No," Neva said, and shook her head.

"Then who's Clare?" Aldine decided to take off her shoes.

"Clar-*ence*," Neva said. "My big brother. He's helping Dad drill seed. They never come in till later. Our hogs died last week."

Aldine grimly added this information to Charlotte's litany about the dust.

"God sent them a sickness, Mama said. So they wouldn't suffer in Kansas anymore. Mama says California is like heaven so I think maybe they went to California. Do you think they could have?"

To her own surprise Aldine said, "If I could come here from Scotland, I guess a pig could go to California."

Neva seemed pleased with this answer.

Aldine sat on the stool beside the water, her feet bare now, and ached to get into the water.

"You're nicer than our last teacher, Mr. Geoph," Neva said, reaching out to clack the black and yellow bracelets again, running her fingers across their slippery curves. "All he did was read the German newspaper and burn buckets of coal in the stove and shout at Yauncy that he was in for a hiding."

Aldine asked who Yauncy was.

"Mr. and Mrs. Tanner's only son. Yauncy's slow and he can't help it. He groans in class, which everybody was used to but not Mr. Geoph." Then she said, "Before that we had Miss Pike, who wasn't nice at all but she got married anyway, Charlotte says she doesn't know how."

Yauncy is slow. And he groaned. Which was why Mr. Tanner said that he was all done growing.

"And Yauncy will not come to school again?"

Neva looked at her quizzically, so Aldine repeated it more slowly.

"Oh. No, I don't suppose so. Mr. Tanner's awfully nice to Yauncy even though Mrs. Tanner isn't really. Everyone says she has a case of nerves that won't allow it, but Mr. Tanner is gentle with him and when Mr. Geoph gave him a hiding for groaning Mr. Tanner took him away and that was that. Yauncy's not right, but he's strong, he can pick up bales easy as you please, so he does that now."

Aldine was relieved, though she wouldn't say it. "And before that?" she asked. "Before Miss Pike who got married?"

"Don't know. I was too little. You'll have to ask Clare or Charlotte."

Mrs. Price put her head in. "Neva," she said. "Leave Miss McCandless to bathe in peace." The smile she directed at Aldine was more dutiful than friendly. "When you're finished, I have something for you to eat," she said, and she took Neva with her when she closed the kitchen door.

Aldine was in the washtub, naked as a frog, when she heard a slamming screen door, then the voice of a man in a room that seemed inches away. She heard Neva say, "Daddy!" and a man's voice, low and rumbly, "Hello, girly." Aldine pulled her knees to her breasts and let the metallic water drip down over her face, holding the cake of Joro tightly as she heard Mrs. Price saying, "Well, that plan of yours worked, Ansel. There's a schoolteacher here from New York City by way of Scotland."

"She's so pretty," Neva said. "She's perfect! Thank you, Daddy!"

"She's *here?*" Ansel asked.

Aldine tightened her grip on her bare legs.

"She's taking a bath on the back porch," Mrs. Price said, her voice low but still audible. "Honestly, Ansel. We can't afford a boarder right now. When is the school board going to start her salary, and where is she going to live?"

The voices moved farther off so that she could hear the humming but not the words. She reached over the side of the tub for a tin cup, and with the cup she poured the tepid water over her hair, her face, and her future, willing it all to become a burn that fed a river that fed an ocean that she could swim in all the way back to Ayr.

12

Of all the surprises in the world, none was more unimaginable to Clare Price than finding a comely young woman kneeling on the rug just before supper, helping Neva with her paper dolls. She wore a black dress printed all over with clamshells. The cloth was thin and shiny and seemed poured over her body. Her hair was black, too, and glossy where the curve of it touched her chin and caught the light. Over the crown of her head she wore a knitted cap of some kind, a flat disk with a black pom-pom. Her skin was freckled white, her arms were long and slender, and her fingers, which were busy folding and pressing a paper dress onto a paper Shirley Temple, reminded him of the naked bodies in the magazine Harry Gifford had given him before Gifford left on a freight train with two other boys who dropped out of school. He wondered how old she was. He wondered if her breasts were as white as her hands, or whiter.

"I'm Aldine McKenna," the girl-woman said, popping up so quickly to shake hands that her bracelets clacked together. "You must be Clarence."

Clay-dance. He barely recognized his own name when she said it—that was how exotic she made it.

"It's Clare," he said out of habit. "No one calls me Clarence." From his lips the name sounded nasal and plain again. He looked down at his hands, oily from tractor work, and wished he'd done a better job of washing them.

"Not even the teachers?" Aldine asked, and then seemed to say, "Beggars thoust will be."

"I'm sorry?" he said.

She said it again, confusing him more, but Neva said, "Because that's what she is, Clare, our new teacher!"

"Oh," Clare said. The young woman smiled and stayed on her feet, as if waiting for him to say more, but he couldn't think of anything more to say. Neva kept dancing on her toes and pushing the black and yellow bangles on Aldine's arm up and down, letting them fall and clack together until finally Aldine slipped them off and handed them to Neva, who pressed the bracelets to her eyes like spectacles and peered clownishly through them at Clare. "They're Bakelite, Clare," she shouted. "Like the telephone!" Then, to Aldine, she said, "Clare remembers things. He can tell you every one of Tom Mix's injuries and recite all the presidents in order including vice presidents!"

She smiled at him. "Well, well. Is that true now, Clarence?" she said in a voice that seemed to flow through him like a warm liquid. "And how many injuries does Mr. Tom Mix have?"

"Twenty-six," he murmured. "They go A to Z."

"Do they now?" Aldine said, and he felt somehow that the friskiness in her tone was coming at his expense. He felt his cheeks going red. He wanted to keep looking at her in the worst way, but he couldn't. He lowered his eyes and turned away.

When they were all seated at the table, Aldine answered questions while dishes were passed. With the bowls of chicken soup, there was a platter of pan rolls and bread. Clare helped himself to a pan roll before he realized there were only five, but he noticed that Aldine more quickly perceived the math problem before them, and took only a heel of bread before passing the platter.

"So," his father said in that broad way that he used at holidays and with guests, "your name is Miss McKenna. Tell us a little something about yourself. How old you are, for instance, and where you come from."

The young woman seemed to realize that the slower she spoke, the better she was understood, so with deliberate slowness she told them that she was twenty-two years of age, had been born and raised in Scotland, and had been most recently living with her married sister, Eileen, in New York, which was how she'd come upon the advertisement in the paper. She had applied for the position in Kansas because she'd liked poetry and music in school and thought she might be able to visit her sister on weekends now and then.

"In New York?" Charlotte said. "From here?"

Clare hated how Charlotte was nearly laughing at the girl. It was a big mistake to make, certainly, but not a funny one.

"I know," the girl said. "I see now that I was ignorant. At home things couldna' be so far apart."

She suddenly bowed her head, and when she looked up again, her expression was of resolve. "I would have come anyway, for all the distance. You see, my sister and her husband and the people in the church in New York wanted to find me a husband, and they found one, but I didna' like him that way."

Everyone was looking at her and leaning ever so slightly toward her, or so it seemed to Clare, everyone except his mother, who did as she usually did, which was to sit back and listen with a judging silence. He said, "It's like Jane Withersteen. In *Riders of the Purple Sage*, except she didn't want to marry a Mormon named Tull."

The young woman seemed confused by this, so he said, "It's a Zane Grey book. There's a swell movie of it with Tom Mix."

"His glorious wounded hero," Charlotte explained, and Clare dropped his gaze and thought the subject was over, but the girl in her funny accent said, "Was there something wrong with the Mormon then?"

Clare laughed. "There was something wrong with *all* the Mormons then. They had lots of wives and were mean to all of them. That's how it was in the book, anyway. We don't know any Mormons personally."

Some moments passed and his father said, "We got just your first letter. I'm sorry we didn't have someone there to meet you. We should have." He'd let his eyes fall on the girl and now he left them there.

"I could've come on our neighbor's horse," Clare blurted, and immediately wished he hadn't because Charlotte countered with a quick, derisive snort. "Oh there's a picture for you—our white knight, Clare, on his black nag, Sally," which prompted Neva to say, "But Sally's *not* a black nag!" and Clare's father in his calm voice said to Charlotte, "Don Quixote rode a skinny barn horse, Lottie, but it always got him there."

The Scottish girl made a pretty sound, and everyone looked at her.

"Rocinante," she said again, in a tone that suggested apology. "I think that was the name of the horse." She let her eyes fall again to her plate, which allowed everyone to consider her.

Something seemed to be happening at the table, Clare thought, some kind of shift that couldn't be seen. It was like watching a play you didn't understand. He nearly began proclaiming about wanted criminals just to dispel the silence, but Charlotte beat him to it.

"Well," she said, "Mr. Tanner's wagon is luxury itself compared to a ride behind Clarence on Sally's bony rumpola."

Charlotte followed this with a high laugh, and Clarence again felt his face color. Only the Scottish girl's presence kept him from remarking on Charlotte's own rumpola. And he wasn't making himself out as a knight in shining armor. More like Tom Mix riding in on Tony the Wonder Horse.

Charlotte turned to Aldine. "Did Mr. Tanner talk a lot about Ed and Billy?" she asked.

Aldine looked up as if startled. "Not a very great lot, no," she replied slowly, "but more of them than anything else."

His father gave out with one of his up-from-the-stomach laughs. "He likes two good mules," he said, and shook his head, smiling. "The question would be who he would choose. If it came down to his mules or his wife," he said and laughed again.

"Mules, no question," Clare said, glad to have something adultlike and cynical to say.

"What about Yauncy?" Neva said. "Who would he choose then?"

"Oh, Yauncy of course," his father said. "I was just joking, Nevie. Mr. Tanner'd save his wife, too, if it came to that."

A silence developed. Spoons clinking on soup bowls. Aldine dipped away from the bowl and sipped quietly from the side of the spoon, and soon Clare was doing so, too. Neva ate her roll and jelly, then began running her tongue in and out of the empty space where her front teeth used to be. Clare broke open his pan roll, spread it with butter, and filled it with plum preserves, and almost before he knew he was doing it, he'd reached past Neva to hand it to Aldine. "Here. Try this. It's just as good as dessert."

"But . . ." Aldine said, and now she was looking at him, which he liked so much it nearly paralyzed him. "I'm full," he heard himself say, though he wasn't. His face was hot. "I had a potato earlier," he explained, which he knew was more or less the same as declaring himself the king of idiots. "A raw one but we cooked it," he said, and then he added, "We took them out with us."

Everyone was staring at him now and he could feel sweat beading on his forehead. He could've kissed Neva when she diverted attention by saying, "Daddy has the best way of cooking potatoes!" and then their father was explaining his method of digging a small hole, covering the potatoes, building a fire above them, and letting them bake from the fire burning down while they worked. He smiled at Clare. "It's something to look forward to, isn't it, Clare?"

Clare nodded. "Yes sir. It is."

"Which goes to show that those two"—Charlotte grinned and nodded toward her father and Clare—"can find some lunatic thing to look forward to no matter how dire the circumstances."

When Aldine sampled the roll and jelly, her whole body seemed to slacken. "Oh, my," she said. "Isna' that splendid then?" As she said this, she looked at his mother, but his mother would have none of it. She became busy with her soup.

"Didn't your folks worry about you traveling alone?" Charlotte said.

No, Aldine told them, her parents were no longer of this earth.

Because nosy Charlotte was nosy Charlotte, Clare expected her to go on asking things, but she didn't. She just nodded and drank more water. A magazine that her friend Opal had given her recommended cold water steeped with mint for shedding weight, but so far the only result he'd noticed was an increased number of trips to the library, which was what she called the outhouse.

"So did you teach in a big school in Scotland?" his mother asked.

"No," Aldine said, and looked down at the oilcloth. "I haven't taught in a school at all before now."

His mother's chin rose at this. "But you went to normal school there in your town?"

"Normal school?" Aldine asked, biting her lower lip in a way that made Clare's own lips feel dry. Her hair, which hung straight down over her ears, was electrified by the dry air, and had been crimped slightly by the knit hat she took off for supper. The whole effect should have ruined her looks, but it didn't. It just made her seem in need of protecting.

"Teacher-training school," his father told Aldine, then turned to his mother. "It was in the letter she sent the school board. They call it something else over there."

"Oh, yes!" Aldine said. "They do."

"I see," his mother said, making it seem somehow as if she saw a great deal. She was still annoyed about something, and there was plenty to choose from. Charlotte probably knew if it was something more than the usual too-much-dust, too-little-money, and too-many-wild-schemes. If there were secrets, Charlotte was always first to find them.

"I'll help Lottie with the dishes," he offered when his mother pushed her chair back and said she was going to make up Aldine's bed in the attic.

Aldine looked abashed. "I can do that myself," she said, but was told not to worry on her first night here, and Clare watched her bite her lip again and refold her napkin with her long white hands and set it on the table just where it had been so that it might seem unused.

~

Charlotte did not disappoint. As she handed Clare rinsed dishes, she told him she'd been with their father in the barn that morning when Mr. Josephson came by to tell him that there would be no money for teachers in the rural schools—"No book money, no salary, no funds at all." They'd better write to that teacher they'd hired and tell her to stay in New York, Mr. Josephson said.

"But it was too late," Charlotte told Clare in a hushed tone. "She was already on the train by then." Charlotte dropped her voice still lower. "Mom doesn't even know yet that there's no money. She's just mad because Aldine is here with us."

"Do you think she'll stay here then?" he asked. He tried to keep his voice absolutely neutral but it was no use. At once Charlotte said in a taunting tone, "Why? What does *Clay-rence* care?"

"I don't," he said. He rubbed at a sticky place on the pot in hand. Then, when enough time had passed, he said, "What's Dad going to do, do you think?"

"What does His Highness usually do?"

Clare set the pot into the cupboard. There had been the time that everyone said no one would watch Shakespeare in Loam County, but then his father had found old copies of *Othello* in the school basement, directed rehearsals on Sunday afternoons, and put on a blackening face-cover for a performance before a full house at the Stony Bank schoolhouse and happily took his bows alongside Desdemona (Georgia Waterman, who was actually swell enough to make somebody jealous). And his mother had said they would not have a Christmas tree last year when there were no gifts to put under it, but his father said of course they would and they did—and a fat one at that—and he had made a wooden tractor and red-roofed barn to go to the winners of the checkers tournament they played through the afternoon.

"Make it work, I guess," Clare said, glad to have a father who was resourceful, especially if it meant that Aldine would be staying in the room directly above his, washing her beautiful white body in a tub that he himself washed in, and eating across the table from him with her long, slender, upturned fingers.

"More specifically," Charlotte said, "make women do whatever it is he wants."

Which was a pot-calling-the-kettle-black circumstance if ever he'd heard one. Charlotte was two years older than Clare, had bossed him as long as he could remember, and didn't care who knew it. She could kill with looks and words. Two neighboring farmers had courted her, Milt Sculler and Albert Flint, but she'd turned them down flat. He'd heard her talking to Albert Flint and she hadn't spared his feelings. "Oh, I just couldn't," she'd told him, "not now or ever after." She'd told Clare she wanted to go to normal school in Topeka, then move out to California and be a teacher, but there was no money now, and who knew when there would ever be again.

To get a rise from his sister, Clare said, "Isn't it in the Bible that women should pretty much always do what men want?" and Charlotte snapped at him with her dish towel while he laughed and dodged.

After he went to bed, he listened to his parents' murmuring voices, pressing his ear against the wall so he could hear first his father explaining, then his mother exclaiming in a slightly louder voice, then his father in his familiar manner proposing ways the shortfall could be ignored or somehow put off, certain that rain would fall and wheat prices would rise. His mother said it would have been easier to turn away a local man, just as she'd said all along, and now what were they going to do?

His father had begun to talk again, but his mother stopped him.

"You'll just have to tell her to go back," she said, and if his father replied, Clare didn't hear it.

He tried to sleep. He went through all the presidents and vice presidents backward and forward. He did multiplication tables through fifteen. He silently recited *Hiawatha* through *Nokomis, the old woman, pointing with her finger westward.* He kept thinking of the girl.

13

In the night, with the cottonwood branch scratching at the bedroom wall and the moon throwing shadows into the room, with his wife snoring gently beside him and with the floor-creaking and water-tinkling sounds of the girl from Scotland using the chamber pot in the attic above him, Ansel Price decided that his wife was right. The girl would have to go back. He would have to tell her how things were with the school board and she would have to go back.

And had the next morning not been a Sunday, perhaps he would have told her she couldn't stay. But it was Sunday, and he rose before dawn because he was too awake to do anything else. Ellie didn't stir. Nobody did. It occurred to him that they all slept soundly now because they'd all been kept awake in the night with their altered thoughts of the house and the world, and what had altered their view of the house and the world was nothing more than the girl's intrusion into it. Rocinante. Now that was something unexpected. All the way from New York City, coming by train and asleep even now in their very attic, a Scottish girl who knew the name of Quixote's horse.

By the time he had fed and milked, the morning's stillness was like a magnifying glass. The cottonwood leaves were yellow as daffodils against a bluest blue sky, and every feather of every chicken in the yard seemed a different shade of red. Indian summer had been his father's favorite season here, and it was his, too. It was hard not to feel hope on such a day, when the wind was not blowing, and the sun was not burning. He found button mushrooms by the creek and brought in late tomatoes from the garden and knew that the smell of them pan-frying in butter would draw the others downstairs.

He tilted the bowl of mushrooms into the buttery pan. He hoped the girl would come down first. There was no easy way of saying to her what needed to be said, but telling her when she was alone would steal less of her dignity, and dignity was something he felt sure the girl cared something about, and the circumstances of her arrival—no one to meet her and a long ride behind Tanner's mules—left her so little of it. But just then Ellie came in from the chickens with a small bowl only half full of brown eggs and frowned at once at his profligate use of butter, and then Neva and Clare were tumbling down the stairs, and after them Lottie, so he rearranged his planning. They would feed the girl properly, and afterward he could draw her outside for a private word, and this, too, was a plan that might have worked had the girl not come downstairs in a pink dress looking altogether freshened and laying her sober brown eyes on Ellie to say in a slow, practiced manner, "Thank you, Mrs. Price, for giving me the particular room that you did. I looked out the window this morning to the most marvelous rising of the sun."

Which anyone in the world would see as a pleasant sentiment, but Ellie just gave the girl's good manners a solemn nod and went back to mixing her pancake batter. The Scottish girl had brushed her hair and her face was pretty and smooth and freckled and the pink dress ornamented with a brown bow at the collar became her in a way that made you think she was spunky and fun despite the worried look that lay back in her eyes, which anybody could see and was probably why Neva was already holding her arm and asking if there were kittens in Scotland. Aldine stood awkwardly by the table until Neva begged her to sit in the chair touching hers, and after one sip of the coffee Ellie poured in her cup, she just stared at her plate.

Ellie had begun serving pancakes with frosty efficiency. Ansel stirred heavy cream with the mushrooms, then wrapped the pan handle with a towel and went plate to plate spooning out portions.

"Yum," Neva said, and the Scottish girl, upon tasting hers, looked up smiling thoroughly and said, "Well, isna' that divine?"

At which he, a grown man and thinking himself well past such things, felt a thrill of self-satisfied pleasure move through his body. He said, "Wait till you taste Ellie's plum syrup," and after tasting the syrup, the girl said that it, too, was divine, though he could tell that Ellie, unmoved, believed that the girl had only taken a cue. He also saw her observe how much of the syrup the girl had poured over her pancakes.

"It's the last of it," Ellie said, as if to Ansel. "No more till the plum bears again."

"We used to get lots," said Clare, who, it was clear, had been sitting in wait of something to say to the girl. "But not so many the last two years."

"*Not so many?*" Charlotte said. "Zero plums is a lot less than not so many."

They ate in silence for a moment, tasting the distilled purple sweetness and feeling the life seep from the room.

"The more reason to savor it," Ansel said and wondered why salvaging the meal seemed so important to him. "And rest assured there'll be more plums next summer, I guarantee it."

"I guarantee it, too, one hundred percent," Neva said, trying to sound somber and adultlike, which made everyone but Ellie smile. When the Scottish girl smiled, you could see the cheerful person she must once have been, or could yet be, given something to cheer her.

"I like that color," Neva said of Aldine's dress. "It's pink as a piggy bank."

The Scottish girl gave out a quick, pretty laugh. "And don't you look glad yourself then," she said in return to Neva, who was wearing her church dress, a yellow cotton as bright as the leaves outside.

He noticed Charlotte smiling and said, "Charlotte made that for Nevie. Lottie sews like there's no tomorrow."

"It's bonny indeed," the girl said, and Charlotte answered, "It is, isn't it, if I say so myself," and sipped from her water.

He was still hungry, and eyed the platter at the center of the table. One pancake left and no one wanting to take it.

"I don't like church," Neva announced to Aldine, her mouth full with pancake. "Do you?"

Ansel didn't have to see it. He could feel Ellie's eyes rising and fixing on the girl.

Aldine held her full coffee cup with both hands, the tendrils of steam lit up by the morning sun. "I love the singing," she said. *Luve,* she said, making the word more powerful, original almost, as if she'd coined it.

"Me, too," he said before he knew it.

There was a silence, and he took a big swig of coffee. He doubted the girl had money to turn around and go back. If she had money, she wouldn't have come at all. He watched Ellie slice her own pancakes into small triangular chunks, hardly sweetened with plum syrup; then he let his gaze drift out the window to the slanted line the barn roof made against the blue sky. He could hear a small wind feeling its way through the cottonwood, finding the weak leaves. He closed his eyes for a moment and watched them fall free.

"Look at the time," Ellie said, and all at once was pushing back her chair and saying to Aldine, "You can come or stay as you like. There's St. Anne's, if you'd rather, but it's in the other direction and you'd have to walk." She was piling plates and untying her apron, tucking a strand of curly hair behind her ear.

Ansel looked around. The buttery mushrooms in heavy cream were gone; the breakfast was over. The smallest kind of sadness but a sadness still. He said, "If she wants to go up to St. Anne's, the Eckerts could take her. They're Catholic."

"They've probably gone already," Ellie said, pushing things ahead. Always, in her little ways, pushing.

"Well, next time," Ansel said.

Ellie shot him a look that said there wouldn't be a next time, but Aldine set down her cup, half full and no longer steaming, and said she wasn't Catholic, anyway, and that she'd much rather see where they went, if they didn't mind.

"Of course we don't mind," he said, wiping his mouth and pushing back his chair as Ellie picked up Aldine's cup of unfinished coffee and set it in the sink.

"Don't you drink coffee, dear?" Ellie asked, trying to keep her tone neutral, as if it didn't bother her to see it wasted.

"Oh, I'm sorry," Aldine said. "It's new to me, is all. At home, we drink tea." She walked quickly to the counter, retrieved her cup, and swallowed the rest.

Ellie told her that wasn't necessary, but Ansel thought it probably was. Everyone at the table had noticed that she'd left plum syrup pooled shallowly on her plate. Wasting coffee would only have compounded the sin.

Still, he thought, something almost boyish unfolding within him, *sin can have its happy by-products.*

So when the girls went upstairs for hats and last-minute adjustments to their dress, he winked at Clare, grabbed the last pancake, and tore it in two. He handed one portion to Clare, and they swabbed their halves assiduously over the girl's dish, sopping up the sweet syrup until her white plate gleamed.

The wind *whuffed* at the windows of the Ford as it moved toward the church, but it was a mild wind, and the world looked newly hopeful to Ansel. He was proud of the new coat of paint on the Methodist church, which he'd helped apply last year. A white clapboard church circled by box elders with their leaves flickering yellow and orange was a good thing to show a foreign visitor. And the people they met going in were all the usual mix of Kansas-curious and Kansas-friendly, asking her name, shaking her hand. Mrs. Odekirk was the first, eyes bright and expecting the best, as she always seemed to do, and he heard himself say, "This is Aldine McKenna, who's just come by train from New York to be our new teacher," sealing his own fate as he said so, and Mrs. Odekirk saying, "Well, this is wonderful! We're delighted to have you." She turned, smiling, to Ansel and said, "You and your big ideas, Ansel Price. We will never doubt you again." Ansel was fond of this tall, stork-like woman. The lines in her face were symmetrical and handsome, like the comb marks in her tightly bound gray hair.

"She's a piano teacher!" Neva told her.

Reverend Bakely turned round. She could play the piano, could she? It happened that Mrs. Tanner, the accompanist, was ill this morning. Did she know any Methodist hymns?

"Miss McKenna is from Scotland," Ansel said. "That's Anglican, right?"

Aldine said no, that actually the Church of Scotland was Presbyterian (a mistake that made him feel like a fool) but she could sight-read, and she didn't mind trying if they didn't mind a mistake or two. So she sat at the piano in her pink dress and brown bow and looked slightly less lost, Ansel thought, when she didn't have to speak or look at anyone. She played well. Even the most tin eared among them could hear that much, and as the congregation registered the surprise of this sudden wonder, he felt suffused with pride in the Scottish girl, and (it had to be admitted) in the fact that he, Ansel Price, had delivered her here.

14

On Monday night, the Prices sat listening to a radio show, some of the family more attentively than others. Mrs. Price stitched shut a hole in one of Mr. Price's black woolen socks; Charlotte had a book on her lap that she read or did not read depending on her interest in the show; Neva played with one of Aldine's knitting needles and leaned close to the big freestanding radio, staring at it as if there were strangers inside she could almost see; Clarence listened with nothing to do, it seemed, but look at Aldine or his knees; whereas Mr. Price sat back with a bemused expression, his interest in the show, as in all things, calibrated somehow.

Aldine knitted. She had begun a blanket with Leenie's baby in mind. She'd spent the day helping with the household work, though Mrs. Price's standards were beyond her—she saw defects in Aldine's cleaning that Aldine could not discern no matter how keenly she stared or studied the chair rung or window glass or chowder bowl in question—so that in the end Mrs. Price seemed to think her more a nuisance than anything else. Whereas Charlotte seemed glad for her company, especially when wiping and rewiping the dust from sills and surfaces with wet rags morning and afternoon. The wind here was horrid but the dust was worse. It got into Aldine's ears and her nose. Her skin dried and cracked and when she asked Charlotte what she did about it, the girl had laughed and said, "Pray that we'll leave!" Which, though Aldine laughed, did nothing to lift her spirits.

The radio program featured a flat-voiced rich man who hoarded his money in his basement and who, besides his stinginess, seemed bland to the edge of flavorless. That did not, however, keep everyone in the radio audience from laughing at every word he said. Aldine couldn't fathom it, and when Mr. Price began to stare off through the window so that now she faced only the scrutiny of Neva and Clarence, she fixed a smile on her face.

The family was suddenly laughing, so she laughed as well, not too soft and not too loud, which seemed to satisfy Neva, but she knew for a fact that Mr. Price saw how lost she was, and what would she tell Leenie about him? That he seemed somehow two men? Well, she would not tell her about the one who was sturdy and tall and entered rooms headfirst, who was rugged-looking to a point just beyond routinely handsome, though he was, but that wasn't the sort of thing you said about married men, and he was forty, at least. His dark hair was receding but his arms were still thick with hair, and his rough fingers were hairy on top. No, she would give Leenie the other one of him, the one who was distant and gentle and full of big boyish hopes, sort of like their own half-daft Uncle Gus, who had no children and raised sheep in Perthshire and trained trees into odd shapes and once, not long ago, brought home in eleven great crates a rusted Ferris wheel that he put right and reassembled. And then when no mother at all would let her child board for the first ride, his barren wife—their sweet Aunt Kathleen—stepped forward and when Uncle Gus sent her around twice and then stopped her at the top, she had whooped in delight and exclaimed at the view, which, Aldine was dead sure, Mrs. Price would never have done for Mr. Price, whatever contraption he might build. She might tell Leenie, too, that when the man stared off (he was doing it now), it was as if he could disconnect himself from the very world round him, but where he'd reconnected himself to in the meantime was the mystery she wished to pierce. And yet when he looked directly into her eyes, he seemed to offer her something—confidence, maybe, or hope—as if she were a prisoner and he had no other way to assure her that he was on her side. Because of that much she was almost certain. He was on her side. He hoped she could be contented.

And then at this very moment, he glanced Aldine's way, but only for a moment, as if he'd felt something on him and had now satisfied himself as to its source, which embarrassed her completely.

She knitted vigorously, eyes down until the comedian on the radio induced further laughter.

Charlotte looked up from her book. *The Harvester*, the book was called, and as she read, she pinched several locks of her springy blonde hair into a sort of paintbrush and swept her lips with it.

Neva said, "I hate it when the show's over. But at least it comes on again Wednesday and that's only two days." Then she said, "How do you do that without looking?" and it took Aldine a moment to realize that the girl was talking to her, about her knitting.

"Oh it's the easiest thing," Aldine said slowly. "I could do it eyes closed in a coal hole."

Aldine thought this might be the moment to excuse herself to go upstairs and write her letter. But as she began to gather her needles and yarn, Mr. Price leaned forward and cleared his throat to say, "I was up to Cyrus Motherbaugh's today."

His seriousness seemed to signify something; his family turned toward him.

"Cyrus no longer owns the fiddle I thought we could get for Miss McKenna," he said. "Sold it last year." Mr. Price tilted his head and lowered his voice. "His father's own fiddle."

The family found this regretful, but, to be truthful, Aldine felt relief. Mr. Price had mentioned the fiddle when it turned out there was no longer a piano at the schoolhouse and Aldine had acted pleased, but really she wasn't sure how she'd use it. Would she play for the children while they read?

"For how much?" Charlotte asked.

Mr. Price shook his head and said he hadn't asked.

Something came into Mrs. Price's face then—Aldine saw it. A careful kind of slyness. "Aldine doesn't really need accompaniment," she said. "She can sing a cappella at school." She fixed her gleaming eyes on her. "I was looking at your letter of application today, dear. You mentioned that you sang a cappella."

Neva asked what *a cappella* meant, and while Mr. Price patiently explained it to the girl, Aldine felt the color rising in her neck and cheeks. She hadn't sung alone, she said. It was in a choir. And they were only a cappella because the organ bellows had failed beyond repair.

"Couldn't you try by yourself, though?" Neva said, and Mrs. Price (really, it was more than she'd said to Aldine the whole day long) said, "Yes, dear, you could just try, couldn't you?" and Neva added, "A real true Scotland song!"

Something had begun unfurling within her then, a feeling that she would just as soon have suppressed, but now, having it coaxed from her (and with spiteful intent!) brought with it a prideful pleasure, just as she had felt, though she cringed to admit it, when she had allowed Dr. O'Malley to look upon her, because she knew (Aunt Sedge's house had mirrors after all) that what she was about to reveal was not without its agreeable aspects. Just as now, though she didn't like to sing alone in front of others, she knew her voice to be quite good, at least within a certain range, so she bowed her head and composed her nerves and then, when she was perfectly ready, began softly to sing: "*By yon bonny banks, and by yon bonny braes.*" As she sang she felt the old trembling want that music dug out of you, a longing that you could finally express and that you dug out of other people as you sang. "*Where the sun shines bright on Loch Lomond.*" They listened, Charlotte with her book folded over her finger, Neva with a broad gap-toothed grin, Clarence with a still, beholding look that, she couldn't help it, put her in mind of Dr. O'Malley, and Mr. Price with face tilted toward the window, eyes closed in an attitude close to reverence. Only Mrs. Price seemed indifferent. She watched for a while, then, as if unimpressed or possibly even disappointed, turned to the basket beside her and withdrew another of her husband's socks in need of mending.

15

On the first day of school, Aldine and Neva had walked in early so that Aldine could get her bearings, and now she had thirty minutes to plan the day.

The building itself was nothing like the upright stone school, two stories high, in which she'd spent her own school years. Stony Bank's country school was just one large room, white on the outside like the Price house, unpainted within, an ancient blue stove in the corner, a blackboard in the front, wooden desks hooked together in rows like immovable sleighs. She studied the portraits of two unsmiling men, one with a white wig, beneath the American flag (it seemed worrisome that she didn't know who they were). If there was one pleasant surprise, it was the relative absence of dust. Someone had been in to clean recently; she could detect the faint scent of soap and ammonia.

Aldine studied the names in the book Mr. Price had given her. He said she was to keep the record book up to date for the superintendent, who came around to all the schools on surprise visits, and who would examine the book when the term ended. Miss Pike had used the book for a year and a half, and Mr. Geoph for the whole previous spring. There were not as many students as she expected.

Berenice Josephson

Emmeline Josephson

Melba Josephson

Jerry Pierce

Geneva Louise Price

Jack Reynolds

Yauncy Tanner

Buster Watson

Harlon Wright

Hector Wright

Phay Wright

What were their ages? Was Phay a boy or a girl? Would they all show except Yauncy? The last thing Mr. Geoph had written about Hector was, *Won't come.* She would ask Neva about the boys when she came in from playing on the schoolyard.

What was missing was the list of the children's Master Lessons. On the desktop, where Mr. Price had told her she would find just such a thing, she saw nothing more than a *Webster's Dictionary* and *Roget's Thesaurus.* In the drawers she found only a ruler, a compass, and a small calendar with *x*'s marked through April 22, 1932, the end of the previous term. A ruled sheet of paper was labeled *Inventory of Books,* with each one listed by title and condition. At the bottom Mr. Geoph had signed his name. Otherwise there was nothing except a much smaller piece of paper on which Mr. Geoph had written: *Recitation Program: Ari. Study Group 1: Ari. Study Group 2: Ari.*

Was this it? Could this possibly be the list of lessons? And if so, what in the world did it mean?

She felt a kind of panic rising within her. Twenty-two minutes. She scanned all the flat surfaces of the room, looking for a folder or anything suggesting more thorough plans. A Master Lesson list, Mr. Price had called it. She tore into cupboards. Odd sets of three or four books, a broom, a pole for the transoms. Heavy paper in different colors. A huge spool of stout string. A rolled American flag on a stick. Boxes of old rulers, pencils, erasers. But no lesson book at all.

Fifteen minutes remained to her, according to the clock, and she had no idea how she might lead the classes. Why hadn't she come sooner to prepare? She'd had nearly two weeks to herself and what had she done with them? Nothing except help with the household work. Why hadn't she studied the children's texts, written herself notes? What had she imagined? But she knew what she'd imagined. She'd returned to it often enough, the picture of herself knitting while the children worked at their lessons, quietly, heads bent over their work, a fire in the woodstove, antelope grazing outside the window. A perfect daftie she'd been. The very embodiment of.

She returned to the page where Mr. Geoph had written his *Summary of Term* and *Inventory of Books*. She tried to match up his numbers with the little row of books on the shelf, saw that only three of the books were *new* and the rest were just *fair* or *poor*, and decided to read the spines. Only one seventh-year reader, one sixth, one fourth, and five third. A red cloth Riverside Shakespeare, just like the one at the Price house, but dustier. Single books on physiology, geography, history, agriculture, and civil government. It was entirely possible that she had overstated her teaching abilities. Lied, even, if you looked at it in a certain way.

Through the window, Aldine could see Neva drawing in the dirt. She made a zigzag, then a curling line, then a *V*. Her name, of course.

Three boys stood huddled in the corner of the yard, hands in pockets, shoulders low in attitudes of resentment.

Seven minutes.

At the end of the shelf she found a slim book called *The Modern Music Series Primer*. Songs were arranged by subject in the table of contents, and her eye skipped past *Work* and *Play* to *Rain*.

Maybe they could do two things at once: summon rain and learn to sing.

At two minutes before nine, three girls appeared on the road to school, their feet scuffling dust. Two had long hair like Neva and looked to be seven or eight. The third one carried a satchel and was tall and regal-looking, with her hair cut in a bob that made her face seem a series of elegantly arranged straight lines. Aldine had seen this girl at church on Sunday, had seen Charlotte catching up to her, and Aldine had wondered whether she herself had been the subject of their conversation—twice Charlotte and the girl had glanced over at her as they talked.

Neva saw them coming and threw down her stick. "Bernie! Melba! Emmeline!" she shouted. "Come see who our new teacher is! She's from Scot-land!"

The Josephson girls then, Aldine thought. *That's who they must be.*

The two little girls ran to meet Neva but the older girl did not quicken her pace, and her gaze as she looked up at the school window to see Aldine was withdrawn and appraising, as if she knew something the others did not. Aldine smiled, anyway, as an experiment, and the girl looked away, slowly, casually, as if she had not seen anyone in the window at all.

Aldine was looking at the clock on the wall when the minute hand—it gave her a start—clicked forward to twelve and marked the hour.

16

Aldine opened the front door and called out, "And let us begin our day," the very words Mrs. Lynch, her favorite teacher in Ayr, had used every morning, but now the children stared at her as if she'd just spoken Hebrew, so this time, when she repeated the words, she added a wave of the hand, motioning them in.

"Where do we sit?" one of the girls called out amidst the sudden shuffle in the hollow room and Aldine said, "Wherever you choose," which none of them seemed to understand, so the oldest Josephson girl said, "Front to back, youngest to oldest."

"Littlest or youngest?" Neva asked, and Emmeline gave her a withering look. "Didn't I just say *youngest*?"

Aldine consulted her list of students. "You would be Emmeline then?" she said to the Josephson girl when they were all seated.

The girl looked up from her desk, her face very calm. "If you mean *Em-me-line*, yes, that is my name. Who I would be *then*, I couldn't say, because I don't know when *then* might be."

Silence, until one of the younger Josephsons said, "My sister's real smart."

Aldine pointed to the books spread out on her desk. "Please come forward and take the one that you should be using this year." She said it twice and then Emmeline said, "I think she wants us to take our books," and then, as they did so, she said, "Not the one you used last year, Phay, unless you want to stay in this horrible little school forevermore."

While the others hooted and laughed, none less loudly than his own older brothers, Phay Wright, a freckled, coarse-faced creature, ducked his reddening face.

Aldine passed out the songbooks, made an announcement, and again Emmeline translated. "I think she wants us to sing the song on page thirty-seven."

"Yes," Aldine said. "Page thirty-seven."

"What about the pledge?" Emmeline asked, and Neva said, "You didn't raise your hand!"

Emmeline raised her hand, Aldine nodded, and Emmeline said, "What about the Pledge of Allegiance?"

Aldine regarded her uncertainly.

"The pledge to the flag," Neva said, looking toward a particular corner of the room. "Except where's the flag?"

Aldine went to the cupboard where she'd seen an American flag wrapped on a short pole.

"Over there!" Neva said, pointing toward a receptacle mounted on a wall near the corner. "Phay will put it up. He always puts it up."

Phay took the flag, pulled up a chair to stand on, and inserted the stick into its receptacle.

"Thank you, Phay," Aldine said, and Phay, walking to his desk, nodded gravely, glad to have his stature to a certain degree restored.

"I'll lead!" Neva said, and Aldine did what the children did, which was to stand upright, stare at the flag, and put a hand over the heart. While they recited, she stood and listened. At its conclusion, they all sat down. Emmeline raised her hand and, once recognized, said in a calm voice, "You don't know the words to the Pledge of Allegiance?"

"Not yet," Aldine said.

"I guess that's because you're not from here."

"Things are new for me, yes," Aldine said. She wanted to say that she learned quickly, because she did, but it would be too demeaning—her saying to her own students, *But I learn quickly.*

She raised her songbook and presented it to them, face out. "Page thirty-seven then. In the key of F." It seemed no one understood her words. She turned the primer around and said, "A-one, a-two, a-one two three four," and began to sing, though only Neva tried to sing along, and then she stopped, too. Aldine sang on, if only to keep these awful children at bay, and in a few moments her whole body seemed to relax and she was not just singing the words but riding them right out of the room.

When she was done, the room fell quiet and one of the Wright boys said, "God almighty."

Emmeline Josephson turned and said, "Hector, that's God's name in vain." Which caused Hector to shrink back.

"This time you will all sing," Aldine said, a tremor in her voice that she hoped they could not detect, and swept her arm toward all of them and then pointed to the page in the music primer. This time, when she began, they sang along dully. Three more songs followed, each sung as weakly as the one before, and Aldine was about to suggest another, simply because she didn't know what else to do, when Neva said, "Maybe we should start our lessons now."

"Yes, yes, of course," Aldine said and began to stare at Mr. Geoph's cryptic note. *Recitation Program: Ari. Study Group 1: Ari. Study Group 2: Ari.*

Did Ari do the recitation of the flag pledge? Is that what it meant? She had no idea.

"Who was Ari?" she said, which baffled the class as much as everything else she said. "Ari," she said again, very slowly. "Who was Ari?"

"Can I look?" Neva said, nodding at the paper that Aldine held.

But when Neva looked at the scribbling, she could make no sense of it, either. "I was in study group 1," she said, "but I don't know who Ari is."

"How do you spell it?" Emmeline asked, and when Neva told her, she said, "That's just Mr. Geoph's shorthand for *arithmetic*." Something cunning came into her face. "But that's not our study plans. Where are our study plans?"

Aldine felt a bulb of sweat roll along her rib cage. This was all a mistake. The most horrible and foolish mistake. "Then let's begin your arithmetic recitation," she said, and when she finally made herself understood, Emmeline said coolly, "How can we recite when we haven't studied anything yet?"

"Sums!" Aldine said in a sudden voice. "Sums!"

Phay Wright said, "Sooms?" and then his brothers became a chorus, saying "Zooms! Zooms!" which caused building laughter until Aldine to her own surprise slapped the top of her desk with her hand so hard that she felt a shock of pain.

This brought stricken silence, in the midst of which Emmeline Josephson cocked her head slightly. "Would you like me to lead them?" she said in a sweet voice that Aldine knew not to trust and yet couldn't at this moment afford to resist, and so they began. "Three plus one equals," Emmeline prompted in a rhythmic tone and the class responded "four" in unison, and so it went, on and on, through the sums of twelves, which only Emmeline and Neva were able to answer assuredly.

During the first recess, Aldine waited until everyone was outside, then seated herself at the teacher's desk. To keep from crying, she squeezed shut her eyes and imagined herself on a sun-warmed rock overlooking the River Doon, eating brown bread and cheese with Leenie and hoping their father, standing in the tea-colored water in his rubberized overalls, would catch fish enough for dinner. And then her mum stirring up a white sauce for the fish and floury potatoes, shaking pepper over the sauce in the skillet, a fat cut of butter melting in the middle of it.

She opened her eyes, took several long, deep breaths of air, and pulled out her knitting bag. She'd managed only a row or two when a sudden thought stopped her.

An idea, from her primary teacher in Ayr.

Aldine went to the storage cupboard, looked in, and felt as she did when she had a recipe and found all the ingredients in Aunt Sedge's pantry. For now, before her, she saw a sheaf of colored paper, a box of old rulers, and a spool of stout string.

17

The Prices were making a supper of boiled eggs, canned potatoes, and pickled beets. The scantness of the offering had caused Clare's mother to send him to the garden to look for a last tomato or two, but there were none at all, and so now he had to choose his way back. He'd come the long way, following the creek, but the shortcut back was by the pasture, where the hogs were buried, and the smell of them was still there. On the other hand he was longing to cast eyes on Aldine, whom he hadn't glimpsed all day, not even at breakfast, so that was that. He would take the shortcut. The game he played was this. Would her actual corporeal self be as fetching as the girl who lived in his mind all day long? Always the answer was yes. Yes, and then some.

When he got close to the hogs, he took a deep breath and broke into a run, but he could never quite outrun the smell. Eighteen dead of cholera. He and his father had piled them up with layers of straw and tried to burn them out of the world, but the fire went out and left a sickening heap of blackened, wasted flesh, so they had to bury them by hand, digging all day, shovel by shovel, with vultures watching just like in a Tom Mix movie, the dirt finally covering ears, snouts and trotters, swollen bellies, and black death. Everything but the smell. Anything could bring it to him, right down to singeing the hair on his arm when feeding the woodstove. A few days after they buried them, the wind had blown enough of the dry, sandy soil that hog parts began protruding. One such protuberance was a snout looking like it was coming up for air, but a day or two later it was gone. Coyotes, probably, or maybe a fox or vulture. Or maybe even Artemis. He'd seen Artemis eating a rat.

His father was sanding the front door when he returned. "No tomatoes," Clare told him and his father said, "No, I supposed not." He folded the sandpaper so that he could reach a corner of the door's inset panel.

"Going to paint it purple this time?" Clare said, a little joke. His father always painted it the same shade of red that his own father had. As he slipped past his father and into the mud porch, Clare said, "Purple or maybe chartreuse," which drew a small laugh from his father.

Even if there were none of the good smells of baking coming from the kitchen, Clare was glad for the voices. All of them, but especially hers.

"Clare! Clare!" Neva shouted when she saw him. "You should come back to school again, it was ever so much fun!"

He smiled at Neva and then, finally, using the delay to tantalize himself, he let his gaze rise to Aldine, whose eyes seemed bright with good feeling.

More fetching than imagined. Unquestionably more fetching.

The table had already been set. The food was carried in. "His Highness is served," Charlotte called out to their father, who came in and surveyed the sparse offerings without a grumble, went so far in fact to profess a love of pickled beets.

Neva said the blessing and the serving plates began to pass.

"So, Nevie, tell us what made the day so grand," his father said. Which meant he'd been listening from the front door.

"The game that Miss McKenna made up for us," Neva said, "with planes and prizes like we've never had before!"

His father turned his bemused look to Aldine, who explained the competition in spite of interruptions from Neva. Each student had been given a long length of string, and tied bits of yarn to it every twelve inches, measured out precisely, until they had fifteen knots. The boys had hammered nails high up on opposite walls and pulled the strings in taut straight lines overhead. Then after each child had made a paper airplane, it was suspended from the first knot.

"And every time Miss McKenna gives us a star on a paper we get to use the transom pole and move our plane up to the next knot and the first one to get to the last knot wins a prize!"

His father was smiling and nodding. "Yes exactly," he said quietly. "That's how it's done." He sounded nearly as impressed as Neva.

"And we all gave our airplanes names!" Neva said. "I called mine *Mr. Benny*."

This provoked laughter and then Clare, feeling a little outside it all, said, "It's a swell idea. It truly is."

Aldine looked up from her plate and let her dark eyes fall on him. "It wasna' my own," she said. "I had a teacher in Ayr who did something like it. Mrs. Lynch she was. She gave away a goldfish in a bowl."

His mother drew a knife through a pickled beet. "And what prize will you give, Aldine?"

A kiss. That was what popped into Clare's head.

"It's a surprise!" Neva proclaimed. "Isn't it, Miss McKenna?"

Aldine gave a laugh that seemed almost musical. "Aye, I'm afraid it's a surprise surely."

Charlotte said, "What did Emmeline Josephson name her airplane?"

"*The Flight of the Fancy!*" Neva said.

Aldine looked up. "There was a bit more, though, wasn't there, Neva? I believe Emmeline christened it *The Flight of the Fancy Pants*, but"—the prettiest smile formed on her lips—"she wrote *pants* very faintly indeed."

Everyone laughed as if this were funny, but Clare knew Emmeline Josephson, and he knew she hadn't meant it as funny.

"The only bad thing was that the lesson book wasn't there, but Miss McKenna had us work from our books and come up one by one to discuss what we'd done."

His father grew suddenly alert. "The lesson list wasn't there?"

Aldine shook her head. "Wasna' on the desktop like you thought it would be. Truly, I looked everywhere until I was frantic. It was not to be found."

~

Clare milked after supper and when he brought in the separator for washing, his father was standing over the wall telephone saying things like, "Good. No, not at all. Did they say where?"

Clare leaned into the kitchen, caught Charlotte's attention, and mouthed a silent "Who?"

"Mr. Josephson," she whispered.

After his father said good-bye to Mr. Josephson, he waited a moment and added, "Good night, Lu, good night, Jeannie." Which was what he always said to the two farm wives who habitually listened in. Then he set the earpiece into its cradle.

"A mystery," he said when he came into the kitchen where Charlotte and Aldine were already cleaning the separator. "Emmeline said that she and her sister left the lesson folder in a desk drawer after they cleaned."

Aldine's jaw set and she asked what desk that might have been.

"Yours."

"Truly now. And in what drawer might that have been?"

"One of the lower ones. Where they thought it would be safe."

"Safe from what?" Clare said. He couldn't help himself. "Safe from the teacher finding it?"

His father maintained his lordly calm as always. "Let's not get excited," he said, and turned from him to Aldine. "You looked everywhere—all the desk drawers?"

"I did," she said, but then her voice slackened. "I'll admit, though, I was a bit agitated with the minutes ticking down."

Clare said, "But if Emmeline knew you hadn't found it, why—"

But his father cut him off. "Enough, Clare. Miss McKenna can take a look tomorrow and we'll see what's what."

Charlotte, who wasn't normally quiet during such exchanges, was notably quiet during this one.

Later, when he stepped out on the porch and heard Artemis barking at some distance, he followed the sound and found Charlotte sitting on a fence rail east of the barn, smoking a cigarette.

"Where'd you get that?" he said.

She handed it to him so he'd keep quiet about it. "That would be none of your beeswax," she said.

He liked the way the smoke felt in his lungs. It made him feel older and more hopeful. He exhaled, gave the cigarette back to Charlotte, and said, "Pretty out here when it's cool and the air's still."

Artemis leaned into his leg and he let his hand fall to her head. Her skin was loose. When he'd come upon her in the barn eating the rat, she'd given him a low growl to keep him away, and then taken what was left of it into her mouth and carried it into a dark corner. There were doves in the rafters. He'd tried to listen to them but all he'd heard were the wet, crackly sounds of Artemis eating the rat.

He said, "Remember when we had barn owls?"

Charlotte nodded but didn't speak.

"It was better when we had barn owls," he said.

From where he was standing he could see the window of Aldine's room. The light was on but she'd pulled the curtains—she was a demon for pulling the curtains. Still, it was nice to think of her in there, writing a letter or reading a book, and maybe if it was really hot up there wearing not much or—a luxurious thought—nothing at all. Later, after she put the light out, she would open the curtains again—she did this every night—and he liked to think of her up there, lying in bed, gazing up at the stars before falling asleep.

"What are you thinking?"

"Nothing," he said. He'd started at the question and wondered if she could tell it.

After the cigarette burned down, Charlotte buried it and lit another, her face different, pretty even, in the sudden illumination. She drew from the cigarette and handed it to Clare. The chickens had settled and so had the cows so there was nothing to be heard now but the crickets. He said, "What do you think happened to the lesson list?"

He wasn't sure, but he thought Charlotte had just expelled smoke through her nose, a new and impressive trick. She said nothing, though.

He said, "I'll bet Emmeline and Berenice hid it when they were there to clean."

Again Charlotte said nothing, which meant, he was pretty sure, that she knew it to be true.

"That Emmeline Josephson is a piece of work," he said in his bitterest tone, and Charlotte gave out a sudden, harsh laugh.

"That's a rich one coming from the little acolyte who couldn't take his moony eyes off Emmeline in school or church either one."

"Well, sure, but that was before."

It was a mistake talking to his sister. She had a cat inside of her and the cat never slept. It was always ready to pounce.

"Before what?" she said, exhaling smoke, then grinning and extending the cigarette to him.

18

September 21, 1932

Dear old Leenie,
Don't worry, I'm fine! I don't have nosebleeds now I'm
used to the air. I have seven students at Stony Bank, four
girls and three lads. There were more lads last year but
Clare says they hopped trains and went off to find work.
One of the girls at school reminds me of Kathleen Hagy
except prettier. But it's all the same in the way of spite
and meanness. This one is called Emmeline and perhaps
you and Will might say a prayer for some sickness to beset
her, nothing mortal please, but plenty to keep her home
in bed. She and another were supposed to leave the les-
son book on my desk for my first day but instead kept it
themselves then put it in my desk next day and said it
was there all along if I had only looked and when I called
her down on it her father steps in and says his daughter
is honest and honorable and oh, I could have screamed.

There. I have just taken a few full breaths.

The Price family is still nice as ever to me. They aren't Mormon anymore but nice all the same. Clare is 16 and ought to go to high school in a big town, like Charlotte did, but there's no money to pay his board. He helps his father on the farm and shoots wee creatures. You won't believe what we ate last night: squirrel. Clare shoots them and his mother cooks them for absolute ages. Made me want to boak at first but it's no worse than Sedgie's Bawd Bree which is what I taught them to make from one of Clare's rabbits. Bang bang bang. Then the skinning. What I wouldn't give for haddock.

You know how we used to wish it would quit raining raining raining? Listen to this song I have been teaching the wee ones in my class:

> *"Rain, rain, do not go*
> *Rain, rain, we love you so*
> *Make us music on the pane*
> *Drum to wild wind's fiddle strain."*

That'd be a laugh on Bellevue Cres. but not here. The Prices have planted wheat like most of the whole county and if rain doesn't come soon, the wheat will die like the corn did in the summer and the wheat did last fall. Every day, Mr. Price gapes up at the sky and listens to the farm report on the radio like he's getting his fortune told. Yesterday, a storm was predicted and it blew up big and black, so bruisy dark we all ran to the windows at school and then when it started chucking I said, "recess!" and we all went out in it, even me. We were drenched but when Neva and I walked home after school, dead certain the fields would be sopping and Mr. Price would

91

be dancing with his wife, we saw it hadn't rained on his fields a drop. Charlotte said it's the hogback's fault. The hogback is a ridge on their property that she says splits every storm and sends all the rain down on other people's fields. Felt wretched for Mr. Price. He looked like Father when Mum died.

Write and tell me about all the barrie jumpers you've knitted for Wee William (or Wilhemina!) to wear the moment he (or she!) is born. I hope you're not feeling as boaky now.

Your own,
Deen

19

On the Tuesday morning of her second week of teaching, while the younger students were reciting multiplication tables in unison, Aldine looked out the window to see dust rising from the graded road to the south. A truck was coming, and as it approached, she saw that it was a truck very much like Mr. Price's and that, trailing behind it, was a flatbed trailer that carried something covered with blankets and strapped down with ropes.

"That's your father," one of the older boys said to Neva, and at once the multiplication tables fell aside. Everyone peered out as the truck and trailer pulled into the schoolyard.

Neva was the first one out the door, calling, "Daddy! Daddy! Clare! Clare!"

While the girls watched and the boys edged close, Clare stepped out of the truck and stretched his arms very casually as a boy will when self-consciously assuming a manly role, then joined Mr. Price in loosening the ropes that held the mysterious shipment in place.

"What is it?" someone asked, but neither Clarence nor Mr. Price spoke. They just kept working the knots.

"It's probably a new outhouse on its side," Emmeline Josephson said, and Mr. Price, smiling, said, "Not that you don't deserve one, Emmeline." Which Aldine wanted to characterize as a backhanded insult, even while knowing it probably wasn't.

When the ropes were loose, he nodded to Clarence, who gave the blankets a flourish, and there it was—a black upright piano.

Aldine was stunned with pleasure. "It's gorgeous," she said, "dead gorgeous. Where in the world did you find it?"

"Mrs. Odekirk," Mr. Price said, and it was clear that both he and Clare were brimming with pride. To Aldine, in this moment, they both seemed boys. "Mrs. Odekirk's arthritis was keeping her from playing," Mr. Price said, "and after hearing you, she thought you would put it to better use here."

He and the boys tipped it carefully on its side and, with Mr. Price at one end and Clare and the Wright boys at the other, they soon had it inside and situated at a pleasing angle to the corners. Clare handed her several books of music, and Phay Wright set the black stool to the keys.

"So who is it would like the first song?" she asked, and then when met with blank faces: "Does nobody play it?"

The children all looked from one to another.

"Then I'll do one," Aldine said, and started on the *Gymnopédies*, which she knew by heart. Her playing wasn't perfect, and the piano was in need of tuning, but, still, it had a rich sound all in all, and the students fell quiet. She felt their eyes on her but she felt all the more Clarence's and Mr. Price's, and when she glanced at them, they each had a particular look, beatific almost, like angels. When she'd finished playing and they made to leave, she wanted to give them each a hug, and she would've, if this were Ayr, but it was not, and hugs and pecks on the cheek were not the way of it here, so she thanked them and thanked them again, and when they laid their eyes on her, she met their gaze one after the other.

"Culture," Mr. Price said. "That's what's needed here, and you've brought it." His tone was earnest, but now a smile creased his face and he said, "Now if you could just bring us a little rain out past the hogback."

20

Ansel and Clare had been clearing roots from one of the new fields when Ansel saw the mules and the wagon. It was Tanner, no question, but his behavior was mysterious. He pulled the mules up short and just sat in the wagon. He didn't wave to Ansel or even look his way.

"Give me a minute," Ansel said to Clare, and planted his mattock.

The ground was hard and cloddy. It took a few minutes for him to cross the field but not once did Tanner turn his way or even seem to move. Nor did he when Ansel called out to him.

Ansel pinched the barbed wire and stooped through. He drew close enough that he could lay an arm on the cart wheel and talk in a low tone, like it was the two of them on the steps of the Methodist church. "Hello, Horace," he said.

Tanner didn't turn, but something in his eyes moved.

"Tell me what's wrong," Ansel said.

Tanner seemed to be shaking his head, but it was hard to tell. It might have been a tremble in fact.

"Are you not feeling well?"

Still Tanner didn't answer. The buzz of insects was in the air and, from the other side of the field, the steady *chunk chunk chunk* of Clare's mattock. A steady worker. It couldn't be said that he wasn't.

"Can I do something?" Ansel asked.

Again a long silence. And then Tanner said, "Take the mules."

Ansel stepped onto the running board and reached forward but Tanner didn't loosen his grip on the reins. "I mean keep them," he said in a whispery voice.

What this meant, Ansel wasn't sure. "Keep them? Until when?"

"Keep 'em and use 'em," Tanner said. "I've got no use for 'em now."

Losing his place. He'd heard Tanner might be losing his place. Which itself didn't carry much surprise. Dirt from his unplanted fields blew onto their own meager plants and would bury them if he and Clare didn't strip-list in anticipation of every wind, digging deep parallel furrows to catch the fine silt blowing low along the ground.

"I can't, Horace," Ansel said. "I can't use them and I can't feed them. I'm sorry, but I can't feed what I've got."

Another silence developed, except for the buzz of insects and the distant *chunk chunk chunk*.

Tanner was so still he might have been asleep. Finally, though, he turned. He looked full at Ansel. His face seemed ancient and absolutely empty. You could cast him as the dead man's ghost. He said, "They're good animals. They've got lots of work left in 'em."

When Ansel got back to Clare, the boy barely looked up. "Whad he want?" he asked, but even when he spoke he kept working. Ansel stared at Tanner's wagon going slowly back the way it had come.

"He's up against it," Ansel said. "Tanner's up against it."

He spat on his hands before taking up his mattock.

21

Charlotte had a photograph album full of pictures she'd taken with the Zeiss Ikon box camera her grandfather Opa had given her mother, but her mother wasn't much interested in it and when she overexposed a roll of the 120, she handed it to Charlotte and said, "Do with it what you will." What Charlotte did was join the Photography Club at Abilene High and take photos galore, which she learned to develop in the darkroom that the science teacher, Mrs. Clough, had set up in the school basement, but now Charlotte had no darkroom at her disposal and they couldn't afford the chemicals if she did, so the camera had been tucked away in her hope chest, but the photograph album with its green leather cover stayed out on the radio where others in the family, Neva especially, would sometimes take it up and finger through it, marveling at the younger versions of themselves.

Charlotte also had a journal, which was handier since it required nothing more than a pen and privacy. She used to keep a girlie diary of her high school days in Abilene: *Went to picture show with Harley and Opal, then had soda and gum. Washed and curled my head.* A litany of valentines, dances, and matinees that made her sad to read now. What she missed was the fullness of things. It wasn't the boys and romance.

She'd had two boys in high school but only let one of them kiss her. She didn't like it but she let him and when he tried to touch her beneath her shirt, she didn't feel at all excited by the maneuvering. She felt clammy and rigid and pushed him away once and for all. After graduation, she just came back home to poor corn and wheat, failing cattle, and dead hogs. No matinees, no jitney lunches, no meetings of the Journalism Club, or the Photography Club, or the Mythology Club (where the girls voted to call her dog Artemis). For that matter, no desire to record on what day she washed and curled her head. Who was there to see it? Not Opal, founder of the Appropriate Dress Club. Not Harley, who'd married Opal one week after graduation and was probably keeping her in Appropriate Dresses with his insurance salary. For company now Charlotte had the voice of KFKB (Kansas First, Kansas Best!) while she fed clothes through the mangle and stirred lumps out of gravy. She listened to the Wonder Bakers while she spooned bread-and-butter pickles into the bread-and-butter pickle dish. She listened to *Roxy and His Gang* while she pieced scraps for a quilt that seemed boring now, so long had she been making it. What possessed her to do one called Wedding Ring? There was no money for new fabric, so she couldn't sew dresses, the only thing that had ever been fun at home.

One day the newsman talked about an editor in Texas who was forming what he called the Last Man's Club. It was for farmers determined not to sell out and leave their farms, so they could vie with one another, she guessed, to be the last man left. It was funny in a not-laughing way. Charlotte already had a friend whose mother was making muffins out of hog shorts. Now her own family had no hogs to feed hog shorts to, and the cows had almost no feed.

In her notebook that night, Charlotte had written: *Reasons not to join the Last Man's Club*, and underlined it twice. Reasons number one and two were, *Hog shorts make horrible muffins*, and *Artemis will starve*.

It wasn't long until she had reason number three: *A farmer in Clark County fell off his tractor while driving it all night. All night! He was ground to pieces, said the man telling the story at the Co-op. I told Dad about it when I came home because he does the same thing, trying to add acres to make up for last year's loss, but he says he lashes himself to the seat with a rope.*

Reasons number four and five were dust and hoppers. She had seen with her own eyes a pitchfork her father kept in the barn, an artifact from the invasion of 1919. Otherwise she wouldn't have believed a bug could eat wood like that.

In the back of the notebook, she practiced journalism à la her junior year at Abilene, using Who What When Where Why and How.

A new teacher, Aldine McKenna, arrived in Dorland from New York on September 1. She boards with the Price Family two miles from Stony Bank School. Miss McKenna has come only recently from Scotland. When Emmeline Josephson, aged 14, was asked to describe her new teacher, she said, "Her speech is very different so I try to translate for the younger children. All she really does is singing and poetry. I don't know how I will pass my eighth grade exam."

Toward the end of October, Charlotte found reason number six. She was helping her mother make pie with the last jar of rhubarb when they got word about Mr. Tanner. Everybody knew the Tanners had been foreclosed on and the auction date was set. Still, Mr. Tanner didn't seem like the kind of man who would hang himself. He went to church and was so gentle with Yauncy, never ever losing patience with him, though it was plain Yauncy would never be able to do more than throw bales. It was Yauncy who found Mr. Tanner in the barn.

Who What When Where Why and How.

She didn't know, so she just wrote: *Reason #6: Mr. Tanner.*

22

Some days in November, his father would ask Clare to walk to school with Neva and Aldine to help light the stove and bring water. If it was really cold he just stayed a while, keeping the fire stoked and trying with uncertain knowledge and carpenter's mud to mend the window where wind eked in. Aldine always started the day by playing the piano and leading the children (and Emmeline, when Emmeline felt like it) through their songs and recitations. A lot of the songs seemed to be about rain. The song he liked best was one he'd never heard before, a Scottish one about some poor guy without shoes or a coat or a hat and all the odd things he wore to make do. She played the piano and sang that one herself while the little kids acted it out. It was *the finale*, she called it, and the way the younger kids were always calling out for "the finale" was a funny thing to watch.

The Miss McKenna of the classroom called him "Clay-dance" instead of Clare, the sound of it flipping his stomach, pushing it closed. She said "aboot" and "dinnae" and "doon." "Coo" instead of "cow." "Hame" instead of "home." When she thought the school needed tidying up, she said she couldn't stand things to be so clarty.

She had looked at him (eyes brown, but not plain brown—deep-river brown with sunlight on the surface) with amusement when he was putting coal in the bucket and she said, "Clay-dance, how aboot you?"

He stood up straight and felt the gaze of all the Josephson girls and Neva, heard their dresses rustle as they swiveled around in their seats.

"How about me?" he asked.

She asked him something that had a few familiar words in it—*poem* and *school magazine*—but the other words took him a minute to translate. He went redder still and rubbed his sooty thumb against a sooty palm.

"One ye especially luve?" she prompted.

"I didn't mind that one in the book by Bryan," he said.

"Bryan?" she asked, her expression meant to encourage, perhaps, though he felt an idiot always. "What did he write then?"

It wasn't so much that he'd liked the poem—he'd just memorized it from boredom—but how could she not know which one he meant? The grammar book had only a few poems in it. Maybe this was why Emmeline Josephson was worried about passing her exams.

"Would you speak a line or two?"

He looked down and began to recite in a hurried, low monotone:

> "So we'll go no more a'roving
> So late into the night,
> Though the heart be still as loving,
> And the moon be still as bright.
> For the sword outwears its sheath,
> And the soul wears out—"

He stopped short. *The soul wears out the breast* was how it went, and he wasn't going to say that, but Aldine was smiling at him as she had never before, as if she were lit up from the inside. "Oh, that's a luve-ly poem," she said, "especially if you slow down a wee bit. It's by George Gordon, also known as Lord Byron." Then, almost to herself, "It can be sung, as well," which of course Neva pleaded for, and so Aldine sang it, and what had just been rhyming lines lifted from the page and hung now in the air, almost touchable.

"Thank you, Clay-dance, for bringing it to our attention," Aldine said. "We'll absolutely put that luve-ly poem in our magazine." She was smiling at him still, something he, in his own paralyzed manner, might have enjoyed more if he hadn't felt Emmeline Josephson staring at him, too, and smiling a smile that she might well have borrowed from Charlotte.

~

One afternoon, his father felt a change in weather, appraised the massing clouds, and said, "It could storm soon." There was hope in his voice, wary hope, Clare saw, but hope just the same. His father prized his gaze from the sky. "Maybe you should fetch coats from home and take them to Neva and Miss McKenna."

Clare didn't wait for his father to change his mind or for the storm to change direction (which it did of course). Still the coats were welcome and, for Clare, the walk home from school was a freezing happiness. Neva hopped and skipped to stay warm, pitching to Aldine every question Clare would have asked if he were not struck dumb by the deep-river gaze she turned on him when he spoke.

"How many brothers do you have, Miss McKenna?" Neva asked.

"Not a one."

A cursive line of geese passed overhead.

"How many sisters?"

"One. Plus a bairn that died."

The air smelled of frozen dust. Neva asked what a bairn was, and Aldine told her.

"How'd the baby die?" Neva asked.

"Don't know, really."

"Did you come here on a boat?"

"Aye."

The sky was thick with snowless clouds.

"Was it big?"

"Enormous."

"Sing that song! The one about Bryan O'Linn."

"If ye'll sing it with me." Aldine turned her eyes to Clare and he felt himself pushed along by currents, brushed by speechless fish. "Do you sing, Clay-dance?"

He shook his head.

"Oh, just try," she said, coaxing him, the black pom-pom quivering slightly on the top of her head as she walked, Charlotte's borrowed coat engulfing the whole of her, except for her boots, small and precise on the dusty road. *"Bryan O'Linn was a gentleman born,"* she began, and Neva sang with her in a high cheerful voice. *"He lived at a time when no clothes they were worn."*

Neva laughed when Clare blushed. "Isn't it funny, Clare?" Neva asked, and she sang, *"But as fashion went out, of course Bryan walked in . . ."* Neva paused dramatically and then finished, *"'Whoo, I'll set all the fashions,' says Bryan O'Linn."*

Clare smiled but he didn't sing, and they walked on. "My nose turned leaky here," Aldine said, touching her glove to her upper lip. "It is this cold in Scotland but my nose never turned leaky."

He understood every word she spoke. They were nearly home. The ground was dry. The air was still. There would be no snow, no moisture of any kind. Aldine snuffled and gave out a small moist laugh. He could have kept walking like this for hours.

"Artemis!" Neva shouted, for there she was, ambling their way, her tail wagging so hard it seemed to rock her bony rump from one side to the other.

23

"He'd thought it all out, they're saying now."

Neva was leaning against the wall. She stared at her fist. Her father's voice, in the next room, was low, like at church.

"He'd dug a big trench and shot the mules so one fell into it and the other one half did. I guess he meant to cover them up but he didn't. He'd gone out to hunt rabbits so no one took notice. Then he went straight into the barn. Mrs. Tanner saw him go in, but didn't think anything about it for almost an hour and then she suddenly wondered where his mules were and why it was so quiet so she sent Yauncy out." A second or two passed. "I guess she feels almost worse about that than the other. Sending Yauncy out."

Quiet. Then her mother's voice. "He knew the Bible. He knew that it was a . . ."

Neva held one box elder bug in her closed hand. Before, she could feel it scrabbling in there but it was resting now. She didn't really want to listen to her mother and father but if she made noise now they would know she had been.

"Mrs. Tanner said he hadn't wanted dinner. He sat with them, though, while they had soup and bread. She said he looked funny at them. Like he was thinking . . . And here afterward she wondered what all had gone on in his mind, sitting there looking at them, how maybe it would be better if they went all together to the sweet hereafter."

Her parents were done talking but they didn't move. Neither did Neva. She opened her hand and looked at the box elder bug. She blew on it but it didn't move. She knew what had happened. Charlotte had told her. Mr. Tanner had an accident in the barn, a bad accident, and had fallen from the hayloft and even though Yauncy tried to save him it was too late.

24

On Sundays, Clare could almost pretend he was courting Aldine, that he'd brought her home to spend the evening with his family, and she was sitting apart from him, knitting on the sofa, only for propriety's sake. Usually his father liked to read aloud after supper on that one day a week he wasn't in the barn or on the tractor. He had read *David Copperfield* the previous winter, followed by Rudyard Kipling's poems and stories, and he had then decided they should try Shakespeare. Too bad they had not done Lord By-run, Clare thought, because then he would not have embarrassed himself.

As his father paged through the Riverside Shakespeare, Neva lay on the floor and drew long-nosed horses that she colored pink and purple. Clare, trying not to stare at Aldine, raked his fingernails across the denim of his pants as if to file them. Charlotte read her own book. His mother sewed under light from the Tiffany lamp. From his place on the wall, Opa Hoffman looked down on all of them like a judge.

His mother still wore her apron, the one embroidered with the outline of a dish-washing bear, and from the way that she kept glancing frequently up at the clock, Clare knew she was wondering if whatever his father chose to read would be over before the start of her radio program.

People told Clare he looked like his mother. It was true they were colored alike: light brown hair, light brown eyes, unfreckled skin that darkened in summer like a jar of tea. They had identical slim noses, too, with a nostril flare that Clare thought made him look effeminate. He thought it was probably his nose that had made Aldine call him "Byronic" a few days after his classroom recitation of Lord Byron. What Lord Byron looked like, Clare would've liked to know.

Clare's father could do accents: English, German, French, or Negro, though he'd stopped doing Irish and Scotch lately because he said Miss McKenna would know him for a charlatan. Finally his father looked up and said they might all take parts in *King Richard III*.

"Oh, please, Dad, not that!" Charlotte said. "Let me pick something a little more fun for the rest of us. Come on."

The book was handed over, and his father slipped off his glasses, laid them aside, and rubbed his eyes.

"What about *Venus and Adonis*?" Charlotte asked. Her father had been moving page by page through the front of the book; she had flipped to the back. "We studied that myth at school. In the Mythology Club."

"What is it, Lottie?" his father asked. "Is it a play? I don't remember it."

Charlotte didn't answer, probably because he'd called her Lottie. She said it made her sound like a big dumb farm girl with pretzel braids. Everyone had called her that until she went away to high school, and now sometimes his father said "Lottie" without thinking. Clare himself employed it whenever he wanted to get her goat, which was fairly often.

"*Venus and Adonis*," Charlotte began, tucking a loose spiral of hair behind her ear. If not for Aldine's presence, Clare would have gone to bed. He was tired, and with Charlotte reading, there wouldn't be any funny parts or accents.

"Who's Venus?" Neva asked from her place on the rug, close to Aldine's feet like an adoring dog. Aldine was knitting a hat just like her own for Neva—a hat she'd told Neva was called a *bud-ay*—and she looked up with a pleasant smile but didn't stop moving her needles.

"The goddess of love," Charlotte said, using her thumb to keep her place. "She fell in love with a handsome mortal but he was killed by a discus."

"That's some oo-ther handsome mortal. I think Adonis is killed by a boar," Aldine said, and Clare took silent pleasure in the way that her pronunciation sounded both correct and poetic.

Neva colored a goggle-eyed pony. "A boar?" she asked.

"Yes, it's very common," Charlotte said, not looking up. "People are bored to death all the time. Especially on farms."

Clare's mother pulled a thread taut and looked reproachfully at Charlotte. "I believe Aldine means a wild pig."

"Hogs," Charlotte said. "Pigs. Boars. Boring people. Anyway, let's just read the story. *Even as the sun with purple-colour'd face,"* she began, *"Had ta'en his last leave of the weeping morn."*

Neva's pencil lead shushed across the paper, Clare peered at Aldine's ankles, and Charlotte read on. It was just harmonious sound at first, something he listened to as he would listen to classical music on one of his mother's radio shows, but then something about the way his father's expression changed and the way his mother lifted her head made him try to change the archaic grammar into meaning.

"The studded bridle on a ragged bough
Nimbly she fastens—O, How quick is love!—
The steed is stalled up, and even now
To tie the rider she begins to prove:
Backward she push'd him, as she would be thrust
And govern'd him in strength, though not in lust."

It was about horses, yet it wasn't about horses. He wished he'd been paying better attention to the verses that came before.

"So soon was she along as he was down,
Each leaning on their elbows and their hips:
Now doth she stroke his cheek, now doth he frown,
And 'gins to chide, but soon she stops his lips;
And kissing speaks, with lustful language broken,
'If thou wilt chide, thy lips shall never open.'"

Clare thought of the magazine he'd gotten from Harry Gifford, of the girls spread across the pages in poses that made him feel this same way, but his mother was sitting there, and his father was sitting there, both of them tensing their eyebrows and lips, and Aldine was looking very hard at her knitting. Her eyes seemed larger, her mouth tighter. But it was Shakespeare, and anything Shakespeare said, you could say in the house. Charlotte was heedless of it all, or—and this suddenly seemed more likely—she was pretending to be heedless, and she kept reading:

"Even as an empty eagle, sharp by fast,
Tires with her beak on feathers, flesh and bone,
Shaking her wings, devouring all in haste,
Till either gorge be stuff'd or prey be gone;
Even so she kiss'd his brow, his cheek, his chin,
And where she ends she doth anew begin."

"Charlotte," his mother said sharply, stuffing the shirt she was mending into her sewing basket. "I don't think this is suitable. Besides, it's Neva's bedtime." She stood abruptly and began gathering Neva's papers.

"No!" Neva said. "I'm not done!"

Clare made himself look at Opa Hoffman's picture until he felt no desire. Charlotte's expression, as she closed the Shakespeare book, was amused, not thwarted, so he was suddenly certain she'd known all about the poem before she'd started it, and that she'd probably gotten a lot farther than she expected.

When Neva's fit about not going to bed got her nowhere, she asked if Miss McKenna could sing her to sleep, please, please, please, and the two of them left the room. It was five past eight. Clare's mother tuned the radio to the NBC Blue Network, where the symphonic music had already begun.

Clare stood and stretched, saying, "Well, good night."

The stairway was cold, as usual. As he climbed the steps, he could hear Aldine singing already. He stood for a moment outside Neva's closed door to hear her tongue flutter against her teeth when she sang the *r*'s:

> "Bryan O'Linn had no breeches to wear
> He got him a sheepskin to make him a pair,
> With the fleshy side out and the woolly side in,
> 'Whoo, they're pleasant and cool!' says Bryan O'Linn."

He put his own tongue to his teeth and whispered "breeches" until he sounded like her, and he wondered how long it would be before he could slip *Venus and Adonis* off the shelf and try to make more sense of its phrases.

25

Opal had bought the fabric, enough for two dresses, on the condition that Charlotte would help her. Charlotte knew what that meant—she'd be sewing the dresses while Opal gabbed and watched—but that was fine by Charlotte. She would get to sew, she would get a new dress, and she would have some company, none of which would be true without the material. Besides, Opal had a funny streak and she was a good listener, especially for all things Aldine.

"You should see Clare turn into a puddle every time she enters the room," Charlotte said, "and Neva starts every sentence with *Miss McKenna*. Miss McKenna says this and Miss McKenna does that."

They'd laid the pattern out on the table and had only two hours before they'd have to take it up and set the dinner dishes. Charlotte was aware of her mother in the kitchen, peeling the apples Opal had brought. Opal had of course offered to help; her mother had of course refused.

"And you'd think that the whole island of Scotland must be free of dust the way she complains of it." She moved her voice up to a thin girlish register. "It's wooonderful here in Pooodunk a'course but wouldna be dead splendid if it were *naw* so *clarty,* don't you know?"

Opal's laughter came up from the stomach and only encouraged Charlotte further.

She said, "In the ooold country we looove to sing a sooong and strike a pooose."

She said, "In New Yooork where you have never been and will never be they have a movie hoose on every bloook."

She said, "Oh Clay-dance, doon't you have the dead juiciest eyes."

"That will be enough, Charlotte!" her mother called from the other room, which only made Charlotte aware of how long her mother had let it go before reining it in.

In a lower voice, Charlotte said, "She'll soon tell us she's descended from the Queen of Scotland."

"Do they have one?"

Charlotte had just put a pin in her mouth but felt it worthwhile to take it out. "Yes, and her name is Aldine."

It was beautiful fabric, the print a maizey yellow with big red-and-orange asters. The dress would be perfect for spring—tiered skirt and ruffled cap sleeves—and the inverted-V bodice with the gathering at the bust would, Charlotte knew, be more becoming on a full figure like her own than on a wispy type like Opal. She bet Opal knew that, too, because she'd suggested that Charlotte wear her dress only on even days while she would take odd so they'd never both be caught wearing it "side by side." A perfectly fine idea, Charlotte guessed, but she couldn't help herself from saying, "But then everyone might think we're just trading the same dress back and forth."

When her mother went out of doors with a basket of wash to hang, Charlotte had the chance she'd been waiting for, and told Opal about, as she put it, "The Venus-and-Adonis Affair."

"You read that *out loud*?" Opal said when Charlotte had filled her in. They'd both privately read the poem last summer, at least the best parts of it, and later conferred about its contents.

Charlotte nodded. She was cutting the fabric now. "Everybody but Neva nearly turned purple. I thought the Mother might expire and I truly thought Clare was going to pop his cork."

This brought raucous laughter from Opal, who shrieked, "What kind of cork?" which caused even Charlotte, who was no prude, to shush her. But her mother had heard nothing—Charlotte could see her stringing a sheet along the line, her mouth full of clothespins.

"Here, you cut this," Charlotte said a moment later to Opal, handing her the scissors. She went to the kitchen and returned with a pencil and slim sheet of paper. Opal suspended her cutting—she was watching Charlotte's every move.

"What are you up to, Miss Mischievous?" Opal said, but Charlotte barely heard the question, so intent was she upon the task at hand.

26

Ellie stood in the pantry, a freestanding shed Ansel had built for her when they were first married, a room where even in summer the air smelled of well water and mold. She was taking stock, not that there was much to take stock of. No pork, no beef, and no chicken, but the holidays were coming—Thanksgiving in four days, then Christmas. She had always been good at special occasions. It was why the Harvey House had been her perfect world, and why a farm miles from the closest town was not.

Ellie would turn forty on Thanksgiving. Her birthday usually fell before or after the holiday, near enough that there was never any time or thought for another celebration even if Ansel had been so inclined. In Shaker Heights, Ohio, the years when she'd been Herr Hoffman's daughter Eleanor and the younger, less lively sister of Ida Marie had been full of birthday parties and pink cakes and presents. At eighteen, she'd worn jet beads to Ida's birthday dance at their house on West Park Boulevard and been paired off with her father's chosen suitor, Monty Pike, a boy with a lot of money and no kindness in him at all, not even for animals.

Becoming Harvey Girls had been Ida's idea because she despised the boys their father picked for her, too. Wouldn't it be glamorous, anyway, a life on your own, a salary, those smart uniforms?

"We won't be on our own," Ellie had said gloomily, picturing them working in the Cleveland station for about two minutes before their father showed up, but Ida said they'd go to some other state, probably Kansas, because Kansas was packed with Harvey Houses.

Like most things done by young people, it was poorly imagined. Only later did she know exactly how far it was from Shaker Heights to Emporia: nine hundred miles. And yet she was happy from the very beginning in Emporia, handing cups of coffee and plates of steaming food across the counter to men leaving on the next train. The tables of the Emporia restaurant—mahogany tables, mahogany chairs—had been set with white linen and silver. The clothes of every waitress were pressed and clean, black and white, like English maids in a movie. She stood every day behind the long gleaming counter, waiting for the sound of Ernie's gong. The train whistle came first, a warning that the train was just a mile away, and then Ernie, who was watching for the first glimpse of the engine, struck that funny Chinese gong. All the orders had been wired ahead and she could hear the cooks stirring, basting, pouring, and frying. There was always something to do, yet there was always time to dream. She'd often felt that the coming train would carry the California hotelier or Hollywood producer who would be so impressed by her efficiency and friendly (but not overfriendly) manner that he would find a reason to stay a few days in Kansas, taking all his meals at the Harvey House and sitting where Ellie Hoffman could take his order for banana pie. And then, after a very refined and respectful courtship, she would become the wife in a household that, like the one of her childhood, required dressing up, formal dinners, and mahogany furniture.

Meanwhile, she would ask: "Coffee, iced tea, hot tea, or milk?" and set the cup in its coded position so the girls behind her would know where to pour what.

Cup upright in the saucer: *coffee*.

Cup upside down in the saucer: *hot tea*.

Cup upside down, tilted against the saucer: *iced tea*.

Cup upside down, away from the saucer: *milk*.

Ansel Price had been working there awhile. A salad man, not a chef or a manager, and he was handsome, though Ida thought that was only half the attraction. "The other half is his faraway eyes that all the girls want to get close to," Ida said. All Ellie knew was that more than one of the girls on her shift had faked an interest in the making of Thousand Isle dressing so Ansel could show them. He sang, too, and played a beautiful old dulcimer that he laid across his lap as he crooned the sentimental old ditty about Harvey Girls and looked into the eyes of all the waitresses who asked him to play when things were slow. Ellie didn't plan to fall for someone like that.

Ida married first—a kind, sunny fellow named Hurd who had thick orange hair and took her away to a town he'd heard about that was north of San Diego and where they never had snow or frost or, to hear Ida tell it, unpleasantness of any kind, but Ellie didn't want to follow unattached. One day, she found herself standing at a window near Ansel Price during a lull. He seemed transfixed—he stared out at the light, swirling snow as if it made him perfectly content. Perhaps that was what had drawn her over. But now the silence, with her standing so close, was discomfiting, and she said, "Good skating weather."

The longest moment passed before he freed his gaze from the snow, and then—this all seemed to happen in slow-motion—he was turning and his dark eyes were settling on hers and he was nodding and saying, "Mmm," which might have meant *Yes, it is good skating weather,* or *I was just trying to enjoy a moment to myself,* or *I have never seen you in quite this light before.*

She had been thinking of the pond near Shaker Heights where she and Ida used to skate, but now she remembered something else. "But Ernie said they went all last year without finding a frozen pond here."

"Mmm," Ansel said again, and his eyes were fixed so intently on hers, and exerted such an unanticipated pull, that she said, "Excuse me," and fled back to her tables without another word.

Three days later when she walked by him in the kitchen, he said, "A word please."

It was so odd and formal that she wondered if she'd misheard him. "Pardon me?"

"I was wondering if you have ever roller-skated?"

She shook her head.

"You might like it," Ansel said.

That evening after her shift she heard scraping noises in the basement and a soft whirring sound and then music tantalizing enough that when Flora Ambrose came upstairs to say there was a nice surprise waiting for her, she let Flora coax her down to the basement, and there, roller-skating in a nice big oval he'd created through wholesale rearrangement of the crates, was Ansel Price.

"Care for a turn?" he asked, his eyes bright. The roller skates were the kind that buckled over your shoes, and he'd found a pair roughly her size, which made her wonder when he'd been assessing her feet. He taught her to skate, and then he taught Flora, and then he asked Ellie to go around with him one more time.

"It's not quite ice-skating," she said, and then when she saw a hint of disappointment in his face, she added, "but it's lots warmer."

When the record stopped, Flora wound up the phonograph and put on a new one: a pretty tenor voice singing "Good Night Little Girl, Goodnight." Ellie and Ansel fell into an easy, graceful rhythm of leaning and pushing and gliding, and she was surprised when the music stopped again so soon, and surprised, too, in looking about, to find that Flora had slipped away, but Ansel Price moved blithely ahead, and as they kept pushing and gliding, she enjoyed the shushing of the skates and, it was true, the warm pressure of his arm. It was so pleasant that she was almost disappointed when he spoke.

"If a fortune-teller looked into a crystal ball," he asked in his soft, deep voice, "what would you want to hear about yourself?"

"I don't know," Ellie said. "Anything except, *I zee you vashing dishes.*"

Ansel laughed, and they skated on.

"How about you? Do want to live in some faraway place?"

He chuckled at that and said, "No, no, I don't think so."

"What then?"

He started out with his own version of her funny foreign accent: "*I zee you in za house where you were born. I zee za wheat growing as far as I can zee.*" But as he gracefully crossed one foot over the other on the curves (she still bent her ankles painfully to steer herself), he started to sound more like himself. "A beautiful girl comes home for dinner even though she doesn't trust you, even though she thinks you're a bit of a show-off. She watches you with your parents and she thinks maybe you aren't so bad. She allows one kiss, maybe two. The two of you go for a ride alone in your father's car—"

It sounded like Monty Pike on wheels, and Ellie stopped skating, pulling her arm from his so she could sit down on a crate.

"Are you all right?" he asked.

"I'm fine," she said.

"Maybe the fortune-teller got a little carried away," he said.

Ellie said she wondered where Flora had gone, and Ansel hardly said a word while she unbuckled the skates.

One day not long after the skating, the lunchroom was nearly empty except for a crippled man and his elderly mother. The crippled man was trying to open the ketchup bottle Ellie had brought him, but he couldn't because his hands didn't work right, and Ellie didn't know what she ought to do. While she was standing behind the counter, trying to watch without seeming to watch, wondering if she ought to just take him a different bottle, Ansel came out of the kitchen and she blurted it out to him. He didn't say anything, but he walked right up to the man's table. "May I?" he asked. He took the bottle and tried the lid, then tried it again. He shook his head and then took it back to the kitchen. When he came back, Ellie heard him say that he'd had to use the pliers on it.

"Where are those pliers again?" she asked him a few hours later in the kitchen.

He looked at her in confusion. "What pliers?"

She felt herself leaning slightly toward him. "The ones you used to open that man's ketchup."

He relaxed then, and his smile made his handsome face handsomer. "Oh, those," he said. "Well, those pliers might be hard to find."

The next time he asked her to do something, he made sure Flora and Ernie went along. They had to be careful because you could get fired for dating an employee, but Ansel was so aloof she began to wonder if he didn't care for her in that way. Once when Flora and Ernie were necking in the backseat, she took his hand and said, "So this house you grew up in. What is it like?"

He told her about his mother, who liked poetry and plays, and who had planned to have a great big family that could put on plays with her and sew the costumes and paint scenery, but he was the only child who survived longer than one year so he played all the male parts and she played all the female ones. She taught him to sing, and his father bought him his fretted dulcimer one time on a trip to Wichita. He didn't mention that his mother was dead and that his father was losing the use of his arms and legs to some kind of illness. That she saw on her first visit and her second, and the third was for his funeral.

She liked watching Ansel stand at the edge of his fields, planting his legs and nodding at whatever she might be saying as he stared off, but then she would fall respectfully silent because she could see his thoughts had floated away like leaves from an autumn tree. He loved the place and she married him because she loved him, and because she thought that was enough. She thought she could enjoy as he did the solitude and simple beauty of a white house and a red barn amidst green fields. She liked the fact that his own child hands had hammered together the gray pieces of wood that formed a ladder up the cottonwood tree, a ladder that she hoped their own children would one day climb. It seemed silly to want money more than she wanted those things, silly to want a big house and mahogany furniture and sterling silver pickle forks.

Her father tried to intervene. He told her that this would be work. Very difficult work.

He told her that he knew she wanted mildness and beauty in her life. "You've never made your own butter, or milked a cow, or cooked for farmhands. It will not kill you, Eleanor. It will be worse than killing you. I know this. I know that it will."

She said, "That's what you said about being a Harvey Girl, you forget."

"I do not forget. It is not the same. That was a job you could quit. A marriage is not that way. Do not marry him now, Eleanor. Please, for me, do not. Give it the time such things need. Let yourself breathe again like a normal person. If in a year you feel the same way, then yes, yes, do what you will. But not now."

She did, though. Sometimes she thought she'd done it just because her father had advised against it. That was how it sometimes was, after you're a child and before you're an adult. But he'd been right. She loved Ansel, but her father had been right all the same.

Having children both helped and didn't help. Even before Charlotte was born she'd begun to wonder if she'd chosen the right man but the wrong place. By the time Clare arrived, she was sure of it, and she began to push Ansel toward a move to California like Ida and Hurd. He could get work as a salad man, then a chef, then a hotelier. He was handsome and competent and assured—he could run any sort of business. Or if he had to farm, he could farm, but in California, where you could farm year-round. *Five crops a year on some of the land here!* Hurd had written. But Ansel, in so many ways malleable, was not in this. "We're happy here, aren't we?" he'd say, and how else could she answer? She said of course they were, because the one indisputable truth was that he was happy here. He was happy to get up before dawn and he was happy to come back from the fields late. He could work for hours on the tractor, work straight through dinner, which she would bring out to him in a basket and wait for him to come to her end of the row and be surprised that it was already two in the afternoon. "What do you do when you're on your tractor?" she asked one day while she watched him eat. He seemed puzzled. "Do? Well, I'm watching the tractor and the row, and I'm listening to the engine, and I'm thinking what else needs to be done this week and next." She had fried chicken for him. He held still a half-eaten drumstick, looked at her, and smiled. "And there's still a little time left over for thinking about my bride." But she knew that what sustained him was his dreaminess, the way he could sit on a tractor or sit in his armchair and remove himself from the real world. He'd always done it, and always would. He had safe places to go. The Scottish girl did, too, she supposed, the way the girl could dry the same dish for a full two minutes, staring out the kitchen window, lost in her daydreams. But all Ellie ever saw staring out the window was flatness and grayness, and all she ever heard was the hollow sighing of the wind.

Once the children were born, she had no time to think about anything except the next feeding or batch of wash. The needs of babies and children were immediate and displaced her own. *We'll come to California when they're older,* she wrote to Ida. *Right now I can't go 10 feet without a fresh diaper.*

They got older, and they climbed up Ansel's cottonwood tree, adding their own pieces of wood to the rickety tree house, and still they went no farther than Wichita. The year that she started feeling peevish all the time, morning to night, was the year Neva was three. Poor Ansel saw it and felt it and wanted to cure it without knowing how. For

Christmas, he bought her the radio. Funny that a man who liked plays and singing could be so annoyed by a machine designed to bring plays and singing right into your living room. She knew from the catalogue that it cost $64.64, but from the minute they turned it on, it was clear he viewed it as an intrusion. "Is that all they can do with it?" he asked. "Why don't they put on real plays?" Some of the music programs were all right with him, but she sensed he preferred to sing himself, with the kids as his chorus. When he came in for dinner, he asked if he couldn't turn it off, and when it needed tubes, he was slow to order them.

Ansel could live in his own world, but Ellie needed other voices. She needed them all day long. She needed them because the house that Ansel was born in, the one that had sounded so sweet and comforting in Ernie's car all those years ago, was as lonesome as the moon. There were no women around who'd grown up in the city. There were no women who'd eaten in or seen a Harvey House. There was no Ida. Ellie had tried to keep standards. Those first years, she'd raised her own turkeys from eggs. She'd cooked Rice Piemontaise, a favorite dish in Emporia, once a week, mincing her own garden onions. One year, she'd sent away for powdered mustard so she could prepare Sauce Robert. One Thanksgiving she'd served both Peach Alexandria and Maple Melange. Everyone pretended to like them, except Clare, who loved mincemeat and, though not saying a word, would suffer nothing else.

And now, four days from her fortieth birthday and four days from Thanksgiving, they could not afford turkey, dead or alive. The pantry held little more than empty jars. No more rhubarb, plum syrup, or peaches. No more rice. They still had canned apricots and two big sacks of flour, luckily, so she wouldn't have to grind up the wheat they used for chicken feed just to make cloverleaf rolls. No more bread-and-butter pickles, no ruby beets. Stewed tomatoes they had in abundance so perhaps she would just have to serve those with chicken and potatoes, which was not the right thing at all for Thanksgiving.

She went back in the house. No one else was there, so she did something she rarely did during the day: she sat down in the chair beside the Tiffany lamp and under the photograph of her father. She took Ida's letter out of her apron pocket and wished she could write an answer that would make her happy again.

> *Dear Ellie,*
>
> *Won't you come for Thanksgiving this year? Heck, come for Thanksgiving and stay till we're toothless and old. I'm planning to serve dinner out of doors this year—it was too hot last year to eat inside. Too hot! Isn't that a change from how things used to be. No silver or china and no Marianne to do the hard work but I like it here so well and I know you would, too. My rock and bottle garden is taking shape and that's where I'll put the dinner table—I have 75 blue bottles now, if you can believe. Folks drink no end of Milk of Magnesia!*
>
> *How is Nevie? Is Charlotte still mopey? I tell you she'd have a grand time of it around here. They're showing pictures at the Women's Club on Saturday nights and they have dances in the park. All sorts of nice boys work at the Packing House with Hurd. Clare could work there, you know, unless you wanted him to go to high school after all. It's not too late! Write and say you'll have turkey and dressing with us. Plus I will bake a red velvet birthday cake if you come.*
>
> *Love and stuff,*
> *Ida*

Why Ida thought they could just pick up and drive two thousand miles was more than a mystery. It had been three years since Ellie had bought a dress or a hat. Her Holeproof Hosiery was on its second life as material for Neva's homemade rag dolls. And now there was Aldine. And all because of Ansel's crazy rose-colored nostalgia for his childhood playacting and singing. Charlotte had seen the advertisement when she'd been cleaning the girl's room, and they'd read it together. *Culturally inclined. Forward-looking.* And now here she was, a Scottish Kewpie doll, eating their food and taking her long baths and sitting up front beside Ansel in the Ford when she went in for Christmas shopping, laughing and casting her spell. Clare was smitten of course, and Neva, too. Charlotte wasn't, though. Charlotte understood the girl's ways as if they were her own, which in many ways they were. But why she'd read that filthy poem out loud was one more of life's dark mysteries because, really, it was as if Lottie knew all along what it was and was having her fun rolling the powder keg into the middle of the room, and Ansel—well, he was a man too sure of his self-possession. During his *Othello* play, she'd watched his eyes following Georgia Waterman around the stage and then when she'd brought it up (knowing she shouldn't and vowing she wouldn't and then finally she did) he'd laughed and said, well of course he watched her, she was Desdemona, the wife Othello no longer trusted, but it was all a role, he knew the difference between a play and real life, et cetera, et cetera, et cetera, and, besides all that, he said, he'd never been a wandering man.

Which, truly, she couldn't rebut.

Still, he hadn't sent the Scottish girl back, as he'd said he would, and as he should have done.

Bringing up Georgia Waterman had been a mistake; she'd seen that clearly. And she'd told herself not to bring up Aldine, either, but of course she had. Ansel was working all the time—strip-listing, working on the machinery, trying to keep the cows standing—but now on Sundays instead of reading he was bringing out his dulcimer, which had seemed a relief after *Venus and Adonis*, but he was singing foolish songs and goading Aldine to do the same, one song after another after another and then, as what Neva called "the grand finale," all of them singing that frightful "Bryan O'Linn" that everyone thought such a lark, especially the part about no clothes that they wore, so finally one Sunday night when they were alone in their room, she could contain herself no longer and said quietly, "Funny how so many of the songs turn out to be duets."

"Not 'Bryan O'Linn,'" Ansel said, and she heard cheer come into his voice just from the thought of it. "Besides, they wouldn't be duets if anyone else would pipe up."

"You know I can't sing," Ellie said.

He said that she had a perfectly nice voice, but she had no intention of trying the songs Aldine performed, with their vibrating consonants and flutey vowels. It was chilling how easily Ansel adopted the girl's tongue, pronouncing the words just as she sang them when he joined her on the chorus.

"It's like I'm not even in the room, Ansel," she said, and at once he wrapped his arms around her and told her that it was only because she was tired that she was thinking such things, a theory that only made her feel more prickly still, and she'd lain there stiff and awake until she could roll away from him and face the wall.

Ellie put the letter away. For Thanksgiving, she would tell Clare to go out for something, squirrel or rabbit. And if he didn't shoot something, he'd have to kill Goosey, one of their last layers. But that wasn't all. There was something else to be done for Christmas, and she would do it.

27

Upon awakening Christmas morning, Aldine took in the sharp chill of her room and cast her eye on the austere gray sky beyond her window. She lay warm in her bed and thought that if ever in time eternal there would be a more cheerless Christmas morning than this one, she hoped not to see it. She used the chamber pot, then cracked her door to listen a bit—she heard movement downstairs, the clank of pans, but no voices—but it was too cold for anything, so she grabbed her book from her satchel and returned to the snug nest of her bed. There were two books in the satchel: *Cyr's Dramatic First Reader*, which she'd brought home to help Neva memorize her parts for the Winter Entertainment, and—the one she had now in hand—the school's red cloth Riverside Shakespeare, which she'd smuggled home for her own diversion.

Aldine had made a bookmark, cut from white paperboard and idly decorated with a teeming and ever-densening thicket of penciled flowers, some with a letter written on each petal to form words (*Seizeth*, for example, and *Breatheth*). She always marked her place indirectly—cunningly, even—in Act IV of *King Henry VIII*, the last play in the volume and within easy proximity of *Venus and Adonis*. Aldine liked this deception; it seemed to enrich the pleasure of the venture. But, this morning, no sooner had she found the portion of the poem she most liked (*Even so she kissed his brow, his cheek, his chin, / And where she ends she doth anew begin*) than she heard the scamper of footsteps on the stairs.

"Miss McKenna! Miss McKenna!" Neva called, and Aldine barely had time to shove the book beneath the quilts before the girl flung open the door and burst into her room. "Sausage!" Neva exclaimed. Really the girl was almost screaming. And (it must have floated in with the girl) Aldine caught the most marvelous scent of cooking meat. "Marmalade, too!" Neva sang out. "And strawberry jelly and oranges and, oh, just . . . *everything*!" She'd taken Aldine's hand and had begun to tug. "Mama says it was Santa but I don't think it was, do you?"

Aldine, pivoting, swung her legs to the edge of the bed, but her movement beneath the twisted covers pushed the hiding Shakespeare suddenly forward: the volume fell to the floor with a violent *ka-thump*.

For a moment they both stared at the immense volume lying there splayed open; then Neva said, "Oh, you! You fell asleep reading, didn't you?" She bent to the floor and folded the book neatly closed. "I do that all the time!"

"I do as well," Aldine said in the calmest manner she could manage, but the demeaning aspect of fooling a guileless eight-year-old did not escape her. She rose and set the book back into her satchel.

"What about this?" Neva said.

She'd picked up the bookmarker decorated with teeming flowers and petals spelling *Breatheth* and *Seizeth*.

"Oh, it's a bookmark I've had for years now," Aldine said, a barefaced lie, and she slid the marker into *The Merchant of Venice* at the front of the volume, eight hundred pages and several climate sectors from *Venus and Adonis*.

Neva was holding out the chenille robe that Aldine had worn the night before for a bit of extra warmth while she read in her room.

"Hurry!" Neva said. "Wear this."

Aldine gave a laugh. "I'll freeze, Neva."

"You won't, though! It's ever so much warmer downstairs. Clare has the fire raging."

So Aldine slipped into the robe, cinched the ropy belt tight at her waist, and followed Neva downstairs, where Mr. Price sat binding a package with twine. Aldine pulled the lapels of her robe together at the collar, but Mr. Price seemed pleasantly surprised by her informal entrance, and when in his low, gravelly voice he said, "Merry Christmas, Miss McKenna," the earnestness of it affected her.

"And Happy Christmas to you, Mr. Price," she said. She glanced at the lively fire beyond the stone hearth. Neva had been right about that—it *was* warm as toast in the room.

"Did you fall out of bed?" Mr. Price asked pleasantly.

Aldine turned, patted at her hair, and wondered what kind of sight she was presenting. "Sir?"

"The alarming thump I heard a minute ago." He was using a serious voice, but there was the smallest smile on his lips. "I thought maybe someone had fallen out of bed."

"Oh, that then," Aldine said and while wondering what mad concoction she might next speak, Neva interceded.

"It was just the book Aldine was reading before she went to sleep, Daddy. It fell on the floor when I woke her up."

And with that, Neva was again pulling her by the hand and as Aldine happily allowed it, she cast an *I-must-be-going* smile back over her shoulder toward Mr. Price.

In the kitchen, Charlotte and Mrs. Price were busily gathering plates, slicing oranges, sliding hotcakes from skillet to platter, and shooing Clare away from the sausages warming on the stovetop.

"Out! Out!" Mrs. Price said to Clare, but her tone was jovial, and Clare, grinning happily at Aldine, grabbed a last sausage before escaping. Aldine joined the women in their work. A festive element had infected them all, none, to Aldine's surprise, less than Mrs. Price. It was nearly too strange to accommodate—Aldine kept watching her from the corner of her eye. Was this what happened to her on Christmas Day but no other? The bounty of food doubtless had something to do with it, but there seemed to be something else as well, an almost eager element to her contentment, as if she were sitting on the pleasantest kind of secret, one that might soon be revealed.

After so many frugal meals, their breakfast felt like a banquet: small cobalt-blue bowls crowded with wedges of seedless oranges, shallow dishes full of jelly and marmalade. One platter packed with small sausages, another with hotcakes. Aldine followed the method of Clare and Neva, who spread their hotcakes with strawberry jelly (though Aldine chose orange marmalade), then wrapped each one around a sausage and ate it without aid of fork or knife.

"Heavenly," she said, and Mrs. Price actually smiled at her compliment.

Mr. Price said, "Nice that"—he gave his wife a mysterious look—"Santa found us this year."

"It is, isn't it?" Mrs. Price said, very coylike, it seemed.

"I think it was a red-haired Santa," Charlotte said, a notion that Aldine couldn't fathom. Nor could Neva, who said, "There's only one and he's got white hair."

They all ate then and for a time no one spoke. Finally Charlotte said, "Do you suppose you could eat like this every morning if you lived in California?"

"You could if you're Tom Mix," Clare said.

"Or William Randolph Hearst," Mr. Price added, and even as Aldine was wondering who this William Somebody Hearst might be, he said to her, "This Hearst fellow's a big newspaper tycoon."

Neva was the first to finish eating, and thereafter sat monitoring the progress of others. Mr. and Mrs. Price were the most deliberate, but when at last they had put down their forks, Neva shouted, "Presents!"

Aldine expected Mrs. Price to insist that the dishes be washed first, but she didn't. She merely nodded and followed the others into the front room. The gifts were simple and various, and of the type, Aldine understood, that were given and received each year. Several ball-in-the-hole games. Found arrowheads. A rubber-band gun. A homemade Parcheesi board. Walnuts for cookies. Tangerines for all (Aldine received two). Aldine gave Neva a knitted long-legged frog and sang the first line of "Froggy went a courtin' Oh" (and wanted, truly, to sing more but felt it would redirect too much attention). As a finale, Clare distributed propeller toys he had made and soon he, Neva, and Aldine were spinning their shafts between flattened hands and gleefully watching them twirl up into the air while Mr. Price stood at the hearth to prevent any wayward toys from a fiery ending.

When everything had settled again, Mr. Price began picking at his dulcimer, and soon was singing "Silent Night," which teased a voice from everyone, even Mrs. Price. A few more carols followed and then a melody that sent a tremor through Aldine.

"Anyone know that one?" Mr. Price asked, and it took Aldine a moment to come to her senses. "It's the 'Carol of the Birds' then, isn't it?"

Mr. Price nodded and kept his eyes on the dulcimer. "I'm afraid I only know the melody," he said. "I was hoping you would know the words."

And so she sang, and she soon had everyone coming in on the beautiful, lilting chorus of *"Curoo, Curoo, Curoo."*

Mr. Price didn't stop after the last verse, so they went through it again, and this time when it was finished, the room fell into serene silence except for the occasional pop and snap from the fire.

Clare suggested a Parcheesi tournament and Mrs. Price said pleasantly, "Not before we have dishes done and dishes made." She addressed the room as a whole. "We have two plump pheasant cocks that Ansel brought home," she said, giving her husband the quickest nod, "and for that we'll have a nice kumquat glaze."

Her eyes were almost unnaturally bright with pleasure.

"It's the most perfect Christmas ever!" Neva said, and Mrs. Price, nodding, said, "Yes, and there's more to come."

Mr. Price, who had just laid his dulcimer into its case, lifted his eyes. "More to come, Ellie?"

She pressed her lips together and nodded.

"More than pheasant for dinner?"

Again she nodded.

He took this in. "Well, don't keep us from it then," he said, and Aldine sensed that his mild tone was wrapped about something harder. "Not on Christmas morning."

Mrs. Price had some sort of surprise for them, that was clear, but she seemed torn between sharing her secret and hanging on to it a bit longer. Aldine was sure she would wait—it was Mrs. Price's nature to nurse on deprivation—but a look of resolution came into her face. "Yes," she said. "Why not?" She was smiling now, smiling at each of her children. "Okay then. Just wait here."

After she departed the room, Mr. Price laid more wood on the fire. It was clear that no one knew what might be coming next, but in a short time Mrs. Price returned with a small wooden crate, which she set down in the middle of the room. Her face was beaming. She took up the lid—the nails holding it had already been loosened—and laid it aside. Then, after one more expectant look at each of her children, she slowly began withdrawing small gifts from the straw packing.

"How did they get here?" Neva shouted. "Where did they come from?" The poor girl was in a state of near hysteria.

"St. Nick," Mrs. Price said, and Neva at once replied, "No. Tell me! Where did they come from?"

"St. Nick," Mrs. Price repeated, "and if you ask again, I'll send them back to the North Pole."

A strange exalted vibrancy had taken over the room, and as Mrs. Price handed out the gifts one by one, each recipient in turn beheld the package, turning it in the hand and regarding it from all angles with such slow brimming expectation that it seemed ceremonious. When Charlotte lifted away the lid from her small box, she found a powder-holder music box that, once she'd wound it, played the first few bars of a stately sonata. For Clare, there was a pair of Carl Zeiss military binoculars; for Neva, a small straw-stuffed monkey with a silver rivet imprinted *Steiff* on the cuff of its green velvet waistcoat; and for Mrs. Price, a double-stranded pearl necklace. "Why, they're . . . *exquisite*," she said in a tender voice as she stared down at them draping over her hands. "But where in the world would I wear them?"

Neva announced that her monkey's name was Milly Mandy Molly, then began poking around in the straw packing of the crate until satisfied that nothing else lay hidden there. "If Santa brought the presents, how come he forgot Daddy and Miss McKenna?"

Mrs. Price didn't seem to hear the question—she was transfixed by the pearls—so Charlotte said, "Santa didn't know Miss McKenna was here, Nevie. And he knows Dad isn't the type for fancy gifts, are you, Dad?"

"No, I'm not," Mr. Price said, and for the first time Aldine became aware of the stiffness that had come over him.

Mrs. Price couldn't keep her eyes off the necklace. Charlotte couldn't, either. "At least put them on," she coaxed, and when with a nod she acceded, Charlotte helped her with the clasp before standing away so all could see.

"Oh, they're truly lovely," Aldine said, but wished she hadn't because Mrs. Price's expression, which had drifted, came back into focus, and she reached behind her neck at once to unfasten the clasp.

"Can I try them on?" Neva pleaded, and Mrs. Price, while tucking the pearls neatly back into their velvet-lined case, said, "You certainly may not."

So Neva wound her sister's music box.

"Beethoven," her mother said, and Mr. Price said something so low nobody could hear it.

"What?" Clare asked and Mr. Price, looking up, said more emphatically, "Mozart."

"He's right," Charlotte said, reading something from the box. *"Mozart Piano Sonata number 16."*

Why the good cheer had gone out of the room, Aldine was unsure. But it had. The room was heavily quiet now. Hot and heavily quiet. Aldine pinched her robe away from her chest for air. Mrs. Price set aside the boxed necklace, rose from her chair, and started for the kitchen. The last time she'd left the room, she'd seemed buoyant; now she seemed wary and deliberate.

"Ellie," Mr. Price said.

Mrs. Price stopped and in just that moment of turning, her expression grew hard.

He scanned the presents in the room before letting his eyes settle again on his wife. "How did this come about?"

Mrs. Price didn't wait. She said, "I wrote him."

A moment passed. "And what did you tell him?"

"What do you think I told him, Ansel." This was not a question. Her voice was low and even. "I told him that we were up against it. I told him that we didn't have a thing for Christmas just like we didn't have a thing last Christmas and the Christmas before that."

She looked as if she might have more to say, but he didn't wait to hear it. He turned and with his lips tight and jaw working and eyes cast straight forward, he walked out of the parlor and through the mud porch and out the yard gate. To the barn, Aldine supposed.

The stillness in the house felt brittle.

Finally, in her smallest voice, Neva said, "We did, too, have Christmas last year. I got . . ." but the dead, cold look in her mother's eyes checked the girl.

Mrs. Price turned then to Charlotte. "Kitchen," she said.

Charlotte rose. Neva did, too. Aldine supposed she would help as well, but Mrs. Price's eyes narrowed on her. "And you," she said, and even more than hearing the words, Aldine felt the hatred pulsing bloodlike within them. "You go upstairs and put some decent clothes on your body."

28

Clare sat alone in an empty parlor that, minutes before, had been brimming with people and presents and good cheer. But it hadn't been trustworthy good cheer. They'd found that out. His father had pulled the drain plug from the room and now there was nothing left.

Clare slipped his military binoculars into their leather case. They were made in Germany by the Carl Zeiss company, the same company that made Charlotte's fancy camera. He had prized the binoculars, but that feeling wasn't trustworthy, either, because now he saw that the gift was part of an insult to his father. Clare didn't snap the case closed; the sound would be too loud. He looked toward the kitchen, where his mother, Neva, and Charlotte were cleaning up without talking. Then they would be making things without talking. He'd been looking forward to the roasted pheasant but he knew that was all spoiled now. He stared out toward the barn, where his father had gone. A loose mist hung low, and everything else was brown and cold and hard outside. He checked the stovepipe that poked from the side of the barn. His father would be getting a fire started in the stove, he supposed, but there was no smoke yet.

Clare took his field glasses and eased up the stairwell, where he had watched Aldine's legs and hips as she rushed away in her nightgown and thin robe, up the stairs and out of sight, throwing her attic door closed behind her so everyone could hear. Then it had fallen quiet up there. He thought he would go up to her room. He would tell her in a quiet, solemn way that his mother was being bad-mannered to her. Worse than bad-mannered even. Monstrous. A declaration along those lines might coax her into tears, and tears might require comforting.

But when he reached the upstairs hallway, he was checked by sudden sounds exploding from the attic room, thuddings and reverberations, hard and furious seeming. She must have put on her thick lace-up shoes and was stomping here and there, slamming drawers, scraping the bedstead out of her way, perhaps even throwing things; that was anyhow what it sounded like. She didn't need comforting. She needed calming, and that was a different task altogether.

All at once her door flew open. Clare stepped back into the shadows of his own room as her hard footsteps quickly descended and her form rushed by; then her shoes were again clacking hard on the wooden stairs and across the parlor floor. The mud porch door slammed closed behind her. Of all these sounds one was missing. She had not closed her attic door. Clare went to his bedroom window. He could see her marching through the low mist toward the barn, a kind of fierceness in her manner. She was going to quit. He could see it in her walk. She was going to demand to be paid and then she was going to quit. Smoke was rising now from the stack on the barn wall, so his father was definitely inside, working on something probably, tinkering, and then she would come in and he would look up and see her and she would demand her money and then whether she got it or not she would quit and then she would leave.

He took out his binoculars, adjusted the focus, and trained them on her moving form. He didn't like it very well, though. Her walk was all grace and smoothness when you watched with the naked eye, but the glasses made her jumpy. But at the mouth of the barn she stopped and peered in and he could see her face in profile. Her tight, smooth face seemed so suddenly close that he held his breath. His watching now seemed almost intimate.

And then a surprise. Her face, which had been hard and determined, suddenly relaxed into a kind of softness. But why? What had happened?

Clare lifted his eyes above the field glasses. She was just standing there at the barn door looking in but even from this distance he could see that something had gone out of her. Her body was no longer rigid; her fierceness was gone. She stayed like that for a few seconds, just standing and looking in, and then she turned and walked beyond the barn past the empty pigpen, through the mist along the cut toward the creek. Artemis stole up behind her and began to amble alongside.

Clare watched them until they slipped down the cut and into the low fog and trees.

He set his field glasses into their case, put on his boots in the mud porch, and walked out to the barn.

His father was bent over the barrel stove, feeding in scraps of wood. Clare came closer until his father heard him and turned.

"Well, well," he said. "Son One."

His father's little joke. There had never been and never would be a Son Two. Clare looked around. "What are you doing?"

His father cast his eyes off into the dimness. "Oh, there's always something needing doing." Then: "How are things indoors?"

"Kind of gloomy." He waited a second or two. "Did you see Aldine?"

"See her where?"

"She came out to the barn. Mom in a real mean way told her to go put some decent clothes on her body and Aldine ran upstairs and put on her heavy clothes and marched out here like she was going to quit teaching and leave or something but she looked into the barn for a few seconds and then she just walked on."

His father looked over to the barn door. Finally he said, "No. I didn't see her."

It fell silent. Clare was trying to make sense of the barn and his father but there was nothing to see or hear. A dove coo-cooing in the rafters was all. "Need me for anything?" Clare asked.

His father raked his fingers through his beard. "You might clean the water pan for the chickens. But otherwise stay or go as you please." He smiled an unhappy smile. "It's Christmas Day after all."

Clare found the pail.

His father said, "Went on walking where?"

Clare had two pails in hand. "What?"

"You said the girl went on walking. Where did she go?"

"Oh. Toward the creek."

Clare pumped and hauled water to the chicken house, then cleaned the mash residue from the pan, which Neva should have been able to do at her age but nobody asked her to. Cleaning the mash sludge made his fingers dirty and cold. Since Aldine had come, he didn't like wiping his hands on his pants so he just put them in his pockets. On his way back to the house he walked past the barn without looking in so that his father wouldn't think of something else he might do.

He tugged off his boots, then stood in the front room, still hot from the fire, *too hot*, he thought. He could hear the clinking of dishes in the kitchen, the dull movement of sullen bodies. They were all in there, he was almost sure. He padded up the stairs. What he was doing was less a decision than a response to a persistent hunger—he felt himself pulled up the stairs in the same way he would move toward the smell of bread baking in the kitchen.

The door was wide open. Her room was a mess. Inside, he took a deep breath and could smell her smell. It was as warm in the room as it might be in summer, but it wasn't summer—through the window he could see the mist-covered corral and, beyond the gray ground fog, the stand of stark cottonwoods. The heat made the smells of her keener, and he felt almost as if he was no longer the Clare he had been until this moment but someone else, less tethered, who was moving in a wondrous dream. He picked up thrown bedding and smelled it before putting it neatly back into place. He pulled smooth the corners of the quilt. He smelled the pillow and pressed it to his face. He closed drawers, then opened others. He saw her threadbare underthings and stared at them a long time lying there in the drawer, and willed himself to close the drawer, but he could not. The slip was soft and had holes along the waistband and smelled of washing soda and borax. He wished he could buy her a new slip, and other things, too. He slid a finger through one of the holes and made it slightly bigger and then he folded it carefully and set it back just as it had been. When he eased open her flowered satchel he saw the Riverside Shakespeare. And then he was holding it. She'd marked her place in *The Merchant of Venice*, which he supposed she was reading. The bookmark was funny, though. All of the flowers, the letters on the petals . . .

It was quiet in the room and yet something made his whole body stiffen and turn.

Charlotte stood in the doorway staring at him.

Her eyes were bright. It was the cat inside her and he was the mouse. She said, "And what are you doing?"

How long had she been there? What had she seen? He felt wooden and numb and yet began to move. He moved toward the door and when she stepped aside, he went past her. He did not say a word. Neither did she. It was not until he was inside his own room with the door closed behind him that he realized that he still had the bookmark in his hand.

He clamped his eyes shut. *Washington*, he thought. *Adams Jefferson Madison Monroe Adams Jackson Van Buren* . . .

~

Ansel put a heavy log on the fire in the oil-drum stove, then set out toward the creek. He didn't try to steal up on the girl, nor did he whistle or sing to announce his presence, but still he was surprised to come upon her sitting on a boulder smoking a cigarette and staring at him. Artemis was looking at him, too, her tail sweeping back and forth, but just looking. Ansel supposed that was how she knew to look up.

"You okay?"

"I am," she said.

The certainty with which she said it kept him from approaching further.

"Clare said Ellie spoke to you sharply."

"She did."

"Well, that's just Ellie." It sounded disloyal. He said, "She deserves more."

This time her voice was less harsh. "I'm sure we all do," she said. She inhaled from her cigarette, then let its smoke spew into the cold air. He'd never seen her with cigarettes before, but it was clear she was not new to the habit. He was surprised how knowing it made her look, and how much that became her.

"But you're okay?" he said. "You're warm enough? Because I'm going back and won't need my jacket."

"It's cold but not so cold," she said. Then she looked around. "I just wanted to be . . ."

Alone. Without question that was the word on her tongue.

"Yes. Of course. But you'll be back in a bit?"

She nodded.

And so he left. Artemis tried to follow, but he shooed her back. The dog would be at least some company and comfort to the girl.

~

Everyone came for dinner, but nobody acted like they wanted to. Neva set Milly Mandy Molly on the table, propped against her water glass so she could see everything. Neva hoped her father would say something silly like "No monkey business at the dinner table," but he didn't say anything at all. Nobody did. Her father said the blessing and everyone mumbled the amens. Plates were passed and people ate and all the time nobody talked. The pheasant with the kumquat glaze was good but it didn't really taste good with nobody talking. She said, "Milly Mandy Molly took a long nap and when she woke up she asked, 'Why is the house so quiet?'"

Nobody gave her an answer, not even Clare or her father, who always answered her questions. They just kept chewing. It was hot in the room but when she went to take the green velvet waistcoat off of Milly Mandy Molly, it made her look naked, so she put it back on.

Finally, when everyone's plate was almost empty, Charlotte's face got that meanness behind it that she got sometimes and she said, "Aldine, if you're missing your bookmark, it's because Clare has it."

Before Neva had even turned to him, Clare's face was red as a beet. She had never seen someone's face go red that fast. He put his eyes down and said, "I took it by mistake. I didn't mean to take it."

"He was in your room," Charlotte said and now everyone was looking at Clare.

"The door was open. I was just straightening up." He didn't look at anybody and even if it wasn't an awful lie, it sounded like one. Finally he looked at Aldine. "Before you left, it sounded like a tornado up there."

Neva could tell her parents were just wondering who should scold him first, and suddenly for no reason she said, "Tornado Aldine!" and Aldine looked at her for a second and then she started a giggling laugh. It was such a wonderful thing, her giggling, then laughing, so Neva was glad to laugh, too, and then her father and Clare were laughing, even if nobody really knew why. Only her mother and Charlotte weren't laughing and somehow that made the rest of them laugh harder. Finally when the laughter was done, Aldine said, "It *was* a bit of a tornado up there, wasn't it then? So thank you, Clarence, for making it tidy." And though it didn't mean that everyone started talking again, at least she and Milly Mandy Molly would have the giggly laughter to talk about when they were alone and it was safe to discuss it.

~

When finally the meal was done, Clare shoved back from his plate and left the table without a word. His body felt as numb and stiff as it had when he'd been caught in her room and he'd walked like a zombie past Charlotte, who he thought would keep his secret if only to barter with it, but she hadn't. She'd spent her secret on humiliating him.

Upstairs in his room he took one last look at the bookmark to memorize its images and words and then he went up to the attic. Her door was again open, but he did not let himself step inside. He wedged the bookmark in plain sight under the edge of the keyhole plate. He glanced into the room. It was orderly now. It was funny that she left the door open again. Probably she was just letting the heat in. It was pretty hot, though, even more than before. It was like all the heat climbed up the stairs and got hotter and hotter where it had nowhere else to go. He went back to his room. He grabbed his jacket and wrapped it around his binoculars and went out. On the way he stopped in front of Aldine and without looking at her he said, "I put it back." She asked what he'd put back and he said, "The bookmark with the writing on it. I put it on your door." Then he went out. By circling around the barn and out to the stand of cottonwoods east, he found a place to hide and watch. They would uproot the trees this summer or next. His father had wanted to do it for three summers now and sooner or later he always did what he wanted to do. But Clare was glad the trees were still there. He found a fallen log among the shrubby cover and from there he could peer out from the trees and keep his military field glasses trained on her window.

~

First she found the bookmark wedged in the keyhole plate. *With the words on it,* he'd said, but there were no words except those written on the petals. *Divination. Seizeth. Disshevell'd. Breatheth. Words, just words,* she thought. Then, when she went to slip the bookmark back into the Riverside Shakespeare, she found a folded note poking from the top of the pages.

It said, *Here come and sit, where never serpent hisses, And being set I'll smother thee with kisses.*

A pen had been used and the printing was plain and careful. It was not signed. *Clarence's work,* she thought at once. *Whose else might it be?* The poor lad was smitten. He had been in her room. He had taken her bookmark. He had brought it back and the folded note with it.

She'd brought the lines from the poem to the light of the window, and now she was staring out. *Smother thee with kisses.* It gave her the smallest bit of a thrill—she couldn't deny it—even if it did come only from Clarence. For it had to be he. He went thick and scarlet in her presence, and that shy beguiled type was just the one to resort to a love verse anonymously delivered. He wasn't a bit hard to look upon, with the deadly shy smile, but he was a babe all the same. She lived in his house, used the same bog, was trusted by his parents to lead no one astray. She folded the note closed. A gesture as useless as it was sweet, and that she might've liked it otherwise changed it not an iota.

But though she'd closed the note, she wasn't ready to release the feeling. The room was more than warm—it was nearly torrid—so she closed the door to the rising heat. She considered opening the window, but that was too much—letting cold air in when so often she'd lain in this room with frozen bones. She took off her dress, the black one with seashells—she'd meant to wear the pink with the brown bow, but her mood after Mrs. Price's words to her had turned dark—and hung it carefully in the wardrobe. She lay then on the bed paging through *Venus and Adonis*, nearly endless though it was, rereading certain of the verses. It was delicious that lines like these rose free as you please from pages that had lain unlocked in the country schoolhouse. Oh wouldn't she like to have plump Mr. Josephson on hand when his sleeveen daughter, reading aloud for one and all, found Venus comparing herself to a park where Adonis-the-deer was invited to graze! Wouldn't that be a taste to savor.

The smallest smile had formed on her lips. *You are bad*, she told herself. *You are bad and rude and randy.* Yet the small smile remained.

She closed the book and went to the window. She stood back a bit but there was nothing but fog and field and bare trees, so who was there to see? When Mr. Price or Clarence were seen out of doors, they were always going out to or coming from the fields to the west, or to the barn in the same direction. It had affected her, seeing him in the barn. She'd gone out to quit or complain or scream—she didn't know what entirely—and then when she'd peered in, there he was squatting down, feeding coal into his stove, calm as could be, one piece after another, and then when he was satisfied, he stood slowly to full height and somehow with his beard and bigness she was put in mind of a tree, a stout sturdy tree just planted there staring into the fire and thinking his faraway thoughts.

Something, a kitchenlike clank from downstairs, brought her up from this reverie and she took away at once the hand at her chest. *Idle hands, the devil's playground,* Aunt Sedge liked to say, and *Busy hands are happy hands* (on this theme, she and Leenie had done some smirky laughing about George Prendergast's happy hands). But still, Sedge had a point, so Aldine propped herself against the bedstead and began to knit. *Slip two, hold in front, knit two, knit two. Purl two, knit two, knit two, purl two.* She was doing scarves, clever ones, with cabling, to give the students for end-of-year gifts—all the girls, anyway, the boys wouldn't want them. She'd thought first of scarf and hat as the prize for the first plane to the end of its string, but she'd never seen such a hat or scarf on a lad, so she'd traded a scarf for a goldfish with a long silvery tail, which everyone seemed to want. Neva, who wanted it most of all and who had been in front of all others, was now falling back because of being croupy so often, or whatever it was that made the cough. There was a lemon downstairs among the Christmas bounty. Aldine wished she had some carrageen moss. She'd always liked picking it at the seashore and drying it on a hot rock and it would be just the thing for little Neva, a hot drink of moss and lemon juice. Well, she would just have to make Neva a scarf of her own no matter how far her plane got, something with the brightest colors she had, to go with a beret just like her own.

She laid down her knitting and opened the note without really meaning to. *Here come and sit, where never serpent hisses, And being set I'll smother thee with kisses.* She couldn't help it. Reading the note was better than reading the poem. It was like having it whispered to her. It gave her a little glow like the one she used to have in school when someone told her that a boy liked her. She let herself enjoy the feeling as she assayed the ups and downs of the letters, the maleness of the writing, and smoothed her fingertip along the indentations in the paper where the writer had pressed down hard.

~

It had been a strange Christmas Day, Charlotte thought. Strange but good.

She was washing the dishes slowly, moving them from wash water to rinse water, setting them in the drainer. They'd gotten the swell food from Aunt Ida and Uncle Hurd and the most beautiful presents from Opa. And her mother had given it to His Highness, given it to him good, which made her feel a little sorry for him, but it was good for him every now and then, when his subjects finally squealed. Maybe they would move. Maybe they would move and have oranges and kumquats and blue skies and people around to talk to.

"Milly Mandy Molly's tired again," Neva said. She sat on the floor with the stuffed monkey curled up in her lap and their mother, who had barely spoken ten words since the revolt against His Highness, said, "Why don't you and she go to your cot and take a nap?"

Neva nodded and carried the doll-monkey away.

They were alone then, she and her mother, which was often the moment when her mother would share a thought, but she wasn't talking today.

Outside the barn, smoke rose from the stovepipe. Her father had gone back in there after dinner and there, she supposed, he would stay. Now the barn would get warm and the house would fall cold. Just then Clare rounded the barn—where had he been?—and went off with a pail toward the cowshed so there would soon be the separator to clean.

He was such a sneak, but really when you thought about it, who wasn't a sneak when it came to internal matters. But today, him sneaking up to her room, that was a surprise. A delicious one, though, because she'd stolen up there for her own reasons and there he was, and wasn't it perfect that she could expose him over dinner and in one fell swoop make him the likely suspect. She was glad that Neva had said that about the tornado and made Aldine laugh, and she was glad he'd gotten out of it with his puppy love intact, because that game was just beginning.

She'd begun wiping the dishes dry. She was anxious now to be done before Clare brought the separator. She wanted to ring up Opal and tell her and anyone else listening what she'd gotten for Christmas. She would tell them how it was made by the Eschle Company in the Black

Forest and she would wind it up and hold it close so they could all hear it and then she would ask Opal if she knew what sonata it was or at least what composer but of course she wouldn't so then she would tell her and anyone else listening that it was Mozart. And then when that fun was all played out, she would arrange to meet with Opal somewhere in private so she could tell her—she'd already worked out the phrase—what strange turns a scheme might take.

29

The days passed, and weeks, and then, on a bitter-cold day near the end of January, something happened. Ansel was in the barn. Outside, the wind was a long, slow, ceaseless moan that sometimes, if he closed his eyes, could put him in mind of a distant train passing, which was strangely comforting and, in any case, the best you could do with a sound like that. From time to time the wind struck the side of the barn as if with a huge flat hand, and the barn shook and made a rumbly sound. It was only four o'clock in the afternoon but his father had built the barn without windows—a mistake that Ansel meant one day to correct—so the dimness made it feel later, almost night. He'd gotten a fire going in the old burner near the workbench and fed in a lump of coal and a few cobs. Artemis had slinked in, ribby and ancient seeming, and settled herself by the fire. "Where's your Lottie, old girl?" Ansel said gently. "Have you lost your Lottie?"

This morning Jimmy Sweeton had stopped by with his center-door sedan filled with everything he could carry. He'd had the haunted look for a while now so it was no surprise. He pointed to an ancient caned rocker roped to the roof. "My mother brought that across the prairie," he said. "Now I'm hauling it to California." His face was a windburned red and he was trying to grin but his eyes were dull and lay deep in his face. He said, "When will you be heading out?"

Ansel said, "Well, it wouldn't be now." He would've added, *Or ever*, which was the truth, but he didn't want to make Jimmy Sweeton feel any worse than he did. Jimmy's wife and children had already gone by train. There was nothing for it now but to go. Ansel reached forward and shook his hand. "I'll be looking for you when the drouth ends, Jimmy," he said, which was what he said to everyone who was leaving.

Before starting the hack again down the lane, Jimmy Sweeton pulled something out of his pocket to give to Ansel.

"A spark plug?"

Jimmy nodded. "Except this one comes with a primer valve attachment. Makes starting a Ford easier when it gets cold . . . as it sometimes does hereabouts." He was again trying to grin. "Won't need it where I'm going."

For how long Ansel had been staring into the fire, he didn't know, but when he heard the Scottish girl's voice, it gave him a turn.

"Mr. Price?"

She was peering into the darkness of the barn with the wind to her back, so it gave the impression of her having been blown there, and under the beret her face was a luminous circle.

"Over here," he said, but as she approached, he turned and poked the fire, afraid to look at her further. He had begun to have dreams about the girl, strange, unbidden dreams, and they stayed in his body all day, like a bird inside a darkened cage.

Aldine stepped forward uncertainly. "My heel broke," she said, and took in the adjustment in warmth, the dog by the fire, the scent of horse and straw and machine oil. *His,* she thought. More than any other place on the farm this was his, and she felt out of place. Though her heel had truly broken, and it really did need fixing, and she surely couldn't pay the cobbler. She'd taken Neva inside the house because she wasn't feeling well—coughing again—and she'd looked for Charlotte but hadn't found her. She didn't want to bother Mrs. Price—that was what she told herself—so she'd walked out to the barn. Besides, if they were alone, she could ask him some questions that were rightly hers to ask. "I thought you might have glue or tacks," she said.

He motioned her closer to the stove and lamp. "Here. Let's have a look."

Aldine sat down on a sawhorse to unlace the boot. She felt him watching her, felt it keenly. Deep beneath her heavy coat she felt her heart beating a little too fast. And what did it mean that she wished her wool stocking less shapeless and ugly? But it was clean, and mended, so there was at least that. She handed Mr. Price the dusty boot and he sat down with it on an old backless chair. While he turned it in his hands, she looked about and, beyond the stove and sleeping dog, she found a surprise: beneath a hanging lightbulb a book lay open on the workbench, a thick book, and something about it—its size, its situation here on his workbench in the barn, the desperation of their circumstances—made her take it for a Bible, but then she saw that the edges of its cover were red, unquestionably red, and it was in the exact moment that she knew it was the Riverside Shakespeare that she felt something within her lifting as if in defiance of gravity. The book, laid open as it was under the soft light, seemed a secret she only now realized she'd been in search of. She needed to pull her eyes from the book—*now! this instant!*—but she could not.

Ansel, looking up from the boot, following her gaze to the book, felt a sordid humiliation suffusing him and then rising through his skin in the form of sweat. *Explain yourself,* he thought. *Tell her why you brought it out.* But he could not. He could not tell her that he wasn't quite sure what all the exotic phrases meant and that he needed to parse them slowly, one word at a time. Vanity, and he knew it. It would be the same as announcing himself a fool, and that was worse than being suspected one, as he supposed he was now. So he said nothing and rustled noisily through several boxes before coming up with a bottle of glue.

"Here we are," he said.

"Good," Aldine said, the wind and her heart so loud she could barely hear her own voice. A rush of wind sent a tremble and moan through the barn. She could feel the pressure of her other boot through her knit stockings, the uneven wood of the sawhorse beneath her hands and legs. She tried not to look at him. The things she'd been hoping to ask this man—what Clare would do next by way of schooling, whether Neva was more than routinely sick, whether the other children, too, would catch it, and, the one big question, whether there had been any news regarding her unpaid wages—all fell silent within her.

Mr. Price cleaned the boot with a rag dipped in rubbing alcohol, took pains brushing the glue onto the sole and heel, then pressed the two back together. He set the boot on the bench and slid a small sledgehammer into the boot for weight. He pressed down on the hammer, which gathered his body into something more condensed and muscular.

Through clenched teeth he said, "I think you might be worried about your salary."

Something in her went out to him, thinking of her when things were so bad for his own self.

"A bit, surely," she said.

Mr. Price grimaced and shook his head but looked at her only momentarily. "I'm sorry. Do you need money for anything? I mean, in particular?"

"No," Aldine lied. She needed postage stamps and something for the dryness of her skin and every kind of underthing, but she wasn't going to mention that. He'd turned aside, was tightening the lid on the glue, and she glanced again at the book lying open there. She wished she could paint. It was the kind of soft illumination and exalted image someone should paint.

"You don't have to stay," Mr. Price said. He did not look at her. He was arranging things in the cupboard. "Working without pay—it's not fair to you, and you're under no obligation."

"But who would teach them?" She closed her eyes, listened to the wind, thought of the book there.

"I suppose they'd find someone," Ansel said gruffly. He didn't know why he said "they." Probably he'd not be a part of the school board after this. He thought the music and poetry Aldine brought to the class were wonderful, perfect, exactly what these children needed, but Josephson complained without end that Emmeline was receiving poor preparation for high school. Ansel moved slightly so that he stood now in front of the book, which was almost as foolish as bringing the damned book out in the first place. When he glanced at the girl, she seemed to be open-ing her eyes and he wondered why she might have had them closed, and for how long. She said, "But we've worked so hard on the Winter Entertainment." Her eyes rose to his. "I couldna' go now."

Ansel lifted the boot a little and studied it. "Probably should have tacked it first. The glue might not be enough." He searched some boxes, found particular tacks that suited him, and knocked them in with quick, efficient taps of a hammer. "It needs to dry for twenty minutes," he said. "Do you want to wait here?"

Did he want her to? Should she, if he did? Or was he merely being kind, thinking about the discomfort of walking through the cold wind in the clarty chicken yard with only one boot? She mumbled about needing to study up for the geography lesson she was teaching tomor-row, make sure she knew the capital of South Dakota.

"Pierre," he said.

"What?" she asked.

"It's Pierre, South Dakota."

Embarrassed, she nodded, and withdrew the book from her bag. "You see my need."

As she stared at her book, Ansel walked over to the tractor and began fiddling with the carburetor. A problem with the air valve was what he thought, because it almost always came down to the dust. He damped a cloth with kerosene and began clearing the dirt and sludge.

He toggled the choke, wondered about taking it down to the vapor control. He dared not look at the girl. He kept thinking of her but he dared not look. Time passed, the wind moaned and slapped and tugged, and once or twice Aldine's book crinkled under her fingers as she turned a page. Once, amidst the *whuffing* and creaking, he thought he heard a sound from the stalls, something other than the normal whisking of rodents. He peered into the darkness, but nothing stirred, and when he glanced over at Artemis, always alert to out-of-the-way sounds, the dog continued to sleep. And then before he could stop himself, he was looking at the girl, sitting on the stool in the firelight, with her thin legs extended. It seemed to him a scene from another century, a time when the convergence of warmth and reading and a lovely young girl and an old dog might suggest the simplest, purest pleasure that a planet had to offer. She did not look up and he let his eyes settle on her as he had never before, until at last she shifted just slightly and shot through him an alarm almost electrical, and he went straight back to work. He tapped free dust from the vapor control, cleaned it, and had nearly completed the reassembly when he saw her stand finally and walk over to the boot.

"It looks dry," she said.

Mr. Price wiped his hands with a rag and stood up, and as he approached did not look at her but kept his eyes narrowly on the boot. He had written the note. She was sure of it. The arrow that had pointed to Clare had all at once changed course. It was aimed now at him. Mr. Price. Which changed its nature entirely, made it more than a boyish notion.

"Do you think it would be better if I went to board somewhere else?" she asked suddenly. Not that she knew who'd take her. Not the Josephsons. Not the Wrights. Perhaps funny old Mrs. Odekirk, who kissed her on the cheek at church and kept asking if Aldine was enjoying her time here. People said Mrs. Odekirk had another house in Emporia that she rented to a doctor, which was why she was so well off. "I could ask Mrs. Odekirk."

"No," Ansel said, with more force than he expected. But he knew why the vehemence. He had done nothing wrong, and he would do nothing wrong. She needn't run away.

Aldine lowered her eyes and raised them in a long slow blink. She leaned against the sawhorse and poked her foot down hard into the boot, which seemed too small now that her foot had thawed. She struggled with it for a moment and then he said, "Let me help."

She meant to say no, but before she could say anything at all, he was kneeling down in front of her and she was looking down at his thick shoulders, his long narrowing back, his wavy head of hair. She had been lonely and homesick for a long time, and something in his tone when he said no was echoing inside her. That he should want her there—that anyone should want her—flooded her with strange thoughts, and he seemed, as he knelt there, to be as full of longing as she was. The boot slipped over her heel, and Mr. Price began to tighten the laces, slowly and firmly. She felt herself trembling and willed herself to stop. She wouldn't come near him again—she couldn't, not after this.

"How's that?" he asked lightly, but when he looked up at her, he failed to make himself look away from her mouth and eyes. It was like permitting himself a drink of water after days of thirst. He didn't move, but kept his hand on the top of her foot.

She wanted to put her hand on his head or his cheek but she didn't quite, managed to extend it only halfway. They were together like that, his hand clasping her boot, her hand outstretched, when the dog raised his head suddenly and then, ambling toward them from the rear of the barn, Charlotte said, "Hullo, Dad."

Ansel stood up abruptly and turned to his daughter. "Hello, Lottie."

She fixed her eyes on her father. "I wondered if you were ready for supper," she said slowly, and it was the slowness that held meaning. Aldine wondered if Charlotte had just come in, or if she'd been in the back of the barn all along. It was like the evening when she'd come out for a tarry and then, when she'd had her first good draw, Charlotte, out of nowhere, was there.

"My boot heel came off," she said to Charlotte, then turned to Mr. Price. "Thank you for fixing it." It sounded like a lie even though it wasn't, and that was Charlotte's fault.

"I'll go in the house now," she said, her face hot with shame, both for what she had felt and for what Charlotte seemed to think.

She picked up her books and turned to the barn door. She wanted to run, and had to keep herself from it. All through supper (squirrel again) Charlotte's cheeks seemed newly pink, her muddy blue eyes bright with a sense of discovery. Mrs. Price said Neva's cold was the second one this month and that she was going upstairs to tape the windows again.

30

On the Wednesday afternoon leading up to the Winter Entertainment, a work party had been called for setting the stage. It wasn't much, in Clare's opinion, mostly just a matter of hanging a curtain. But he and Neva had cooked up the idea of the block and tackle, and that could be something to remember. He bet it would in fact. He hadn't expected his father to approve, but he did, and Aldine, too, though its purpose was not to be revealed to the general public until the night of the performance. That was the part Clare liked about the plan. The surprise element.

He had come this afternoon to help with the stage-setting, along with his father, and the two younger Josephson girls had stayed after school as well. Neva wanted to be there, but was too sick. This morning she'd lied about not feeling sick just so she could go to school and stay for the work party but her coughing had given her away and so she had been kept home, crying and coughing a gurgly cough and wailing about the unfairness of the world. That was when his father volunteered himself and Clare, as if that would somehow make Neva feel better, which was faulty thinking, in Clare's opinion, not that he would say so.

At the moment, he was setting a pulley to the schoolroom's ridge beam, a job that required his perching atop a tall stepladder. The ladder was rickety, so his father stood holding it. Clare was glad he'd been allowed to set the pulley—usually his father wanted to take the lead in such things, especially when women were present, and today Miss McKenna (as Clare thought of her in the schoolhouse) was here, the most important presence of all.

Clare had poked a long heavy screwdriver through the eyebolt and was using it to crank the bolt tight, an aching job that required him to stretch and reach with each turn and though he wanted to stop and rest, he wouldn't, because he wanted neither his father nor Miss McKenna to see him giving up. He was relieved when one of the Josephson girls needed his father's help with a knot.

"Just hold still," his father said to him, and stepped away.

He sat. The whole room seemed different from up here, looking down at his father working at a knotted bag and at Berenice and Melba shaping clumps of wool and pasting them on the curtain that had once hung in Mrs. Wright's living room, before having been stored in the cellar. Charlotte had shaken off the mouse droppings and washed them and sewed them together for the stage curtain. Charlotte had said she would do that much and by that implied she would do no more. She hadn't come to the work party, though she could have come easy enough. Emmeline Josephson was absent, too. He'd seen her walking away when they were driving up. Maybe as soon as a female got to a certain age she couldn't like Aldine, and maybe that was because once a male got to a certain age he couldn't help but like her. He bet it was all one and the same.

Clare stared at the curtain and the wool, then squinted his eyes. The curtain was supposed to look like a winter sky with snowy clouds but even when squinting, all it looked like was an old curtain, with funny lines of sun-fading and lumps of uncarded wool on top.

His father had brought some wood for the stove so the work party would seem cheerier, and it did seem cheerier for the warmth and also for the fact that Miss McKenna had taken off her long heavy cardigan sweater and now when she stretched and knelt and leaned you could see the smooth contours of her body beneath her long thin dress.

"You falling asleep up there?" Ansel asked mildly when he returned to the ladder, and he could see it gave the boy a start. He'd been watching Aldine.

Clare stood, slid the heavy screwdriver through the eyebolt, and raised both hands to it.

"A few more good turns," Ansel said, and stood idly holding the ladder and taking things in. The goldfish twirled lazily in its bowl atop Aldine's desk. Neva's paper plane trailed Emmeline Josephson's *Flight of the Fancy* by the length of only one knot. She wouldn't catch up, though, he knew, not with so many school days missed.

"It's not so bad," Melba said of the old curtain, and Aldine said, "It will do, though, won't it?"

They were quiet then and the silence spoke volumes, in Clare's opinion.

Then a voice from behind said, "It's *wonderful!*"

Everyone turned and there was Neva, looking shrunken and small in their mother's winter coat. She held Milly Mandy Molly by her long monkey arm.

"It's *wonderful!*" she said again. She stepped forward and couldn't keep her eyes from the curtain. "They're the clouds Jack Frost will blow on! It's the sky he'll fill with snowflakes!"

Miss McKenna went at once to Nevie, knelt down, and reached her arm around her shoulders. His father drew close, too. "Did you walk?" Berenice asked, and Melba said, "You look all-overish, Neva. Are you frozen through?"

"No, but she is," Neva said, nodding at her stuffed monkey.

Clare was watching his father put a scoop of coal in the stove when the front door flew open and in walked his mother, looking like a wronged goddess. "There you are," she said in a tight, cold voice and for one odd moment he thought his mother was talking to Miss McKenna, but she stepped forward and roughly pulled Neva away from Miss McKenna's embrace. Then she picked up a ruler.

"Hand," she said.

Neva set the monkey gently to the floor and held out her open hand, but his mother couldn't do it. She couldn't strike Neva and she couldn't forgive her, either. She squeezed out the words one by one. *"Never ever ever do that again. Never ever ever do . . ."* Neva covered her eyes with her hands but his mother kept saying it until his father stepped forward and wrapped his arm around Neva and said softly, "The girl knows now, Ellie. She knows."

31

The night of the Winter Entertainment, the air was blessedly still, and the moon was almost full. It shone on the eastern fields in the usual way, enormous and unknowable, lighting Charlotte's path to the truck. Clare had helped Neva glue flakes of mica all over the cut-paper raindrops and snowflakes and tiaras that were required for the program, and as Charlotte laid them in the back of the truck, she stopped to look up at the constellations she knew, a short list that began with Orion and ended with the Pleiades. At the single night meeting of the Mythology Club, Harley's dad had allowed them to look through his telescope and she had stared at Jupiter while Harley's dad was saying, "There's a storm on Jupiter that could hold two earths like peas in a pod."

A storm so big it could hold our whole world twice over and so enduring that astronomers had been watching it since 1665—that was what Harley's dad had said. She scanned the sky for Jupiter, trying to remember if it shone in the west or southwest, and when she found the brightest of the white lights, she imagined storms more powerful than the ones that swept Kansas, winds blowing unchecked on an even larger plain. She felt the shiver she sought, the tiny fragile nothingness of herself, and then it was gone, replaced by the wool blanket she held in her hands, the paper props, and the excitement of having somewhere to go after dark. She didn't care if it was Aldine's big moment to show off. Charlotte had washed and curled her head for this. She had cleaned the dust off every stitch and crevice of her Sally shoes. She had patted her forehead and cheeks with the face powder her mother kept on her dresser. She was going to enjoy herself.

Charlotte had arranged to ride to the school with her father in the truck, thus ensuring that he would not take Aldine. Clare would drive Aldine, Neva, and their mother in the Ford. When she'd written out those lines from *Venus and Adonis*, she didn't mean them to induce Aldine to flirt with their father. Far from it. She'd intended it to be a little trial for Clare and maybe even a boost, and, sure, she had to admit it, a little amusement for herself. It was Clare's handwriting she'd imitated; no one would've thought anything else. Her father's penmanship, when he wrote down in the account book what they earned and what they spent, was better than her own. How for the love of God could Aldine have failed to notice that? And how could her willful ignorance have knocked down the perfectly sturdy walls of Charlotte's plan and left them far behind? Really, it was as if Aldine could control men just by willing it so.

Charlotte had been in the barn that day because the barn was a place to go when she wanted to get away from everybody and it was too cold to go outside. She read sometimes, if there was something to read. Sometimes she napped in what had been the horse's stall with Artemis curled beside her. She added things to her notebook. She'd been napping that day, in fact, or she would have told her father she was there. The first thing she heard was Aldine's singsongy brogue, and when Charlotte peered out through the rails, it was like watching a play, except with bad lighting.

Now they were all coming out on the porch, chattering to each other and pulling on coats, the bright scent of Joy in the air, the perfume from Opa that her mother saved and portioned out by the half drop, so this was a sure sign that she wanted to make the event a special occasion, too. Neva's hair was French braided and pinned into loops that she kept taking off her mittens to touch. Charlotte had moistened Neva's cheeks and eyelids with cold cream, then crushed a little mica between her fingers and touched it to Neva's face, a trick Charlotte learned in Dorland. Neva would be both a fairy and a snowflake in the play, provided that her cough stayed quiet. Clare wore a tie with his old plaid barn coat and it looked as if he'd oiled his hair. His pale face was moony and handsome in its own way, and Charlotte felt a little sorry for him, remembering that he had stayed home while she was larking around with Opal in Abilene, that he'd been waiting for a turn that didn't come. And her plan to play Cupid had failed, too, at least for him.

Aldine stepped out of the house, but she might just as well have stepped from the pages of *Vogue* or *Harper's Bazaar*, beaming with expectant pleasure, ready to take her place in the spotlight, all dark hair and eyelashes and ungodly thinness, her feet small and graceful even in laced-up boots. It wasn't fair to despise Aldine for this, but she did just the same. Aldine never met Charlotte's gaze now, not since the day in the barn. Charlotte knew her father hadn't done anything with Aldine that afternoon, but there had been something odd about her father's look, something that reminded her of that day in the post office when she caught him seeming like someone other than her father, and there was something too meaningful in the wretched way he held Aldine's boot, kneeling before her, telling her she shouldn't go. No, he hadn't done anything wrong, but he'd been *poised* to, and she couldn't stand it, she just couldn't, and without even knowing what she was doing she'd felt herself standing up and walking toward them and saying, *Hullo, Dad*. She didn't blame her father. He was just a man and inside every man was a boy, and as could easily be seen, every boy could be twirled on his own axis by the right girl. And Aldine was the right girl for just about every boy in the county. So the blame went where it belonged—to Aldine, for being pretty and skinny and spritely and talking in that trilling way that everyone with a thingie found so charming. For visiting her father alone in the barn. For living with them month after month and seeing everything they did not have. And she blamed herself, too, just a little, for making the dumb love letter and slipping it into her book.

"Time to go," her father said, cranking the Ford for Clare and then hopping into the truck. Without a look at anyone else, Charlotte quickly slid in beside her father and, under the storm of Jupiter, they drove toward Stony Bank School.

32

Neva didn't care if Emmeline rolled her eyes. Neva loved the Winter Entertainment. She and Melba had the best parts. The songs were vivacious. Her Ray Fairy costume was vivacious. Melba was a vivacious Cloud Queen. That was one of their hard spelling words, *vivacious*, but it was ever so perfect.

She adored the program that Mrs. Odekirk had typed twenty times so that each member of the audience could have a "nice memento." She and the Josephson girls (except Emmeline, who said she would work on her math instead) had glued each sheet to stiff purple paper that Mrs. Odekirk had gone to Kress in Dorland especially to buy, and Neva planned to keep hers forever and ever.

A Winter Entertainment

February 1933

Presented by the Students of Stony Bank School

Laura McNeal

***

POEM: "THE WAVES OF THE SEASHORE"

BY GENEVA LOUISE PRICE, MELBA JOSEPHSON, AND PHAY WRIGHT

PLAY: "THE SNOW STORM"

BERENICE JOSEPHSON—*JILL*

EMMELINE JOSEPHSON—*MOTHER NATURE & SUN QUEEN*

MELBA JOSEPHSON—*CLOUD QUEEN*

GENEVA LOUISE PRICE—*RAY FAIRY*

HARLON WRIGHT—*JACK FROST & OLD OCEAN*

PHAY WRIGHT—*JAMES*

SONG: "RAIN DROPS"

BY ALL

SONG: "BRYAN O'LINN"

BY MISS MCKENNA AND ALL STUDENTS

THE END

She went behind the curtain rigged up by the work party but mostly by Clare and her father. Emmeline wore a long, gold, drapey dress that had been her great aunt's, with green velvet leaves that fluttered along the sleeves and hem. She had waved her hair and she let Miss McKenna powder her face and rouge her lips and she wasn't fooling anybody. She was excited in spite of herself.

Neva said her part of the poem to herself and tapped her foot to keep the beat.

> "Roll on, roll on, you noisy waves,
> Roll higher up the strand.
> How is it that you cannot pass
> That line of yellow sand?"

She hadn't known, when the inspector came last week, that this beat was called iambic tetrameter, but she knew it now because the inspector told her. She didn't like the inspector because he didn't like Miss McKenna. You could tell from the straight line of his mouth and his stiff mustache. He had frowned at the planes on their strings along the ceiling and he didn't stop frowning while Miss McKenna explained what they were. Neva had come up to him when he was alone and told him that Miss McKenna was the best teacher she ever had and the man stared down at her with his stiff face and said, "Well, missy, you haven't had many teachers yet, have you?" Neva hoped the inspector was struck by lightning and never came back again.

She felt a cough coming, held her breath until she'd fought it back down.

"Roll on, roll on, you noisy waves," she whispered again, rubbing her index finger ever so lightly across her fairy wings so she could feel the powdery bits of mica. The grown-ups were loud on the other side of the curtain, and she liked it when she heard her father's laugh and her mother's hellos to Mrs. Odekirk and Mrs. Wright. She could also hear

Yauncy's funny nasal voice and that was a nice surprise. Nobody had seen Yauncy since Mr. Tanner fell out of his hayloft and broke his neck.

"About ready then?" Miss McKenna asked, her shiny black hair glistening around her face. She was like an angel, she really was, dropped down from heaven for them. She kept going child to child, adjusting crowns and wings and collars. Neva felt the clogging of her windpipe again, and held her breath again. If she coughed, her mother would come behind the curtain and ruin everything, especially the magical surprise, because that was what it was, a magical surprise, Clare pulling on a rope threaded through a pulley way up on the highest beam and lifting her up into the sky. She could hardly believe it was going to happen but it was. When the Sun Queen called, "Fly, little Ray Fairy, down to the ocean!" Neva was going to fly. It would be the most magical thing ever done in the entire history of Stony Bank School.

Neva inhaled, and felt the cough seizing her, and stumbled out the door so she could cough where no one would hear her. But Miss McKenna followed her out.

"Are you all right?" she asked when Neva finally stopped coughing. "Your father gave me the Pinex just in case." She held up the little bottle of cough syrup.

Neva took a sip, not very much, and held it in her mouth, because the syrup looked good but wasn't. Clare said it had more alcohol than rum but Charlotte said how would he know? All Neva knew was that it burned when it went down. She closed her eyes, swallowed, and hoped it would take the other stuff in her throat down with it. She opened her eyes and took a deep breath. "I'm fine now," she said.

33

No one could have foreseen the connection, was Ansel's opinion. Especially not Aldine. Those who blamed her for what happened were ready to blame her for anything—like Josephson and his daughter. Everyone was enjoying the night well enough before the rope trick, laughing and clapping at their own bright-cheeked children as they recited and sang and bowed in their blue-gray glittery getups. He felt a swelling flood of fondness and gratitude move through him when Neva said her solemn lines about the ocean waves and Ellie hooked her arm in his, leaning against him in a way she hardly ever did anymore.

He'd loved coming into the schoolhouse, finding it warmed by the stove, the funny stage curtain hanging at one end of the room, the paper airplanes strung up overhead. In his chair next to Ellie, he closed his eyes and inhaled. He'd sat in this very schoolhouse as a boy, and while sitting here had fallen in love with books and singing and any number of little girls, but what he had really been doing, he thought now, was falling in love with this place, and all that it was. Him so small and so different then. But not entirely so.

Aldine's program itself was charming everyone. They all chuckled at wispy Phay Wright, dancing on his tiptoes and saying, "Mother Nature!

Mother Nature! Will you send us some snow?" Ansel had no idea that the youngest Wright boy could be such a ham, pretending to ice skate across the floor, showing Emmeline's regal Mother Nature how he'd pack a snowball with his hands.

Emmeline looked almost benevolent when she smiled at him and said, "Well, child, I will see what I can do for you. My plants and seeds need a snow blanket. I will send for Jack Frost. Jack Frost! Jack Frost!"

Harlon Wright appeared stage left in a union suit covered all over with paper snowflakes—and so did Old Ocean and the Sun Queen, both of whom were played once again by Harlon and Emmeline, who were breathing so hard after their costume changes that they could hardly speak their lines. Old Ocean said something about calling the Ray Fairies, and when Neva came running out shedding mica from her blue gown and paper wings, he couldn't keep himself from clapping a little.

"Here is the vapor for you," Harlon told her in his deepest Old Ocean voice, holding a pitchfork that was tipped with paper triangles so it would look more like a trident—a clever touch, in Ansel's view.

Then Neva cried gaily, "I will *fly* with the vapor!" stretching out the word *fly* and spreading her arms dramatically, triumphantly. They could all see the rope, of course, and she was wearing a harness that looked like Clare's work, so it was no surprise when someone on the other side of the curtain (Clare, it turned out, had slipped away from his chair) pulled Neva-the-Ray-Fairy up into the air in fits and jerks while she, with visible effort, lifted her legs and stretched out her arms in the posture of flying. Her expression was serene, as if her ability to think of this ungainly suspension as flight could make it actual, and for a moment Ansel felt a swelling pride in his daughter's happiness, and in his son's ingenuity, and in Aldine's influence on them all.

Ansel would remember that sentiment, and wonder at its completeness and purity, and also its brevity, because in the next instant everything changed.

Old Ocean didn't quite finish his line, something that began "I shall soon—" when Yauncy Tanner began to groan and bawl and point, standing up so suddenly from his chair that everyone around him stood up, too, in surprise or confusion or maybe fright. The sound reminded Ansel of a cow when calving hurt it deep inside. Yauncy was taller than plenty of men and all of the women, and he was heavier, too, than most. "Et oun!" he yelled. "Et oun!"

That was when the similarity struck him, and likely other people: the rope looked like the one Yauncy had found his father hanging from that day in the barn.

Neva didn't know what was the matter, and Emmeline just stared at Yauncy, her wreath of artificial daisies slightly crooked and her cheeks pink from makeup and heat. Aldine, standing to the side of the stage, looked paralyzed, but Mrs. Odekirk stood up on her stork-thin legs and took Yauncy's hand, the one his mother wasn't already clinging to, and said, "It's all right, Yauncy. She's not choking." Yauncy was still agitated, frantic even, moving toward the stage, and Emmeline backed into the curtain, as if Yauncy were coming to grab her, so Ansel could only think to help Neva get down. "Let's get her down, then," he called gently to Yauncy, and he stepped around Mrs. Odekirk and around little Phay in his snow clothes and reached up to hold Neva by the waist. Neva had by this time lost her angel-flight pose and was hanging like a lamb in a winch, looking not a bit grateful for his interference with her big moment, but she didn't fight him, either, as he held her tight and undid the hook and set her gently down on the wooden floor.

"See?" he called to Yauncy. "She's right as rain."

Yauncy sat back down but Mrs. Tanner was silently crying, a handkerchief balled in her hand, and when Mrs. Odekirk sat down, she kept Yauncy's hand on her lap, patting it in that benign, confident way she had.

Ansel nodded at Aldine, who was just staring out, hand to throat, and he mouthed the words, "Go on," nodding again when she didn't move, trying to coax her into a prompt that would get the play moving again. Every time he looked at her he felt the desire to hold her and kiss every part of her, a longing that he tried to convert to some acceptable feeling, like friendship or paternal care. "Go on," he said again gently.

Aldine stepped across the stage, finally, and whispered into Emmeline's ear, and Emmeline said miserably, "Blow upon the clouds, Jack Frost! Fill the air with snowflakes!"

Harlon wasn't dressed as Jack Frost. He was holding the pitchfork-trident. Still, Emmeline's line had roused him, and he pushed open the crack in the curtain. After some rustling, he came back out with handfuls of mica and cut-paper flakes, which he began awkwardly to toss, and a bucket appeared behind him, above the curtain, and began to shake sawdust down onto the stage.

Neva looked at Berenice and Melba, but none of them spoke. It was Phay who finally remembered the line and shouted it. "Hurrah!" he said gamely. "Hurrah! Here comes the snowstorm!"

Aldine started clapping, so Ansel joined in, and others, too, but with restraint, and the children bowed in uncertain little waves. A few of them, including Neva, smiled despite the confusion. The older ones, who Ansel guessed knew how Horace Tanner died, might have known what had disturbed Yauncy, or they might have thought it was yet another time when Yauncy was different and flubbed things for himself or others, hopeless to blame or help. Mrs. Tanner gathered up her coat and stood to go, thinking either that the event was over or that it was over for her.

Perhaps fearing that the other parents would leave, Aldine said, "And now we hope you'll all enjoy our next entertainment, a song called 'Rain Drops.'"

Mrs. Tanner didn't sit back down, but pulled Yauncy along with her, not roughly, but firmly. He let go of Mrs. Odekirk's hand.

"Please don't go, Mrs. Tanner," Aldine said. "It's all right."

But Mrs. Tanner just shook her head and kept walking, and people let her pass, looking like they wished they could put on their own hats and coats and disappear into the dark.

Aldine had to wait while the two Tanners went out the door, the sound of Yauncy's big feet loud upon the hollow floor. The children shuffled out holding paper raindrops as big as their heads, but they sang uncertainly now, in hushed voices, and could not keep together well enough for all the words to come through. Ansel thought that would be all until he saw that the last song on the program was the song he'd so often heard Aldine singing to Neva, the one he had sung with her himself before Ellie chided him. He wished it wasn't included, or that Aldine would see that calling it a night would be best for all, but she didn't.

She looked scared, but she stepped forward and said, "Our last number is a Scottish ballad I've taught the children. I hope you'll enjoy it—it's about making do. Emmeline Josephson, who has excellent hand-writing, has ta'en the trouble to write out some of the last verses for you so you can sing along at the end. If you like," she added, and Ansel tried to give her an encouraging nod when she glanced at him.

She seated herself at the piano and looked toward the curtain, one edge of which was gripped by a small hand. The hand belonged to Phay, who held a sheepskin, and who in a wavering voice introduced them to Bryan O'Linn's troubles. The props for the song were funny: a feed sack, a graniteware pot, a turnip from somebody's root cellar. The women in the audience, stilled by Mrs. Tanner's grief, managed to smile as the children sang about Bryan's lack of hosiery, trousers, watch, and shoes. On the last verse Aldine sang alone, a cappella, with her hands still on the piano keys.

> "Bryan O'Linn, his wife, and wife's mother,
> Were all going over the bridge together,
> The bridge it broke up and they all tumbled in,
> 'We'll go home by water,' says Bryan O'Linn."

173

He knew the parents in the audience had smiled and clapped, not with gusto, but at least enough to be polite, and he knew that the children had enjoyed putting on most of the show, but that was not what any of them would remember. They would remember the rope, and poor Mrs. Tanner walking away with her damaged boy, and the way Aldine had nonetheless kept the show going, probably so she could sing at the very end and show her voice to such advantage.

34

It wasn't so bad, the play, she didn't think now, though it all seemed bad while she hung there in the air. The next day, at the very beginning of school, Aldine had told the children that they had all performed beautifully and that what had happened with poor Yauncy was no one's fault, least of all theirs, and then Harlon Wright said, "I thought Yauncy was the best part of the show!" which got a big laugh from his brother and wasn't nice, but it did help to put the sorry part of it aside and allow them all to think about the good parts if they wanted to.

It would be a short day, which made the other children happy but not Neva. She liked being at school with Miss McKenna and doing her lessons and being warm and singing songs. And today would be the day for the airplane prize because there were a week's worth of tests and papers coming back today and her plane and Emmeline's were almost nose and nose with only three more knots to the finish. On Miss McKenna's desk the goldfish with its long ribbony tail hovered and stared and sometimes did a graceful turnabout.

Right after the pledge and the singing, Miss McKenna pulled the tests out of her bag and looked them over dramatically.

"If I got hundreds on every one of those, I'll be right in the thick of it," Phay Wright said, and Harlon said, "If you got hundreds on every one of those, my name is Agnes Turpentine," which was a new one in Neva's book and for some reason made her laugh. Maybe it was nervousness.

"I'll pass out the hundreds first so you can move your planes," Miss McKenna said, and everyone watched while the different students received their papers one by one and then used the transom pole to move their plane.

"Emmeline," Miss McKenna said, "receives three perfect scores."

This was met with a general groan, and Emmeline, smug as a queen, moved her plane ahead the three knots to the finish line. Which meant Neva needed four to tie. Almost before she'd made that computation, Miss McKenna said, "Neva receives three perfect scores."

Neva looked down at her desk. Phay said, "That's good, though, Neva. That's real good."

She rose and moved her *Mr. Benny* plane to a spot just behind Emmeline's. She didn't look at Emmeline. She knew what Emmeline's face would look like if she did, all rosy and glorying and pretending to be nice.

She could hardly remember the rest of the day, except she'd made it a vow not to let anyone know how bad she felt because she didn't want Emmeline Josephson to have that satisfaction, so she was taken by surprise when Clare over supper said, "So who won the goldfish?" and all of a sudden the dam broke and she was crying like a baby and running from the room with her face burning in shame.

That was the bad part.

The good part was the next day when Clare walked all the way to town and went to Oswald's Five and Dime and traded this and that and came home with a goldfish in a bowl that was just for her. She named it Goldo and said it might go on stage with Groucho, Harpo, Chico, Gummo, and Zeppo.

35

At first Ansel thought the huge cloud rising might mean rain. It was from the southwest, the right direction for a good hard rain. Storms like this were violent in the beginning, with lightning and thunder and gusts of wind. These things fell upon you before the rain.

But there was no lightning or thunder. Just darkness billowing, a roiling cloud that went, he suddenly realized, from earth to sky, not sky to earth.

Artemis barked at it, but Artemis always barked at storms. The chickens quarreled their way to the coop. It was noon on a Saturday, the middle of February, and he assumed everyone was home. Clare, Ellie, Neva, and Charlotte came first to the porch or windows, then the yard, expecting the sucking mineral cavity of air that brought rock-hard showers. Not until the mountainous clouds reached them and he saw larks trying to outfly the wind did he realize the air was all dirt and no water, as if hell had come up from the ground. In the next moment they were blasted with dirt, almost swallowed by it, and they covered their eyes to run for the house.

For a few minutes they just stayed in the living room, wiping their eyes and faces, tasting dust on their teeth, breathing in the particles that swirled through the air. No one even sat down. They were used to blow months, used to spitting dust out like tobacco juice, but this was something different. The dust blotted out the sun. He kept staring out at it. He couldn't close his eyes. If he closed his eyes, he would imagine the world ending. Things like that happened. Not ending, maybe, but close to it. An asteroid, then dust, then the world turned into another place. It happened to the dinosaurs; why couldn't it happen to humans?

"Is it smoke?" Ellie asked. She was holding a potato and a peeler, which she didn't set down. "Is there a grass fire, do you think?"

"No," he said. "It wouldn't have so much dirt in it."

"Maybe we should be in the cellar," Clare said, leaning down so he could peer out the window. "Maybe it's a tornado."

Ansel was still staring out. Tornadoes were dark, it was true. "But it came from the ground, not the sky," he said. "It's the ground blowing."

"But why is there so much of it this time?"

Neva's eyes were enormous, and when she coughed they all stiffened, afraid that it would be like the night she couldn't stop for over an hour and had to gasp deep to get any air at all. He said they should breathe through wet handkerchiefs for a while, like when you were filtering out smoke. He got them all to sit down, and with the handkerchief pressed to her mouth, Neva's coughing stopped.

"Shouldn't someone go up and see if Aldine's okay?" Clare asked.

"Yes," Ansel said, glad he didn't have to be the one to suggest it. "Charlotte, you go."

"She isn't here," Charlotte said through her handkerchief in an even voice. She had one hand on Artemis, who normally wasn't allowed in the house.

"What do you mean—where is she?" Ansel couldn't keep the annoyance out of his voice, even though Ellie had asked him to go easier on her. "Why didn't you say so before?"

"I forgot," Charlotte said. What made her words cheeky was the indifference with which she delivered them. "She said she was going to work on a geography project at the school, but that's not what she's really doing. What she's really doing is reading one of my books and smoking her cigarettes with ivory tips."

They were all looking at him over their handkerchiefs like the monkeys labeled *Speak no evil*. He bolted up and said he was going to the school. He didn't wait to see what Ellie would say about it. Aldine was an outsider. This was no better than a blizzard. She could stumble out of that school and be lost in a minute. He clapped the wet rag back over his mouth and pulled the door tight behind him, to keep the dust out.

36

What Aldine noticed first was the loss of light. The page she was reading turned gray, as if night had fallen. Her tarry glowed like a pinched candlewick. At home, such darkness meant one thing, and she thought, *It's going to chuck it doon.* A good rain would be a relief to everyone and most especially to Ansel, though she had told herself to call him only Mr. Price in her head now.

Did she love him? When she was alone, she let herself remember his face that day in the barn or his fingers playing the dulcimer. It was like turning on a faucet. You let it all pour out and wash over you. Then she turned it off and went on being what she was, a teacher in his house who would never do any of the bad things Ellie and Charlotte suspected her of doing.

Not until she stood up and looked out the wavy glass did she become afraid. She could barely see the American flag on its pole, flung out by gritty winds, and she wondered if Mr. Marvin, who lived on the nearest farm and raised and lowered the flag every day of the year, would come to take it home. She could hear what sounded like rocks pit the wall of the school, a rattling, angry assault of airborne pieces. She opened the front door without stepping out, and into her nose and mouth came the smell of pulverized loam and a taste like burned chalk. The road leading back to the Prices' had disappeared. She set the door closed, and looked around. She drew close to the stove, where she had built, as she usually did on these cold Saturday afternoons when she stole away, a comforting fire, one that now gave merely adequate heat. She opened the door to the stove, threw her cigarette butt into its orangey mouth, and crouched there with the door ajar, watching the coals for a long moment. A sudden burst of wind blew right into the roof and shot down the stovepipe, throwing freezing air and lit cinders out onto the floor. It was as if the stove had spit at her, and she flung the door closed before she stomped out the live red crumbs.

She went again to the window. In the yard, the flag was like a reddish waving shadow and then as she stared at the strange thing that it had become, it vanished. She kept staring at the spot but she could not see it at all.

Going out in it would be an idiot's business. That much was sure.

The blue curtains they'd used for the Winter Entertainment were still folded up on a back shelf, and she prepared herself like an animal in a burrow, laying them out in layers until she had a makeshift bed. She watched for spiders but not especially. She covered herself with the last panel, even her head, and hoped, as she hoped nightly, that when she woke up it would all be over. What the *it* was, she didn't know. The winter. The pennilessness. The aloneness. The badness. The curtains smelled of mothballs and clarty sheep, still clotted here and there as they were with the wool that had served for winter clouds, which no one believed looked a bit like clouds except Neva. Neva did. Aldine laid her head on the novel she'd been reading and fell into grainy sleep.

37

The truck started when Ansel tried it the third time, his hands gritty, the seat gritty, the whole machine rocking slightly in the brown wind. Things whose position he thought he knew—the coop, the western fence—were hidden like furniture in a room when the lights go out. He drove slowly, blindly, and came within sickening inches of the porch and then the cottonwood. Creeping along the road, he knew that he would only be aware that he had veered from its relative safety if he struck something or sank into the sand that lay in drifts along the edges. His nose was raw and—a disquieting surprise—he tasted blood in his throat. Still, he had found the road, and the road was straight. There wasn't likely to be another car headed for him even on a clear day, so he drove slowly ahead for what seemed the right distance to the school, and then kept going and going and going, praying and squinting and searching and yet certain that he'd somehow passed it, until, at last, he spotted what he thought must be the edge of the school fence. He did not feel any pride in finding it. He felt only gratitude. He rolled slowly forward until he banged into something that turned out to be the flagpole.

He forced the car door open against the wind and choked his way across the schoolyard, glad they had decided to sink the flagpole so close to the building, and glad when his outstretched hand touched something solid. He tried not to breathe as he felt his way along the boards of the outer wall, remembering the direction of the door but not the distance, tripping on the steps and scraping his knuckles. "Miss McKenna?" he shouted, and when he climbed up the steps and found the doorknob, he felt himself caught like a thistle in a barbed wire fence.

He had to close the door behind him and use the rag on his eyes, then his nose and mouth. It was like having the flu, this storm. The dust gave him a sense of bodily pain and a thickness of mouth that was physically nauseating. Then he could see the bundle on the floor, a dark, twisted shape, her pale, lovely face rising in the center of it. "What is it?" she asked. "Is a tornado coming?"

"No," he said, though he couldn't be sure. A ferocious gust hit the side of the school and he said, "Come on. I'll drive you back to the house."

"No," she said.

"What do you mean?"

Instead of answering, she lay back down. "I can't."

That was a surprise.

"Do you want to sit here a minute and see if it dies down?"

"Yes," she said, her smooth, pale face sideways on the blankets. He couldn't figure out what the light-colored clumps were. It looked like maybe she had torn the stuffing out of thick blankets. Then he remembered the play.

He didn't really think the storm would die down. A normal wind could blow for ten or twenty hours. Once, a wind had blown for one hundred hours. If it blew for even three, the sun would go down and it would be even harder to get home.

"All right," he said. "We'll wait a minute."

They listened to the wind against the walls. It made him think of being in the barn with her that afternoon and he felt both dread and happiness.

After a while, she said, "Do you believe in fate, Mr. Price?"

"I suppose so," he said. "In a certain way."

"How?"

"I don't believe in using it as an excuse. But things shape us. We're led to certain things and have certain gifts."

"I think I shouldn't have come," she said.

"That's my fault," he said. "I'm sorry you feel that way. But you've done a lot of good."

"No. I haven't."

"Don't say that." The wind was a *whuffing* sound, then a rising, swarming rush. He wondered if there was anything diagonal in the walls for lateral stress. He eased close to Aldine and bent near and still, as you would make yourself near and still with a spooked horse. She reached out and touched his shoe.

Ansel's knees didn't bend that easily and they were starting to ache. He sat down on the floor so that he could lean against the wall, but he laced his hands together so that he wouldn't reach out to take her hand. George Washington and Benjamin Franklin peered from their frames with placid eyes.

Aldine took her hand back as if embarrassed. She said, "When Leenie and I were growing up, we had an aunt who wasn't married. The story our da told us was she'd been in love with a Japanese man who didn't come to fetch her until it was too late."

"What do you mean too late?"

"I don't even know! We always thought it was because she was too old. When you're a child, people can seem old. We saw the man once, when he came to ask her. And then he went away again, and she went on living alone. Leenie and I, we were always planning to meet our Japanese man at the right time, and go off with him, and not be alone for years and years, wearing fascinators and trying to get other people's children to like us."

Ansel wasn't sure what a fascinator was. "You're still young," he said. "You'll be happy."

"Like you and Ellie?" she asked.

He thought about that. Did he and Ellie seem happy? By some measures they were. As happy as anyone was at that stage of things. And now here he was beside Aldine, and she was curled up inside the old curtains and he felt an overpowering urge to caress her.

Ansel tried to look only at his hands or at the walls. The wind shook the building, seeping through the cracks.

"I'm so cold," Aldine said, and he looked unwillingly at her eyes and mouth. Her smooth hair fell forward around her face and because she was still lying down, it was like seeing her when she first woke up in the morning, as if they were in bed together. Ansel stood up. He intended to do it quickly but found himself stiff and old feeling, as he often did lately. He said he would put more coal in the stove, but the bin was empty when he looked.

"I used what was inside already," she said flatly. "I was going to tell you when I got home that we needed to fill up."

With his wife, his daughters, or even Clare, he would have had the warmth of his body to offer. Even to imagine this with Aldine was to go dry-mouthed with desire, so he waited a moment before he said, "Another reason to leave now. Before it gets colder and darker."

Aldine simply curled herself smaller inside the pile she'd made. She tried to remember the Venus poem. Something about kissing where there was no hiss of death. The wind was nothing if not a hiss of death, and if Ansel had copied down those words for her, if he had felt what she thought he felt that day in the barn, would he act on it now? From a distance adultery seemed so obviously wrong and resistible, and yet what she craved now was the man before her, with his large hard workman's hands, his sturdy limbs, his quiet way of being. She loved him. If he were not married, he would be her Japanese man—that was the truth of it. And then she had a terrible thought: What if Aunt Sedgewick's Japanese man had been married? When she met him the first time, or even perhaps later on? She had always assumed that poor Aunt Sedge made the wrong decision, that she was just too timid to seize her own chance at happiness.

"We have to get back," Ansel said. "They'll be worried." He remained standing, and she remained on the floor. "Miss McKenna," he said, and he reached his hand out to help her rise, willing himself to make this ordinary gesture, telling himself it would make their relations courtly and chaste. She put out her hand and the touch of it was something he tried not to let his blood race toward. As long as he said nothing, did nothing, the feeling would go away. Her hand was cold and small, and she tightened her grip on his hand without making an effort to stand.

"I'm afraid," she said, the only words that expressed both how she felt and how she was allowed to feel. If he had moved his hand or his body closer, she would have met him eagerly, but he was just looking at her and his face was so grave, so sorrowful, that she only held on to his hand and waited.

He pulled her up, and she thought he would pull her into his arms. George Washington and the flag. The flag and Ben Franklin. Aldine's own script on the chalkboard, the white words she had copied out, *oil broil hoist coil.*

"Pull that blanket you were using up around your head," he said hoarsely. "Shut out some of the wind while we run for it." She reached down to pick up a blue curtain panel and draped it over her head.

"Take my hand," he said, "so you don't get lost. I'll lead you."

She took it, but he didn't move. She stepped forward and pressed her body against his, laying her face against his chest, her arms clutching him. When his arms caught her to him, something like a sob shook her, and she couldn't tell if it came from relief or fear. He held her very tightly until it passed, and she felt a dark measureless want.

38

Charlotte told Emmeline, and Emmeline told her father, who must have told the inspector, that Ansel Price nearly died driving to the school to fetch a teacher who was using school-owned coal to heat herself on a Saturday afternoon. "She was smoking, too," Charlotte had added. The novel that Emmeline and her father found on the school floor early Monday morning was *The Harvester*, just as Charlotte said, and inside the front cover of the novel was Charlotte's handwritten name.

Charlotte knew that her father would not have said that he nearly died, but that was how it had seemed to her and her mother during the five hours that they waited in the suffocating brown gloom of the house. They had peeled potatoes and cooked them in gritty water, and they had told Neva not to worry, but they had worried. Neva was too sick to stay alert during the strange dark afternoon, slipping into sleep until she coughed herself awake, then drifting off again.

Her father's explanation, that he couldn't get the truck to start, that they'd been sitting in the truck in the schoolyard most of the time, that darkness fell and then the wind stopped, at which time the engine turned over just fine, was logical enough, but Charlotte didn't like the way Aldine slipped up the stairs wearing that old curtain over her head like the Virgin Mary or something, her face pale, her eyes red, not even bothering to say, "Sorry," or to ask, "How are you?"

39

While waiting for the inspector to arrive on Friday afternoon of the following week, Aldine went about the empty schoolhouse wiping dust off the bookshelves with a damp white cloth and a pail of water. It was good to work. It kept her warm. They had brought coal for the stove, but just the littlest bit, not enough for even a week. She had to stop and refill the pail with clean water every five minutes or she streaked the varnished shelves with mud instead of cleaning them. The shelves would be gritty again by Monday, but it gave her something to do.

As she worked she was aware, as she had been aware since the day of the storm, of a difference in her skin. All over her skin was the desire for Ansel, which was like the electricity that clung invisibly to her cracked fingers, which pulled her skirt against her legs and stuck her hair together and sparked on metal. In Ansel's truck she hadn't been able to stop shivering, had cried unintelligibly and tried to open the door again so she could go back inside the school, which at least didn't rock back and forth in the wind, but he gathered her body against him and said, "Shh. Shh. Close your eyes, Aldine, and don't look."

He'd never before used her Christian name, and it made his voice sound different—closer, more intimate. "I can still hear it!" she cried. "I can still hear the hissing sound!"

"Sing then," he said, but she cried harder and dug her hand into his shirt.

"I can't," she said. "I can't."

"Shh," he murmured, just as if she were his daughter. "You'll be all right. We'll just wait it out, is all, just wait it out." He had said that over and·over until she stopped trying to open the door and held still. She was more or less in his lap by then, and although they were both gritty and there was on his neck the smell of dirt and the smell of sweat, she kept her face against his skin. It surprised her now that she hadn't kissed him. She wanted to kiss him now, it was true and shameful, but in the truck, in his arms, there had been a nearly guiltless intimacy to his embrace that soothed her.

Outside, Aldine heard the motor of a car. Then a few seconds of quiet, followed by a car door slamming. Footsteps on the stairs, and then the inspector entered the schoolhouse without knock or greeting. His manner was brusque. He brought the winter in with him. He removed his hat and took up a stance ten paces from Aldine. He stared at her for a moment, and said, "There have been reports of impropriety."

Aldine looked at her pail of dirty water, not at the man with the stiff face and brushy mustache and fancy hat. "Impropriety," he said again.

"Meaning?" Aldine asked, looking up now. That she had worked for five months without pay was not mentioned. That was improper, if you asked her.

"The use of the school premises for non-school activities. The burning of coal for personal comfort." The inspector might have added that Mr. Josephson had lowered his voice to mention a rumored impropriety of another sort, but that was always the problem with these unmarried schoolteachers, wasn't it? It was the devilish bind the boards were in— they couldn't hire a married teacher, had to fire one who got married, in fact, but unmarried women, especially those who were young and fetching, could get into trouble in a farm town just as quick as they could in the city. One more reason why, in his opinion, the country schools needed consolidation. Board them up, that was the thing now. Board them up and consolidate.

The girl had looked away from him in clear impudent disdain, and now squeezed her rag into the pail, leaning forward a bit, her thin dress pulling tight, her skin so milky and smooth it seemed nothing had ever touched it, not even the sun. *There's talk she's set her eye on Mr. Price,* Mr. Josephson had said in his murmuring voice.

"So," he said, and when the girl turned her round, pretty face to him, he felt in a raw way the nature of her sin whether actual or contemplated, one only the necessary step to the other, and he wondered if this was the way it was in Ireland or wherever she came from—that you set your cap for a man, married or not.

"As of today," he said, "the school is closed for the near term." He was glad to see the hurt in her eyes, the way they lost their impudence. "You'll need to complete your assessments of each pupil for the incoming teacher."

Aldine suffered his words like a series of blows, and felt her skin flushing from both anger and humiliation. That this stout, stupid man with his stony face and his hairbrush mustache who knew not one blessed thing about her and her schoolteaching could make her feel like a chastened child made her livid. "I didn't pockle the bloody cool," she said. The muddy water had whitened the cracks in the hand that shook as she pointed at the stove. "I've no place of my own, have received no money at all, and have lived with a family that has not been paid to keep me. It's the school board that has pockled my pay."

"The board will consider your salary in the context of recent events," the inspector said evenly. "There is the matter of deducting for the coal, of course, and also"—he seemed to be savoring his command over the situation—"other matters."

"Other matters?" she said. "And what other matters would there be?"

The inspector set his hat on his head and turned the brim until it was just so.

"Deducting for the coal, you are saying to me?" She was yelling now. She couldn't remember when in her life she last had. "You can't take something from nothing!"

If her words or tone influenced the man, he didn't show it. He kept walking. It was a large car he drove away in.

She finished the damp-ragging, she didn't know why. Then she straightened the books and used the transom hooks to take down the planes and strings. She would save Neva's for her, but she would burn the rest, with Emmeline's going first. She was sorry the hideous girl had the goldfish. She who'd won it the only one in the class who hadn't wanted it. She cleared her desk so that it was just as she had found it five months before; then she put a bit more of the coal in the stove and held her hands over it. If they gave her nothing, where would she go? How could she buy a ticket? How would she leave?

She pulled the red cloth Riverside Shakespeare from her satchel and laid it on the very pile of books where she'd found it that first day of school; then she seated herself at the desk and opened her grade book. She would do the assessments, carefully and completely. She would not give the school board one thing more to excuse their failure to pay her the wages she deserved.

40

While Ansel drove the straight oiled road toward Wichita, Ellie sat in the backseat with Neva's head in her lap. She'd stroked the girl's forehead until she'd finally fallen to sleep and now Ellie sat without moving in order to let her sleep on. From up front, Ansel didn't speak; he had barely spoken since leaving the place. He hadn't accompanied her a week ago Monday when she'd taken the girl to see Dr. Gilling in Dorland and he hadn't believed the diagnosis when they returned. "Dust pneumonia," Ellie had told him, and waited for the words to sink in, just as Dr. Gilling had with her. Dr. Gilling seemed to feel bad about the pronouncement, but Ellie, strangely, felt a kind of relief, first to have a name for the sickness that Neva could not shed and, second, to know that it was a sickness that came with a cure. It was only after these two reactions that the astonishing implication of it all had risen within her: Leaving Kansas was no longer just an option. It was a necessity. "Leave Kansas," Dr. Gilling had said. "Kansas is going to kill her." She'd recited those very words to Ansel, and didn't know whether he hadn't trusted the doctor's judgment or simply did not want to believe it. He had insisted on seeing a specialist he'd heard about in Wichita and when Ellie, feeling defiance accruing within her, asked him how he thought they would pay for this specialist in Wichita, he had waited a long while before saying, "Maybe we can borrow it." Which of course meant calling her father, and she had tightened her lips and said, "Okay then." So she'd called him, and he'd listened in silence before finally saying, "So! Your daughter is sick and your husband will not get her to safety."

"He will," Ellie said. "He just wants to be sure the diagnosis is right."

"And your husband has no money to pay your child's doctor bills?"

Ellie didn't answer. She could hear breathing on the line—Lu Walls and Jeannie Simpson, listening in—and then at last her father said he would send the money through Western Union. "And also, Eleanor, I am going to mail you a check for one hundred dollars. Do not cash it except for the expenses of leaving that place."

She had begun a sentence that started with, "I don't need—" but he cut her off by saying, "Good-bye, Eleanor."

After he hung up, she heard the muted clicks of Lu Walls and Jeannie Simpson disconnecting. She went looking for Ansel in the barn; that was where she most often found him these days. He was bent over the tractor, tightening something with a box wrench, but she sensed he was aware of her approach, a sense confirmed when he stopped tightening and stood stock-still as her footsteps in the oily dirt drew closer. Why did she say nothing? Why did she wait for him to turn? To see the disappointment in his eyes that it was her? Because that was what she saw—fleetingly, faintly, but she saw it. He was let down to see her instead of someone else.

"That was funny," he said. "I was just thinking of Charlotte and then your footsteps sounded like hers."

He was lying—she was sure he was lying—and that only deepened her disappointment in him.

"My father's sending the money," she'd said in a neutral voice and Ansel had nodded and turned away and fitted the wrench to the head of another bolt. She'd said nothing about the one hundred dollar check and the conditions required for cashing it. He would find out soon enough. She should have mentioned it because Lu Walls and Jeannie Simpson would already be telling everyone who would listen, but she hadn't told Ansel.

Now, this morning, in the backseat of the Ford, Neva coughed, opened her eyes to find Ellie's face, and closed them again. Ellie snugged the blanket over the girl's ears, then stared out at the passing landscape, the flat line of the horizon separating endless beige from endless gray. What if the specialist said she had something else? This was the fear she had been fighting since the appointment had been made. What if the specialist didn't think that curing Neva would require them to leave Kansas and the Scottish girl and all of the rest of it behind? What would she have to do then?

41

That afternoon, the sky was as white as frost, and Clare was clenching and unclenching his toes on the front porch, wishing he had a hot sugared roll to eat, the kind his mother had once baked three times a week. He could taste the butter, the sugar, the cinnamon, the tang of yeast.

The door opened behind him and Charlotte walked out in her coat, singing her new favorite tune, which the radio seemed to play ten times a day. "Not much money, oh, but honey, ain't we got fun?" She slapped him on the shoulder and announced, "We're going to California!" She couldn't keep from smiling and rising up on her toes a little.

"What?" Clare asked. He looked at the frozen wheat field, the brown rise of the hogback ridge against a pale blue sky, the empty pigsty, and the outhouse. At such moments, their smallness in the world seemed pitiful. Charlotte threw a handful of dried corn to the last three chickens.

"Mom's inside writing to Aunt Ida," Charlotte said. "If you ask me we should have gone years ago."

Clare had always wanted to go to California, too, but that was before Aldine appeared.

"Why now?" he asked.

Charlotte shrugged. "Two reasons, I'm guessing. First is what the doctors said about Neva. That she can't survive Kansas, which is ironic, in my opinion, because who can survive Kansas? That's what I'd like to know. Doctors ought to fill out all their prescription forms with the words *Abandon Kansas* and put an exclamation point on it."

Charlotte watched the chickens searching for more corn but they had eaten it all.

She said, "Know what the doctor in Wichita told Mom? He said that he treated a man last week who couldn't breathe right, and after the doctor pounded on his chest, the man coughed something up. Know what it was?"

"I don't think I want to," Clare said.

"Dirt. He had a big plug of it inside him. Like a cork, he said." She shook her head.

Clare picked up a stone and chucked it toward a fence post. It missed. "Is that reason number one and number two?"

"No. The second reason is the storm. Dad trapped with Aldine like that."

"So?" Clare wished he'd been the hero who'd staggered out through the wind and driven blind in the brownout and found himself unable to restart the car until the storm stopped; then for five whole hours Aldine would've been his and his alone.

Charlotte pulled her coat tighter and fingered the place where she had very neatly darned a moth hole. "People talk," she said. "And the coal she burned up was the school's, not hers to use as she pleased. That's why they've closed the school. That and the lack of funds. I heard about it from Emmeline."

Clare slowly ran his tongue across his gritty teeth. "I'll bet you did," he said.

After a while Charlotte said, "You're supposed to kill Goosey for dinner."

"Goosey is a layer."

"We can't take a layer to California, can we?"

Clare didn't mind shooting squirrels or rabbits, but he hated butchering chickens. "All she's good for is boiling," he said, but not very loud. He wondered what would happen to Aldine if they all moved to California. They could take her along, maybe. More likely she'd go back to her sister in New York, maybe all the way back home to Air, Scotland, where there was a river called Dune. He wished he could go such places. When he pulled the ax out of the chopping block, Goosey went on pecking at the ground, her naked pink back a record of troubles with roosters now dead.

"*Bryan O'Linn had no hat to his head*," Clare sang to her, and she shied a bit.

> "He thought that the pot would do him instead,
> Then he murdered a cod for the sake of its fin,
> 'Whoo, as good as a feather,' says Bryan O'Linn."

He fingered the dust in his pocket. He sank the ax in the block, scaring Goosey enough to make her half fly clumsily toward the front porch. The wind was starting to pick up, and he crouched down on the dirt to keep warm, thinking that he would go through the presidents and vice presidents once before he caught her.

42

I wrote to Ida this afternoon," Mrs. Price told Aldine at supper, her face rosier than Aldine had ever seen it. "That's my sister," Mrs. Price added, though Aldine already knew who Ida was: the one in the photograph on the marble side table who looked like a well-fed, cheerful, darker-haired Ellie Price. Aldine knew, too, that the family was leaving, probably to California. Charlotte had told her, barely able to suppress the gladness in her voice. She and her mother had won. Ansel had lost.

"She lives in Fallbrook, California," Mrs. Price was saying. "Lemons grow there and I don't know what all." Mrs. Price pointed to the wooden box she kept papers in, a crate decorated on one side with a peeling dark blue picture of oversized lemons and white flowers. *Lofty Lemons*, it said. *Fallbrook, California.* The box had always been there, but Aldine had never known that it came from someone they knew.

"Do you think they have Silver Shred there?" she asked. As she looked at the bright yellow lemons, impossibly round and large, she longed for a spoonful.

"Silver what?"

"I guess you'd call it lemon jam. It's marmalade."

Ellie shook her head. "I've never heard of it. Ida sent those lemons a long time ago, but she never sent jam. She does accounts at the packinghouse."

"I wrote to my sister, too, in New York City. I suppose Mr. Price told you."

She saw from Mrs. Price's face that Ansel hadn't told her, a fact that for some reason pleased her. She'd told Ansel that she asked her sister for a loan of enough money to buy a train ticket back to New York. She'd also made it clear that she still expected to be paid by the school board and she was sorry when Ansel had said, "That's only right," and "Fair is fair," but gave her nothing by way of timetable for when such payment might be forthcoming.

"Leenie would've had her bairn by now and I'm dying to see it," she said, looking only at Mrs. Price while she spoke, not at Charlotte, though what she really felt was Ansel's presence across the table, his dark hair and his arms, the sleeves of his work shirt rolled up to the elbow.

A silence began to set in.

"Did you know there's a storm on Jupiter that's been blowing for two hundred and sixty-eight years?" Charlotte asked no one in particular.

No one answered, so Aldine out of courtesy said, no, she couldn't imagine it. She still expected, when she looked out the window, to see dust billowing up like a brown, vaporous sea that would bury them as the volcano buried Pompeii.

"At least our storm didn't last that long," Charlotte said. Her tone was benign but not sincerely so. She just wanted to bring the topic round to what happened at the schoolhouse, wanted everyone to have to think of it again, but Ansel deflected her.

"No, Lottie, it didn't last that long," he said, and then remarked that he'd been asking around to see if he could rent out the farm. The Tanner, Osborne, and Heapson places had all been sold at auction for a tenth of their worth, he said, so he wouldn't get anything for his property, or for his equipment, either.

"Rent to who?" Ellie asked. "You can't rent something that blows out from under you." Her forehead seemed unusually high and stark because she'd tied a navy-blue scarf tightly over her hair. Just looking at the scarf made Aldine's scalp itch because she did the same thing when she didn't have time to wash her hair.

"I heard a tenant might be moving onto the Tanner place," Clare said.

Ansel took a forkful of boiled chicken and pushed it across the gravy on his plate. His serving, like Aldine's and everyone else's, had been a meager pile in the center of the plate. Aldine thought he must be ravenous, being twice her size. She was hungry every night now.

"Opa's sent a draft," Ellie said. "I have only to go to the bank with it."

Ansel didn't look up but his fist stiffened on the fork. Clare had once told Aldine that, for a wedding gift, Herr Hoffman had given Ellie a silver serving spoon engraved with her first name instead of her newly acquired initial. Aldine pressed her lips together and took a drink of silty water.

"Did you hear about the Stuyvesants?" Charlotte asked. She had finished her stew and was pressing the fork down in the gravy, then licking it. It was what they all did.

Mrs. Price gave Charlotte a warning look. "Now is not the time, Lottie."

"What?" Neva asked, her big eyes glossy with fever, her mouth ajar so that you could see a pair of oversize teeth pushing their crooked way from her gums. "What happened to the Stuyvesants?"

"Nothing," Mrs. Price said. "Can you eat another dumpling, Neva? Please? Look, I cut it into little pieces for you."

"Tell me first," Neva said, regarding the dumpling.

Mrs. Price shook her head. "Absolutely not," she said.

Neva looked pleadingly at Aldine, who shrugged and smiled and said, "Listen to your mother now."

Charlotte had already told Aldine in morbid detail how five members of the Stuyvesant family, who lived on a farm not ten miles away, had died of ptomaine poisoning from eating apricots canned without sugar. For the first day they were just fine, she said, and they went about their business, but then they developed double vision. The four-year-old, the eleven-year-old, an uncle, a sister-in-law, and the mother had died, in that order.

On the table, as usual, was a jar of home-canned fruit. Aldine had been hoping they were peaches, and that they would be dessert. Now that Mrs. Price had opened them, she saw that they were small like apricots.

"Should we be eating those?" Charlotte asked.

"They're perfectly good," Mrs. Price said. "I put in lots of sugar." With the engraved silver spoon, which was so large that syrup splashed on the tablecloth, she dished out two slippery, menacing globes for each person. When she came to the last plate, which was Neva's, she hesitated. She put the jar down and went into the kitchen, returning with a smaller jar of peach pit jelly and a heel of bread.

"Not pit jelly," Neva cried. "I want apricots!"

"No," Mrs. Price said. "When you're sick, you can't bear up as well. You can't take chances."

"What chances? I want apricots like everyone else!"

"You can have them in California."

It was all so hopeless. The family was going to California, to the town where lemons grew, and Aldine wouldn't have a place to live. She didn't want to eat the apricots, but Mrs. Price stuck her fork in the center of an apricot's round back and sliced. Then she ate a piece. Ansel didn't bother to cut his, but simply moved the orb from plate to mouth, chewed, swallowed, and said, "Flavorsome or I'm a fool. What's the matter with you all?"

Aldine cut her apricots into small pieces and ate each piece in the faith that if she died, he would die, too, a strange and silly thought that shamed her. Everything she could see in the next room—the petit-point rug, the cherrywood secretary, Herr Hoffman's photograph, Mrs. Price's radio, Tiffany lamp, and marble-topped occasional table—all had a fragile, abandoned look about them, as if they were the furnishings of a ship that was tipping and taking on water. She remembered how she had stood in that exact spot one September day, bangles clacking, feeling Neva's little fingers pulling her forward. It seemed a long time ago.

43

Charlotte had told Clare the story about the Stuyvesants while he was washing up for supper, but apricots were his favorite, and he didn't want her to think she'd scared him so he ate them. They tasted all right. But now, in bed, he felt something besides the usual hunger. It was a kind of dizzy fog. He wondered if it wasn't the first sign of ptomaine poisoning. Probably it wasn't but possibly it was. This possibility kept him awake, and when he was awake, he thought of Aldine. He imagined tiptoeing up the stairs, standing at the foot of her bed, and staring at her as she slept. He thought of this all the time. He could never think what he might say if she woke up, but what he wanted to say was something that would turn her into one of those women in photographs who smiled mischievously above naked, round breasts.

He'd never tiptoed upstairs. Always before, he'd thought she'd still be here a week or month from now and now everyone was leaving before anything could happen.

He folded back his blankets, stood up, and tested his stocking feet on the wooden floor. He began to walk. The stairs to the attic didn't creak beneath his weight, at least not until the top one when it was too late to go back. He stood very still and listened for wind. It was not blowing tonight.

When he pushed open the door and stood within it, the room was much as he imagined it, only more beautiful, for moonlight slanted through the window and washed across the iron bed in the center of the tiny room, the figure under the blanket, the dark hair on the pillow. She was turned away from Clare, but she turned suddenly at his approach, as if she'd been awake all along.

"I'm sorry," he whispered. "I didn't mean to scare you."

"What are you doing here?" she said, but without real alarm. She kept her voice low, too.

"I can't sleep," he said.

She was staring at him through the dimness. She did not seem afraid.

"I thought maybe—" He was listening to his voice, wondering what he would say next. "I thought maybe you could do like you do for Neva. Sing that song about Bryan O'Linn."

"What?" She sat up and held the blanket over her upper half. She slept in something with long sleeves. She would, given the cold.

"Bryan O'Linn, his wife, and wife's mother," Clare whispered, too embarrassed to sing the lyric, "were all going over the bridge together."

Aldine watched him.

"I can't remember the next part," he whispered. This was a bald lie and he supposed she knew it.

"You have to go out of here," she said in a low voice. "I've had enough trouble."

"Please," he said. "Just sing it to me. Then I'll go back down."

Aldine was quiet. Her face was pale in the moonlight, and her fingers clutched the blanket. "Come here then," she whispered and when he'd sat down, she sang in the smallest, purest voice.

"Bryan O'Linn, his wife, and wife's mother
Were all going over the bridge together,
The bridge it broke up and they all tumbled in,
'We'll go home by water,' says Bryan O'Linn."

Her voice made him feel dizzier. He found himself wondering whether her nightgown went all the way down to her feet, or only to her knees. He shivered. "It's so cold up here," he said. "I could bring you an extra blanket."

"Go back doonstairs," she whispered. "Clarence, you must."

Clay-dance. That was how his ear would always receive it.

"Don't make me go," he said. The quilt she had on the bed was made from Opa's old suits. He touched the end that was nearest him and whispered that when he was little, he'd pretended each rectangle was a field and the far edge was the track for his train of stones. "See?" he said, pointing to a herringbone patch. "This here's wheat." He pointed to a mustard-colored patch near her thigh. "This one's corn." He slowly moved his finger to the black patch that was lying like a hill on her foot. "And this," he said, "has just been plowed for a kitchen garden." He left his hand there. She didn't speak but retracted her foot.

"Aldine is a beautiful name," he whispered.

She said nothing. He had repeated the name to himself many times, alone and in private. This was the first time he'd said it in her presence.

"Aldine," he whispered. "I just wanted to tell you, before we leave—" He stopped. Her eyes looked enormous and black. "If we die, for example, I would want you to know."

"Know what?" Aldine asked, her voice even quieter than his. Clare realized that his breath was visible in the moonlight and his hands were freezing.

"When you sing," he whispered, "I fall in love with you."

Aldine watched him. He wanted to move closer, to be near her face, but she didn't move, and he felt immobilized, his hands still touching the wool of the blanket.

"I could taste the sugar, couldn't you?" she whispered. "And there was no mold on top. They said Mrs. Stuyvesant scraped mold off the top."

"Yes," he said. "I could taste it."

"The mold?" She pronounced it "moold."

"No. Sugar. I could taste the sugar."

It was quiet. He wondered how you made a woman want you back. He did nothing except go on feeling his own suppressed, pathetic wanting, and after several more silent moments, she said he should go back to bed. He supposed he should feel upright and gallant for standing up and saying good-bye but all he felt was humiliation.

44

The next day, Ansel sold the last cows and brought back from town a letter for Aldine. *That was fast*, was his first thought upon seeing the envelope, but he saw at once that something was wrong. Aldine sister's name was on it—*Mrs. Wm. Cooper*—but the return address was in Salt Lake City, which didn't make sense. Aldine said her sister lived in New York. There had been nothing at the post office from the superintendent's office, which was an aggravation. Why couldn't they send the girl the money she earned, or at least tell her when they would?

"A letter for Miss McKenna," he called into the house from the mud porch when he arrived home.

Ellie appeared from the kitchen wiping her hands in her apron. She'd been packing, he knew, and her hair was limp, oily, disheveled. "She's gone to Newton with Sonia Odekirk."

He waited.

"They were going to have lunch at Woolworth's."

"Good for her then," he said, and he meant it.

Ellie's expression was stony. "At least someone will have a good meal and a pleasant day." Then, with a rigid set to her chin: "Sonia might've asked Lottie, too."

"Lottie's seen Newton. The girl never has."

Ellie gave her head an impatient shake, her way of saying, *Nonsense*. "The truth is, the girl could've helped for once." She looked at her hands, inky from packing plates in newspaper. Then, looking tiredly at Ansel: "What did you get for the cows?"

He looked down. "Less even than I feared." A lie. He'd gotten exactly what he'd feared, and then slipped half of it into a hidden niche of his wallet. So he told a lie he could never have told if they were staying on—Ellie would've ferreted out the truth or stumbled onto it, one or the other—but they weren't staying on. They were leaving the home place.

Ellie nodded without expression, and why would it be otherwise—she expected nothing from him or his cows or his farm. Her gaze shifted to the letter he held at his side. She extended her hand to take it from him, and he was surprised by his instantaneous impulse not to give it up, but he did. She looked down at it and said, "Money, let's hope."

In a low voice he said, "She deserves it, God knows."

Ellie studied him, saying nothing, until his gaze slid away. When he looked again, she'd turned and set the letter on the center table, where Aldine would see it. From the kitchen he could hear the clink of dishes and a low desultory exchange between Lottie and Ellie.

"What about these?"

"Wrap them and stack them. We can only take so much."

He was rigging up the trailer behind the car when Aldine came walking up the drive, bundled head to toe, like something in a beautiful, wintry old-world painting. She smiled at the sight of him and it came upon him in a rush, the feel of her against him in the truck, the way all the tension and fear had drained out of her and how he had just held her and closed his eyes and felt all his own troubling worries slip away, too.

"Sonia might've brought you up to the house," he said.

"She wanted to. But I wanted to walk the last little bit." She regarded the trailer. "You'll be packing up then?"

"Mmm. Just what we need for a while out there. We'll come back. We're not leaving for good."

She looked at him and said nothing but there was kindness in her eyes, and concern, and—this was the hard part—he didn't know what else.

"Cold," he said, just for something to say.

"But peaceful," she said, letting her eyes rest on him a moment more before gazing back down the lane she'd just walked. "You can almost *feel* its peacefulness when the wind isna' blowing everything away."

And then her keen eyes were on him again. "You know, way inside you, down in the bones."

He *did* know—he felt exactly so himself even if he couldn't have found such a pretty way to put it. He said only, "You enjoyed yourself? In Newton?"

"Oh, yes, very much. We had the grandest time in Woolworth's. I especially liked the area with a funny name, where they have buttons and stays and such."

"Notions."

"Yes! *Notions.*" She released a small musical laugh. "And then we sat at the counter for chocolate malteds and cheese sandwiches that were ever so—" She must have realized what she was saying, for she checked herself and seemed now, by expression, to be begging forgiveness.

"They make a good malted there," he said. He knew Ellie was probably watching from the kitchen window, and maybe Lottie, too, but he couldn't help himself. He let his eyes settle fully on hers. "It would have been a shame if you'd left Kansas without tasting . . ." *A malted from Woolworth's* was what he'd thought to say, but instead he said, "something indulgent like that."

"Mmm," she said, looking at him, and just that—her gaze and her low murmuring—sent blood stirring through him wildly.

"A letter came for you," he said, forcing gruffness into his tone. "Ellie put it inside."

"Well then," she said, searching his eyes for a moment and then dropping her gaze, and without another word she went inside.

An hour or so later, when they all sat down to supper, Aldine was not among them. Ellie said the blessing, and began to pass a plate of biscuits and a bowl of syrupy apricots, which was all there was, but the room was thick with the girl's absence.

"Where is she?" Neva said. Her small voice had been coarsened by coughing.

"I'll go and see," Ellie said, before anyone else could.

After she'd left, Clare said, "Do you think she's all right?"

Ansel picked a biscuit from the plate and was surprised by his hand. It was trembling like one of a man sick or aged. Everywhere it was nicked from working in tight spaces with tools, and under the black hair, red scabs and pink scars showed, and there it was, his solid hand, trembling.

"Dad?"

"What?" he said, more sharply than he intended. He set down the biscuit and rested his flattened hand on the table.

"Miss McKenna," Clare said. "Do you think she's all right?"

"I think so. She received a letter today from her sister, which might mean good news."

"But the postmark was from Salt Lake City," Charlotte said. "I thought her sister lived in New York."

Neva clacked the Bakelite bangles on her wrist—Aldine must have finally just given them to her—and said, "I don't want to go to California."

"I do," Charlotte said, her blue eyes bright. She made an impish smile. "It'll be looove-ly."

To his own surprise, Ansel's hand rose and slapped down hard on the table so that the plates and silverware jumped and clattered. A heavy silence followed until Ansel at last mumbled an apology. He looked up from his plate and scanned the rooms. "It's just that . . . it's no one's fault—except my own and Mother Nature's—but I never thought we'd be leaving the place."

It fell quiet again until they heard footsteps on the stairs, a stern series of clicks on the planks. It was Ellie, and only Ellie.

"There's no money from her sister," she reported. "It's worse than that even. Her sister wasn't writing in response to Aldine's letter. She hadn't even received the letter." Ellie cut through an apricot, then stilled her knife. "If it weren't so sad, it would be funny," she said. "The sister was writing on her own, in hopes of borrowing money from Miss McKenna."

"From *Miss McKenna*?" Ansel couldn't keep from saying.

Ellie nodded. Aldine's sister and brother-in-law had been called to Salt Lake, she said, and they'd spent all their money on the baby and travel and hoped that Aldine might help them through. Ellie shook her head. "In the letters she wrote them, she never mentioned she wasn't being paid."

There was silence until Clare said, "She should just come with us to California."

Ansel took a bite of biscuit, but it seemed to lie hard in his mouth. He took a bite of apricot to help it down. He tried to sound hesitant when he said, "I suppose we could do that."

"Goodie!" Neva said, but no one responded, and she said it again, louder.

"Where would she sit in the car?" Charlotte asked. She looked actually alarmed. "Where would she live when we get there?"

"If there's work for us," Clare said, "maybe there'd be work for her. They have schools, don't they?"

Neva said, "She can have my place in the car. I could sit on her lap."

Ansel picked a final crumb off his plate. He could almost hear the terrible wrenching of his family as it pulled in opposite ways, he and Clare and Neva on one side, Ellie and Lottie on the other, and the girl in the middle. But they had an obligation, didn't they? They had brought her out here, and now her problems were theirs, too. *So why not bring Aldine along?* he thought, and then, to his surprise, he heard himself say it: "Why not bring the girl along?"

When Ellie stared at him with reproachful eyes, he stared right back. He wanted to be near the girl. That was all, nothing more. Was that wrong? And being near was all that he wanted. To be near was enough.

"I'm sure Miss McKenna would prefer to go back home," Ellie said in a quiet, controlled voice. "The school board is just going to have to meet its obligation here so she can go back to her own family." She paused. "In the meantime, though, she could work in Emporia at the Harvey House."

Ansel was incredulous. "The Harvey House?"

She nodded.

"They couldn't be hiring, not now, with—"

But she cut him off. "They aren't hiring. But they will hire her."

Her father. Her father had arranged something.

"But a waitress," he said. "She came here to teach school, not wait on tables."

"You married a waitress, Ansel," Ellie said. "It was good enough for me and it was good enough for you." She set her face. "It's a paying job when paying jobs are hard to come by."

"And your father had nothing to do with this?"

Ellie looked away and told Neva to eat her biscuit.

"But will she be okay," Clare said, "being all alone like that?"

"Gil's still there," Ellie said, "and two girls are getting married. It's a good place to work. She'll have girls to talk to"—she paused—"and I'm sure Gil will look after her."

Neva pushed her food around on her plate and said, "Can you get me a job there, too?"

Ansel was seeing Ellie in a way he had never seen before, and this new incarnation cost her sympathy. He said, "It isn't Mother you need to ask, Neva. You'll need to take your case to Opa. He solves all our family's problems."

He waited for Ellie to say something, or even to meet his eyes, but she did neither. So it was true.

Ansel went out to finish packing the trailer after supper, but he was so reluctant to complete the task that his progress was slow. At last, when everything was set and roped, the house was dark and black clouds had cut off the moon. He backed the trailer into the barn, which felt like some kind of sad joke. Putting the trailer inside to protect it from rain. The wind had begun to blow. He closed his eyes and stood smelling the barn and listening to the creaking boards and an owl's low chortle and *whoo*. He'd used up all the firewood. He found the sledgehammer and knocked some planks from a stall and cracked them into shorter lengths. He got a fire going in the stove and stared into it, moving only as needed to feed in more wood. He did this for a long, long while.

When finally he walked back to the house, it was very late. Neva and Ellie lay on the bed arranged for Neva near the cookstove in the kitchen. He stood in the door frame wondering if they were asleep.

"Trailer safe?" she asked through the darkness.

"Mmm. Unless the barn blows away." She didn't reply, so he said, "Are you staying down here again?"

Neva shifted in the bed, and Ellie waited for her to grow quiet again. "It's better if I can be here to put more water in the kettle," she said. "Keep the air moist for her."

"Sure," he said. "That makes sense," and he turned to go upstairs alone.

He lay fully dressed on their bed. Last night, he'd heard creaking on the stairs and then low voices overhead. Clare's voice, he was sure, and the girl's. Clare hadn't stayed long—Ansel thought he heard the girl sending him away. Still, Ansel had left his bedroom door ajar. To hear Clare, if he should pass again, that was what he told himself. But on this night, no matter how still he lay, or for how long, his body would not give itself up to sleep. The windows shivered under the wind. He got up and looked in on Clare—the boy didn't stir—then he went downstairs and found Neva and Ellie both snoring gently. He stood watching them for a while, and wondered what had gone through old Tanner's mind at dinner the day he shot his mules.

When Ansel climbed the stairs, he supposed it was to return to his bed, but he did not return to his room. He moved past it, and eased up one step after another, toward the attic.

Aldine's door was closed fast. His turn of the knob produced a click and a squeak, and by the time he'd pushed the door open, Aldine was sitting bolt upright in bed, the covers pulled tight to her neck.

"Oh, it's you then," she whispered, relaxing her hand on the covers. "I was afraid it was Clare."

"I need to talk to you," he said in a stiff whisper.

She swung her legs about so there was room for him to sit on the bed.

He raised his hands and held on to the doorjamb as if holding against something pushing from behind. "No," he said, as much to himself as to her. "Not here." The wind shivered the window glass, slid through the wall cracks. His skin felt different. It seemed as if some crusty everyday part of him suddenly dissolved, or was suddenly shed, and what was left was a new skin meant not to repel but receive. He closed and opened his eyes in a slow blink. "Put on your coat," he whispered, and hearing how gruff it sounded, he tried again. "Please put on your coat and come with me."

45

Clare didn't know what awakened him. The wind, he supposed. The moon had risen outside his window, and he could see the long horizontal crack in the plaster of his wall and the nail that had once held his photo of Tom Mix and his horse Tony Jr. Clare removed his hand from the warmth of the blanket to look at his Tom Mix Straight Shooter signature ring. He'd had a wooden Tom Mix gun, too, with a revolving cartridge, but he'd traded it for Neva's goldfish, gone now to Opal. The ring had looked like copper and silver in the ads, but it was just painted tin. He'd found the ring and the diagram of Tom Mix's injuries among some clothes while packing and slipped the ring on his pinkie, unwilling to throw it away. He remembered how similar his hand was to Aldine's in size if not smoothness and a sudden impulse came to him and took hold: he would give the ring to Aldine as a pledge that he would send for her once he had enough money. She should have someone to count on, and why shouldn't he be that someone? Clare pulled his pants over his long underwear and crept up the stairs.

The door to Aldine's room was not quite closed, and when he pushed it open, he saw the flat mattress and blanket. Aldine was gone.

He hurried down the one flight of stairs to his parents' room. He would tell his father that she had run away. They would go after her, bring her back, make her safe. "Dad," he whispered, and whispered again, louder, but he was looking at an empty bed.

He nearly yelled. He felt like yelling. Where was everyone? He had the sudden fleeting fearful sensation he remembered from fairy tales when parents sent their children off, or abandoned them in the woods somewhere. He listened to the house and heard nothing but wind. He eased down the stairs slowly and still listening.

From the doorway of the kitchen, he could see his mother and Neva curled up together on the narrow bed. He didn't speak or move. He held his breath. But his mother shifted in the bed and looked up, as if she had felt someone in the room.

"What is it?" she asked. "Can't you sleep?"

"I'm fine," he said. "I have to go out and relieve myself." That was the way she had taught him to speak of bodily functions, the only phrase they could use.

"All right," she said, and returned her head to the pillow.

He was quiet when he left the house and quiet as he approached the lit barn. He knew a place where he could look into the barn without opening the door, a wide enough crack between planks. Why he went to that crack instead of opening the door was a question he would ask himself later. He wondered whether the car was there, and this was the quickest way to find out. If it was gone, it was simple. His father had taken Aldine to the station already and he would not get to say good-bye to her.

When he brought his eye to the space between two boards, he saw at once that the car was there. Then he saw Aldine's back. She was wearing her gray wool coat, and her hair was pressed down under her beret. She sat on a bale of straw. His father had lit a lantern and was talking quietly to her, partly obscured by more bales. He heard him tell Aldine, "You'll like working there. Lots of people your age."

He could hear Aldine crying, but she didn't answer.

"Here," her father said, extending his hand, "this will get you started." And when she wouldn't take it, he said, "It's okay. I got more than I hoped for the cows."

She didn't touch the money his father set on her knee.

"Take it please," his father said, but she didn't.

"I should never, ever have come here," she said in a small, bitter voice.

"Oh, don't say that."

"But what I don't understand is why. Why did you do it then?" Aldine asked.

Clare watched and waited. He would forgive Aldine anything, but it wasn't fair of her to blame his father. His father hadn't been the one to fire her. His father hadn't been the one to withhold her pay.

Aldine brought her hands up to her face, then leaned forward at the waist. Clare couldn't see her head when she did that, and his father had drawn back out of sight.

"Writing me that note. Why did you do that?"

There was a scraping sound, like a boot on the floor. "I just thought we could do better with an outsider," his father said. "Someone who knew poems and played music. And my pal Terence Tidball told me I could run a classified ad for free so . . ."

She raised her head and looked up at him. "No! I didn't mean that. I meant, *Here come and sit, where never serpent hisses*," she said, enunciating each word. *"And being set I'll smother thee with kisses."*

Clare recognized the lines, and the poem they came from.

"What?" his father asked.

Aldine didn't answer. She was sitting up straight again. She was no longer crying. "Someone in the house gave me a note with those lines on it. I saw that you had the Shakespeare book out here that day when you fixed my boot, and I thought—"

Aldine stopped talking for a few seconds.

"I thought you meant . . . ," she said, her voice almost strangled.

"Oh, Aldine," Clare heard his father say softly, "I couldn't write a note like that."

Aldine was staring at his father. She stared and stared. Finally she said, "I guess it was only Clare then."

She fell silent and Clare felt the cold in his nostrils and fingertips, in the knuckles he held against the rough wood of the barn.

"Aldine," his father said again.

"I know. I should've known you'd ne'er think of me that way."

"But that isn't true," his father said, and Aldine kept her face down and Clare watched his father reach for her hand.

It was a clumsy gesture—even Clare knew that much—but like something released from gravity she rose up into his arms, and he began to kiss Aldine in a way that Clare had never imagined one person might kiss another. It was shocking and alarming and dreadful. They looked ravenous for one another, and Clare stepped back, weakened in the legs, his body beginning to shiver violently.

Clare turned and walked toward the house. His legs felt heavy, like he was wearing boots of ice. Somehow he opened the yard gate, then the door to the mud porch, then the front door. He made no attempt at quietness.

"Clare?" his mother said in a calling whisper. "Clare?"

Clare said nothing and took himself upstairs.

46

Ansel didn't think anymore. He wanted to hold her as he had held her in his truck, with a love he could call pure and protective, but this time she didn't tuck herself against him. She looked into his face as he pulled her up, and this look drew them into a kiss. He touched her hair and pressed her closer to him, and it was as blissful as the dream. What he saw in Aldine's eyes was not rebuke or annoyance or boredom or fatigue. She wanted to be near him, part of him. He could be what someone wanted again. He moved his lips from her mouth to her neck, from her neck to her shoulder, then back again. There was no wind rattling the barn. There were no crops dying in the fields. There were no hogs dead in the ground. There was no family asleep in the house.

47

When he woke up on the last morning he would ever spend in Kansas, Clare didn't know what to do with his Straight Shooter ring. *My last morning here* was the way he thought of it even though his father said things about returning. That sounded to Clare like the kind of thing a person would say when he needed to believe that the everlasting change he was about to make wasn't really everlasting. Clare went over to the nail sticking out of his wall and tugged on it. It slid out easily, dribbling crumbs of plaster on the floor. The wall was chalky underneath the yellow paint, and he fingered it, then hacked at the plaster with the nail. There was horsehair in the plaster. His father had told him it was there for binding and strengthening. He'd always thought his father was trustworthy and now he knew he wasn't. This knowledge was like a hand and the hand was wrapped around a fact. The fact was that Aldine cared for his father. Clare dug into the wall with the nail until the hole was big enough for the ring. Once he had pushed the ring into the hole, he pushed the nail into the palm of his hand again and again until he broke the skin and a small bulblet of blood formed. Then he set the nail on the windowsill, back behind the curtain, and went downstairs.

His mother was awake and busy, trying to get the last of the edible food together for breakfast and for the car. "Just eat a biscuit," she said to Clare. "And there's a little bit of preserves we need to finish."

He nodded. Normally he would have happily eaten a biscuit and he would have happily finished the preserves. The kitchen was clean as a whistle. It seemed strange to him that his mother would feel the need to leave it just so.

"Where's Miss McKenna?" Neva asked. Neva was wearing her good dress for reasons unknown. Her wrists stuck out of her coat sleeves and her hair puffed out on one side but not the other. She had decided to take her Shirley Temple paper dolls with her, he noticed, along with Milly Mandy Molly and she was eating a biscuit that dropped crumbs on the pile of paper clothes she held in her lap.

Ellie wiped out the biscuit pan with a towel and put it back in the cupboard, then removed it and put it on the counter. "Your father already dropped her off at the station. She's off to be a Harvey Girl." She opened the cupboard and put the biscuit tin inside it once again.

Neva began to wail and Clare's back prickled all over with chills. "But she didn't tell me good-bye," Neva said. "She said she would tell me good-bye. And I want to go to the Harvey House, too. You promised we would!"

"And we will," Ellie said, folding the towel into thirds and hanging it on the towel bar as she always did. "But we'll go to a different one. Where Aldine's going is east, and we're going west."

Neva kept crying. His mother opened the cupboard and peered into it without comment.

"Where's Dad?" Clare asked.

"Barn."

Clare went out to the porch with a cold biscuit to avoid hearing Neva. The air was freezing and the car was parked out front, facing the road. Wind whipped at his face and tore at the wooden trailer, packed with quilts and crates, including the one that said *Lofty Lemons*. The crate that had once enclosed the new radio had been lined with a horse blanket for Artemis. Krazy Kat would come, too. The other cats were staying behind. The hogs and chickens were dead and the cows were sold, so that was it. Opal had told Neva she would take care of her goldfish until she came back. Artemis wasn't in her crate yet, and she came walking up to him, nosing his hand with her wet black nose. "We won't leave you," he told her. The dog began licking the drying blood on his hand.

While he petted her, he heard a fluttering sound. A stone had been set on the porch, a round rock that they'd brought back from a trip to the Arkansas River and used sometimes for home plate. The little beret for Neva lay underneath it, finished, along with a scarf. A piece of paper had been folded into the brim, and Aldine had written in her schoolteacher script, *Please give these to Neva, my favorite student. Aldine.* He brought the small beret to his nose. It had the faintly yeasty scent he associated with her hair. Inside, he could hear Neva crying and beginning to cough. He took the hat and scarf and note inside and set them beside her.

"There," Ellie said, her face hard the way it got when Neva coughed, or maybe because the beret reminded her of Aldine. "You see? She did say good-bye in the best way she could."

Neva pulled the hat over her puffed-up hair and smiled a little.

"Clare's going to take you out to the car, Neva," Ellie said, deliberately smoothing her voice. "We're almost ready to go." She took off her apron, hung it on the nail where it always hung, then seemed to think better of it and tied it back on.

"I hate California," Neva said, and rubbed at her wet cheek. "I don't want to go there."

"It'll be warm," Clare said. Neva in a fit had strewn her paper dolls. Clare helped her pick them up and slip them into their paper wardrobe. "Come on," he said, and she let herself be lifted into his arms. He leaned close to Neva's ear. "You'll get better there right away," he said. "You'll get so big I won't be able to pick you up."

He set Neva on the cold seat of the car and waited for his father to come out of the barn. He dreaded the moment that he would look at his father and his father would look at him. He stared at the house. It made him think of a large silent animal they were leaving to die. Charlotte and his mother came out with things in their hands. Charlotte was holding her notebook, and his mother carried the Tiffany lampshade she'd said she was going to leave behind. There had been a lot of talk about what to take and what to leave, what was too heavy and what was too hard to pack. They had to leave the sofa, the armchairs, the washing machine, and the stove. His mother wanted to take the radio, and that's when his father had said, *But we're coming back, aren't we?* and his mother had fallen silent and there wasn't any more discussion about the radio or coming back, either one. In the end, the only machine they were taking was the Singer. It was small and had its own carrying case.

Clare liked the lampshade, but doubted it was going to be easy to hold in the car all the way to California. It was big, for one thing, and the thick pieces of glass—amber, blue, ruby, and emerald—were divided by heavy lead. He opened the car door so his mother could get in, but she just set the lampshade down on the seat next to Neva and turned to walk back to the house. "Help me," she said. He didn't want to, but he did. He followed her back up the steps, through the door, and into the living room, where the furniture stood waiting as if this were an ordinary day. His mother unfolded a sheet and draped it over the radio. "Help me pull it taut," she said. He held the sheet, and she took a roll of gummed tape out of her pocket. She dipped her fingers in a cup of water and moistened a length of the brown paper, and then she taped the edges of the sheet to the floor. It stuck in some places, but Clare could see it wouldn't hold.

"I have to keep the dust out of the tubes," she said.

"Well, we used it the whole time we were living here," Clare said. "Never got dust in the tubes then."

"Because I dusted it," his mother said, but it didn't really make sense. Nothing did.

"That ought to keep out the dirt," Clare said just to say something, patting the top of the radio. He thought suddenly of Aldine in the barn, kissing his father like that. He could hardly believe it. Even having seen it, he could hardly believe it.

His mother nodded and looked around one more time before walking out to the porch with her mug of tape-moistening water. She was done. She was ready to go. She'd been ready for years. She set the mug down by the front door. "Come on," she said. "I want to get going. Before this wind picks up." But she still stood looking around.

Neva and Charlotte watched from the car, and Charlotte was angrily mouthing, "Come *on*!"

"Where's Dad now?" Clare asked.

"Still in the barn, I guess," his mother said.

He looked at the blank face of the barn as he walked and he climbed into the backseat with Charlotte. She was stiff and set and ready to go, too.

"Look at my hat, Charlotte," Neva said, curling herself around so that she could hold both hands to the sides of her new beret.

"Looks familiar," Charlotte said. She fiddled with the frayed edge of her notebook, and Clare wondered what he would learn if he stole it and read every word. The air in the car smelled like moist wool and gasoline.

"It's like Miss McKenna's, dummy," Neva said.

Charlotte sniffed and said, "And where is the wee Scotch lass?"

"On her way to Emporia," Clare said. "Dad took her to the station already."

Their mother pulled open the car door, her wavy hair blown across her mouth for a second. Then she sat down next to Neva in the front seat and closed the door. Clare looked at the porch. The mug was still by the front door. That wasn't normal. Nothing was.

"She gets to be a Harvey Girl," Neva said in her high voice. "And I don't."

Charlotte sniffed again. "Huh," she said doubtfully. "Is that why Dad isn't here?"

"No," Clare said. "He's already back. He's in the barn doing something."

Charlotte's eyes looked a little buggy, like they always did right before she told on Clare for smoking or missing school. "Well, I hope she has a loooove-ly time," she said, her voice hard and meaningful. "Though I know she'll miss our papa."

From the front seat, his mother turned to give Charlotte a rigid look. "We don't need any more meanness this morning, Lottie."

Charlotte squinted her eyes a little. "Don't call me that. And I don't think it's mean," she said slowly, with particular emphasis on each word, "to point out that she was gaga for him. And—"

His mother cut her off. "Enough," she said. She held the heavy lampshade and stared straight out the windshield.

The four of them breathing in the car staled the air and fogged the windows. Artemis barked from her wooden crate, pulling at the rope Charlotte had tied to the trailer. Clare thought of what he could say about the barn and his father kissing Aldine and he knew that he wouldn't. He didn't know what it meant. Maybe if he said nothing, it would mean nothing. He wiped at the window with a fingertip and thought suddenly of Mr. Tanner. A hardness like a peach pit formed in his stomach. "What did Dad say he was doing in the barn?" he asked.

His mother seemed not to hear. She sat with the lampshade and turned her wedding ring around and around on her finger, which she always did when she had nothing to do but wished she had.

Clare said, "I'll go tell him we're ready," and stepped out of the car and walked steadily toward the barn, just as he had the night before, except that now he went to the wide barn door. "Dad?" he called.

No one answered, and when Clare thrust his hand into the gap between the door and the frame, he grabbed in the wrong place, where a rusty, broken clasp poked out. He knew that it was sharp, had been told several times to remove the clasp, and now it ripped into his finger. When Clare got inside, he held his index finger between his lips and looked with dread into the half darkness, to where his father was standing. He was holding a rifle.

"What are you doing?" Clare asked.

"Forgot that," his father said, nodding vaguely. A few feet away the dulcimer case sat in the packed, oily dirt. His chin was bristly and his winter coat was muddy. He looked like he hadn't slept. Knowing the reason for that made Clare feel queasy, and a little mean.

"We should go," he said. "They're all in the car."

"I'll be along," Ansel said. He continued to finger the rifle.

"Okay," Clare said, but he didn't go. He felt the blood on his finger and brought it to his mouth again.

"Cut your hand?"

"Mmm."

"That clasp needed coming off." His father said this but he did not seem to be thinking about this. He seemed to be thinking something else.

"I kept forgetting," he said. "It'll be the first thing on my list when we get back."

His father was quiet. Then he said, "Wait for me in the car. I'll be along."

"They're all in the car and it's cold," he said. His father didn't move. "Please, Dad," he said. "Please put the gun down and come with us."

Ansel lifted the gun and pointed it at the rafters, where owls and other birds roosted. He raised the rifle slightly and cocked it.

To shoot doves in the barn would be cheating. Clare knew this. His father did, too. He had stropped him for it once.

"Please, Dad," Clare said again.

His father sighted and fired. One bird fell with a dull plop. The other plowed the air and circled, terrified, but it couldn't find a way out. It returned to the same beam where it had been sitting before.

"You have to drive, Dad," Clare said. He walked toward his father. His feet felt heavy again, like they had last night. He held out his hand for the gun. His father didn't speak or move. Clare wrapped his hand around the barrel, which still pointed up.

His father didn't move. Clare pulled on the rifle, and his father let go.

"Okay," Clare said. To what he was saying okay, he had no idea. "Okay."

His mother came to the open door of the barn with a wild look on her face. She saw that everyone was standing up, unbloodied, and she saw that Clare held the rifle. She brought her gloved hands up to her mouth, and then put them down again. "Ansel," she said, as if starting a pleading sort of sentence, but she went no further.

Clare walked over to the dead bird and picked it up by the legs. There was nothing to do with it. He set it back down in the soft dirt for the barn cats.

In a coaxing way, his mother said, "Neva's going to freeze to death in that car, Ansel."

Clare walked toward the door, listening for his father's footsteps behind him. When Clare finally turned, he saw his mother wiping her nose with a handkerchief, and he saw his father step out of the barn. His father didn't have the dulcimer, he didn't close the door, and he didn't look at Clare. The way he walked toward the car put Clare in mind of a stick that has fallen into a river without much current. When his father sat behind the wheel of the car, and his mother once again had the glass shade on her lap, Clare closed his car door. Neva was asleep. Charlotte's face was set, writing something in her journal. As the car began to move she did not even look up.

Two hours passed without a word. Familiar farms and houses and little towns gave way to unfamiliar farms and houses and towns. They passed through Garden City and had almost made Colorado when Neva awakened and said, "We forgot Krazy Kat."

His father looked over at his mother, who said, "We're not going back." A few seconds passed. Then, over his shoulder in a soothing voice, his father said, "Krazy Kat will be happier there, Nevie. It's her home. It's all she's ever known."

PART TWO

48

With every mile that passed, Charlotte felt better and better. They were actually going. They were not turning back. She kept her notebook at hand and jotted little reminders of the sights. She intended to write all about her fantastic journey to Opal and Emmeline, and perhaps also to Mrs. Gilman, the English teacher who'd once said she had a gift.

March 1, 1933

Dear Opal,
Guess where I am? In a cabin camp at La Junta, Colorado! Neva keeps asking about her goldfish so if you write don't include news of its demise. Permission granted for happily ever after story however fishy! I hope the dust hasn't been so bad in Dorland. We went over to have dinner at the Otero Hotel this evening and my was it regal. Prices to astound. My mom said we should just go back to the cabin and heat some soup but my

dad said, no, it was what she'd been wanting forever, to be in the Harvey House again and we had the cow money so we could afford it this once. I had Tournedos of Beef Marco Polo and Mom had Lamb Chops a la Nelson. The price includes dessert so I had Brandy Flip Pie. Was too delicious for words.

Your vagabond pal,
Char

March 2, 1933

Dear Emmeline,
Boy is Colorado nice. Tell your dad he was right that this route would be the nicest. Today was all paved roads (much easier on the derriere) and we've been lucky with the weather. It snowed some in Pueblo but didn't stick. I sure like Santa Fe. We found a brand new Harvey House while walking about and it sure was pretty. It's called La Fonda and the girls wear Mexican skirts and blouses instead of the regular black and white. My mom thought it looked like fun and I was half afraid she'd indenture me. We're staying at a cabin camp, though, not the La Fonda. Dad says we have to for Artemis. We forgot Neva's cat and she breaks out crying ever so often over that, but it's for the best Mom says.

Your roving reporter, Char
P.S. I don't know if you heard that the Scottish Songbird went to Emporia to work at the Harvey House. Tell your dad in case he goes there on business and needs to avoid. Dad says she still expects to be paid!

March 4, 1933

Dear Mrs. Gilman,

I wanted to write and thank you for all you taught me. I'm sorry I didn't get to come to Abilene and say good-bye. My sister's been sick and the doctor said we'd better go before the dust kills her. For her health, we are moving to California to live with my aunt and uncle and then to farm there, lemons probably, but maybe alligator pears. (Watch out for them! Ha ha.) On the way, we sure have seen some pretty country. Yesterday we drove from Santa Fe through Albuquerque to Gallup, which was a rough road. Then we crossed into Arizona and it took all day to reach Phoenix. I waved to it for you and said you sent your regards. It is as you say a very cosmopolitan city (hope I spelled that right! We're staying in a camp cabin and there's a Bible but no dictionary). My dad says we'll get to California tomorrow.

    Sincerely yours,
    Charlotte Price

49

New Mexico and Arizona lasted forever. California looked just the same, Neva thought, but it smelled better. She was tired of eating stale bread and cantaloupes and watery soup, tired of sitting, tired of being poked by Charlotte and falling asleep with her neck bent over. She missed Miss McKenna, who was much nicer to her than Charlotte was. She looked at the hills outside the car, sandy and bare except for pokey cactuses, but the hills didn't look like people at all. They looked like stones piled on top of one another. What if it was all a sneaky trick? What if there was no sleeping Indian like in the postcard Aunt Ida sent, no hilly green feet, no gigantic grass-covered head?

She closed her eyes and when she woke up, everything had changed. The earth on either side of the highways was soft and damp with rain, and there were gentle hills everywhere, as green as can be, even though it had still been winter in Kansas. She thought she saw shoulders and stomachs in the distance, raised knees furred all over with green bushes. It had rained a lot here, it looked like, and in some valleys the clouds hung low like fog.

"Is that it?" Neva asked, rubbing the window to make a better porthole. She wasn't supposed to ask anymore, but their father said they were getting close.

"No, Neva," her mother said, leaning forward to check.

"Those hills over there," Neva said. She thought the two hills looked more like the belly and face of a pregnant woman, but maybe the Indian was fat. She found the postcard on the floor and studied the tinted slopes.

Her mother looked a bit longer out the window. "No," she decided. "That's not it, Nevie."

More miles passed, the green grass by the road striking them all dumb. When they finally spotted a large black-and-white sign with an arrow, Charlotte whooped. "Fallbrook!" she said. "My God, I can't wait to get out of this car."

Neva expected Charlotte to get in trouble for saying *My God*, but she didn't. "Where is he? Where is he?" Neva almost screamed, kneeling on her seat and rubbing the whole window with her sleeve.

"The arrow just points to the town," Clare said. "I don't think you can see the big stiff from here." That was a mean thing to say, in Neva's opinion, but he leaned toward the window and helped her look.

Neva started reading the signs out loud. *"Sunkist Lemons,"* she said. *"No Trespassing."* They passed a yellow house that she hoped was it and a falling-down white one that had a dog chained up in the yard. Then a red-and-white sign with a chicken on it said, *"Fresh Eggs."*

"That's it," Ellie said. "We turn there."

The car filled with a feeling like Christmas morning. "Well, yaw-hoo," Charlotte said, sticking her head out the window and breathing in. "I am never, never going to leave California."

Neva wanted the car to go faster so she could get out and play in all that grass, but the muddy lane was so rutted and puddled that the car jolted, then slid into a furrow and ground to a stop.

"I guess we'll just have to walk," her mother said cheerfully, opening the door. She managed to stand up with the leaded glass lampshade, then set it carefully on the seat. Her heels sank in the mud but she didn't stop to clean them. She didn't even stop for Neva as she hurried up the hill.

Neva still wore the beret that was just like Miss McKenna's. She let Artemis off her leash and walked into the grove, where she stopped under a lemon-studded tree. The bark was so thin it looked like brown skin, smoothly covering a trunk that divided in two and then came together again in a twist. Grass like fine hair grew under her feet, and when she reached out to touch a lemon, it came off in her hand, smelling just like candy.

"Don't *pick* them!" Charlotte said in her mean way, but then there was the sound, higher up the hill, of a screen door slapping, and Charlotte, too, left Neva behind.

From the house she could hear her aunt saying, "Poor duck, poor duck," and a man saying, "Welcome to California!"

Neva crouched down beside the tree and found she could see the bit of yard where people were hugging and laughing. Uncle Hurd was a round man, shorter than her father and dressed like a railroad man in a blue work shirt and overalls. The whole time he was talking and listening, he kept rubbing his hand over the dog's face and ears.

Aunt Ida looked like her mother except with darker hair and bigger arms, legs, and cheeks. She didn't touch Artemis at all but you could tell from her face lines that she liked to smile. She looked around and Neva could hear her saying, "But where's little Neva?" and Neva knew she should go up and be kissed but instead she just sat very still.

"She's probably shy," Clare said. "She'll come along."

"Neva? Come and eat now! I've been cooking for two entire days!" Ida called, and the adults—her father last of all—began drifting toward the square white house, out of Neva's view. Her stomach hurt, and she was hungry, but the grove was so glittery and green. She looked up, and she saw blue sky. She looked back down. A ladybug was crawling on a long stem of grass that arced like a bridge. She put out her hand and extended a finger to the ladybug. Up at the house, Uncle Hurd was laughing like Santa Claus, "Ho ho ho."

When the ladybug lifted its wings and spun away, Neva stood up and crept to the side of the house. The wooden shutters had been painted bright pink, which gave the house a fairy tale look. A brown chicken shied away from her, and then another. The white plaster wall was warm where she leaned against the corner to peek at the front yard. Rusty machinery and old cars were everywhere. It was too organized to be a dump, though. Sparkly blue bottles had been wired to the branches of a little tree. Some of the bottles were pale turquoise and small like they'd once carried perfume. Some were medicine blue and so heavy that they made the branches droop. More glass bottles, clear and brown and green, had been sorted by color and were heaped in wire crates. Stones lined a winding path that Neva followed. Rainwater glistened on everything, and Neva picked up a clear perfume bottle shaped like a girl's head.

"Neva!" Charlotte called. She opened the screen door and looked disapprovingly at Neva. "Come in here. We're going to have chicken and biscuits now."

Neva set the girl's glass head down and went in to sit at a round table covered with a printed tablecloth and all sorts of food.

"Do you like it so far, Neva?" Aunt Ida said to her from the other end of the table and Neva looked down and said, "I like that blue-bottle tree."

Neva didn't like some of the food, such as mashed sweet potatoes, but some she did, like the fried chicken, which was just like her mother's. Her mother looked happy, and her father seemed almost like himself again, telling a story about starting the car on a steep hill in Colorado. They all ate three helpings and then Uncle Hurd walked her father and Clare around the place, standing before one rusty machine after another, telling them where he got it, what it used to be, and what he planned to make with it. Neva sat down between the piles of stones and glass bottles and made little houses by arranging them into rooms and furniture. The glass girl lived in the biggest house, with a broken Blue Willow cup for a bathtub and a three-legged china elephant as a pet. The women were washing up inside, and Neva could hear the watery thudding sounds and the high laughter of her mother and Charlotte, as if they had never left their cats behind or sent Miss McKenna away in the middle of the night. She wondered suddenly where Milly Mandy Molly was.

Uncle Hurd came up to Neva's crossed legs and crouched down. His work boots were thick and heavy-looking, and he wore a turquoise ring whose stone was larger than the space between his knuckles. He looked down at her houses and said, "Nice setup you've got there." He was grinning so hard she couldn't look at him. "You like California?"

Neva nodded, knowing it was what she was supposed to say. "Can you see the sleeping Indian from here?" she asked.

"Just the head," Hurd said, pointing beyond a car with three wheels. "See that strange hummocky thing over there?"

Neva stood up and followed his finger to a hill like a camel's hump. It might have been the same shape as the head in the postcard. She wasn't sure.

"You can see the whole body from that hill," he said. "Shall I carry you over there?"

"All right," Neva said. She let him put her up on his shoulders, and she held on to the hand that wore the ring.

"Ansel?" Uncle Hurd called. "You and Clare want to come see the Chief?" Neva kept her eye on the Indian's head as Uncle Hurd walked, trying to see if the Indian's face would be clearer than it was in the postcard. Uncle Hurd huffed a bit as they climbed a hill that gave off a green prickly scent.

When they reached the top, he didn't have to point. She saw it. She could see the hummocky hill, only now it was connected by a valley to a high table that looked exactly like a chest with a pair of hands crossed high up by the neck. The chest sloped down to the Indian's flat belly. His long legs connected to a hill that poked up like feet. She couldn't see the stones that made eyes or the tree that made his nose, but the body was huge and wonderful. Clare whistled and said, "That's swell as anything." Even her father said, "Sure enough."

"Beyond that lies the ocean," Uncle Hurd said. "Some days, from the really high hills, you can see it. The air has to be perfectly clear. Morning is the best time to look."

Suddenly Neva reached out her arms for her father. He came close so she could move from Uncle Hurd's shoulders to his. That was better. She could see even farther. She sat on her father's shoulders and imagined the sea on the other side of the sleeping Indian. The hillsides around them were planted with rows of orange and lemon trees. Clouds with rough gray edges hung down into a clear blue sky. It made her think of the curtains for the Winter Entertainment and then she wondered if this could possibly be the same earth as the one Kansas was on, and she touched her knitted cap to see if it was still there.

50

"No nail polish, no gum, no makeup," Mrs. Gore told Aldine. She was the head waitress; Ansel's friend Gil was the manager. "No smoking, no cursing, no drinking. And absolutely no men in your room."

There were four other waitresses, Aldine was told, and one of them was her roommate, Glynis Walsh, who looked too young to be on her own. She was even shorter than Aldine, with freckled skin, a raspy voice, and dark brown, wavy hair cut close to her head. It was midafternoon and Glynis and Mrs. Gore were wearing stiff black-and-white dresses that, to Aldine's eye, made them look like nuns. The badge on Glynis's apron said 4.

"You'll start out as a ten, like everyone else, and work your way up," Mrs. Gore said and handed Aldine a badge, a starched apron, a black long-sleeved dress, black stockings, and a pair of black lace-up shoes that were shockingly ugly. Mrs. Gore was at the top of the system: no badge at all, just a pin that said her name. You wouldn't call her pretty; she was instead the type Aunt Sedge would refer to as handsome. She and Leenie always knew what that meant: a plain sort made less so by community stature. Mrs. Gore said, "It's not seniority but hard work that moves you up. Do you play softball?"

Aldine shook her head.

"Well, you will when it gets warmer. We all do. We have uniforms and you can play any position you like except pitcher. I'm the pitcher." She ran her finger across one of the window-blind slats and frowned. "Curfew's ten o'clock. Sneak out and you're gone for good. Don't date Harvey employees, and don't think I won't find out. Glynis can help you with lunchroom protocol if you forget, but you need to put on that dress right now and comb your hair so I can run through the routine with you before the evening train."

Aldine's head buzzed with exhaustion. She'd slept some on a bench in Dorland, where she'd waited five hours for an eastbound train, then had taken little naps with her head against the train window. Less than a whole day since she'd been in Ansel's arms, and now he was gone. Fallen woman, that's what she'd be in books and such. She wondered if she could be a fallen woman even if she didn't feel like one.

"I'll help you with the apron," Glynis said. "And the cup code. Cup code's hard the first day."

Aldine nodded. At least she knew that much—Neva had taught her the cup code.

"Don't worry, dear," Mrs. Gore said, touching Aldine's arm and softening her voice. "I know you're tired but it's best to dive right in. Did Mr. Dorado tell you that for the first month of training it's just room and board? The sooner you start working, the sooner your pay starts. I'll meet you downstairs in ten minutes."

"Did you sign a six- or a twelve-month?" Glynis asked when they were alone, holding open the black dress like she was waiting for Aldine to undress.

"Six," Aldine said, dropping her coat onto the bed, which she was glad to see was covered with a good thick blanket.

"That means you get a fireman," Glynis said. "For twelve months, you get an engineer."

Aldine didn't understand, and she was tired of not understanding, so as she sat down to take off her shoes she asked, "What do you mean?"

"It's a joke the railroaders tell. For six months of service, Harvey Girls get to marry a fireman, but for twelve months they earn an engineer!"

Aldine forced a small laugh that sounded like a hiccup. She took off her stockings. "Which will you get?"

"Oh, none of 'em. I want to move to the Grand Canyon. I've put in for a transfer twice but all the girls want to go there, Gore says." Glynis sat back on her own small bed, still holding Aldine's uniform on her lap. She scratched her ankle and said, "How'd your folks feel about you coming here from Scotland?"

"They're no longer living."

"Oops. Sorry. I thought Gore said your dad put you on a train."

Aldine shook her head. She unzipped her dress but didn't take it off.

"My parents make me write them twice a week. They wouldn't have let me come if the drought weren't so bad. My sister ran off when I was nine."

"Oh," Aldine said.

"By the time we finally found her, the man had took off and left her."

Aldine waited for the end of a story she didn't want to hear.

"She died."

Aldine couldn't help worrying about the time. She wanted to know why the sister died but she just said how awful it was and held out her hands for the uniform.

"Homely, isn't it," Aldine said.

"Hoom-ly?"

"Ugly," she tried, though she didn't say that word in the American way, either.

"You shred it, Wheat," Glynis said. This turned out to be just one of her queer catchphrases, along with "Mitt me, kid," which she said at the end of a busy shift, and "dead hoofer," which she called the clumsier railroad men who asked her to dance at the weekly romps. While Aldine zipped herself into the dress and wriggled into the cross straps of the apron, Glynis checked the finger waves in her own hair, then pinned Aldine's black bow to her collar. "Well, there'll be some eyeballs rolling after you in the room," she said, and Aldine said, "Oh. Should I do something different then?"

Glynis laughed. "Not a thing. You'll be out-tipping us all before the week's out."

Downstairs, Mrs. Gore recited the lunchroom rules: no flirting with customers, never carry a glass in your hand (always on a tray), the cup code, the code for various salads and dishes, each of which she would have to memorize because at no time would she be writing down the orders—Harvey Girls didn't take notes but kept everything in their heads.

By the end of the seemingly endless day Aldine had worked three not-busy rush times ("used to be murder," Glynis said, "before times got hard") and had heard about every celebrity Glynis had seen come through on the Chief: Will Rogers, Tom Mix, Shirley Temple, and Gloria Swanson ("togged to the bricks," Glynis said). Aldine did not know who most of these people were, but she knew Clare had liked Tom Mix, so she asked if he was nice.

"Hard to tell. He just sat and ate while all his group swilled and whooped it up. It wasn't my table. But he left a big tip and when he went away he said to Betty Smart, 'That was good pot roast.' Those were the only words anyone heard him speak the whole time."

Aldine had heard about Betty Smart, the neighbor girl with whom Glynis had been hired ("my folks felt better sending me with the neighbor girl, and anyway they like to hire two good friends 'cause then you won't get homesick and quit"). Betty had married a railroader, though, according to Glynis, and gone on to a plum job at La Castañeda, the sort of job that Aldine ought to try for once she learned the ropes.

"I've heard of girls seeing the whole country that way," Glynis said. "Arizona and New Mexico and Texas and even California."

The word *California* was like a poke in the stomach. What if she kept hopping and skipping west until finally she was serving pie in California? Would that be good or bad? Bad, probably. That's what her head said. But the rest of her was ready to go.

"Stick with me, kid," Glynis said into the dark, her raspy voice silenced by the approach of a thudding freight train, the first of a dozen that would shatter the night and seem, in Aldine's dreams, to be headed right for her iron bed.

51

It seemed to Clare that California changed everyone except Neva, the one person whose life it was supposed to change. Neva still ate too little and coughed too much. Charlotte was happier—she was sewing new clothes and wearing Aunt Ida's jewelry. Instead of worrying and nagging everybody, his mother more or less ignored them all. But she was happier, too, singing to herself as she cooked with Ida, smiling and gossiping about people he'd never heard of. His father stopped reading aloud. He stopped reading to himself. He stopped shaving. His beard began to take over his cheeks and neck. He worked picking fruit six days a week and on Sundays he sat in Ida's bottle garden smoking cigarettes (Uncle Hurd smoked, so Clare supposed that was why he'd started) and watching the horizon, usually with a hand on the head of Charlotte's dog. Clare figured his father was thinking of Aldine, but when Neva asked him, he said, "Oh, just things, Nevie." Charlotte asked him, too, what he was always thinking about, and he turned to her and said, "I think you know."

His voice was so low and serious it seemed to set Charlotte back a little. She said, "The place, you mean."

He turned his eyes slowly away from her and in the same serious, low voice said, "Yes, I'm thinking about the place."

Once, when Clare asked him if he wished he'd brought his fretted dulcimer, his father considered it a moment or two and then said, "No."

Clare had hoped to go to high school, and everyone agreed that he should, but not right away. Better, Hurd and Ida said, to start fresh in the fall when he could start right alongside all the others instead of jumping in when the school term was almost done. Clare didn't argue. He picked fruit together with his father and after supper he sometimes walked alone to the town library, where he could read magazines and, each week, write a letter to Aldine.

> *Well, we finally made it to California. It's every bit as pretty as they say. Did you get to Emporia all right? My mom says being a Harvey Girl was the most fun she ever had.*

He didn't know why he was writing to her, or why he still thought about her all the time.

> *Write and tell me what it's like. Neva wears the hat and scarf all the time even though it's too hot for it.*
> *Yours ever, Clare.*

The next week:

> *We sure miss you. Specially Neva. She asks about you alot. At first her cold seemed to go away but now she's had a repeat and I know a word from you would mean alot.*

Then he added,

Remember when I said I loved you I still do. I think of
you all the time, please let me know how you are. They
say California is the place to come for cures, but Neva is
still poorly and my dad—

He was going to say that his father had a cough but he didn't want Aldine to write only out of concern for him. Clare started the letter over, leaving his father out of it, and the part about him loving her. He sent the letters care of the Emporia, Kansas, Harvey House, and he checked at the Fallbrook post office whenever he could to see if she had written back.

"You and your dad are the waitingest pair," the postmaster said one afternoon in May. Bart Crandall had a lazy eye, a limp, and a twisted hand. It was quite a package, in Clare's opinion. Little kids were scared of him even though he was always passing out candy. Butterscotch usually, but saltwater taffy today. Bart had managed to court and marry a plump woman named Florrie, who worked for Western Union, so they knew everybody's business, just like the telephone operators in Kansas.

"Waitingest?" Clare asked, twirling open a taffy wrapper.

"Both coming in, checking for General Delivery," Bart said. "I sure hope the money comes for you."

"It's not money," he said. Bart Crandall nodded and waited and Clare said, "We lost track of somebody back in Kansas."

"Family?" Bart Crandall asked.

"Mmm," Clare said, nodding, while the postman smiled and studied him and waited. Clare put the taffy in his mouth as a kind of stopper. He began to chew.

"Cousin of some kind?" Bart Crandall asked.

Clare shrugged and pretended to laugh and pointed at his mouth full of taffy. Before making for the door he bawled a thank-you that resembled a sound that Yauncy Tanner might make. That seemed about right to Clare. Because in letting Bart Crandall fish facts out of him, he had been an idiot and a swell one at that.

52

The snow started falling on Emporia after passengers left on the 2:24 westbound. It fell on the lead-dark tracks, on the roofs and windows of parked cars, and on the hunched shoulders of men and women caught out in the weather. The quiet that always descended in the wake of train departures, a slow, tired cleaning of plates, tables, and floors, was deepened by the whiteness outside, as if the snow were a sleep that invited them all.

"Dreaming about Los Angeleez?"

Glynis's raspy voice from behind. It gave Aldine a start.

"No," she said, "not at all." She glanced out. "Though the snow falling on the street like that puts me in mind of Ayr."

Glynis gave a cheerful little laugh and said, "Well, kid, stop dreamin' and get crackin'," before heading off with a bin of dirty dishes. It was a line that Gilbert Dorado used. Mr. Dorado had been Ansel's friend, and Mrs. Price's, too, when she was still Eleanor Hoffman. Mr. Dorado was nice, but he moved from restaurant to restaurant and always called Aldine "our fair lass" because he had never learned her name.

In the beginning it felt odd to be called "kid" by a girl younger (and shorter!) than herself, but Glynis's steady everyday friendship and her confident certainty in all matters of conduct had altered Aldine's view of her, and made it more accommodating. Still, Glynis traded on confidences, both the giving, which she yielded readily, and the getting, which she sought relentlessly. She'd pointed out to Aldine the purveyor of sheet music who had last summer, by means of a note written on a coaster, suggested a riverside "rendezvous" and she told her about the railroad man who came in twice a week and after his meal would withdraw from his vest a packet of off-color postcards and then select one to leave for his waitress, "which," Glynis said, "I will not say did not sometimes amuse me but then he left one that could not be abided." Aldine felt obliged to ask the nature of the offending card. "Too offensive," Glynis returned. "I cannot say." But of course she did. "You've got a safari tent occupied by newlyweds. Flap's closed, see, so it's dark inside but a curious elephant slips his trunk inside and the bride in happy surprise exclaims, 'Ye Gods, Charlie!'" Glynis's tone was disapproving. Aldine wanted to laugh—it was the kind of thing that in their younger days she and Leenie might've laughed themselves sick at—but she couldn't laugh now because of Glynis's somber presentation of it all. "Next time I waited on him I told him to eat his dinner and keep his filthy cards to himself. "You see, don't you?" she said to Aldine but didn't wait for a reply. "If my father and mama taught me one thing," she said, "it's that you have to draw a line or the men will run roughshod." This was a common theme for Glynis, who returned time and again to the tragedy of her sister.

As much as Glynis needed to tell her stories, Aldine preferred to conceal her own.

About her own sister, she had been very brief. "I lived with her in New York before I came to Kansas," she said. When letters came for Aldine—four or five from Clare and two from Ansel—Glynis asked, "From your sister?" and Aldine just shook her head and tied them together with a pink ribbon she found left behind in one of the booths at the Harvey House. She hadn't wanted to share the letters, but Glynis had prompted so relentlessly that Aldine finally read them aloud. She started with Clare's letters because they required no explaining. "He sounds sweet as molasses," was Glynis's response after the last one, "and almost as slow."

"No, he can recite anything," Aldine said, and began rewrapping the letters, but Glynis said, "What about the others?" so there was nothing for it. She lifted Ansel's onionskin pages out of the slit-open air mail envelope, and tried to keep her hands from trembling.

> *"Dear Aldine,*
> *If I had not kissed you or declared how I felt, there would*
> *have been no wrong in insisting that you come with us*
> *to a place where you'd be among friends. Please let me*
> *know if you get this letter because then I'll know Gilbert's*
> *watching over you all right.*
> *Ansel"*

"Oh, Gilbert would watch over you all right," Glynis said with a sniggering laugh, "if he was ever here. But it's such a sad, beautiful letter . . . Why did Ansel have to go to California?"

"Work. His farm was failing and he had work out there."

Glynis lay silent and still for a minute on her bed opposite Aldine. Then she said, "What did he mean by 'coming with us.' Who's 'us'?"

Aldine pretended she didn't know. She said Ansel had a brother he was close to, and to change the subject said, "I guess I should tell him that Gilbert has a different job now."

"Happy journeys describing it. From what I hear he just goes from Harvey House to Harvey House flirting with all the plump girls. Have you seen the girlfriend he plays house with? You'd think she'd be plump enough to take care of a dozen Gilberts, but oh no. I'd never marry a Mexican, Italian, or Frenchman for that very reason—the vows don't mean a hill of beans to them."

"I thought you said you would never marry a Catholic," Aldine added. Glynis could get carried away with all the types she wouldn't marry, and Aldine wanted her carried away.

"Correct-o," Glynis said. "Catholics or Jews, either one. And to tell the truth I haven't liked what I've seen of Bohemians." But she was eyeing the packet of letters Aldine was trying to put away. "What about the last one?" she said.

Aldine slipped it out, but it was too hard to read aloud. She started, but her voice faltered, and she just handed it to Glynis.

> *Aldine, I know I wronged you. I forgot myself. Still I*
> *can't bear not knowing if you're safe. Please write back*
> *and tell me that the money I gave you was enough and*
> *you're serving coffee, having fun.*

He had signed it simply *Ansel.* Then without a P.S., he'd added, *It is terrible and wonderful the vividness of your face in my mind.*

Glynis handed the letter back. "It's like the words are soft but the meanings are hard. He said good-bye to you, didn't he?"

Aldine lowered her eyes and nodded. Glynis came over and sat beside her on the bed and when she turned to hug her, Aldine was surprised at the urgency with which she turned to receive it. She was soon crying lavishly, as if a dam had given way. Glynis's words were consoling. It was going to be okay, she said. Aldine was lucky she hadn't run off with a man like that. "We'll stick together," she said, "get a good transfer together. You'll meet a man ten times nicer than that. You didn't write back to him, did you?"

Aldine shook her head miserably.

"Good," Glynis said, "because writing back would just make forgiving himself all that much easier," and then she said nothing else but hugged Aldine until the last tear had fallen.

Aldine was ashamed at how much of Ansel she'd given up, and she was horrified by the sordid figure that Glynis had turned him into. She was glad at least that she hadn't mentioned the nausea. She'd never been one for keeping track of dates, but she wished now that she was. She hadn't been on, it seemed, in over a month, maybe six weeks. She didn't boak, like Leenie had, so it was probably just the change of weather or some mild form of flu, but whatever it was, it wasn't Glynis's business or anyone else's.

The snow had covered everything now, had turned everything dirty into a soft, comforting white. It was Aldine's job to drain the giant coffee urn and wipe the spattered silver, to place washed coffee cups on trays that could be carried to the tables for the 5:13 eastbound. If customers appeared in the meantime, she would stop what she was doing and serve them, but few in Emporia could afford restaurant meals, and fewer still dined at 2:30 in the afternoon, so she was surprised to see a man in a dark coat stop at the door, remove his hat, and come in.

She recognized him before he'd finished brushing the snow from his coat and hat. It was the ginger hair, she supposed, and the upturned nose and the freckles; they were all the same despite a general thickening of his features and limbs. Still, she thought she might be seeing things. Had she ever asked what part of the states Elder Lance came from, to what part of it he would return? Had he mentioned farming? She thought he had.

"Can you wait on that man?" Aldine whispered to Glynis while Mrs. Gore's back was turned. The room was hushed and brown and warm, and the gleaming surface of the counter reflected Aldine's white sleeve as she lifted her hand to indicate Elder Lance.

Glynis looked across the room. "Sure, kid. Your wish is my command."

Glynis headed for the booth. Aldine turned her back and made a serious business of rubbing the coffee urn with a flannel cloth. Glynis soon returned to say, "He wants Finnan Haddie and 'a big ol' glass of buttermilk,' but I should tell you that he asked me if your name is by any chance Aldine McKenna."

Aldine knew that she shouldn't turn her head, but she couldn't help it, and when she looked at the booth by the window, Elder Lance waved his hand at her and smiled in the snow-lit air. Aldine looked around for Mrs. Gore, saw that she had left the room, and lifted her hand in what she hoped was a noncommittal way.

Glynis poured buttermilk into a glass and looked mischievously at Aldine. "Old beau I'm thinking?"

Aldine shook her head and used the flannel to rub water spots from a silver knife.

"Want to take him his big ol' glass of buttermilk?"

Aldine said no, she didn't. Instead of putting the glass on a tray, Glynis just stood there grinning. "I guess he's coming to fetch it himself," she said, and a moment later Elder Lance was at the counter. When Aldine turned, he began to smile, to lean his head back with amazement. The teeth were still the same gingery brown. "Ye gods and little fishes," he said. "Aldine McKenna—am I right?"

His remembering her full name was a surprise.

"It's me," she said, and smiled in the most guarded way she could. "How are you, Elder . . . ?" She knew his name but preferred him not to know it.

"Lance," he said. "Elder Lance. At least that's who I was. Now I'm just Roy." He drew from his vest pocket a small card that said *Roy T. Lance, Farm Implements.* "That's another person I used to be. I'm in college now." He stopped talking, shook his head, and spread his blunt fingers wide on the lunch counter. "Ye gods and little fishes," he said, softer this time. "Aldine McKenna." He sat down on one of the stools and said, "Can I just eat here?"

"Course you can," Glynis said, setting his buttermilk before him.

Elder Lance turned from Glynis to Aldine. "Well, this does beat everything," he said. She wondered if he'd ever stop shaking his head. "This really takes the cake."

Through her demeanor, Aldine tried to suggest that she would have to be curt. There were jobs that were hers to do, and there was the strict no-flirting rule, and there were the stories about how fast Mrs. Gore could have you on the street.

"You know I just saw Leenie and Will," Elder Lance said. "I ate at their house, what, two weeks ago. The baby's real sweet. Spitting image of Will." He was nodding. "Absolute spitting image."

Aldine couldn't look at him because of the brown teeth, but his words had a stiffening effect on her. Outside the window, the April snow kept falling and deepening. She had not written Leenie because she couldn't think of a way to tell Leenie and Will where she was living, what she was doing.

Mrs. Gore entered the rear door of the lunchroom with a vacuum cleaner that had been sent out for repairs. She set it down in the corner, made sure that Aldine saw it there, and left again.

"There's your haddie," Aldine said and went for the plate the cook had set on the ledge.

"They're not going to believe that I saw you! They told me you were in Kansas, but they said Loam County. They don't know Kansas, I guess."

"No, they wouldn't," Aldine said. Glynis was removing soiled table-cloths and shaking out fresh ones, but Aldine noticed she was sticking to the nearer tables. Aldine resumed polishing silverware, but Elder Lance was not one for subtleties. He went on talking.

His mother had been pretty darned ill, he said, squeezing a lemon over the white ruffled flesh of his fish, down in Olpe. She was all right now. She was a corker. He was studying to be an engineer at Brigham Young University, which was a beautiful place—she ought to see it. It was just over the mountain pass from where Leenie and Will lived in Salt Lake.

Aldine had only an image from Leenie's moth-brown photo of the Salt Lake temple, the spires like masts, the windows like portholes. She wondered if Will and Leenie had gone there and done the magic things that would keep them together even in death, and if they had done the magic for her parents.

"I thought Leenie said you were working as a teacher here, living with a Mormon family."

Glynis was smoothing out a cloth and pretending not to listen. Aldine hadn't told Glynis that she lived with a family at all. On the windowsill the snow was rounding into the corners, the way you might find them in a cozy holiday card. She wished she were out in it, catching the lacy formations you could see for an instant if you caught one on your sleeve.

"How was that, with the Mormon family?" Elder Lance said, bringing her back.

"They had to leave their farm because of the dust storms," Aldine said and kept her eyes on the silverware. "Their little girl had what they call dust pneumonia."

Elder Lance forked a bite of haddie, dragged it through sauce, and popped it in his mouth.

"Why'd you stay here, then?" he said, still chewing.

"Seemed for the best. And I'd heard this could be fun."

"Is it?"

"Aye. Sometimes. I love the big room."

"Luve the big rroom!" he said with shocking loudness, rolling his tongue to sound, as he imagined, like her. "I do miss those accents! You know, where you oughta be is Brigham Young. Lots of girls go there, you know, and the boys would go for that accent."

Aldine didn't look him in the eye as she frowned and said, "Aye."

"Hey, why don't you come back with me!"

"What?"

Glynis dropped a fork onto the table and looked up.

"I bet Will and Leenie'd be ten times happier to have you with 'em, and this way you don't have to make the trip all by yourself."

"Oh, I couldn't do that."

"Right," he said, forking another bite of haddie, his pink face rosier yet with embarrassment. "Of course not."

She didn't know why he thought she could buy train tickets on impulse and enroll in university. She studied his suit for signs of money, but it wasn't the best wool. The lining of his overcoat sagged, his scarf had been knitted by a mother or sister from cheap yarn, and his hat had been rubbed smooth along the brim. "It isn't that," she said, meaning it wasn't that she thought he was being forward. She tried to think, as Glynis walked toward yet another table with an armful of linen, of how to say that she, like most people, couldn't afford to quit her job.

"I have to stop talking or I'll lose my place," she said, flashing him an apologetic smile and walking away. She didn't want to go to Salt Lake City. She didn't want boys to "go for" her accent. What she wanted most of all when she carried a tray of empty cups to the window booths was to look out the window and see Ansel Price coming up the way to fetch her, magically free of Ellie and his marriage so he could hold her and be as he was in her dreams, when the warmth of him was like the sun through closed eyelids.

Elder Lance (she could never think of him as anything else) left a good tip, especially for a counter customer, and his good cheer was unassailable. He would tell Leenie where to write her, he said, and he wished he had a camera so he could take a photograph, and it sure was good to see her once again.

53

That evening, when Aldine could find no more reasons to stay locked in the bog, she came back to find Glynis waiting cross-legged on her bed in a pair of man's pajamas, gluing a picture of Clark Gable into her scrapbook. The radiator was warm and ticking, so the boiler was working. It wasn't always. Glynis would glue anything in her scrapbooks—a drawing of a little boy she said looked just like her brother Charlie, an Easter poem from the *Ladies' Home Journal*, a picture of a red-cheeked girl doing Highland dances in a green plaid kilt. Beneath this she had written, in her girlish print, *Like my dear friend Scottish Aldine*. Glynis looked up now, checked the tightness of a hairpin, and said, "What a day, huh?"

"It was," Aldine said. She leaned against the radiator and yawned. She was ready for rest and silence and hoped Glynis saw it.

But Glynis merely nodded at their shared tin of scavenged cigarette remnants and said, "Butt me, will you, kid."

This was a surprise. House rules forbade smoking in the rooms, and Glynis was not the type to invite trouble. Aldine hoisted up the window and the cold night air rushed in. The roofs were layered with snow, all white except for a large circle of amber under the streetlight. It was startlingly pretty.

"Well?" Glynis said once they'd lit and inhaled.

"Yes?"

"The funny-looking one with the tragic smile."

"I met him in Scotland," she said. "He was a missionary there." She wanted to stop right there, but she knew Glynis would hector until she told the story through, so she did tell the story, but only in the barest outlines.

"So you never joined?" Glynis asked when she was done.

Aldine tweezed a bit of tobacco from her tongue and said no, she never did.

The room was small and plain. They weren't supposed to put anything on the walls, though holes in the pink plaster were evidence that other girls had made themselves more at home. She had thought more than once that she'd like some photographs on the walls, of Ayr and of Leenie and Will, and of Neva and Clare and, truly, before all others, of Ansel, though she had none of him or, for that matter, any of the Prices, and he was married so of course she couldn't. Aldine removed her apron and hoped Glynis was done talking.

"I guess your sister'll send for you now," Glynis said, pressing down on Clark Gable's forehead.

"I doubt it. She has no money." It was cooler now in the room with winter stealing through the open window. Aldine rested her hands on the embossed curves of the radiator and breathed in the heat. The thick iron ribs smelled like scalded milk, and the steady warmth was one way that her life had improved since becoming a Harvey Girl.

"What did he mean about a Mormon family you were living with? You didn't tell me you were a schoolmarm."

"They weren't Mormon," Aldine said.

"What town was it?"

Aldine didn't want to say, but Glynis would know if she made up a town.

"Dorland," she said.

"That how you met Ansel?" she asked. She looked up from the pages of her Hollywood magazine, and Aldine pressed her palms against the radiator. She nodded.

Glynis studied a gauzy photo and turned the page. "I guess you were living with his family."

Aldine nodded again, and Glynis kept looking at her. Aldine's fingers were red at the tips, and she curled them into her palms.

"You ought to write your sister," Glynis said.

"Yes"—Aldine stubbed out her cigarette on a cracked saucer—"I ought." She closed the window and left the radiator for the coolness of her bed. She turned her face to the pink plaster wall and pulled up the covers. She would write Leenie just as soon as she was sure she wasn't pregnant. She felt an approaching freight train before she heard it. From the east, heading west. She'd grown to like the trains passing slowly and heavily through the night, liked to think where they might carry her. Finally this one was gone and the room was still lit.

"Are you going to moon over Clark Gable all night then?" she asked Glynis, "or can we get to sleep now?"

"Clark Gable is okay," Glynis said. She'd had her story from Aldine and evidently didn't like it. Her voice was sullen.

"Except Mr. Clark Gable is Catholic," Aldine said—she didn't know why—and she soon wished she hadn't.

"He's not," Glynis said. And then, lower but not so low that Aldine couldn't hear it: "And he's not a family man, either."

54

Initially Charlotte didn't think much about the man. He was a little mysterious, that was all—a tall, brown-headed figure (all bone and tanned skin, like a man from the Far East) wearing funny metal-rimmed spectacles. He owned the packinghouse and was a town big shot of some sort and sometimes came Sunday afternoons to stand under a tree and discuss who knew what with Uncle Hurd before departing in his black Packard.

After dinner on one such Sunday, Charlotte was at the dining room table laying out pattern pieces for a new dress. Charlotte liked every part of sewing: unfolding the tissue paper and smoothing it out over the fabric, the heavy snip of the scissors as she cut through layers, the gnawing sound the Singer made as she stitched one strange geometric shape to another, the burned-soap smell of the iron as she pressed the seams open. The more complicated the pattern was, the better she liked it: she had made lined jackets, covered buttons, handkerchief hems, and pleated sleeves. The dress she was doing now would have a huge collar that lay open to display not one but six inset buttonholes. She was pinning the tissue to pink pongee when she heard Artemis barking, then someone opening the screen door. That was when the man stepped in and removed his hat from his brown head.

"This is my niece Charlotte," Ida said, sweeping in behind him, her big arms draped with pearl bracelets and a gold chain that held, in each link, a different charm shaped like the birds of California. "Just arrived from Kansas. Charlotte, this is Mr. McNamara, who owns the packinghouse."

Charlotte nodded. Mr. McNamara held his hat in his hands, and she noticed that his hands, like the rest of him, were long and bony. There was something distinctive about him, something more than his double-breasted suit and red tie, which she was almost certain was silk. It had to do with the way he regarded her, but in what way he regarded her, she wasn't exactly sure.

"That's a striking color," he said, touching the thin, soft fabric on the table in a way unexpected from a man. He looked over the complex arrangement of material, pins, and pongee; then he unhinged his gold spectacles from his face, took out a soft cloth, and began to clean the lenses. "You don't by chance have a teaching certificate, do you?"

Ida said, "Mr. McNamara's on the school board. President, in fact."

Mr. McNamara held his spectacles up to the light to inspect the lenses he'd just cleaned. The lenses and their thin frames were shaped like octagons, which was a new one for Charlotte.

"I'm afraid not," she said. "I was planning to go to normal school in Topeka, but things didn't work out."

He nodded, tucked away his cleaning cloth, and carefully hooked his spectacles behind his ears. "And is your sister doing better here?"

Charlotte wondered how he knew about her sister. "Yes," she said. "A little better, anyway."

She didn't know what else to say, and she was a little alarmed when Ida said he should sit down while she cut him a piece of pie. She hoped he would go out into the living room, or maybe even follow Ida into the kitchen, but he simply sat down on one of the high-backed chairs

Ida kept on either side of the buffet and said, "The domestic arts are becoming the lost arts. Or so I fear. Did you learn to sew at school?"

"No," she said. "At school we didn't do any home stuff. I liked mythology. We had a sort of appreciation club for it."

"A mythology appreciation club?"

There was something in his voice, amusement or disbelief, she wasn't sure which. "Yes," she said. "That's what it was. We started with six members but it didn't take us long to boil down to three."

She meant this as funny, and he smiled, and fell silent.

"We had a photography club, too," she said. "We had a darkroom at the school and everything." She realized with irritation that she'd lost track of where she was on the pattern.

"So you have a camera?"

"Sort of. My grandfather gave one to my mother, who didn't like it, so I guess I inherited it."

"What kind?"

"Zeiss Ikon box camera," she said and he let out a low whistle of respect and said, "That cost your grandpa a pretty penny."

Charlotte felt a strange flush of pride. She decided not to mention that she'd stopped taking pictures because they couldn't afford the chemicals for developing.

He stroked the brim of his felt hat and was looking at her in that way again, the way she not only didn't understand, but wasn't even sure whether she disliked or liked. "Have you seen our high school?" he asked.

"Yes," Charlotte said, not looking up. "Uncle Hurd showed us all around. It's swell." She slipped a pin through the tissue. She was sorry to have said *swell* to the president of the school board or whatever he was.

"Pie, James," Ida said, emerging with a cup of coffee and a huge wedge of lemon meringue. It reminded Charlotte of her mother saying, to practically every guest they'd ever had on Thanksgiving, that when the industry standard was to cut a pie into six pieces, the Harvey House cut theirs in four. Ida had clearly had the same training. "Let me clean off the table for you," Charlotte said, folding up the edges of the pink pongee.

"Please, no," Mr. McNamara said. "Don't spoil your work. I'm happy as I am." He set the coffee cup on the buffet beside him and rested the plate of pie on his knees. The meringue looked two inches thick.

"Charlotte's a brilliant girl," Ida said. She was one of those women who always wore makeup and perfume, and she had moved off the conveyor belt at the packinghouse and into the office, where pay was higher. Hurd was a supervisor, so between them both, Charlotte was pretty sure that they had more money than their junk-collecting hobby would suggest. Ida never let her permanent grow out too far, but even as Charlotte admired her, she saw, with fear, that she would have big arms like that, too, one day, and shop from the pages in the catalogue marked for the Mature Lady. Mr. McNamara was a fastidious eater—a small bite, subtle chewing, napkin daubed to the corners of his lips—which suggested a degree of culture past any experience she'd had in Kansas. She remembered Aunt Ida telling her that she'd met Mr. McNamara at a Rotary supper, which had led to dinner at Ida and Hurd's, and after a tour of Ida's bottle garden, he said he would give her his blue Milk of Magnesia bottles straight after he finished dosing himself and save her the trip to the dump. She had laughed and said, "Oh, but I live for the search, James, the search for buried treasure." Charlotte wondered if he'd brought her a sapphire bottle today, and sure enough, when she went into the living room to find her pincushion, there on the table where her aunt generally set a vase of flowers was a clean, empty Magnesia bottle big enough to dose a horse.

"You should see how many novels Charlotte reads a week," Ida went on.

She could feel his eyes settle on her. "So how old are you, Charlotte?"

"Eighteen," she said. "Well, next month, anyway."

"And what are your plans?"

"College," Charlotte said at once, then added: "Though I guess that's more a hope than a plan."

"Mmm," he said. He wore a constant half smile that she took for inner peace (annoying) or amusement (even more annoying).

Ida sat down opposite Mr. McNamara, took a sip from her own cup of coffee (black with two teaspoons of sugar), and said, "She can't make real plans until her family's good and settled. Then she'll probably go to normal school or university. Things are different now for women, don't you think?"

He nodded mildly. "That's why we built the Practice House. So many girls now are not learning what they need to learn at home."

The Practice House had been on Charlotte's tour of the high school: a cute little cottage at the top of a hill where girls could learn to dust and iron and mop. Charlotte had been incredulous at the time; what were the girls doing at *home*, then, she wanted to know? Did they all have servants, or were they just slow learners, or what? It was the craziest idea she'd ever heard, like building a barn at the school and filling it with cows.

Ida smiled warmly at Charlotte. "Charlotte made the curtains in my kitchen. Also that skirt she's wearing."

Charlotte didn't like to think that Mr. McNamara would now be looking at her skirt. She kept her eyes on the pattern and sat down—unbearable to bend over now—to measure the distance from the selvage to the long black line on the pattern that helped you determine straightness of grain, then immediately forgot how many inches and eighths of inches it was.

"Have you seen the sewing and cooking labs, Charlotte?" Ida asked. "They're nicer than most homes!"

"I did see them," Charlotte said. "They're awfully nice." As if the Practice House weren't enough, there was a huge building with a high ceiling like the great hall in a castle, and in that building were black-and-white-tiled mini-kitchens, each one with a stove and a por-celain sink, and two rows of sewing machines and four big tables for cutting out patterns. The machines were brand new, with ruffling attachments that Charlotte had never seen in person, and they smelled intoxicatingly of machine oil.

Ida collected the plate and took it off to the kitchen and did not immediately return.

"What else did you like in school?" Mr. McNamara asked. It seemed to Charlotte that he was giving her the same beatific smile he'd given his lemon meringue pie.

"Astronomy," she said, and then—why, she wasn't sure—she looked right at him. "I liked that a lot."

His eyes seemed to dilate, or readjust, or did she just imagine it? At any rate, his gaze shifted into the emptiness of his hat. This first tingling hint of her own powers was shocking to her, and strangely exhilarating. When he again looked up, he asked in a soft voice, "Have you ever looked at the night sky through a telescope?"

"Once," Charlotte said, remembering the cold night, the spray of stars, squinting at Jupiter.

"And did you enjoy it?"

"I did." She'd never in her life flirted with an adult, but she had a sudden comprehension that she was doing it now. "Very much."

"Well, then, you'll have to come and look through mine."

Charlotte took this in, looking at him, then stretched the tape measure from the grain line to the edge of pink pongee and stared at the numbers. "Thank you," she said, and she knew the polite thing would be to say, *That would be nice,* but she decided not to say it. She wondered whether she would be alone when she looked through this telescope.

"Do you know your constellations?" he asked.

"Some," she said. (A lie. She knew a great many.) "But I'd like to learn more."

He smiled his small smile and looked at her again, and suddenly she had it. The way he was looking at her was a knowing way. But what did he know? She had the peculiar, not unpleasant feeling that he knew something about her that she herself didn't yet know.

Mr. McNamara stood. "I'm sure I'll see you again," he said quietly.

"Mmm," Charlotte said. "Why wouldn't you?" She added a shrug and a smile. "It's a small town, after all."

He nodded and disappeared into the kitchen to say his good-byes to Aunt Ida. He left that way; she heard the back door open and close. It was a warm day and she could see Aunt Ida's bottle tree from the window, the smallest of the cobalt decorations no wider than her pinkie, the largest like a quart of milk. She'd discovered one day that the bottles had rainwater inside them, rainwater that, when she tipped one of the small bottles upside down, felt warm on her fingers and dripped prettily from her fingertips. She'd tipped one bottle after another, letting the sun-warmed water touch different parts of her bare arm until, suddenly conscious that someone might be watching her, she stopped.

55

After the bad time with Bart Crandall, Clare limited his visits to the post office to once a week, on Saturday, when it was easy to walk into town. He would offer Bart Crandall no further information about the person they'd lost track of in Kansas. He just approached the counter, took a taffy or butterscotch, and waited for Bart Crandall to say, "Nothing this week," or "What's the name I should be looking for?" to which Clare just gave a friendly nod before departing, but one day in May the dreary sequence was finally undone. The moment Bart Crandall caught sight of Clare coming through the door, he raised an envelope and held it out for him.

McKenna, the return address said. *Harvey House Emporia Kansas.*

"Thanks," Clare said. He tried to keep the eagerness out of his voice. He bet it was in his face, though.

"Is this the relative—A. McKenna?" Bart Crandall asked.

"We'll find out, won't we?" Clare said. If he had to say something, this was the answer he'd practiced to say. He'd learned it from Mr. McNamara, and it was a good one. He grabbed a butterscotch from the saucer, thanked Mr. Crandall, and was gone.

The town's small library was housed in the clubhouse of the Fallbrook Women's Club. Clare went inside, took several books from a shelf, then sat at a desk removed from regular traffic. Tearing open the envelope seemed ungodly loud, but no one shushed him, and he wouldn't have cared if they did.

Dear Clare, the letter said.

> *I am well and happy and I thank you for asking. I appreciate hearing all your news especially about your family. I am glad that all of you are happy in California which sounds like paradise itself.* She went on in this neutral tone for several more sentences before signing, *Your teacher (and friend), Aldine McKenna.*

A postscript was then added. *If Charlotte has taken any photographs of each of you in California I would love to have some for my scrapbook.*

Clare touched his finger to the paper she'd held in her hands and written on and even brought the stationery close to his nose but there was nothing of her in its scent. It was restaurant stationery. *Harvey Houses*, it said at the top, *Civilizing the Old West.*

He read the letter three times. After that he knew it word for word, but there weren't really any words for him. The only thing with meaning was the P.S. Aldine had never had a scrapbook, as far as he knew. And *photographs of each of you.* Not of *all* of you. A picture of his father. That's what she wanted.

He waited three days to write back. *Be cheerful*, he told himself. *Cheerful and chatty.*

> Dear Aldine,
> *Neva misses you but she is much better, even I can tell. This makes all of us happy especially my mother but all of us really. I might go back to school in the fall but right*

now my father and I pick fruit all day and can eat all we want. The strangest of our news concerns Charlotte who is dating a regular adult man about town. Doesn't that beat all? Mr. McNamara's tall and skinny with no hair whatsoever, forty years old at least, and he wears little gold rimmed glasses in the shape of hexagon or maybe octogon. I keep waiting for my father to put an end to it, but he hasn't yet. Mr. McN's taken Charlotte for 3 rides in his fancie Packard once all the way to the ocean and Ida says he's the catch of the town, kind of like the king here. She said if Mr. McNamara didn't have bigwiggy (her word) friends up north, Fallbrook never could have built such a fine big school. She said he got the funds because he was at Stanford U. with Congressman Somebody or Other. We all like it here, especially Charlotte and my mother who never mention Kansas except to say they're never going back. Neva misses you, I can tell you that, and I miss Kansas a lot myself though of course not a bit as much as my father who I think will die if he doesn't get back.

He'd written that last sentiment almost without thinking, and he knew at once how much it might mean to her, and then—he couldn't help himself—he added, *I guess you always had your heart set on my dad.*

He shouldn't have added that. It was a mistake and a sorry one at that. But he was at the bottom of a full page. He wasn't going to rewrite a whole new letter. He was ready to be done with it. He addressed it to *A. McKenna*, and under *Yours always,* he signed his name as she'd always said it: *Clarence.* Then he dropped it into the drab green corner mailbox.

56

All that spring Ellie was aware of Ansel's restlessness and disquiet. He worked steadily, resolutely picking fruit in the orchards—Hurd had told her this—and was polite but spoke only when he had to. He ate his lunch with Clare but Clare told her that he often gave him half his lunch. He wasn't hungry, he said. He'd begun smoking cigarettes, too. In the late afternoon after his work shift, he would sit on a rock in the shade beyond the blue-bottle tree where an arroyo—that was what the locals called it—afforded a long downsloping view to the east. For hours he would sit there with the dog and smoke and look off. He couldn't like it here. She understood this as she might understand the troubles of a bear brought to a place without winter. It was as if the rhythms of these hours and shadows and seasons were not his, and never could be. She understood this, but allowed herself not to care, just as he had allowed himself not to care when she was imprisoned by the farm.

She had been looking for a place for them to rent. While Ansel scanned the newspapers for news about rainfall and farm yields in Kansas, she browsed the *House for Rent* advertisements. She told Ida that she didn't see any reason to leave a town where she only needed to dust the furniture once a week, and where if you set a cup of coffee down on the counter, you didn't come back to find it covered with the topsoil of your neighbor's wheat field. They ate like royalty, especially on the weekends, when she and Ida made any number of elaborate meals: fresh corn chowder, say, with pickled beets, strawberry salad, and a ham stewed in kumquats the color of the sun at twilight.

While Ida worked during the week, Ellie took up the cooking and enjoyed having fresh ingredients close at hand. Everything grew here: not just oranges, lemons, and limes, but also avocados, guavas, apples, plums, and apricots. When Ida came home from working all day at the packinghouse, Ellie might serve fresh beef tongue, fried apple cakes, spring onions on toast, and guava pudding. Everyone exclaimed over the food, except for Ansel, who ate little and kept up merely a stiff cordiality. Neva ate more, and Clare, too. Since taking up with Mr. McNamara, Charlotte limited her portions (and was looking trimmer for it) but one night, after a supper of pork chops with plums, wilted dandelion greens, fried yams, and orange sherbet, Charlotte looked at her and, with what seemed like true wonder in her voice, said, "I had no idea you could cook like this."

That very night, sitting alone with Ida in the dimming kitchen, Ellie said, "I haven't felt this way since the Harvey House."

Ida gave her sister a smile. "You do seem happy."

Ellie wouldn't have thought she could be happy if her marriage had so many holes in it. "Happiness of a kind," she said. "I think I'm contented."

Ida nodded.

Outside, they could see Ansel smoking under the blue-bottle tree. Ida said, "Did we do anything to get his goat?"

"It's not you." Except for her and Ida, the house was empty. Hurd was in his workshop welding. Charlotte had walked into town. Clare was helping Neva with a tree house. And Ansel was staring off. "He just misses Kansas," she said. She looked at him out there. "Sometimes when he's out there smoking I think he'll just stand up and start walking east and never look back."

A moment or two passed. "What would you do then?" Ida asked. Her expression was hard to read. Was she worried for her, or did she think Ansel's leaving would be a blessing for them all?

"I don't know," Ellie said. "Do what I do now, I guess." She thought about it. "In lots of ways, he's already gone."

On the table between them stood a blue bowl filled with lemons. She had polished and arranged them herself to look like something in a painting. She picked one up and turned it in her hands. It was one of the odd-shaped mutations, normal on one end but split at the other, so that it appeared to have a beak. "Have you ever made lemon marmalade?" she asked.

Ida said she never had. "Want to try?"

"Maybe sometime," she said. She turned her head toward the sound of someone hammering out of doors, probably Clare. He'd promised Neva he would try to replicate their old tree house—she supposed he was pounding footholds into the side of a eucalyptus tree. She said, "There was a schoolteacher who lived with us who craved some special kind of lemon marmalade."

"This would be the famous Miss McKenna that Neva is always talking about?"

"*Infamous* is more the word."

Ida's Geiger counter was as good as ever. "Do tell," she said.

And so she did, up to a point. She mentioned the girl being fired for impropriety, the girl burning the school district's coal on Saturdays so she could sit in the schoolhouse reading novels, warm and snug, and she mentioned Ansel's having to rescue her one Saturday when a black blizzard came up. Through these descriptions she never called her Aldine; she referred to her only as "the girl."

"So where is the girl now?" Ida asked.

"Harvey House. In Emporia, our old haunt."

Ida was staring into her as if trying to figure Ellie out. It reminded her of how Ansel looked when he was staring at a tractor engine that wasn't running right, and he didn't know quite why.

"Gil is still there," Ellie added. "He gave her the job."

"Gil's got a full-time lady friend now," Ida said, "so he might leave her alone."

Ida nodded and waited for more, but Ellie changed the subject. "The other day I was trying to look through the windows of that old hotel on Main Street. It looked like there was a restaurant there a long time ago."

"More than one," Ida said. "First one went great guns for a while and then the highway route changed and times got bad and it kept changing owners and getting worse and worse. You know who owns it now? James McNamara, believe it or not." She laughed. "That man didn't get rich by sleepwalking, I'll tell you that. He bought it just by paying off the taxes on it, at least that's what I heard."

In Ellie's opinion, the El Real Hotel was the only building besides the high school that was even half as pretty as a Harvey House. It was brick, for one thing, a pale pink shade, and stucco roses and swoops decorated the curved roofline. The windows were leaded glass orna-mented along the sides with Spanish-style wrought-iron curlicues. She asked what Mr. McNamara was going to do with it now.

"We'll find out, won't we? If anybody asks, that's just what he says. He told Hurd that the bricks, flooring, and fixtures were worth more than he paid for it, so he'd knock it down for salvage if it came to that."

"It's a beautiful building," Ellie said, and she meant it. Something had begun unfolding inside of her when she heard who owned it. Not an idea exactly. More the kind of climate in which an idea might grow. "You don't think he'd really knock it down, do you?"

"Oh, he might. He'll do what it will make him money to do."

Ellie set the lemon back in the bowl and fell silent.

"Ellie?" Ida said. Her expression was playful and coaxing. "You've got that scheming look . . . What are you thinking?"

She looked at Ida. "I don't even know," she said. Which was true. It was just a feeling, and a vague one at that. But she knew one thing. She needed money.

"Do you think there'd be any work for me at the packinghouse?" she asked.

"Oh, sweetie, that's awful work. I did it years ago when I was still full of vim and vigor, and I could barely handle it then."

"But can you ask?" she said. "Just to see?"

57

A Thursday, the workday done. Four days down, two to go. Ansel took them week by week. He and Clare were riding in the back of the flatbed truck with three other men, all of them tired and quiet. Clare whistled something that did not sound quite like a tune. The other three pickers were men up from Mexico. They sat with their legs stretched out before them and two of them slept. Up front, in the cab, the crew chief, Oscar de la Cueva, drove slowly with his right arm extended along the back of the seat, gazing left and right to appraise the conditions of the passing groves. Even without fruit hanging, Ansel could recognize all the trees now: Mexican and Bearss limes, Mexicola, Fuerte, and Zutano avocados, pummelos, Fuyu and Hachiya persimmons, Marsh grapefruit, papayas, strawberry and lemon guavas, macadamias, blood oranges, pomegranates, olives, almonds, satsuma mandarins—everything under the sun, was the way he thought of it. "God's own garden," Ellie called it, but what she really meant was, "God's garden compared to Kansas."

When Oscar de la Cueva stopped the truck at the end of the lane leading to Ida and Hurd's place, Clare in one swift set of motions braced his arm to the side rail and vaulted to the ground. Ansel stepped stiffly onto the tailgate and eased himself down. Clare waved to the crew chief and yelled thanks, but Ansel didn't bother. Of the three remaining men in the back of the truck, the two that slept seemed to keep sleeping. The third stared forward without speaking. Clare had already started up the lane toward the house.

Ansel began to walk off the stiffness in his legs. Clare stopped to throw a couple of stones at trees—his way, Ansel knew, of letting him catch up.

"Did better today, didn't we?" Clare said as he approached.

Ansel nodded. He felt the cough coming on, held his breath waiting for it to subside.

"I mean, not good exactly, but better."

"That's right," Ansel said. He was able to breathe now. "We did better." The boy was indomitable. They were picking the last of the navels, going grove to grove, hauling ladders tree to tree, pulling down the fruit one by one until the canvas bag slung over your shoulder seemed to pancake the plates in your spine, and then you picked a dozen more for good measure before humping the fruit down to the bin that was yours and Clare's, and stood barely more than half as full as any other pair of pickers. That was just how it was. It was tree-climbing work, and they'd never worked in trees, but Clare wasn't giving up. He would barely set his ladder before racing up, reaching far out to one side, then another.

"You ought to be more careful," Ansel said one day while they sat at the edge of a grove eating their sandwiches and drinking their coffee.

Clare said, "Well, we get paid by the box."

Ansel gave him that. "But you go and kill yourself and your mother will be disappointed in us both." He was going for humor, but he meant it, too.

"I just do it the way they do," Clare said, and glanced toward the other men. They squatted now, eating tamales they'd warmed over coals.

The Mexicans brought little rugs to spread in the shade of a tree for a nap after lunch. Ansel missed the occasion that Kansans had always made of a dinner. He encouraged Clare to bring a cloth for a nap, but Clare always wanted to get back to picking. Ansel didn't mind the picking—he liked the look and the feel of the fruit in his hand—but the pace of it, the insistence on quickness, deprived him of the time to think and daydream that tractor work afforded. And he found now that having time to think and dream was as vital to him as food or water, though—and he knew this as a regrettable truth—any space he had now for thinking and dreaming always got filled up with Aldine, which shamed him. So they went back to picking even while the men from Mexico took their siestas, but it didn't matter—he and Clare always picked less, and he had the feeling that the Mexicans resented the fact that he and Clare were picking these trees alongside them instead of their brothers and cousins. He didn't blame them. They knew what he knew: that without Hurd's help they wouldn't have the work.

As they walked up the lane toward Ida and Hurd's house, a car from the opposite direction wheeled into view, a black Packard he recognized at once as McNamara's, except Charlotte was sitting beside him, her head thrown back in laughter.

Ansel turned slightly so as to speak to McNamara when he slowed, but he didn't slow. The black Packard kept speed and passed by.

They watched them go. Charlotte glanced back from the Packard's front seat.

"I don't think he saw us," Clare said. When his father remained grimly silent, he added, "I don't think Mr. McNamara recognized us."

When they got to the house, Ansel didn't go inside. "If you see your mother, could you tell her I'm out by the bottle tree?"

He'd found a relic of a chair on the road one day and had brought it home. He sat in it now. The dog came and laid her head on his knee for a second or two before settling at his feet. He'd rolled and smoked one cigarette and started another before he heard footsteps behind him. He didn't turn but when he felt her close by, he said, "I saw Charlotte with that man today. Do you know where they were going?"

"If you mean Mr. McNamara, he's taking her to see the place where she will be the domestic arts teacher." Ansel flicked a glance at her and she said, "Mr. McNamara has offered her a job."

Ansel stared down through the trees. "That's good for her. Still, it makes me worry that we'll be beholden."

She didn't respond for a few moments, and he could feel it, the distance he had put between them and the way she had started, already, to build a wall around herself.

"We already are beholden, in a way. How do you think I got my job?"

He swung his gaze to her. "Through Ida and Hurd."

"Who went to Mr. McNamara."

"I didn't know that."

She seemed to soften a bit. "It's not a bad thing, Ansel. With my money and what Charlotte will soon be making, which is good money, by the way, real good money for a girl her age, and with every little bit you and Clare make we'll soon be able to rent a place of our own."

Ansel said nothing. There was nothing to say. He didn't know if it was worse to hear her say it or to realize she was right. *Every little bit you and Clare make.* He looked off, saying nothing until she went away. He lit another cigarette and drew deeply of the smoke and slowly exhaled. He brought his hand up as if to rub his nose but it wasn't to rub his nose. It was to smell the tobacco on his fingers. That night with Aldine he'd brought her hand to his face and smelled the tobacco on her fingertips and then, in a kind of ecstasy he'd never imagined let alone experienced, he'd sucked the taste of it from her fingers, one after another.

58

Disparaging Ansel was something Glynis never grew tired of. Did he forget he was married? Did *you* forget he was married? What kind of man, and on and on.

"Glynis," Aldine said, "we must agree to speak no further of this. I do not speak to him. I do not write to him. What more is there to do?"

Glynis didn't answer, but made it clear that she wouldn't desist until Aldine's degree of disapproval matched her own. To accomplish that, her tight-lipped expression said, more talking was certainly required.

More than once Aldine had thought about Mrs. Odekirk. She had encountered her on Neosho Street one summer afternoon when the temperature was 104. Mrs. Odekirk, her skeletal frame perched on slender legs like a white heron, had hugged and kissed Aldine so affectionately that Aldine might have been her own daughter. "Let me look at you," she kept saying, the heat pulsing through everything, turning Aldine's black pocketbook into a patent leather stove.

"The Josephsons said you were here!" Mrs. Odekirk said, the lines in her face symmetrical and handsome, like the comb marks in her tightly bound gray hair. "Loam County is all but deserted now. I can't drive anymore, so I sold my car, and I've come to live in my mother's old house here in Emporia." One hardened hand curled into itself with arthritis. With the other hand, she touched a handkerchief now and then to her narrow, bony nose.

Aldine smiled and moved farther into the shade of the bank building.

"A doctor rents the front house so I live in the back cottage. Convenient really for someone of my age. Oh, please come and visit me, Aldine. Better yet, take one of my rooms. Keep me company."

But she didn't go visit Mrs. Odekirk, or stay with her, because when her circumstances could no longer be hidden, she couldn't bear the look that would come into Mrs. Odekirk's eyes. So she said to Glynis, "It was wrong of course, and who could deny it? But it's a wrong that's made only if two make it, so enough about him."

And it was enough about him, but only for the night.

The days passed and within her stockings her legs swelled and then one day a letter came from poor sweet Clarence and it ended with, *I guess you always had your heart set on my dad*, and as she stood in the post office reading these words, she felt suddenly as if all her clothes and disguises had been stripped away, and there was nothing left of her, nothing at all, not even her secrets.

Clarence knew? How could Clarence know? And if Clarence knew, who in all the world didn't?

But then as she was serving luncheon she thought—and this, she would tell herself later, was how dauntless hope could be—well, probably Clarence had indistinctly sensed his father's distant attention to her, as a spurned admirer will sense such things. Sensed and then, in his letter, guessed. And walking home that evening while Glynis chattered about lousy tippers and Clark Gable and Jean Harlow, she thought, *Yes, it surely had to be that, a guess, and nothing more.*

59

In good weather some of the Harvey Girls enjoyed going to the park by the Cottonwood River, or seeking the cool of the Carnegie library's basement reading room on Sixth Street, or playing ball on Mrs. Gore's teams, but as far as Aldine was concerned, there were just two things to look forward to, and going to the movies at the Granada was one of them. She loved the darkness and hush and smoky haze of the movie house, and she loved settling into the lives of the people on the screen. She liked love stories (she'd seen *Today We Live* twice) and some crime pictures, but she didn't like cowboy movies. She'd gone to *The Rustler's Roundup* just to see why Clarence worshipped Tom Mix, but had come home befuddled. The cowboy star was old and squeaky-voiced and stiff as plaster; that was her judgment, anyway. The pictures changed in the middle of the week, but Aldine learned to wait until Friday, when the blond-haired boy named Harry was in the booth. He and one of his friends would come once a week to the Harvey House for coconut cake and he would always sit at one of her tables. One day, when his friend was in the bathroom, he'd introduced himself and asked her if she liked the movies and she laughed and said that was a funny question wasn't it, because who didn't? He said he worked at the Granada every night but Wednesday and Thursday, and he gave a discount to adorable waitresses, and Aldine, who couldn't deny his spunk, said, well, when she next saw an adorable waitress, she'd pass on the news, and he said he thought the only adorable waitress he'd seen had already gotten the news, meaning her. That Friday she ventured to the Granada and found him sitting illuminated in the glass booth. He grinned at her, gave her a ticket without taking her money, and that was the way it was whenever she went to the Granada ever after. It was no sin, not by her accounts. She was saving her money, so why wouldn't she wait a day or two until a friendly face was in the booth? And when Harry and one of his friends sat at one of her tables, she always gave them a lovely piece of cake, and a pretty smile besides, but she had to charge them full price all the same. If she didn't, Mrs. Gore would sack her in a second, and she needed the job.

One night she took Glynis along to the pictures on a Friday, and Harry smiled at Aldine, ignored their coins on the counter, and spooled out two tickets to pass to Aldine. Then, pushing their coins back toward them, he said, "Don't forget your change," and Glynis was such a little fool she went inside saying right out loud, "Wait a darned second, we didn't even pay!" Aldine shushed her, and the Shirley Temple short wasn't even over before Glynis got up and left. "I paid the boy and now I can watch in peace," she hissed into Aldine's ear when she got back, so that was it, she didn't go to the pictures with Glynis again.

Aldine was saving her money but for what, she didn't know exactly. She didn't want to go back to living with Leenie, not like this, and she surely didn't want to go all the way back to Bellevue Crescent. What would she say to Aunt Sedge? *You were right. I shouldn't have gone away.* She didn't feel ill, at least, not in any boaky kind of way, and she hadn't begun to fatten and waddle, thank the good sweet Lord, but the day was coming, and then she'd be out of a job and would need all of her savings and more besides to tide her over.

The second thing Aldine looked forward to were her visits to the post office, and the guilty thrill she felt when the postman returned from the General Delivery bin with an envelope in his hand. She stopped by the post office every day and she always went alone. She told Glynis it was to see if anything had come from her sister, but that was only a sliver of the truth. Ansel had sent three letters and each one not only made fresh her feelings for him, but drove her further into her dreams of a world in which there was no Ellie, no guilt, just a far-off place she thought of as their Japan. When one of his letters came, she touched it there in her pocket as she worked, and back at the house she took it to the bog where she could read it again and again behind a locked door.

> *If I had not kissed you or declared how I felt.*
> *It is terrible and wonderful the vividness of your face in my*
> *mind.*
> *Please write back and tell me . . .*

But she could not write back. She could have written mad, hot-house letters to the man who lived in her imagination, but she could not write back to Ellie's husband. That did not, however, mean that she could be kept from reading and rereading his letters, touching her finger to the paper he had held, letting her finger follow the beautiful loops of the cursive he had written.

The darkness of the movies, the romantic figures on the screen, the pleasant haze of cigarette smoke. And the thrill when the postman returned from the General Delivery bin with an envelope in his hand. That was all there was to get her through the days.

The days passed. *Scarface, As You Desire Me, Tarzan the Ape Man.* She learned that sucking on ginger candy helped a little bit with the morning sickness, and she didn't know what to do at all about the bulging veins in her legs and feet, and thanked her lucky stars for dark stockings. *Grand Hotel, Horse Feathers, Shanghai Express.* There were no letters for her in General Delivery until one day the postmaster handed her an envelope addressed in a childish cursive that could belong to no one in the world except Neva.

Dear Miss McKenna, it began.

> *It is ever so much warmer here and there is no dust blowing only fruits of all kinds which Clare and Dad pick from the trees every day. Mama works in the packinghouse with Aunt Ida and Uncle Hurd. Charlotte is going to be a teacher now, she will teach sewing and cooking which Clare says is a laugh and a half because Charlotte hates to cook. I miss you so much. I'm going to go to a big school but I just know there won't be paper planes to go to the next knot if you get 100. I wish we could come back but I have stopped coughing and Mama says I will start again if I go back. Dad has another story. He says he has borrowed my cough and likes it so much he's not going to give it back. Mom likes it here best of all. Dad does not like it one bit. Everyone can tell how bad he misses Kansas. That's the one bad part, that and the fact you and Krazy Kat aren't here. Okay. I love you, Miss McKenna, and I hope God is watching you and Krazy Kat.*
>
> *Your friend, Neva*

Every repetition of the word *Mama* was like a sharp cut in her stomach, and she read it over and over again to inflict the pain on herself so she would stop longing for what would hurt Neva so much.

60

One night after the dishes were done, and Ansel was off somewhere smoking and brooding about the girl—or so she supposed—Ellie walked out to find Hurd in his shop. He wore leather work gloves and was setting long pieces of rusty metal out on the ground, then staring down at them, rearranging, staring again. His orange hair was flat with sweat.

When he saw Ellie, he nodded toward the metal and said, "What do you think?"

She studied the splayed metal on the ground. She had no idea what she thought.

"What does it look like to you?" he asked and when she didn't answer, he said, "Doesn't it look just like a stork?"

"It does a little," she offered, "now that you mention it." She smiled. "It reminds me of Mrs. Odekirk back in Kansas, and she looked like a stork."

Hurd laughed, prized a slender piece of metal from beneath a nearby pile, regarded it for a moment, then used it to replace what she now saw was meant to be the bird's bill. "What do you think?" he asked and Ellie said she had to admit, that made it look more like a stork.

Hurd went over to his glass of iced tea and held it toward Ellie. "Want a snort?"

She declined, and he took a big gulp, wiped his mouth on his blue sleeve, and waited. He knew Ellie wasn't the type to idly watch him assemble his trifles.

"I was wondering, Hurd," she said carefully. "I'm grateful as anything just to have work, you know that, but if there were any extra hours, it would mean a lot to me."

"More hours?" Hurd said.

"I'm saving up. Well, *we* are. Toward our own place."

"Well, I don't know, Ellie. That'd just mean you'd leave us faster," he said, but she knew that was just so much talk.

"You and Ida have been beyond kind, Hurd, but we can't stay forever. And the sooner we have our own place, the sooner Ansel will stop thinking about Kansas."

Hurd's expression and emotions usually rode genially along on the surface of things, but his round freckled face softened and when he spoke his voice was low. "I don't think you'll ever take Kansas out of that man, Ellie. It'd be like removing his veins."

She said nothing, and in the next moment Hurd was himself again. "I'll do a little checking," he said, "but no promises."

"Thanks, Hurd," she said, and that was just one more reason she wanted a place of her own, so she could finally stop saying thank you all the time. She walked through piles of scavenged metal toward the other end of a former olive-pickling barn, where Hurd, with encouragement—and, she suspected, financial backing—from Mr. McNamara had turned a storage bin into a darkroom for Charlotte, and on her way out, Ellie poked her head into it. It was dark as a coal hole until she found the cord to an amber light and plugged it in. A series of photographs hung clothespinned to an overhead line, images of the ocean and a fishing pier and some houses, all looking golden in the room's amber light. There was a price tag showing on one of the jars of chemicals and Ellie went over to look at it. Thirty-five cents. Mr. McNamara bought her the paper and supplies but Ellie had no idea they were that expensive. Thirty-five cents a bottle times how many bottles? She began pulling them out to count them, and when she pulled the seventh one out, a piece of wood behind it fell forward, and revealed a small cubbyhole. Ellie peered into the darkness and tried to tell herself that it wasn't a cubbyhole at all, but the only way to disprove the notion was to reach in, which she did with unease. Almost at once she touched something papery. What she pulled forward was a large brown envelope. She unclasped it and tilted it forward, and a sheaf of heavy papers slid out facedown. Ellie turned them over. They were photographs of a woman. That was her first thought—*photographs of a woman*—and she would remember it because until this moment Ellie had never before thought of her daughter as a woman. But she looked like a woman in the photographs, a woman sitting on a rock by a stream with her back to the photographer and wearing almost nothing whatsoever.

Her first thought was to leave these photographs where they lay, so Charlotte would find them and wonder who had seen them, but what if Hurd found them first—what would Hurd and Ida and who knew who else think of their family then? So she squared the photographs and slid them back into the hiding place, secured by the piece of wood and the weight of the chemical jars in front of it.

A full day passed before Ellie found a chance to speak privately with Charlotte, and by then her thoughts were more measured. It was dusk and they were walking a dirt lane that split the lemon grove. Artemis ambled along just behind. Mr. McNamara had taken Charlotte for a drive that afternoon, south on Highway 395 to a little town called Escondido that Charlotte said was full of orange trees and fruit stands. Her tone was flat and matter-of-fact.

"Did you have a good time?"

"Mmm."

A few seconds passed before Ellie said, "Do you have feelings for Mr. McNamara?"

Charlotte hitched her chin just a little. "What kind of feelings?"

"Romantic, I guess." This was difficult. More than difficult really.

"I don't know about romantic," Charlotte said. "Romantic might be taking it too far."

"Are you friendly to him?"

Charlotte looked at her as if trying to parse her meaning. "I'm not overly anything—friendly or unfriendly," she said. "I like going places, he likes taking me places, but, Mom, he's a grown man."

"Exactly," she said. "Are his intentions honorable?"

Charlotte gave a hearty laugh. "Oh, God, Mom. He asks me to marry him practically every Sunday."

This was more than a surprise. "And what do you tell him?"

"I don't tell him anything. I don't say yes and I don't say no."

"And what does he say to that?"

Just below the surface of Charlotte's face brimmed something looking very much like pride. "He says he'll just go on asking every Sunday until I say yes."

They walked on a bit before Charlotte, sensing something, drew up and looked behind. Perhaps thirty yards back, Artemis sat staring at them, looking abashed, but not taking another step.

"Tired," Charlotte said.

"We'll have to put her down soon," Ellie said. She watched as Charlotte returned to the dog and led her to a shady spot under a lemon tree. She and Ansel. He was always putting off shooting a dog, too.

"We'll come back this way, girly-girl," Charlotte was saying to the dog. "You can go home with us then."

Artemis looked at her and, without otherwise moving, let her tail thump the earth.

Ellie said nothing as they walked on. She already had more to chew on than she could readily process. But after a time it was Charlotte who said softly, "What would you do? About Mr. McNamara, I mean." And in that tender voice Ellie heard the Charlotte that she had once been, the girl who still wanted guidance from her mother.

Ellie wasn't sure how to say what she wanted to say, which was that a certain amount of pragmatism in such matters was no sin, so finally in a small, tired voice she said, "Well, Lottie, I would marry the man who can provide what will make you happy."

Charlotte waited and then asked, not in a challenging voice, but with a slight tremor, "Is that what you did?"

Ellie reached down and picked up a stone that she pretended to study. She had thought so, and she had been wrong, but she couldn't say that. What good would it do? Mr. McNamara was nothing like Ansel; Charlotte was not Ellie. "I trust you," Ellie said decisively, pretending that was an answer to the question and trusting that Charlotte didn't really want to know. "You know what will make you happy, and you'll find it for yourself, with or without Mr. McNamara."

61

Clare had built the tree house for Neva but she hardly ever used it. It wasn't really a tree house, anyway. It was just a series of wooden cleats leading up to a planked platform, but it was a shady place to sit in the evening or on Sunday and no one ever came there. Clare could sit high up on the platform, lean against the smooth trunk of the eucalyptus, stretch out his legs, and read one of his Zane Greys. Once a hawk had glided into the eucalyptus and alighted not ten feet away, sitting there hunch shouldered and watchful before swooping away with a keen beating of wings. Clare had watched any number of creatures pass beneath the tree house—roadrunners, rabbits, coyotes, a bobcat—all of them unaware of his eyes upon them from above. Sometimes he would make his hand into the shape of a gun, aim with his index finger and, bringing his thumb down, whisper, *Ka-blam.* Just that little whisper was enough to still a rabbit and cock the head of a coyote. Sometimes Clare would smoke a cigarette stolen from his father's stash. He'd smoked his father's leftovers, too, when they first got here, but his father no longer allowed it. He might have bronchitis, he said, and he didn't want Clare to get it, too.

On this particular day Clare had finished *Tonto Basin*, as he knew he would, so he'd also brought *Riders of the Purple Sage*, which he'd read so many times that he knew the first lines by heart. It was still his favorite and its familiarity was reassuring to him. It made him feel safe. He pinched a leaf from a branch, crushed it with his thumb, and held it close to his nose so he could take in the lemony smell. Silver Shred was what she called it. He wondered how he might buy a jar of Silver Shred. He could ask the librarian, Mrs. Goddard. She was nice to him even if nobody else much was. Living in California and closer to town, he thought he would have friends, but he didn't. He'd never really had them in Kansas. He didn't know how to go about finding them. When he went to town, people either seemed to think he was invisible or, if they did look at him, it was warily, as if he might be some kind of predator. It was true that some of the girls smiled at him but he was too shy to smile back so they soon quit. Only Mr. McNamara ever waved to him on the street and he was almost afraid to wave back, because of who might see him. Once, when they needed extra workers at the packinghouse for a day, Clare had been chosen, and at the noon whistle, he took his lunch bucket out to the tables where he supposed his mother would be, but she wasn't. There were three wood-plank tables set beneath the massive sweet-smelling pepper trees. Two of the tables were packed full of workers, but the only one sitting at the third table was a boy just a little older than himself whose name Clare knew to be Caleb. Clare sat down and nodded across the table at the boy, but he didn't nod back. Clare's mother had told him that as a newcomer in town, if he wanted to find friends, he needed to put his best foot forward, so he persisted with, "You're Caleb, right?" The boy still said nothing. His small eyes were set in a wide, tapering face that put Clare in mind of a possum. He kept staring at Clare with that possum's face, and Clare began having a hard time enjoying his sandwich. Finally the boy said, "Is that Hurd your uncle?" Clare nodded. The boy again said nothing for a time. Then—it was as if so many words and thoughts had collected in his brain that he could no longer keep them there—he said, "Well, McNamara is a scroungy, pitiless son of a bitch and your Uncle Hurd is his stooge, which is just exactly how come you and your family have yourselves all the plum jobs."

Clare felt dazed. It was like he'd been hit hard in the face. All he'd managed to say was, "What do you mean, *his stooge*?"

The boy's face, already drawn pink, drew pinker. "I mean he's the fat orange-haired mick that watches and watches to see if anybody falls down drunk on Saturday or misses church or sneaks in late to work or takes home a couple of punked avocados, and if he does, McNamara knows by Sunday. Because you know what Sunday is?"

Clare said he did not. He was trying to get his bearings.

By now an older woman from the other table had hurried over and put her hand under the boy's arm as if to escort him away. "Shush now, Caleb, just shush now," she said, but the boy would not be shushed. He shook his possum head and spat onto the wooden floor. "He knows by Sunday because besides being the day of the Lord, Sunday is when McNamara goes out to your fat uncle's place and gets all the fat-face gossip." He stood and swung his leg over the bench to leave, but checked himself. "Do you know Olive Teagarten?"

Clare shook his head.

"Well, I do. And McNamara knew she was knocked up almost before she did."

The boy then rose and moved to one of the other tables, where the workers scooched sideways to make room for him while Clare ate alone. He saw the boy at work one more time, and then never again.

From then on, Clare had viewed Hurd's round happy face differently, and Mr. McNamara's, too. He hated seeing that grown man with Charlotte, hated it more than he could say. Why did grown men do that—chase after girls half their age? Clare squeezed his eyes tightly closed. He took a breath and began reciting to himself: "*a sharp clip-clop of iron-shod hooves deadened and died away and clouds of yellow dust drifted from under the cottonwoods out over the purple sage . . .*"

He opened the book to check. He'd gotten everything right but *purple*. The purple came in the next line, when Jane Withersteen gazed down the wide purple slope with dreamy, troubled eyes.

62

Ellie regarded her hands, the skin cracked and the cracks dark with ink. This was the fourth straight day she had stayed late at the packinghouse pasting labels on boxes to earn extra money. It was almost eight o'clock when she punched out and walked alone down the steps from the loading dock. Ida would have kept something covered for her supper, but Ellie had worked her way past hunger. All during her lunch break, sitting away from the others on a crate in the east-wall shade of the packinghouse, she'd stared across the lots at the pink bricks of El Real, so now, instead of walking straight home, she stepped over the railroad tracks and picked her way through the weeds and broken glass of the vacant lots. The fennel weeds were five feet tall and bushy, each one as dry as a broom straw. She snapped off a gray cluster to roll the beads between her fingers and smell the sweet oil it left, a scent that was exactly like licorice. She glanced back at the packinghouse when she reached the El Real, to see if anyone was watching, and then she reached out to the doorknob. It turned, and she let herself in.

The sun was low in the sky and the light was horizontal. The wrought-iron curlicues on the window bars became serpentine shadows on amber walls above a short lunch counter and a stack of cheap wooden chairs. She'd thought more than once of asking Mr. McNamara whether he'd be willing to rent the building, but she wanted to see it for herself first, see if it was the sort of place where you could serve green tomato pie and Spanish cream.

She ran her hand over the varnished wood of the lunch counter. There was dust all right, but she knew how to clean up dust. She studied the dust on a six-burner stove. It was no Harvey House, but even with the dust, the chrome gleamed faintly in the twilight. The floor was a black-and-white checkerboard that would look smart when scoured. Truly, it was all much nicer than she'd imagined. She looked up at the stairs. They were solid and carpeted up the center and looked elegant, really, except for the leathery carcass of a mouse halfway up. She reached the top just as the gold light of the setting sun winked out and left the interior in shades of blue. The first door she opened went into a hotel room furnished with a dusty striped mattress, a pine wardrobe, a nightstand, and scattered black droppings of mice. There were four other rooms more or less the same, and bathrooms at each end of the hallway, so it could be an apartment, she thought, if she cooked the family meals in the café kitchen.

There was the matter of money of course, but June had been a good month at the packinghouse and she'd made three dollars most days, sometimes four. From that she had managed to save twelve dollars now.

She was checking the window latch in the back bedroom when she heard the door open downstairs. A liquid burst of fear shot from her stomach to her head. She stood perfectly still, smelling the crushed fennel on her fingertips, hoping that whoever it was had not seen her open the door and let herself in. She heard shuffling footsteps, then a man's voice.

"As you can see, nothing's been taken out. It's just as it was the last time you looked at it." It was McNamara's voice, his quiet even modulation.

"What's changed is the times," another voice said, a man's, as if calling across the room. His voice was gruff and unfamiliar. "Nothing's what they were. Including rents."

Mr. McNamara responded in a voice too low to be heard from this distance.

Ellie folded her arms across her stomach and shifted her weight to her left foot. She should never have sneaked into the building like this. She could hide out upstairs and hope they didn't find her, but if they did, it would be the worst kind of humiliation. She took a deep breath and stepped forward to the head of the stairs.

"Hello? Is that you, Mr. McNamara?" she called down, trying to make her voice sound breezy. "I heard you were renting this place and I stopped by on my way home."

The restaurant below was lit, and as she descended, Mr. McNamara stepped to the foot of the stairs and looked up with frank curiosity. She hoped her hair wasn't frazzled.

"Well, well," he said, but his tone was not unfriendly.

A stranger—cowboy boots, rodeo-style neck scarf, hat in hand—appeared behind him. As she made her way down with one hand on the rail, she felt vaguely as if she were making an entrance.

When they were all standing in the empty restaurant, she said, "I'd heard that you owned it and didn't know what to do with it, and"—she glanced at the other man, who stared back without smiling—"I've always had the idea of running a café."

Mr. McNamara was leaning forward slightly, smiling and nodding. "What kind of café?"

She glanced down and, seeing her chapped hands, held them behind her. "Breakfast and lunch," she said. "Hearty foods and specialty dishes and desserts."

Mr. McNamara was nodding thoughtfully. "And maybe hamburgers and malts for the high school crowd in the afternoon."

It was quiet and the overhead chandeliers, only one of which was working, made the room seem golden. She'd almost forgotten the man in the rodeo scarf until he said, "All right, then. I'll take it."

Mr. McNamara turned to him. "Well, that's just fine, Mr. Schutt." He smiled through the briefest pause. "And you'll be taking the hotel, too? Because I imagine that if Mrs. Price were to open her café she would be interested in using the hotel as apartments for her family, with maybe even a boarder or two, just to supplement."

The other man's expression sharpened. "You never said anything before about having to take the rooms, too."

"I know that, Mr. Schutt," Mr. McNamara said. His voice went beyond patience; it was condolence itself. "But you can see what an advantage renting the whole building would be for all concerned."

The man took this in, then said, "I wouldn't say for *all* concerned," and, slapping on his hat, he walked out of the building.

It was quiet again. "I'm terribly sorry," Ellie said.

"For what? This is all just splendid. The town needs a good café. In fact, it is just *exactly* what this town needs."

"But . . . ," Ellie said, and let her eyes drift toward the door the man had just walked out of.

"Oh, don't worry about Mr. Schutt. He's been looking at the place for the last year and a half and all he ever wants to do is knock me down on the rent."

Ellie chuckled at this for the sake of politeness; then she took a breath and said, "Well, about that rent . . . what exactly were you thinking?"

Mr. McNamara scanned the disused restaurant, as if considering its possibilities. He was wearing his slim gray suit, and, to Ellie's eye, his smooth brown head was somehow distinguished-looking, as if to grow hair was to let yourself go. "Well," he said finally, "you're going to need some seed money, for supplies and machinery and so forth, so my suggestion is this. I'll put up the money and provide the building and, once you start turning a profit, I'll take twenty percent until you pay me back, and ten percent thereafter." His smile stretched wide. "How does that sound to you?"

"The percentage . . . that would be in addition to the rent?"

"No, I mean instead of the rent," he said. His expression was warm and genial, as if presenting her with this gift gave him as much pleasure as he knew it would give her, and just like that, Ellie felt lighter than air, as if she might float away.

A café. Her own café. She already had a name for it. She wouldn't say it out loud, not yet, but she had it. *The Sleeping Indian.*

It grew dark as Mr. McNamara drove her back to Ida and Hurd's. The whole way they talked about Charlotte.

63

Already Oscar de la Cueva had dropped the rest of the pickers at another grove, but he'd told Clare and his father to stay on the truck and then driven slowly to this place at the end of a long dirt lane, a small grove of Valencias bounded on each side by a windbreak of shaggy eucalyptus. He and his father rolled a single bin off the truck and stood staring at the trees.

"Thanks for the favor, Oscar," Clare said. He gave it the sound of a jest but it wasn't really a jest. The trees in this grove were too closely spaced. That forced the limbs upward in their search for sun and light. Tall trees meant sparse fruit and slow picking.

Oscar de la Cueva ignored the remark. He said to Clare, "They tell me to tell you that tomorrow you go to packing."

Clare wasn't sure what he'd heard. "Packing?" he said. "Or picking?"

"*Pack*ing," Oscar de la Cueva said.

"Just for a day or two? Like before?"

"No. You stay in packing." He squinted at Clare. "Just you." He glanced at Clare's father. "Not papa."

Working in the packinghouse was what all the pickers wanted. The pay was better but the best part was, you could work even when it rained. Probably this was why Oscar de la Cueva waited until the other men weren't there. He didn't want them there when he announced that one of the worst pickers had been promoted. Clare looked at his father, who was pretending still to appraise the trees they'd be picking.

"No," Clare said suddenly. "We're together. My dad and me. We're a team."

Oscar de la Cueva's eyes slowly closed and when after a long moment they opened again, they were on Clare. "Tomorrow you go to packing," he said in a low, even voice. "Only you." He gazed away again. "And today you and papa pick this grove. These are my trees. You pick my fruit and you see what you see."

He drove away without another word. Clare and his father shouldered their bags and their ladders and began picking their way into the grove. It was bad work. Even the lower branches were hard to pick because one tree grew into the next. The upper branches were all but impossible to reach, but Clare tried. He didn't want Oscar de la Cueva pointing to unpicked fruit. Twice when Clare stretched out from the top of the ladder, he looked down to see his father with his foot planted at the ladder's base and his hands on its rails so it wouldn't slip.

"We'll never finish this grove if you hold my ladder all day," he said and his father nodded and said, "We'll never finish this grove if you break your neck."

When they sat down to eat lunch at noon, the heat lay like a membrane and held everything still. Clare felt like he'd already worked a full day. The sweet juice from the oranges bit into the cracks and scratches of his hands and smelled like boiled punch. His boots were stained and wet with the juice and his hair was brittle with the broken webs of orb spiders. His father unwrapped his sandwich and said that it was good he was going to the packinghouse. "You'll make more, you'll have shade and cover, and there won't be any ladders for you to fall off of."

"But I like being outside. That's what I've always done, Kansas or here, worked outside with you."

His father cleared his throat, turned away, and spat phlegm. Then he said, "We're here now. It's like your mother says, we've got to make adjustments. Besides, school will start soon. You should be in school."

Clare started to say more but his father raised a hand to cut him off, so that was that. As he gazed down through the trees the air seemed to shimmer with heat. The ham-and-butter sandwich he was eating tasted limp and salty, like it had been steamed, and a swallowtail butterfly seemed almost to stagger through the air. He unwrapped his second sandwich, but had no appetite for it. The butterfly landed on a thin, pliant bough and opened and closed its wings and suddenly Clare was thinking of the yellow meadowlarks that used to sit on the fence posts on the farm and sing with their black beaks wide open. He used to be able to whistle their squeaky, flutey, watery song, and that's what he'd done to amuse Neva before Aldine came. He put his lips into a tight O and sucked in his breath. When he finished the ripple of notes, his father was staring at him, looking like his own ghost, and then he smiled a little. "I miss that," he said.

Clare wrapped his sandwich back into its wax paper and went back to work. His arms were protected but you couldn't pick with gloves on. There was nothing for it but to search out the next orange even while grabbing the one at hand, a process repeated again and again and again. He heard the rattle of his father's ladder as he reset it against a nearby tree, but he wasn't coughing. That was the good thing. It was hard to work or think or anything when he was coughing. The packinghouse would be better, sure it would, but it was hard to think of his father out here alone. He was like the monkeys on Monkey Island at the zoo in Independence, marooned by a moat and a fence, always looking out like they remembered where they used to be. He'd often heard his father talking to Hurd about wheat prices and rain, and then, no matter what Hurd said, his father would nod and conclude that things were about to come round again in Kansas. His mother said nothing even if she was within earshot of such talk. Charlotte couldn't hold her tongue, though. She would always say she wouldn't go back for all the tea in China except maybe to visit in her dotage and late dotage at that, and his father would light another cigarette and look out over the moat nobody else could see.

"I'd go with you," Clare said on one such occasion and his father had glanced at him with soft eyes.

Clare trudged to the bin, drained his bagged oranges into it, and headed back up the row. He had just begun to set his ladder at the next tree when he smelled something wonderful in the air. Corn roasting, he decided. A Kansas smell. He left the ladder and followed the smell. He heard footsteps behind him—his father was coming, too. Just beyond the windbreak of eucalyptus, a line of smoke rose and curled. In the shadows a rough hut had been assembled from discarded wood and tin, and a girl sat tending the fire with a baby in her arms. She wore a blanket over her shoulders in spite of the heat. The smoke and the crackling of the fire must have masked Clare's approach, but when a long piece of tree bark snapped underfoot, the girl's head jerked around, and for one fleeting instant he thought that this was an animal wrapped in a shawl; that's how alarmed and darting and feral her eyes were.

She stood to face them. The end of the long stick she held in her hand was blackened and smoking slightly. In her other arm, she held the wrapped baby. "Who're you?" she hissed. Whatever his advantages in size and strength might be, they were lost to her ferocity.

Clare nodded toward his father and the orange trees behind them. "We're picking the grove, ma'am, is all. Me and my dad. And I just smelled the good smell from your fire." He smiled in hopes of disarming the girl, but her expression was unchanged.

"What's your name?" she demanded.

"Clare Price," he said and thought some kind of recognition flickered in her eyes.

"And that's your father there with you?"

"Yes, ma'am."

She seemed to be making some kind of calculation.

Clare said, "I've got an extra ham-and-butter sandwich if you like that kind."

The girl ignored the question. She kept the baby in one arm and the smoking stick in the other hand and then, as if having made some kind of decision, she stepped toward him in a way that made him want to move back. He didn't, though. He stood fast.

"You want to hold my baby?" she said.

He did not want to hold her baby, but he thought it would be impolite to decline. "I'm not sure I know how," he said.

"It's easy," she said. "You can't hurt him." She tossed the smoking, charred stick back toward the fire and taking another step forward, she presented the baby.

It was swaddled in a dirty blanket and he could not bring himself to take it, but he didn't have to. His father abruptly stepped forward. "I've held a few infants," he said, and then, taking the baby and peeling away the blanket, he said, "What is its name?"

"It's Caleb," the girl said, watching his father's face. The girl's eyes were bright. "Caleb Junior," she added. "After his father."

Only later would Clare make sense of her words. At the moment he barely heard them. He was staring in shock at the baby in his father's arms. It was wooden and bluish and unmoving. When he then looked up at the stricken set of his father's face, he knew he was right, that the baby his father was holding was not alive. His father pushed it back into the girl's hands and, stepping away, almost fell. Then Clare turned and began to run. Not just him. Even his father. Behind them, the girl's calls and laughter did not seem human.

64

Hurd said, when Ansel described the whole horrible encounter in the grove, that the Teagarten girl had given birth to a stillborn baby at home, which could happen to anyone, but the rest of it you could lay at Caleb's door.

They didn't say more about it because there wasn't much else to say, and later Ansel took two sheets of onionskin paper from the desk near the time clock, folded them in threes, and slipped them inside his shirt. He meant to write his old friend Gil to find out about Aldine but as he walked, he thought, too, about one more letter to Aldine.

At the post office counter Ansel asked Bart Crandall for a stamp and envelope.

"Air mail or regular?" Bart Crandall asked in a neutral voice as if it made no difference to him, but it did. One meant *This is routine* and the other meant it was not. But Ansel didn't care.

"Air mail," he said, and took the stamp and envelope to a far counter. He unfolded the onionskin paper—it was spotted slightly with sweat. He took out his pencil but just held it. He could feel Bart Crandall's eyes on him from behind, but he didn't care. He stared out toward the street. The last time he'd composed from a post office, it was in Dorland and he had written the advertisement that Aldine had happened upon in New York City and used to make her escape, and now look what he'd done with her. He, Ansel Price, who had thought himself an honorable man.

For one long tantalizing moment, he thought he might think of what to say to her, but he could not. He addressed the envelope to Gilbert Dorado, of the Harvey House, Emporia, Kansas. Then he wrote:

> *Dear Gil,*
>
> *Just checking on the new girl we brought you. Not much news about Kansas in the California papers. Everything all right there with Miss McKenna? Still got work for everyone? Plenty of avocados growing around here so let me know if Fred Harvey needs a case.*
>
> *Your old amigo, Ansel*

He sealed the envelope, licked the stamp, and rolled the heel of his hand over it to secure it. Then he dropped it through the brass mail slot marked *Air Mail*. Even before he reached the door he heard the scrape of Bart Crandall's stool on the wooden floor, and Ansel didn't have to see it to see it: Bart Crandall going over to the canvas bag that stood open under the air mail slot, stooping over, peering in, taking out the letter to see where it was off to.

65

Charlotte didn't know what to do about marrying Mr. McNamara, so one day when she was alone in the Practice House, she tore out a page from a composition book and drew two columns. At the top of one she wrote, *Plus*; at the top of the other, *Minus*.

In the *Minus* column she wrote, *Leaving everybody*, though truthfully when she thought of leaving her parents and Neva and Clare, it didn't seem so bad, really, and *Closing Other Doors*, by which she meant all the other lives that would never be hers, not if she married Mr. McNamara.

His Christian name was James but she'd never called him that, and he'd never asked her to. So she kept calling him Mr. McNamara until it just seemed normal to turn Mister into a nickname. "I'd like to nibble your ear off," he might say, for example, and she would say, "I happen to need that ear, Mister." Or he might say, "I'd like to undo this particular button right here," and she would say, "Not tonight, Mister." Once when they were at a diner and he needed cheering up, she leaned forward to take his hand and say, "You're my funny, sweet Mister, aren't you?" and he said yes, and that he was glad he was.

In the *Plus* column she wrote *Car* (she loved riding in the Packard and she loved the way people looked at you even when they were trying not to) and *Goddess-ness* (the first time she went riding with him he said he wanted to treat her like a goddess and from then on, he pretty much had) and *House* (he would build her one on a knoll at the top of an avocado grove) and *Job* (because the last thing she wanted to do was stay home cleaning that house) and *Resolution* (because, well, you got married and that would be that).

She knew she'd left out two important things but she didn't know where to put them. Finally she made a new column and wrote *Irrelevant* at the top and below it, in place of *Love and Sex*, she wrote *X & X*.

She laid down her pencil then and looked for a long time at the page and its three columns. She did not mind that she would not be seeing him that night. He had driven to Los Angeles and wouldn't be back until Thursday. She never knew quite what he did on these excursions. It didn't matter whether he was going to Los Angeles or San Francisco or, as he did once, Mesa, Arizona, he merely said that he was going to go "look into something." She liked that he went away like that; it made him mysterious, and it gave her a little breathing room. She took up her pencil and wrote that as a last addition to the *Plus* column: *Breathing Room*.

66

There was a hummingbird that kept mistaking Ida's blue bottles for flowers. Ansel had come to know the hummingbird by the motorized whir of his wings and his sudden precipitous dives. The bird pierced lavender stalks with his hypodermic beak, his throat a flashy crimson, the luminescent green of his back almost reptilian, his aim greedy and precise. He drank and then he whirred away, returning at least once to hover in confusion above a bright, impenetrable vial of blue glass.

Ansel liked being out here, beyond the reach of Ida's voice, and Ellie's, too. He could still hear them talking, but he couldn't make out the words, which was fine by him. Usually Ellie stayed inside once they'd finished the dishes, playing cards or listening to the radio, but tonight he heard the back door squeak and footsteps heading his way.

"I heard you coughing clear from the kitchen," she said.

There was no chair near him, so he stood up and stepped on the stub of his cigarette, waving his hand toward the chair to offer it to her, but she shook her head.

"You've had a long day," she said. "Sit and rest."

"I thought I might sleep outside tonight," he said. "Because of the coughing. I know it wakes you and the kids. Probably Ida and Hurd, too."

"Ida says you ought to go see the doctor."

"It'll pass," he said. "Colds always do." The hummingbird had left when Ellie walked up. Now dozens of crows were flying above the low, dusky hills, calling to one another, gliding down into the tallest of a knot of oaks.

Ansel felt the quick tightening of his chest and then the thickness gathering there like some horrible phlegmy stew bubbling, beginning to boil, and then all at once he was bent over in a convulsion of thick, raking, bilious coughs that finally subsided. Sitting back down in his chair felt like a concession, but there was no getting around it. He inhaled and daubed the tears in his eyes. "See?" he said in a hoarse, broken voice, forcing a smile. "Better to sleep out here until it does."

Ellie looked away from him and snapped off a stalk of lavender and ground the blossom between her fingers to release its aroma. She was always picking plants and shredding them, as if that was the way she figured out what they were. In Emporia, on one of their first walks, she kept leaning down to pick dandelions, running the palm of her hand over the fluff instead of setting it free with her breath.

She said, "I think we should move, Ansel."

He turned to her. "Back?"

She didn't look at him. "No. To town. Mr. McNamara has offered to rent us the hotel on Main Street, and I think we could open the café together, you and I. Everything's there already—the equipment, the tables, the pots and pans. We can start over, in our own place, and it'll be like the Harvey House."

It would never be like that for him, and that wasn't the time he wanted to go back to, anyway.

"Ansel?"

"I can't, Ellie. I came out here for Neva, but this place isn't ours. It isn't mine, anyway. It'll never be home." Her face stiffened even before he finished.

"I've signed a lease," she said.

"What kind of a lease?"

"I've rented the whole thing—the restaurant, the rooms upstairs, everything."

"With what?"

"I've been saving," she said.

He understood. He was sure he understood. "And writing to your father."

But she said evenly, "My father has no hand in it, Ansel. Mr. McNamara is putting up the seed money and he's given us terms that are more than fair."

"Why would he do that?"

"He thinks we're the kind of family that can make the town better," she said. "And he thinks the town needs a café."

To this Ansel gave his head a bitter shake and she said, "He speaks well of you, you know. How you're willing to go out with the picking crews at your age to help your family." She paused and then seemed to have some trouble saying the next part. "He calls you a good example."

Ansel didn't know what the saddest moment in his marriage was, but that might have been it.

"I'm sorry, El," he said.

It was quiet and he listened to the sounds of the oncoming night. The crickets were starting. The coyotes would be out soon, working together, screaming in chorus as they converged on a rabbit or cat. He took a breath and didn't feel the catch of a cough. He could say more if he knew what to say and how to say it, but he didn't, so he turned and started for the tree house, where he thought there might be a blanket.

"Good night, Ansel," she said after him, and without slowing or turning around he said, "Good night, Ellie."

67

Neva didn't really like polishing and cleaning, but she liked the busyness of it all, her mother telling Charlotte and Clare what to do, and the trash going out into the alley and new things coming in the front door. She'd helped with the cleaning, but she'd gotten tired of it and pretended to be wheezy from it so she sat in front of the hotel on a little stool with Milly Mandy Molly and read a book, and if anyone walked by, she gave them one of the little cards that Mr. McNamara had made up. She loved the little cards. They said, *Sleeping Indian Café* at the top, and then:

Home-Style Food

Breakfast, Lunch, and Supper Specials

Ellie & Ansel Price, Proprietors

When people asked when they would be open, Neva had been instructed to say, "Soon! Keep watching for progress!"

More than once she'd heard herself compared to Shirley Temple.

Sometimes if she got tired of handing out cards, she'd go inside and climb the stairs and look out the window of the room that was going to be hers and Charlotte's. It wasn't the best room—Clare's was the best, because it was right by the outside stairs and you could see the Sleeping Indian from one of his windows—but her and Charlotte's room had a mirror on the closet door that was as tall as Charlotte. When they first saw the rooms, they were full of trash and things like dirty cups and empty bottles and soiled rags that made you think it was where the Murderous Hordes had stayed when they were passing through. But today her mother and father and Ida and Hurd and Clare and Charlotte and even Mr. McNamara came with barrels and shovels and brooms and cleaned everything out. Her father worked all morning and into the afternoon, but his coughing got worse and her mother made him go home. Mr. McNamara had perfect round beads of sweat popping up all over his bald head no matter how often he wiped it with his handkerchief but he and Clare were doing the hardest work and she was surprised how Mr. McNamara was always smiling and winking all day long, even after his shirt was wet and dirty and one side of it hanging out of his pants. "That was fun," he announced at the end of the day when all the rooms were finally spic-and-span, and then winking at Uncle Hurd, he said, "We menfolk may have to go quench our thirst," and off they went. Clare took Neva and went back to see if his father was feeling better. He was. He started to walk back to town to keep helping but they told him it was all done now.

From the window of her and Charlotte's room, you could see Main Street down below and a line of fat palm trees across the street. The window faced east. Her father told her that. "Know how I know?" he'd said with fun in his voice, so she said, "No. How?" And he said, "Well, if I squint and look out that particular window, I can see Kansas."

That was a funny idea so she'd asked what exactly he could see in Kansas and he said, "Everything," so she asked if he could see Dorland and their house and their barn and Krazy Kat sleeping in the hayloft and he said yes to every one.

68

One afternoon after the westbound for Albuquerque had pulled from the station and the coffee urn had been cleaned and polished and the tablecloths were all smoothed and set for the next incoming train, Glynis approached from across the vast room. Aldine, refilling salt and pepper cellars, saw her coming and noticed at once the stiffness of her face. She was afraid someone in her family had died or fallen gravely ill, so she set everything down and met her in the middle of the room with the idea of offering consolation.

"What's happened then, Glynny?" she said.

"I don't know." Truly, she was on the verge of tears. "It's Mrs. Gore. She thinks you're pregnant, but I told her you weren't." Her glistening eyes fell on Aldine's. "You're not, are you?"

Aldine took a quick breath, composing a lie, but she couldn't do it. She let her eyes fall.

For a few moments there was nothing but the sound of the clinking and tinkling of the other waitresses going about their work. Then Glynis said, "Well, she says she wants to see you."

69

School, as Clare experienced it in Fallbrook, was nothing like school in Kansas. The high school was a big handsome building the color of sand, a line of palm trees in front of it, straight and stately and foreign. There was, to begin with, the strangeness of seeing his sister coming out of the faculty room or the Practice House as a teacher while he was still a student. Queen of the Practice House, he'd heard someone call her, and The Big Cheese of Spic-and-Span. (She laughed when he related this, but he knew she was pretending.) The bigger surprise was how he took to the schoolwork, especially the algebra and the chemistry. At the country school, he'd always been the one helping the younger ones in math and science, but no one had remarked particularly on his capabilities. Now he was sitting with kids his own age, and he was doing very well.

There was a girl in Clare's Latin class, Lavinia Gulden, whose hair was the same color as Aldine's, though she was not as pretty. She had a long serious face and matronly clothes and fingers that were unusually long and white, like Aldine's had been. In class each day, after writing down the daily quotation and the verbs to be conjugated, Clare looked at the back of Lavinia's head and tried not to think of Aldine. Once,

Lavinia turned around, saw Clare looking at her, and smiled. Clare smiled in what he hoped was a disinterested way and studied his Latin notebook.

Usually the best way not to think of Aldine was to do some algebra or chemistry. You couldn't do those subjects and think of anything else, not if you wanted to wind up with the right answers, and Clare found that he did. He liked doing better than the other kids, the ones who had all the friends and the fun.

"You know what you might think about?" Mr. Petring, his chemistry teacher, said to him one day. "Pharmacy school." It was a fine profession, Mr. Petring said. His own uncle had been a druggist and wound up with a grand house on an eight-acre walnut grove. Clare had nodded. It was preposterous of course, a Kansas farm boy going to pharmacy school, but he couldn't stop thinking about it. He left school each day just after noon so he could bus and wait tables at the café, but when things thinned out, he worked all the harder on his studies. A pharmacist. What would Aldine think of him if that's what he were to become?

70

Mr. McNamara had been right. Fallbrook *did* need a home-style restaurant. And Ellie had been right, too, in thinking that customers would like the white aprons, genial politeness, and brisk efficiency that she'd learned in the Harvey House. She'd started with one waitress and had already added another, each of them working from 5:30 when they opened until 4:30 p.m., an hour after closing.

Mr. McNamara had contacts everywhere, and had set her up with suppliers of beef and poultry, and with Mr. Ames, who went every morning to the farmers' market in Los Angeles, and with Mr. Balize, who supplied secondhand china and cutlery that was good as new. She liked ordering supplies and cooking the food and hearing the hum of customers and, at the end of the day, she liked opening the cash register and balancing accounts. Some days they were ahead ten or twelve dollars; other days, the good days, as much as twenty or even thirty.

One day Mr. McNamara drove her and Charlotte and Neva and Clare out to the highway, but he made sure Charlotte and Ellie were sitting up front. After turning north off of Mission Road, he drove a half mile or so and told them all to cover their eyes, which they did.

Then he reversed direction on the highway, pulled off to the side, and came to a stop.

"Okay," Mr. McNamara said. "Now."

Ellie's eyes rose to the billboard in front of her.

Sleeping Indian Café, it said in huge red letters within a feathered arrow pointing toward town. *Steaks, Chops & Home-Made Pie. Breakfast & Lunch. Closed Sunday.*

"It's wonderful," Charlotte said. Her voice was soft and full of affection. "Really, Mister. It's wonderful."

"I can't see!" Neva said from the backseat, almost beside herself. "I can't see!"

Mr. McNamara stepped from the Packard and opened her door. Clare stepped out, too, and was standing there nodding and smiling. They all were.

"Just look!" Neva screamed, pointing up at it. "It's us! Right up there! It's us!"

It was a dream. That's what it seemed to Ellie. A dream from which she hoped never to awaken.

71

Neva didn't like her new school. She didn't like the way the grades were all separated, and she didn't like the way there was no stove in the room, and she didn't like the way her teacher, Mrs. Hartshorn, called everybody Miss So-and-so or Master Such-and-such. When Neva raised her hand, Mrs. Hartshorn never called on her, and when she didn't raise her hand, Mrs. Hartshorn might very well pass over all the raised hands and say in her old crab apple way, "Miss Price will now recite."

Neva had made a plan for that. The next time she knew an answer, she cast down her eyes and acted like she was hoping like anything that she wouldn't be called on, and then when Mrs. Hartshorn said, "Miss Price surely knows the answer," Neva looked up with bright eyes and said, "Yes, I do. Columbus is the capital of Ohio!"

But a knowing look had come into Mrs. Hartshorn's face, and Neva knew that her plan wasn't any good after all.

It was no better on the playground, where the games were new to her. Dodgeball, tetherball, kickball, she hated them all, and instead would take her school bag and go to the far side of the building where no one else was. She would take Milly Mandy Molly out of the bottom of her bag and set her up where she could watch. Neva spent more than a week breaking twigs from a juniper bush and making a tight fence for a new fort. "It has to be tight," she said to Milly Mandy Molly, "because right over there, under the juniper bush, the Murderous Horde is going to come, so the fort has to be strong." She was nearly done with the fence and was arranging longer branches for the tall corner turrets when two boys found her there and looked at the fence and asked what it was.

She didn't look at them. She knew they didn't like her and she knew she didn't like them. One of them wore black shoes and the other wore brown.

"It's just a play fort," she said.

"Fort what?"

She had named it Fort Prickly Hedge but she wasn't going to say that because she knew they would turn it into something dirty. "I don't know. It's not Fort anything."

"Maybe it's Fort Okie," one boy said and the other said, "Or Fort Okefenokee."

Neva still didn't look up at them. "We're from Kansas," she said.

"Well wherever Okie place you were, you came here to steal jobs."

Neva set another branch for a corner post and said quietly, "That's not true."

"Is too true so get used to it."

The brown shoes stepped closer.

"Not either true," she said so low she hardly knew whether she'd said it, but it didn't matter whether she did or didn't because the boy said, "Your Okie mother came in and took away another's job and then she gets overtime, which no one else gets, even those working years and years."

"Who says that?"

"Everybody says that," the boy said.

"What's that?" the other boy said, and there was something so queer in his voice that Neva looked up and followed his eyes to Milly Mandy Molly leaning against the fence. "Is that monkey yours?"

The boy with the brown shoes laughed but it wasn't a nice laugh at all. "You bring a stuffed monkey with you to school?"

All at once their shoes were moving toward Milly Mandy Molly and Neva sprawled out and grabbed one of the boys' legs and tried to wrestle him down, but this just made them laugh harder and it wasn't very long at all before they had torn off Milly Mandy Molly's green velvet waistcoat and were shaking the straw from a hole in her stomach.

72

Ansel had begun coughing when he was near the top of the tapering wooden ladder, but he worked his way down to the ground and stood bent over until he was gasping for the next breath and tears ran down his face. Two of the Mexicans appeared but would not come too close. "*Consunción*," one of them said, and kept staring at him.

"No," Ansel said when he could, waving them away. "I'm okay."

He made it through that day and the next.

They were living in the hotel now. There was no denying that the girls had made it nice, and there was plenty of room. He'd taken the room farthest down the hall so he wouldn't wake anyone with his coughing, or with his getting up to walk, either.

After coughing in a Valencia grove one day, he spit out the phlegm and stared at it. It was hard to tell, in the soft dirt, but that night in his room he had to spit in his white handkerchief, and it was unquestionably red. From then on he'd begun washing his own handkerchiefs, and drying them on a towel under his bed, but one day Ellie found one he hadn't yet washed.

"What's this?" she asked and he replied that he'd cut his hand and used it to staunch the cut, but she had always been good at recognizing mistruths and he had always been bad at telling them.

October was a slow month, with gusts of hot air blowing over dry hills. There was not much fruit to pick, though he did a fair amount of pruning, cutting the limbs from one whole grove of avocado trees down to their trunks, then spreading white paint over them to kill disease. The white trunks were like sculptures of unfinished men, the limbs stopped abruptly in the act of reaching out.

On the first day of November, he stopped into the post office and Bart Crandall, watching him, said, "Got something for you."

Ansel thanked him and glanced at the letter and stepped out into the street without opening it because it was from Gilbert Dorado and bore the insignia of the Harvey House. His mind whirred but he kept his face expressionless on the way to the hotel and tucked the letter into his back pocket before he walked through the café door, almost deserted at this hour, though it smelled pleasantly of meat loaf and onions. Dr. Quigley was at the counter eating a slice of pie and Ellie was at work cleaning the counter. Quigley liked to come by at the end of the day for a slice of lemon meringue pie and a cup of coffee and Ellie never liked to finish her day at the café without putting a gleam to it all. Ansel nodded first at Quigley, then at Ellie and made his way to the stairs. He never sat down in a booth or at the counter when he was still wearing his picking clothes and smelling, as Neva put it, of "dirty sugar," but it was more than that. He dreaded having a coughing attack in the restaurant with a customer present. Today this worked to his advantage—it permitted him to go directly upstairs and open the letter behind the closed bedroom door.

It was brief—even briefer than the one he'd sent. Gil had taken pains to write legibly, though, printing in block letters:

> *Estimado Anselmo,*
> *I send my hellos to your family and youre so beautiful wife.*
> *New job for FH sends me every which way. It's no busy but*
> *we are still working. The Scottish girl was very good work-*
> *er but Mrs. Gore fire her when she turns up family way.*

He read and reread and reread.

"Daddy?" Neva called. She knocked on the door and he heard the knob turn.

"Don't come in," he said. "I'm changing."

She let go of the knob.

"Mama told me to come up and tell you to get presentable," Neva said loudly. "She said Mr. McNamara's coming to talk to you."

"When?" he asked, sitting down on the bed and reading the last line of the letter again.

"She said hurry."

"Okay," he told Neva, but he sat holding the letter.

He read it one last time, searching for details that weren't there, then folded it back into the envelope. Even on the second floor, the building smelled of meat loaf and onions. He looked around for a place to put the letter and couldn't find one.

Feet were thudding up the stairs again—too fast to be Ellie, he guessed, but he stood up to unbutton his shirt and stuffed the letter in his pocket.

"Daddy!" Neva said again, knocking harder this time. "He's here. And he's all dressed up. Mama told me to get you right now!"

As he descended the stairs, Neva and Ellie were attending McNamara, but Ellie made her excuses and shepherded Neva out with her. Dr. Quigley had left, and his dishes had been cleared away. McNamara sat at a center table with an iced lemonade, and Ellie had left a cup of hot, honeyed lemon juice for Ansel, in case he began to cough. McNamara wore a linen suit with a seersucker vest and ivory shoes.

"Mr. McNamara," Ansel said, extending his hand, and McNamara said to Ansel what he'd never said to Charlotte: "Please, please. Call me James."

So on a hot November day that was like Kansas in summer, at five o'clock in the afternoon, James McNamara asked Ansel Price for

Charlotte's hand in marriage. Ansel took this in and while sipping his hot lemon juice considered the irony of a man renting a building to a married woman without consulting her husband and then asking that same man for permission to marry his daughter. But he said merely, "And I suppose Charlotte is agreeable."

"Yes," he said, and Ansel heard pride slipping into McNamara's voice, giving it a fullness missing moments ago. "Yes, she is."

Charlotte was not at home, but Ansel sensed Ellie listening through the kitchen door, and probably Neva, too. He knew he was supposed to say, *Well, good then, I couldn't be more pleased* and be done with it, but for a few moments he picked tenderly at one of the small linear scabs on the back of his hand, and then looking up, he said, "And you don't think Charlotte will grow restless?"

Unquestionably this took McNamara by surprise. "Excuse me?"

"The age difference," he said.

"Ah," McNamara said. He sipped his lemonade. He did not smell of sweat or the grit on orange peels, a distinction he seemed to relish. He looked at Ansel and said, "I'm going to tell you something that I have told no one in this town other than Charlotte." He paused. "I married once before, and I chose badly. Her family . . . Well, she came from bad stock. They were nothing, *nothing*, men and women without background or bearings. Still, I was determined. I understood the meaning of 'for better or for worse.' My wife however did not. So that was a very different kettle of fish. Charlotte is a majestic girl. *Majestic.* She is her father's daughter and she is her mother's daughter. Your wife's father is a very distinguished man, as I'm told your own father was sturdy and sure. Sound blood flows in Charlotte's veins, and it shows." He picked up his glass of lemonade, then put it back down. "Charlotte and I have discussed all this. My point, Ansel, and it's no small one, is that I believe in Charlotte and she and I believe in the vows of marriage. For better or for worse. Like my own parents. Like you and Mrs. Price. You see what I mean, don't you?"

Ansel nodded as if he did.

"Could she grow restless? Yes. Could I walk out this door and be run over in the street? Yes. But I don't think either possibility is likely." He smiled and said, "I look both ways when crossing a road. I believe ours will be vows that will endure."

Ansel heard himself say, "A father couldn't ask for more than that," though he wanted, somehow, to ask for more. He said, "What happened to your first wife?"

"I don't know. She and her fellow made for New Mexico. That's all I know. You notice I don't give her name. I haven't spoken it since the day she left." He straightened his back and pushed his glass half an inch away. He was ready to be done, but Ansel took another sip of honeyed lemon juice to coat his throat.

"Do you remember a girl named Olive Teagarten?" he asked.

McNamara said he did.

"Why did she stop working for you?"

"With child, as I recall." His voice had changed. This was his business voice. "Unmarried and with child."

Ansel nodded. "But wouldn't that be the time to give her a hand instead of turning her out?"

"It might seem like it, yes, but then you no longer have the line that can't be crossed." His eyes scanned the room before returning to Ansel. "You see, Ansel, you have to think of your other employees of this type. You need them to know there are lines that can't be crossed."

"Of this type?" Ansel said but before McNamara could reply, Ellie was pushing through the door carrying a pitcher and asking Mr. McNamara if he would care for more lemonade.

"No, I don't believe so, Ellie," he said, scraping back his chair and standing and smiling a broad smile. "But I'm happy to inform you that your husband has granted me my fond ambition of marrying your daughter."

Ellie let out a small murmur of pleasure, and in the next moment Neva had poured through the door and, hearing the news, said, "When will it be and what will I wear?"

McNamara went to one knee to speak to her eye to eye. "You'll wear something fetching, we'll see to that, and, as for when it will be, I suggested tomorrow"—he winked up at Ellie—"but Charlotte said she needs time. She wants to sew her own gown." He stood again and looked toward Ansel and Ellie. "We'd like to plan on the Friday after Thanksgiving, if that meets with your approval."

Ansel, in rising from his chair, heard the slightest crinkle of Gilbert's letter in his pocket. "That seems just fine," he said.

"Can we invite Miss McKenna to the wedding, Daddy?" Neva asked, slipping her hand into Ansel's.

"No, sugar," he said, something he hadn't called her in years.

"That was my teacher in Kansas," Neva told McNamara. She extended her arm. "She gave me these bracelets made out of Bakelite."

"She sounds splendid," McNamara said, and without missing a beat or stiffening in expression, Ellie told Neva not to get ahead of herself—they had plenty of time to think about the guest list. She turned then to McNamara and in the rosiness of her cheeks Ansel saw that this marriage, too, like the move to California, like the acquisition of the café, was all part of the wall she'd built to protect the life she wanted, and which didn't require him. "Won't you stay for dinner?" she said. "It's meat loaf, grilled onions, and mashed potatoes."

But the man had gotten what he'd come for. "I'll have to take a rain check on that, Ellie," he said, setting his cap on his head. "Just let Charlotte know I'll stop by around seven." He smiled at Ansel. "We're going to go see a movie. The new Buster Keaton is playing."

73

They'd gone instead to see Marlene Dietrich in *Blonde Venus*, which was playing in Escondido. It was a thirty-minute drive, and they passed the time talking about the wedding. Charlotte liked thinking of the dresses and the decorations and the food. Mr. McNamara's interest was in the guest list and even more especially the honeymoon, but Charlotte didn't mind this. She'd learned that there would be a good deal of compromise in this marriage, but as far as she could see, she was getting the better end of the bargain. She turned her knees toward him on the seat and said, "I never dreamed I'd come to California and get a job and be married in two seconds flat."

Mr. McNamara gave her a wide sidelong smile. "And I never dreamed that a Kansas dust storm would blow a goddess all the way to Fallbrook." He winked. "Buttons please."

She laughed and said, "Two and that's all."

With two buttons undone, she felt like a model for one of those racy true-crime magazines. It surprised her how easy (and secretly pleasing) it was to do such things for him, but it was every bit as easy and satisfying to deny him the larger favors he wanted. She stretched and yawned in a way that he liked. He'd begun buying her underthings, and the brassieres he plumped for were so flimsy she often thought she'd bust right out of them. "Eyes on the road, Mister," she said, "or you'll get us both dead."

74

The next day, Ellie told Ansel she'd made an appointment for him with Dr. Quigley. "I heard you coughing half the night," she said. "We're going to have a wedding. You can't cough all the way up the aisle when you're giving Charlotte away."

Ansel *had* been coughing during the night. And when he wasn't coughing, he was trying to find his bearings now that the world had shifted. Aldine was pregnant. That was the fantastic refrain. Aldine was pregnant. It seemed so unlikely. And yet not impossible. He'd read and reread Gilbert's letter. The image of the Teagarten girl kept coming to him unbidden, the hut she lived in, the dead baby wrapped in her arms, the strange look in her eyes. Until opening Gilbert's letter, staying in Fallbrook had seemed the right thing—it meant honoring his family, which they deserved, and it meant bringing no further dishonor to Aldine, which she deserved, too—but Gilbert's letter changed everything. If the baby was his, he needed to be there to help, and if it wasn't—well, she might still need his help.

"What time?" Ansel asked.

"Four o'clock," Ellie said. "Right after work."

On the day of the appointment, he was pruning deadwood from Valencias in a grove near De Luz when Oscar de la Cueva picked him up early. Ansel was glad of that. It afforded him time to wash up and change into fresh clothes before walking to the little cottage that served as a hospital. Alone in the small examination room, he took off his shirt as the nurse had asked him to do, and sat down on the metal table. The facing wall was covered with framed diplomas and commendations issued to Morris A. Quigley from Boston College and the University of California. The room must have once been the pantry or some such. There wasn't a window to look out of; all there was to look at were the gilt-lettered commendations. Presently Dr. Quigley entered, smiling in a friendly way and saying, "Mr. Price," and drawing a folder down from a cupboard. Friendly, and yet he had not offered his hand.

Ansel had met Quigley, of course, but their dealings had never gone beyond a nod and hello. Ansel regarded Quigley's shoes, which looked right out of the box, though he knew they weren't. Neva had told him that Dr. Quigley wore two pairs of shoes, one to and from the office and another that he wore only at the office so they never got dirty. The doctor's chin was dimpled and, though he looked to be no more than forty, his hair was already silvery. He was a widower—a quiet, serious one, according to Ellie, who set aside a piece of lemon meringue pie every day so he wouldn't be disappointed when he came in after the café was closed. Quigley called it his standing order, and Neva said he was a good tipper and nice to everybody, "especially Mama."

"You know that lemon meringue pie your wife bakes?" Quigley said now as he labeled the folder with Ansel's name. "Sometimes I'll be thinking about that pie all day long."

"It's good pie," Ansel said. He always knew which days Quigley came and which days he didn't, because when he didn't come, Ellie gave the leftover pie to Ansel. Those days, he'd noticed, were few.

Quigley leaned over his folder with pencil in hand and asked for Ansel's full name, date of birth, and past medical conditions.

"I don't get sick much," Ansel said. "Only this little cough of mine."

Quigley nodded and wrote. "Your last visit to a doctor?"

"Thirty-six years ago," Ansel said. "Got kicked in the head by a milk cow." He grinned. "I was fine and would not have gone. It was my mother's decision." He paused and smiled. "That milk cow was saucy."

Quigley gave this a polite laugh, not the broad, knowing laugh Kansans generally gave it. He closed the folder, and hooked his stethoscope over his ears. It felt strange and unpleasant to sit bare chested on the table and breathe the scent of another man's hair oil while he listened to you inhale. Quigley wore a blue bow tie and the knot looked intricate. The only man Ansel had known in Kansas who knotted a bow tie was Fitzimmons the banker.

After a time, Quigley sat back. "Have you ever coughed up blood?"

Ansel shook his head, but from the expression on Quigley's face, Ansel guessed that Ellie had told him about the handkerchief. "You'll need to give me a sputum sample," he said. "We just need to rule out tuberculosis."

Even before Ansel could absorb the shock of hearing the word spoken to him, straight out, from a doctor's lips, Quigley was handing him a paper titled *Rules to Be Observed for the Prevention of the Spread of Tuberculosis.* He scanned the set of rules that followed. *Patient's utensils marked and separated. Patient must spit only into sputum cups. Sputum cups boiled every day for 10 minutes. Contents burned.*

Ansel looked up. "I don't have tuberculosis," he said, and extended the paper back to the doctor, but Quigley wouldn't take it. "It's just a bad cold. I'll recover."

"I imagine you're right, Mr. Price, but we'd better do the test."

Ansel felt a sudden need to buy time, to figure out how to get out of here. "Kind of an old-fashioned illness, isn't it? Tuberculosis I mean," he said.

"It's come back into fashion," Quigley said. "Especially where you're from. All the dust."

"What about Neva? Did you do the test on her?"

Quigley's expression relaxed as he nodded. "Of course. She's negative."

He'd done the test on Neva? Ellie had told him that Dr. Quigley had said that Neva was fine, but she never said anything about taking a test for tuberculosis. Ansel got up and reached for his shirt. "This is all kind of sudden," he said. "Just give me a day or two to get used to the idea."

"There's nothing here to get used to, Mr. Price," Quigley said. He took a deep breath. "It's not just your own health we're talking about." He paused so that this could sink in. "Without a negative finding, you should be immediately quarantined."

Quigley's fingernails were flat and clean, just like McNamara's. There was nothing wrong with Quigley and McNamara, except for their clean fingernails and the smoothness of their lives. Ansel knew this, and yet it did little to moderate his resentment of either one of these men. Quigley went to the cupboard behind him and took out a piece of cardboard, which he folded to form a rudimentary cup. "Just spit into this," he said, "so you can prove me wrong."

"It's just a cold," Ansel said, buttoning his shirt, "and if it isn't gone in a day or two, I'll come back." In a day or two, he would be gone and he could forget all this.

"Mr. Price," the doctor said. His voice was firmer. "If the health department thinks the café might be a source of TB, they'll shut it down, no ifs, ands, or buts."

The doctor stood holding the improvised cup. Ansel wanted out of this room and this town but between him and the door stood Quigley with his little cardboard cup.

What if I told you I don't give a tinker's damn about that restaurant? Ansel thought about saying and then pushing him aside and stepping through the door, but that wasn't really true. He wanted Ellie to be happy. He wanted a good life to be hers if he left.

He took the cup and spat into it.

~

Since opening the café, Ellie had begun serving the family supper on the table closest to the kitchen. Often she would make a casserole or potpie with leftovers from the day's cooking. Tonight it was a beef pie topped with browned biscuits that everyone except Ansel ate with relish. Charlotte and Neva and Clare kept up a stream of newsy chatter—a broken window at the Practice House, a perfect score on a history test, an unwed girl going to Los Angeles to get swallowed up in who knew what. When there was a respite, Clare asked how many lunches they'd served that day, a question he always asked.

"Twenty-four," Ellie replied quietly.

Clare looked up from his beef pie in surprise. "Twenty-four?" His face was brimming with approval. "That's swell, Mom. That's a record, right?"

Ellie nodded and laughed. "And one of the bankers said he wanted to patent my Duchess Potatoes."

Charlotte and Clare both gave small laughs; Neva wanted to know how you patented a potato, which brought more laughter.

Ansel could not help but marvel at his wife. She would even hum popular tunes now—"It's Only a Paper Moon" was the one he heard the most—while doing the dishes. Always before he'd found her bustling cheer discouraging, but now he found a certain compensation in the transformation: it was one more reason that argued for his leaving.

It was nearly eight o'clock before the dishes were done and the children were gone and they were alone in the café. By then, the room had a scrubbed aspect, like the face of a person who was ready for church, but Ellie was still working the surfaces with a damp rag. "Charlotte sewed up Neva's monkey," she said. "Really you can't even tell."

He nodded. He'd asked Neva what had happened to the doll, but she wouldn't say, and everyone else seemed happy to leave the matter untended. That was the way of it here, with him on the outside looking in, seeing only parts of the room, hearing only some of the conversation, and it was his fault, he knew that. Ellie was holding up a glass, tilting it to the light, searching for fingerprints when she said casually, "How'd your appointment go?"

"Fine."

"And is he doing the test?"

"He said if I didn't, the café would close." He waited just a moment. "I suppose he told you that, too."

"He's trying to help us, Ansel. That's all he's trying to do."

"I know," he said. "I'm going back, Ellie. I think it's the only way."

She kept rubbing the glass. "You mean after the wedding?"

"No," he said, "tomorrow. I'll check the house and see if things are looking up. Maybe it's turned the corner, the whole drouth situation, and I can start again in spring. Besides, there are some papers I have to sign at the bank."

"What papers?" she asked.

"Something wasn't signed right and needs witnessing." He wanted her to accept that it was a good lie, a defense she could offer to anyone who asked.

"And you can't take care of it by mail? Or after Charlotte's wedding?" She seemed to understand him; he wasn't sure.

"No, I can't."

She set down the glass and stood perfectly still. She'd grown comelier in her happiness, and it came fresh to him how he had once loved her, but it was like thinking of two people he'd known a long time ago.

"I'm sorry," he said again.

A moment or two passed in silence. "But you'll be back for Charlotte's wedding, is that right?" When he didn't answer, she said in a keener voice, "This is Charlotte's wedding, Ansel. She expects you here. So does Mr. McNamara, and so do I."

He nodded, and then he said it, so he would hear himself say it. "Yes. I'll be back for that."

The headlights of a single car passed on the street and he wondered what they might look like to the driver of that car, a man and wife in their café talking at the end of a long day. In his mildest voice he said, "Did Quigley test you, too?"

She nodded. "I'm fine."

"It's just a bad cold," he said.

She walked over to the Hardy's Drugstore calendar on the wall and turned the page to November. "Thanksgiving's the twenty-third. Wedding's the twenty-fourth. You need to be back by the twentieth." She was looking at him now. "For appearances' sake."

Just like that, he thought. Just like that, they had come to an agreement.

She let the lifted calendar page fall back into place. Without looking at him, she said, "I'm guessing your first stop will be the Harvey House."

He didn't answer.

There were footsteps on the stairs and they both looked up to see Charlotte, who was wearing her movie-star bathrobe (no one had to tell him it had come from McNamara). There was also a funny expression on her face, as if she'd heard some of their conversation.

"I found the dress I want to make," she said, holding a magazine open with her thumb. Ellie didn't say anything, and neither did Ansel. "Wanna see it?" she asked, and she held the picture up for Ellie, who reached out to take the magazine, and then passed it to Ansel. After he'd looked it over, he nodded and said, "You'll look beautiful, Lottie."

But there was a terrible stiffness in the room—it was impossible the girl didn't feel it. He stood up to go. "Good night," he said, and they both murmured, "Good night."

75

The next morning Ansel stood with Clare outside the packinghouse waiting for their ride. Hurd was picking up an order of crates from a man in Del Mar and Ansel had arranged to ride along as far as Oceanside, where he would catch his train that afternoon. He wasn't sure why Clare had insisted on riding along, but he wished he hadn't. He didn't want him asking questions there weren't good answers for. So while they waited for Hurd, Ansel stood a few paces away from Clare and stared off. It had broken a mild, clean day but there were changes in the making. Steely cumulus clouds were rolling in, shadowing the hills and turning them violet, the kind of clouds he prayed for in Kansas. He heard a grinding downshift of gears, and turned to see Oscar de la Cueva's flatbed turn into the lot with Hurd behind the wheel.

Ansel picked up his bag and grinned at Clare. "Maybe we should say our good-byes here, champ."

They were almost eye to eye now. The boy seemed to have grown three inches since they came here. "Naw," he said. "I want to see you off and I want to see the ocean."

Hurd pulled the truck close and grinned out at them, rotating a toothpick in his mouth. "You hobos looking for a ride?" he said.

Ansel nodded. "I appreciate this," he said. Clare nodded to Hurd but neither smiled nor spoke. It was lost on nobody that Clare hadn't really warmed up to his uncle. Or rather that he had, but then something had cooled between them. But why exactly, Clare would never say.

Ansel stowed his gear in the back of the truck, then climbed into the cab with Clare in the middle, but no sooner had he pulled the door closed behind him with the three of them sitting closely packed together than he felt the familiar hitch in his throat, the first pesky command to cough that could be ignored for a few seconds or maybe even a full minute but would finally be obeyed. "You know, Hurd, I think I'll ride in the back."

Hurd registered surprise. "The hell you say."

"Yeah. If I'm going to spend the next few weeks in Kansas, I need to enjoy the California weather while I can. Besides, this is Oscar's field truck. I've ridden in the back so many times I've got the boards broken in to my particular specifications."

He fought back a cough and swung open the door, but before he could start to close it, he'd begun coughing. He coughed and spat several times and only when the coughing began to abate did he realize Clare was standing behind him.

"You okay?" Clare said.

"Yes." He was surprised at the frank apprehension in the boy's face. "Go ahead and sit up front," Ansel said. "Hurd will want the company."

But Clare climbed into the back with him and once they'd settled themselves in the truck bed with their legs extended and their backs to the cab, Clare tapped on the rear window and gave the thumbs-up sign, and soon they were rumbling through town. There were several tarps in the bed of the truck, folded and tied loosely with rope. Ansel tightly refolded two of the tarps so each had a cushion beneath him. Then when Hurd turned the truck onto the highway and they gained speed, he took another of the tarps and wrapped it around them for warmth.

They didn't talk. The road noise was too keen and constant for that. He looked back at the highway trailing behind them. He looked off at the passing fields and groves and houses. He looked up at the splintered beams of light that found their way through the massing black clouds. There was a beauty here, but he could only view it as a traveler would.

The highway descended south out of town, curving beside a creek that fed into the San Luis Rey River. Oaks and white sycamores lined the banks. From the rains the week before, deep ridges cut the bluffs where water had flowed through reddish soil. Hawks were out hunting, and Ansel spotted two of them perched on broken limbs within a few yards of each other. The truck hummed along. Ansel experimentally took a slightly deeper breath and didn't feel the tickling cough-trigger. He breathed deep, and still nothing. It was as if the cough command had slid away. He felt something he could hardly remember feeling. He felt warmly . . . what? Not happy exactly, but contented. Clare was looking off the other way, and Ansel was regarding the soft swirl of his hair when the boy suddenly turned to him with a wide pure smile, and Ansel found himself nodding at the boy, nodding yes to everything he had been, and had become, and would one day be. He wondered if this wasn't as pure as love could be, the admiration of a son by a father, and then he wondered if in leaving he would lose Clare's regard forever.

Perhaps twenty minutes later the countryside gave way again to clusters of houses, and a sign and then another. Clare shed the tarp and stood to peer over the cab. Ansel also stood. He had never seen the ocean before, and was surprised to sense it an instant before it lay before him, the way you could sometimes sense the presence of a wild animal. Vast and imperturbable, shimmering with silver light, the water covered everything in the distance, from one end of the earth to the other.

Clare grinned at him. "It's swell, isn't it, Dad? Isn't it swell?"

Hurd pulled the truck slowly to a stop by the train station, which perched on a bluff within view of a long wooden pier that ventured a hundred yards into the waves. "It is," he said. "I'm glad we saw it."

"It's something, isn't it?" Hurd said, staring off at the water as Ansel and Clare swung down from the truck. Ansel couldn't stand for Clare to leave now, so he was glad they began walking alongside him to the platform. "Ida likes to come here once a summer and douse herself," Hurd said. "She brings home buckets of shells. Me, I just sit under an umbrella and take in the sights." He gestured toward the expanse of cold sand and wagged his eyebrows. "In the summertime, there are plenty of sights."

Clare stuffed both hands in his pockets as he strolled along, and kept his eyes on the ocean, grinning. The salty air made his cheeks red and his hair more boyish, flapping a bit in the breeze. "We should come here again when you get back, Dad," he said. "We could go in the water."

"Sure," Ansel said. "I'd like nothing more than that."

Clare watched the waves and Ansel could see him imagining the future as it could never be.

Hurd issued from the station wearing a smile. "Wonder of wonders," he said. "Train is on time." He made a show of looking at his watch. "But we won't be, Clare, if we don't get a move on." He nodded and winked at Ansel instead of shaking his hand, then told Clare he'd go bring the truck around.

A shorebird screeched and the ocean rolled forward and sucked away. Hurd wheeled the truck to the near corner of the parking lot.

"Okay then," Clare said and stuck out his hand, but Ansel put one hand on the sleeve of the boy's coat and tapped the boy's shoulder with his other, so there was none of the skin to skin contact forbidden by Dr. Quigley's *Rules to be Observed*. Clare seemed confused by this, but nodded and tried to grin and then he was walking away. But he turned back once.

"Hey, Dad," he called. "Check on Mom's radio. Mom and I covered it up pretty well but she seems worried about it."

"Sure," Ansel said. "I'll be sure to do that. And you be sure to keep up with your studies."

The boy nodded. He liked school; the studies were no problem for him. "See you at the wedding!"

Ansel nodded.

Hurd's information notwithstanding, the train was late, but Ansel didn't mind. When he'd looked toward the parking lot, the packing-house truck was turning out onto the street and for a moment the form behind the wheel seemed more Clare's than Hurd's, but that was impossible, or at least unlikely, and besides, they were beyond him now. All of that was beyond him. He waited a long time on the platform, lost in his thoughts, idly watching the storm advance above water that was a pale, gemlike green only when it rose up near the shore and the light showed its emptiness. By the time the rain began to sluice down, he'd found himself a seat in a nearly vacant passenger car. The rain fell with such force that even as he watched, a channel formed in the sand and a stream of silty water churned down the beach into the sea, where waves pushed the new water back onto the sand. The train began to move.

76

Clare gazed at the dashboard and said, "Dad let me drive a truck like this in Kansas."

Uncle Hurd's expression slowly opened, and Clare wondered if he thought the idea coming to him was his own. "Okeydoke, then," he said, "why not?" and slid over so Clare could take the wheel.

Clare *had* driven a truck like this, but only over the rutted farm roads of Kansas. Still, he turned from the parking lot and shifted through the gears without difficulty, and they were on their way. Clare discouraged Hurd's happy yakking, which was hard for him to take when he was picturing what his father might do in Kansas, by concentrating on the open road.

When the rain began, Hurd merely reached across the seat, switched the wipers on, and said, "Maybe your dad will take some of this rain with him."

Clare acknowledged that he should.

The wipers smeared the window and made a pulsing click-clicking sound that felt somehow connected to the beating of a heart.

"Well, look at that," Hurd said. "It's beginning to hail."

Clare hadn't even noticed. He'd been thinking about his father at the station and not hugging him, about him going away to their house, and to where Aldine was, too. Clare would later try to remember the sequence of events as they then occurred but all he could remember was squinting through the windshield imagining Aldine holding on to his father in the barn when, at a turn in the road, he felt the metal cab sliding slantwise as he pulled the wheel gently and then too hard to the right, and felt in the great mass in which they were riding the strange uncorrectable momentum and, for a shorter moment than it would later seem, glided ahead in the sensation of detachment, and then hearing the slow crack, which was softer in his memory than he thought it must have been, given that the tree sank so deeply into the truck. And then? And then he didn't know. He'd gone somewhere else.

77

Ellie knew the plan but couldn't bear to picture it. Dr. Quigley intended to nail Clare's leg back together as if he were a wooden marionette. Nurse Roover would hold the leg steady and Dr. Quigley would *introduce the nail*—that's how he'd put it—and she would sit in the next room where she couldn't hold Clare's hand or see Clare's face or, really, be Clare's mother, which was what at this moment she wanted most to be.

"We'll give him nitrous oxide first," Dr. Quigley had told her. "Then we'll introduce the nail."

It had to be nailed because the neck of the femur was lacerated (at first Ellie thought he was saying Clare's neck was broken, but he said no, he meant the neck of the femur, the slender curve of the thighbone) and they would need to secure it with something called a transfixion nail, a piece of metal three-sixteenths of an inch wide. He used his fingers to show how narrow that was, how minuscule, really, but she registered the fact that he didn't show her the actual nail. He said he had used the method several times, that it was very effective, very safe, the only way to make sure that the edges of the bone stayed together. That was important, Dr. Quigley said, in order to avoid deformity. *So that's what we're doing,* she thought. *Avoiding deformity.*

A calendar hung on the wall before her, a hunting calendar featuring a wet spaniel mouthing a limp duck. Ellie studied the spaniel and the duck and the grid of days that represented the month of November. Hurd sat nearby, staring at the floor, his clothes dirty and wet, his fingers crusty with blood. He'd sat with Clare's head in his lap in the backseat of a car driven by a stranger.

"My fault," he said now to Ellie without looking up. "Not the boy's, not anybody's, just me."

"No," she said.

Hurd stood and walked heavily down the hall. Toward the bathroom, she supposed.

A woman's voice from the inner room seemed to say, Oh good Lord.

Would a nurse say that? Say, Oh good Lord?

∼

Dr. Quigley had thrown Miss Roover a look when she exclaimed at the damage. He'd flexed the knee, swabbed it with iodine, then drawn the skin upward. It was more than Roover normally saw, but the woman was a nurse for crying out loud, and the boy's mother was just on the other side of the door. He made a short vertical incision, less than an inch but bisecting the greater trochanter and external condyle. He pushed the nail to the bone while Roover held the boy's leg. "Steady," he whispered and when he glanced up, he saw she had her eyes squeezed shut. He tapped the nail with his bone mallet until he felt it transfix the bone. There the skin had to be drawn upward—he had to cut it so the nail could pass through without piercing the skin. Piercing the skin would cause acute pain, he knew, the kind of pain Ellie would imagine in any case when she saw the nail projecting an inch on either side of Clare's leg. That was the hard part, the mental acceptance of a nail driven through flesh and bone, making visible the grisly stuff you could normally hide beneath layers of plaster.

It mattered to him what she thought. He wanted to make sure she didn't see the nail right away. He watched as Nurse Roover covered the wounds with dressing soaked in a solution of iodine and sterile saline. He'd asked her to prepare a dram of iodine, a pint of sterile saline. After the wet dressing, he fastened the spreader to the ends of the nail and showed the nurse how to wrap it with dry gauze and cotton, firmly but not so firmly that Clare couldn't flex his knee. Ellie would have to do this after the first forty-eight hours—it was clear the Prices couldn't afford to keep the boy in the hospital for six weeks of bed rest. Six weeks, at least. And every other day Ellie would have to change the dressings. But he could come by to help a bit with that.

~

Hurd dozed in his chair. Ellie studied the spaniel. She studied the duck. Through the door she heard tapping sounds, squeaks, metallic clicks, Dr. Quigley's muffled voice. Each noise pricked at her mind, and she smelled what she thought was blood. Bits of debris and muddy footprints had dried on the waiting room floor, and the dirt made what was going on in the next room feel uncontrolled.

Finally the sounds from inside the room ceased, and a short while later Dr. Quigley came out. It went well, he said, looking from her to Hurd, who was straightening in his chair. Nurse Roover hurried past them, her wrinkled face pale, her hands wrapped in a towel, and went into the kitchen. Water ran. The hospital was really just a made-over house. Where they sat now, she guessed, had been a living room, the operating room was once a bedroom, and Nurse Roover was using the kitchen to wash the blood off.

"You should go home and come back in the morning," Dr. Quigley said. He wore a pale pink shirt under his white coat, and his shoes were Mercurochrome brown. There were spatters of blood on the white coat. She appreciated his slightly mournful expression. He was not brusque the way Neva's doctor in Kansas had been, and he'd been among the very first to patronize the café, and he loved her pie.

"I'd rather stay," she said. "I won't be able to sleep at home."

She expected him to insist, but he went into the examining room and returned with a blanket and a pillow. "You might prefer the sofa," he said, pointing to a green cloth couch that was more like a bench than a bed, but it was long enough to stretch out on. Hurd said he'd better go home and give Ida the news, and he promised to look in on Charlotte and Neva. Ellie didn't expect to sleep, staring in the dark at the closed door that lay between her and Clare, but she did, and awakened to bright sunlight and the sound of Nurse Roover's footsteps on the hard linoleum.

Ellie glanced toward Clare's room and asked if she could peek in. Nurse Roover nodded and said, "But don't wake him," so she tiptoed in and stared quietly at Clare in his white metal bed. He looked both frailer and larger than Ellie had expected, perhaps because she didn't see him lying down much anymore, certainly not stretched out like that on his back. As a baby he'd slept curled on his side, and as a child, with all his limbs flung out. She wanted to touch his forehead but didn't. She looked at his hoisted leg. Whatever was broken was hidden under layers of gauze.

The room was comforting because it was so obviously a bedroom once, with a big window that let in the morning light. She still felt surprise to find herself in California, marveled when she looked out and saw trees, fruit, and green hills, all of it fed by water, none of it suffocating in dust. The window by Clare's bed looked out over a small orchard: one tree each of lemon, orange, grapefruit, and persimmon. The persimmon tree, still dripping with rain, was the prettiest: all its slender brown branches studded with bright orange fruit. The leaves had fallen off but the fruit remained, as though someone had hung masses of red glass balls on it for Christmas. When Ellie looked hard, she could see that most of the persimmons had been pocked by hail or crows' beaks, and the crimson scraps of skin hung down to tempt more birds. Even as she watched, a crow came and picked at the flesh, then stood on the branches and bent forward with each hard caw, its body like a black pump handle.

Clare stirred and, a moment later, opened his eyes. He saw her and at once mumbled, "I'm sorry."

He'd gone through a phase in childhood where all he did was apologize, saying "sorry" even when he stirred in his sleep, or when his elbow brushed hers at the kitchen table. "Don't say that," she said, her eyes filling with tears she had to dab at before she could crush his hand in hers. "It wasn't your fault, so don't be sorry. How do you feel?"

Clare closed his eyes, opened them again, and flinched. "Don't tell Dad, okay?" he said. "Crashing Mr. McNamara's truck . . ." His voice trailed away.

Mr. McNamara had met them at the hospital. He said not to mind about the truck; he thought it would be fine. He just hoped Clare would be okay. Ellie told Clare all this, but she wasn't sure what he heard. His eyes had again fallen closed.

78

Ansel stepped off the train slowly, reading twice the carved letters that said *Emporia* before he let go of the railing. The original limestone building, the one he could have sketched in his sleep, was now surrounded by red brick. The old place had been without shade or shelter; you were either indoors, or you were out. Now a series of arches stretched from the depot to the tracks. He walked to the corner of Third Avenue and Neosho Street and saw that the rest of the town was not much changed, except for the hard, dry browns and grays of it all. The drought endured. From the train window, he'd seen mile after mile of blown dust and abandoned buildings.

It was midday. Streaky clouds that Ellie called mares' tails spread their feathery ice across the sky. Bare cottonwoods and maples, their shapes as familiar to him as his own hands, fringed the tracks where town ended and the prairie began. The air was cold and bright when the sun hit it slantwise, the way air was supposed to feel in November, and he felt that after a long time of wearing someone else's clothes he had once again slipped into his own.

He walked east in the direction of the Harvey House and noticed that he still felt beneath his feet the steady a-way, a-way, a-way rhythm of the train, a pulse that was stronger than his own light footsteps. When he stood, at last, before the heavy glass-and-mahogany door of the old lunchroom, he took a breath and stifled a cough. The place had seemed grand in the old days, a place of bustling wealth where passengers gave off an electrical surge of anticipation. He had been young then, with no responsibility but to do his job, amuse himself, and stay loosely on the lookout for the right girl to marry and take back to Dorland. It was a strangely unhampered life. There had been plenty of time, plenty of food, plenty of people, plenty of cheerful girls, and then, in the end, one more interesting and serious girl, whose name was Eleanor Hoffman.

The ceilings, when he pushed open the door and walked in, were still elaborately patterned, the walls around him still of that height and breadth that meant no expense had been spared, but there was about the dining room a stillness that smelled of brown gravy and old steam.

It gave him a turn when a girl came out of the kitchen in the same uniform Ellie used to wear: black dress, white apron. Funny how it hadn't changed in all this time. "You can seat yourself at the bar," she said. Her voice was raspy and she looked even younger than Aldine, which was odd because she had a 2 on her apron badge, and seemed almost to be in charge. She was looking him up and down, assessing whether he was a tramp or paying customer, he guessed. She gave no sign that she took him for a customer.

"I'm looking for Gilbert Dorado," Ansel said. "He around?"

"You aren't here about a job, are you?"

"Nope. Gil's an old friend."

The girlish woman nodded. "That's good because we don't have jobs," she said, studying him a bit more. "I have to say that ten times a day."

He took this in and gazed across the room at the empty tables with their white tablecloths, heavy silver place settings, empty goblets and cups. Aldine had been here, and now she was gone. It was lunchtime but not a soul was eating. "I expected more people to get off the train here," he said.

"Was the train full?"

"No . . . no it wasn't." He'd been glad of its relative emptiness, truthfully, because twice he'd been seized by fits of coughing and the Chinawoman traveling with her children had been able to move away from him.

"Sometimes they are, but usually they aren't," the waitress said. "I'll go find Mr. Dorado. You going to want lunch?"

He wanted lunch, but he couldn't waste money on it here. "No, but thank you," he said.

"Well, the menu's right there," she said, pointing to the bar, "if you change your mind. I'll be back."

He looked around, took it all in. For months Aldine had walked across this room, carrying trays, touching the silverware that lay within his reach, talking to strangers, thinking . . . well, who knew what she was thinking. He rubbed hard at his forehead. It hurt him physically to remember her slender hands, the way they curved up at the fingertips like a hawk's wings in flight.

Ansel sat down on one of the stools and opened the menu. *Beef Steak Frascati*. He'd watched Ernie cook so many of those he remembered it A to Z. Breaking an egg yolk on each tenderloin, sprinkling it with pickled capers, minced onions, parsley, and garlic salt. The rich taste of seared beef in a pool of Bordelaise, the way the salty capers spilled onto your tongue.

"Selmo!"

Gilbert Dorado walked out of the kitchen smiling hugely, his funny shock of black hair thinner but still flopping over one eyebrow, his short body with big feet pointing outward as he hurried close. "Selmo! Selmo! Selmo!" he said. "At last you've come for your cooking lesson! I'll teach you everything I know!"

"Which is damned little, if I remember right."

He'd stood, and was grinning, too, but when Gilbert extended his hand Ansel leaned back, smiling and appraising. "New mustache," he said, softly knuckling his own upper lip, "and maybe a few new pounds"—he touched his own stomach—"down here."

"No!" Gilbert said. "Not an ounce! Well, maybe an ounce. But not a pound! Certainly not a pound!"

The waitress with the 2 badge had again drawn close, as if waiting for an order, but taking everything in, too.

Ansel glanced vaguely toward the window and remarked on the drought.

"Drought, depression, wind, dust, death," Gilbert said. He smiled and shook his head. "Maybe God doesn't like us so much anymore."

That thought lay in front of them for a moment, and then the waitress said, "He don't care so much about a girl's tips, I know that."

Gilbert gave a small laugh and turned to Ansel. "So!" he said, changing subjects. "How is the beautiful Ellie?"

"She's good," Ansel said. "She's opened a café out in California that's doing just fine."

"A café! Always the smart one, Ellie. It's what I should do, but, no, it's me and Fred Harvey till death do us part."

Ansel laughed and felt the tickle in his throat.

"How many kids? Two?"

"Three," Ansel said and gave Gilbert the quickest summary. The waitress standing nearby made him feel funny talking about his family, he wasn't sure why. "So, Gilbert, did you ever talk somebody into marrying you?"

"Me? Nobody! Nobody thinks I'm a good bet! But I *am* a good bet!" He grinned at the waitress. "Tell my old friend Selmo, Glynis. Tell him that I'm a good bet!"

The waitress gave Gilbert a thin smile. "I'd rather not fib if you don't mind." She had a strangely husky voice, which, along with her searching eyes, gave her an exotic aspect, as if she could tell fortunes or read palms.

Gilbert grinned and shrugged. "Then bring my old friend Selmo some of your hot coffee, Glynis. And maybe an apple croquette." He turned to Ansel. "Cook fried maybe a few too many and"—a wink—"we don't want them lying around when Mrs. Gore comes in."

Once the waitress was gone, Gilbert said, "So, Selmo. This is unexpected. A pleasure of course, but an unexpected one."

Gilbert's black eyes were curious, but unsuspicious. Ansel turned from them and regarded his own gnarled hands folded on the varnished wood countertop. "I'm going to check on the place," he said, "but first I'm here for business." He forced himself to look Gilbert in the eye. "Papers to sign at the bank, in front of a witness."

Gilbert began shaking his head. "The bankers!" he said. "I'd like to line them all up in front of a wall and shoot them!" Glynis was strolling toward them with a coffee urn and a small plate of crispy croquettes. "Tell the man, Glynis. Tell him how I would line the bankers up in front of a wall and shoot them."

To Ansel's surprise, the waitress gave out with an actual laugh. "He even chose the wall," she said.

"Yes! I showed it to this girl so she'd know how serious I am about the bankers!" He began heaping sugar into his coffee. "So, Mr. California. Did you bring us some of your fancy avocados? I think you promised us fancy avocados."

"Wrong season," he said. "Spring's the best time for avocados." He caught the waitress staring at him again. Maybe he looked ill. The Chinawoman on the train had herded her brood to the farthest corner of the car. But the waitress named Glynis merely said, "You're from California, then?"

Ansel nodded. "For now, anyway."

"Place called Fallbrook, right?" Gil asked.

The girl said in a slow voice, "My old roommate used to get letters from there."

Ansel tried to keep his expression neutral. "From California, you mean?"

"No, from Fallbrook." Glynis kept her eyes fixed on him. "A Scotch girl. Name of Aldine. You wouldn't know her, would you?"

Ansel nodded at once, and said, "Yes, I do," and took two sips of the boiling coffee before his throat felt wet enough for him to go on. "You a friend of Miss McKenna's?"

"Mmm," Glynis said, glancing at Gil, then back at Ansel. "Really close friends."

Ansel looked at the girl, waiting for her to say more, but she said nothing more. The black coffee and rich croquette on an empty stomach were making him feel light-headed and queasy, but he sipped more just for something to do that wasn't talking.

"But you got my letter, right, Selmo?" Gilbert said, smoothing his mustache and looking both concerned and confused. "You know she's not here anymore."

"I know," Ansel said, determined to follow through. "I thought you might know where she went." He didn't know what to say. He wanted the waitress named Glynis either to tell him something or to go away, but she didn't go away. "I feel—I feel responsible for her," he said, and he knew that if his words didn't give him away, the way he'd blurted them did. Still, this was what he'd come for. There was no going back. "She was in our house," he said. "The school board couldn't pay her and she had to come here. She had no money and nobody to look after her. It didn't sit right with us."

Half-truths to hide a bigger truth. He felt the shame beginning to rise within him again. He looked out the enormous windows of the restaurant, hoping to see where he should go next, but the windows faced the train tracks and the loading docks, the stained gray buildings that had become even shabbier since he left twenty years before.

Glynis said, "Is your name Selmo?"

Ansel turned, but already Gilbert was saying, "I just call him that. From Anselmo." He set a knuckled hand to Ansel's shoulder. "His name if he'd been luckier with his place of birth."

"Anselmo?" Glynis said.

"Ansel," Gilbert said. "That's his sorry gringo name."

Now the girl's eyes were drilling into him. "Ansel," she said. "Your name is Ansel?"

"Yes," Ansel said, not sure what he was admitting to, or how Aldine would have presented him to a friend. "Where is Miss McKenna now? Where did she go?"

Glynis seemed to be considering her words. "I'm not sure," she said, "but one time before she stopped working here, a man came in and talked to her. He seemed to know some of her family. She was really nervous around him so I asked Aldine about him after he left. He was a Mormon missionary who knew her family. So, you know, when she left, I asked if she was going to live with her family."

"And?" Ansel asked. Things like this worked out all right sometimes, with the baby passing as the child of the married relative. It might've been the safest thing to do.

Glynis had been gazing out at the large empty room, but turned now to Ansel. Her eyes were indifferent and cold. "She said she'd rather die," she said.

Ansel felt a kind of agitation rising. "So where is she then?"

He thought he saw a kind of defiance come into her face. "I don't know," she said.

A lie. Ansel was sure this was a lie. He glanced at the clock on the wall and pushed away his coffee cup. "I'm going to have to get to the bank," he said. He smiled at Gilbert. "How much are you charging for coffee and a croquette these days?"

"Nada," Gilbert said. "But maybe something more to eat, Selmo? You need your strength to deal with these *insolente* bankers."

Ansel was already standing. "How about a rain check?" he said. "I'll eat better when I've finished my business."

Glynis leaned on her hands and said, "It's nice to put a face with a name."

79

Out of sight of the Harvey House, Ansel walked past the bronze doorplate of the Emporia Savings & Loan, smudged by many hands, and then went next door to a grocery, where he bought sardines and bread. He walked south in the cold air until the houses and sidewalks stopped, and he stood facing a large new park planted with stubbly brown grass and young cottonwood trees, in the center of which a pond threw brightness back at the winter sky. *Peter Pan Park* said the carved plaques in each of the two pillars, which were made of stone in a style that suggested a child's idea of a castle. The park had not been there when he lived in Emporia, and he was surprised to see groups of shabbily dressed men loosely gathered near a stone boathouse. Ansel walked to the far side of the pond and ate his sardines standing up under a rattling maple.

He looked west, beyond the pale water. A few hundred miles in that direction his house stood unoccupied, his fields abandoned. He wanted to go there, see how things looked. He wanted to find Aldine, and take her with him. He had to talk to Glynis again, but away from Gil, who had driven all the way to Ellie's father's house to attend their wedding.

He rolled the uneaten portion of the bread into its paper bag and walked back toward the Harvey House, past groups of bundled-up people hurrying past him in clouds of their own chilled breath. They were leaving offices and shops, he supposed, and the cold reddened their faces and turned them inward. Few looked at him, and those who did gave him only the quickest glance before again looking away.

Near the platform, within the covered archway, Ansel leaned against the cold stone wall and waited for Glynis to come out, or for the train to come, or for a better idea to present itself, whichever, he thought, came first. The architects who'd added the covered archway had only made a cold place colder. He was miserable, his fingers and toes registering what it was like to be on the plains with winter coming on. The wind bit at his ears. He began to cough his deep raking cough. From the nearby shadows something large was suddenly moving—a man who had been crouching there, still and unseen by Ansel, silently rose and moved away.

Minutes passed, perhaps a half hour. Numbness crept over him; even when he coughed, he didn't feel the customary pain in his ribs. Finally the door of the restaurant flashed gold in the wintry sun, and Glynis came out, her head wrapped in a bright green scarf and her chin snugged down inside the collar of a dark coat. She was alone.

The moment he stepped from the shadows, Glynis saw him. He raised his chin in greeting and she nodded, a letter in her gloved hand. She didn't seem surprised to see him.

"Thought you were going to come back and eat," she said.

"There might not be time," he said. "But I wanted to ask if you know anything else about where Aldine is."

She looked not so much at him as into him. Her brown eyes narrowed and her thin, finely shaped eyebrows drew together. "Are you still married?"

"Yes," he said. "But—"

She cut him off to say, "And you think you're in love with Aldine?"

To Ansel, this sounded less like a question than an accusation. What this girl—what was her name?—seemed to mean by love was something sneaky and side-doorish and vulgar.

"No," he said, "not the way you mean it. It was more like . . ." Like what? A father? A brother? But it wasn't like that, either. "It was . . . more like my heart went out to her," he said.

The girl's cold eyes settled on him. "You felt sorry for her, you're saying, and then you had your way with her?"

"No," he said, "that wasn't how it was—"

But the girl was done talking. Her worst expectations had been met. Her face had again gone bland. "I need to get to the post office before it closes," she said.

He walked in the direction she walked, his open mouth pulling the biting-cold air into his lungs. He stopped to cough, then had to trot to catch up.

"Do you have pneumonia or something?" she said over her shoulder.

"Just a bad cold." He gulped air. "I'll be fine."

The girl said nothing, but she did slacken her pace. Still, he had a hard time keeping up.

They stepped off the street and his foot broke through a brittle skin of ice into a shallow puddle of frigid water. "I just wanted to know how she is," he said.

She kept walking steadily forward. "Yours weren't the only letters, you know. They came from both of you. But I could tell by the way she treated your letters that you were the one she loved, not the boy." She glanced at him. "Clare, right?"

He nodded, and she seemed pleased by her own abilities of recall. "I remembered it because it's a funny name for a boy. It's a nice enough girl's name but I'd never give it to a boy."

The sky was pink as she pushed on the door of the post office. It was a surprise that Clare had written her letters, and yet it was not, but he couldn't think of that now. He needed to say the words that would allow this girl to trust him. She walked ahead of him into the big tiled room and stood behind two others waiting in line. It surprised him to remember the post office so well: the black-and-white pattern of the tiles on the floor, cracked near the counter where something heavy had fallen once, the brass edges of the counter deeply buried in the wood, like fingernails in flesh. The door behind them opened and another patron joined the small line, nobody speaking. When it was Glynis's turn, she pushed a letter across the varnished oak counter. There was something almost fierce in the gesture, and he looked down to see the words *McKenna* and *Salt Lake City, Utah*. The postman touched a stamp to a wet sponge, pressed it crookedly down, and then canceled it, saying, "That'll be two cents, miss."

Glynis pushed the two cents across the counter and the letter was gone.

When they had gone out into the cold blue twilight, he said, "I thought she told you she'd rather die."

"People say that," Glynis said. "But they wouldn't."

"So she's gone to her sister's," he said, full of despair instead of the relief he expected—after all, her sister would take care of her. But that wasn't what he truly wanted. He wanted her to be with him.

Glynis kept walking, and Ansel kept walking with her. "The other letters," she said after a time, "the ones from Clare, she left in a drawer. Yours she put in a little box. I used to hear her crying when she read them, especially as it got plain, you know, what had happened to her." Glynis shrugged her black woolen shoulders and touched her red nose with an embroidered handkerchief.

"Please give me her address," he said. "I *do* love her. In the purest way. I want to find her and make it right."

362

She stopped under a streetlight and studied him again. He was aware, this time, of her smallness beside him. She was looking up at his face, and he was looking down into her determined eyes. A car went past them, popping through ice that had glassed a pothole. She came to some conclusion but said only, "Well." She removed a stubby pencil from her bag and then a scrap of paper, which she held against the brick wall of the post office as she wrote an address for him.

80

Mrs. Odekirk always went to bed early, but on that Tuesday night Aldine was sewing a crooked yellow blanket stitch along the edge of a cream-colored flannelette baby jacket and wondering if she could sneak a tarry. She felt as heavy as a turtle and dragged herself like one. Her swollen feet even looked like fat old turtle feet. She dreamed some nights that she had fallen over the rail of an ocean liner and was plunging through pale green freezing water, her belly a cannonball. She was prone to little nightmares even when she sat working on the tiny frocks Mrs. Odekirk had set her to making. She'd be sewing, and then she'd be dreaming, and that's why Glynis's soft knocking seemed at first like a subterranean noise. But when she hoisted her turtle body and scuttled to the window, there was a person on the back step, and that person was Glynis, her breath coldly visible as she turned her face toward Aldine.

"I saw him," Glynis said and walked right in, taking Aldine's wing chair even though the pincushion was right there on the footstool. Glynis had crocheted a pair of booties for the baby last month, and before that, a yellow bib.

Aldine lowered herself onto the stiff velvet love seat and pointed at Mrs. Odekirk's closed bedroom door. "Asleep," she whispered.

Aldine liked Mrs. Odekirk, and had visited her several times before Mrs. Gore fired her. When she was turned out of her quarters, she'd come here, and Mrs. Odekirk, without asking any questions, had offered her a room.

"I saw him," Glynis repeated in a whisper that was almost a hiss.

"You saw who?" Aldine assumed it was some man Glynis didn't like. The giver of the randy postcards came to mind.

"Ansel," Glynis said.

"*Here?* You saw Ansel *here?*"

"This afternoon. He came to look for you at the Harvey House."

The words pulled her like river water. "Where is he now?" she asked, holding herself fast against the love seat.

"He's gone. He went off."

"Went off *where?*"

Glynis let her gaze slide away. "I didn't know what to do."

"What *did* you do, Glynis?"

"He wanted to know where you were," she said, her words trailing off. Her air of dramatic regret made Aldine want to shake her.

"Didn't you tell him that I'm here?"

Glynis shook her head. She touched a snag on her skirt with the green finger of her gloved hand.

"Why not?" Aldine stood up and as she did so reflexively touched her belly.

"I don't know. I thought you'd be better off. But then later he did seem to care so much that I felt maybe I'd done wrong and that's why I'm here now."

"What did you tell him? You're not making any sense!"

"I wrote to your sister," Glynis said, looking up tearfully. "I knew you wouldn't do it, that you were too ashamed, but I know how it feels to be looking for someone. I thought she should have the chance to help you. After Ansel came to the restaurant and I told him I didn't know where you were, I decided to write to your sister. Then he—Ansel— found me on my way to the post office, but that was when I was still thinking he should just let you be."

"So you just told him you didn't know?"

Glynis let her eyes drop. "I gave him your sister's address."

Aldine was horror-struck. "He came here looking for me, and you sent him to Salt Lake?"

Glynis nodded less distinctly. "He didn't say flat out that he'd go find you there. Honestly, he didn't look very good. I mean, well enough for much travel."

"He looked tired, you mean?"

"Maybe," Glynis said. "But more sickly I think."

"What kind of sickly?"

"He said it was a cold."

Aldine could think of nothing to say, so she pressed her fingertips down hard on her closed eyelids.

"He's a married man," Glynis said. "What would you have done if I'd sent him here, anyway?"

Aldine shook her head and said nothing. Ansel had come to find her, and she didn't get to see him. That was all she knew, and it was too much. "Please go," Aldine said.

"I'm sorry," Glynis said. "I'm very, very sorry."

Aldine didn't look at Glynis or answer her but instead pressed her hands harder over her closed eyes, felt the heaviness of her body, and listened to Glynis go quietly out the door.

81

Aldine went out within the quarter hour carrying a small suitcase, wearing her frayed coat, scarf, and gloves. The night was silent except for dogs, and the cold air seeped through her clothes as soon as she began walking toward the tracks. She hoped the unsmiling doctor was deaf in his sleep, like Mrs. Odekirk, and that the plain reflective squares of the neighbors' windows would let her pass by unremarked upon: half turtle, half woman. The curtains were drawn, the lamps were dim, the sidewalks barely visible because there was no moon. Stars like specks of ice, like the mica that had stuck to her hands that night of the Winter Entertainment, were strewn in their billions but gave no light.

The South Avenue houses were large and judgmental, fronted by elms and American flags, but on First and Second Avenues the houses were crude narrow boxes between stores, the trash piled up in cans on untended front yards. She paused a moment, feeling the baby within her. At first, he (as she thought of him) had been a strange hardness inside, an oval mass that kept her from bending properly at the waist, more like a piece of internal pottery than a living thing. But then the fluttering had started and she'd not been able to stop thinking of the fairy tale wolf that had swallowed a whole family of white kid goats, stuffing himself with their quivering bodies and then falling, as the story went, asleep. In a few weeks, or maybe less, her baby, like all those goats, would come out whole.

She kept one arm folded over her belly and ignored the ache of her feet as she forced them, swollen and creaky, to leave the sidewalk for the gravel beside the tracks. Her entire head seemed to pulse with fear, and her footsteps crunched the night silence that had enveloped her on the street. The immense depot loomed above her, a few of the dormitory windows glowing orange behind cheap muslin. The window she had once shared with Glynis was dark.

Ahead of her a group of men stood around a barrel, the flickering light from the fire casting jagged light on their faces. They stopped talking and watched her coming toward them, each face too dark yet to be identified as Ansel's.

"I'm looking for a man," she said, and one of them snickered in a low way. "A newcomer," she corrected.

"We're all new enough," said the hollowest one, high-voiced and snaky.

Aldine could feel them appraising her condition, thinking their knowing thoughts about why the man she was looking for might have run away. Still, she made herself ask again. "He just got here today. His name is Ansel Price and he might have been asking which train to Salt Lake."

They shook their heads so slowly they might not have been answering her at all.

A man who hadn't said a thing, bareheaded and wide jawed, removed his hands from his pockets and looked at her with a different kind of knowingness. "Far from home, are we, lass?" he said, a name she'd not been called in so long that it was like he'd spoken her true name. The vowels and consonants were like a code between them and something unlocked in her head.

She nodded and her eyes were wet. "Far."

"I'll go have a wee chat for ye," he said, and he left the barrel for a group of men, who, while he talked, glanced over at her and then told him something she couldn't hear. She wanted to put her cold hands over the fire but stayed back, feeling with each vertebra the suspended weight of her abdomen, so heavy that she couldn't decide whether to lean forward or lean back.

As the Scotsman walked back toward her she sensed that he had learned something, and when he met her eyes she was sure. "What?" she asked.

"They said there was a man asked about Salt Lake. They said they'd show us where he is."

All the hope that had been pooling in her chest ran fast and hot now, as if it were lava rolling down into the sea. She followed the Scotsman, and he followed a lanky man in a soldier's canvas coat, and they walked past buildings without windows or names until they stopped by a crooked door that might have been red or dark brown once. The lanky man opened it and let them go by, the sour, dank smell of bodies reaching her as the warmth of the room came out. A stove of some kind was lit, and some men slept on the wooden floor, three or four of them it looked like. She didn't know which one they were headed for, and it was too dim to see.

"What's the name?" the Scotsman asked, and she said, "Ansel."

The bodies on the floor didn't move and the inhabited but silent room frightened her.

"Ansel," the man repeated for her, louder. "Are ye here?"

Now a body did move, rolling slightly, and they walked toward it. She got close enough to see his face—yes, it was his wide forehead, his jaw, his mouth. "Ansel?" she said, and he turned his eyes toward her.

82

It was not a fit place to be found sleeping, so he stood up quickly. He picked up the bag he'd been using as a pillow and led her out into the cold where he could be himself again, not one of these men. A skinny-eyed tramp said, "Found ya, didn't she, Pop?" and snickered.

He and Aldine walked along the tracks to the sidewalk, breath mingling in cold isolation, her small gloved hand in his. "You're here," he said. "We can go to the farm now."

"I'm living with Mrs. Odekirk," she said.

"Sonia?"

"Yes. She has a house here."

"Why did Glynis say you'd gone to Utah?"

"She was just leading you away."

He tried to trap his cough but the cold dragged it out of him. She kept close, so he turned away. "I'm sorry," he whispered when he stopped and had his breath again. "I'll be fine now that I've found you."

They walked silently past the narrow houses and the spilling trash. They began to approach the wide, squat invincible houses, where even the shadows felt more virtuous and safe. He had still done nothing more than hold her gloved hand. In front of a looming house and fenced lawn, he reached for her other hand and held it tightly so that they came to a stop. "Wait," he said. He wanted to look at her face. "We need to go," he said. "We should leave right away for the farm. Can you travel?"

"What kind of travel?"

"Just a car. We need one. Maybe Gil—" He wondered if Gil had a car for work now. Perhaps he could give them a ride.

"I need my things," Aldine said. "And I can't just leave without saying anything to Sonia. We could stay with her for the night. I'll make a bed for you, and we can explain everything in the morning. I'll tell her that I ran into you, that you were sick and had nowhere to go. She'll understand. Oh, and the front house is a doctor's. She rents it out to him for living and office visits. I send out billings and the like, so he's promised to deliver the baby free of charge."

"We can't stay," Ansel said. He couldn't explain to Sonia Odekirk— much less expect her to understand—that he, a friend and member of her church, was the father of Aldine's baby, so he had now left his wife and three children to do the right and proper thing.

The pickets of the fence beside them loomed like teeth. Somewhere an unseen animal scurried and dug. "I can't go there," he said. "Come with me now to the farm."

"But what will we do?" Aldine said, her face worried, her eyes black. She stepped closer to him.

Her round dark eyes sought something in him, groping almost like hands. He wanted to pull her to him under the black-leafed maple and kiss her. He felt better and stronger than he had the whole trip, almost weightless, and the night had a richness to it that seemed full of possibility. He would keep Aldine with him at the farm and he would get well, and everything else could be sorted out from a place where he was himself.

Instead of kissing her on the mouth, he kissed her neck, her ear, a bare space where the shawl slid off her shoulder. The future lay like still water in his mind.

"I'm going to the farm," he said. "I have to check on the radio and the house. Krazy Kat. You can come with me."

"But how would we get there?" she asked.

He had planned to go by train. Aldine said again the part about Sonia's house, the nice doctor, waiting until light, all the while letting his hands and his kisses travel over her neck and body. If only he could go with her to the house with all of its rooms and furnishings. He could go on touching her there. They would not be anyone's charity.

"Dr. Stober has a car," she said, pointing at a Nash parked across the street. "He doesn't use it much. How far is it to the place?"

"About five hours."

"He let someone use it once. A friend of his. He never drives it."

Ansel didn't know what to say.

"Or we could just stay here with Sonia, as I said."

It would not look right, Ansel knew. He wasn't sleeping under anyone else's roof ever again.

"You think he would loan it to you?" he said.

She looked dubious and then determined. Then she turned, and he was watching her dark, swollen form slip into a side door of the doctor's office. He closed his eyes. He felt he was living a dream or, really, that a dream—a strange, not unpleasant dream—was lifting him away and was carrying him along, and because Aldine was part of the dream, the dream was perfect, and it was pleasant to be carried along on it.

"I've got it," she whispered, and he opened his eyes. He was sitting down. He didn't remember sitting.

She held a small tin box, and when she opened it, she held up a key. "I wrote a note to tell him we'll—I didna' say it was you, just me—that I'll bring it back."

He rose heavily to his feet and she was at once close to him again. Her hair smelled sweet, and even through his heavy clothes, and hers, he felt the smoothness and roundness and fullness of her body.

He climbed behind the wheel. She sat close beside him, as she had done once before, and the ignition flared at his touch.

83

Ansel's house stood quiet in a quiet night. Blown brush and dirt and debris had collected everywhere but, still, the sight of the house calmed him as it always had, the same four windows and the same red door he had glimpsed from his mother's lap, his father's truck, the back of a sleigh, a tractor seat. The cottonwood leaned over and touched the roof. As the car rolled over the rocks and dust of the drive, the headlights swept the barn and caught the startling eyes of an animal.

"Krazy Kat," Ansel murmured in a low, pleased tone, and Aldine said, "Won't Neva be glad!"

He had never let go of her the whole ride, both of them wide awake in the darkness as the black fields rolled by. They were happy riding along and they were happy now, stepping out of the car. The cat watched them for a moment, then ran into the barn. That they would enter the house together and have no impediment made Aldine tremble. Her ears roared with it.

A long strip of tape flapped over the front door, but other strips still held, and Ansel broke the seal by tugging hard on the knob. Aldine's foot struck a coffee mug left standing on the porch and it rolled away. When Ansel's fingers found the light switch, the living room lit up before them: dust and mouse droppings everywhere, the sheet-wrapped hulk of the radio, its edges taped to the floor, the sprigged love seat in its place below the window, a paper costume for Shirley Temple where it had fallen by the stairs. Ansel said nothing, but led her up the stairs. There were times when his illness seemed to exhilarate instead of drain, when fatigue became eagerness and he knew he had turned the corner. The bed was not made up, but there were a few blankets in the cupboard, the quilts his mother had made and Ellie had not wanted. It was cold in the room, and he didn't want Aldine to be cold. He spread them over the bed as she watched.

"We shouldn't kiss until I'm better," he said.

"Not on the mouth," she said. She unzipped her dress, and stepped out of it.

"I'm gigantic," she said, but he shook his head so that she felt his rough chin brush her ear. She didn't feel grotesque now, not in the cocoon of blankets that they pulled over them, warming the air with musty blue cotton. His body made her feel small and rightly formed because it was his baby that her belly held. His hands were rough as they moved over the skin of it, then over the skin of her breasts and back and neck and face. She let herself touch the back of his head and his shoulders and then downward. She let herself think only of the present and of what she had wanted all this time.

84

When Sonia Odekirk couldn't find Aldine, she stepped out her back door and up the sidewalk to Dr. Stober's office. She was convinced the baby had started coming in the night and she'd slept through it, though why Aldine hadn't shaken her awake she couldn't understand.

It was a bright day with a bit of wind, the kind you had to push against when you walked. Weeds cowered, stood back up, were flattened again. Blue sky swallowed gust after gust above the black roof of her house, where in childhood there had been a flag, where now there was a gunmetal socket for a flagpole. She hurried up the wide front steps, pulled open the lace-curtained door that said *Myron L. Stober, M.D.* in black letters, and closed it as fast as she could to shut out the wind.

Dr. Stober was sitting at his desk reading the *Journal-Post*.

"Have you seen Miss McKenna?" she asked.

Dr. Stober looked over his glasses at her, one hand on the newspaper page he'd been about to turn. "No," he said.

A normal person would have said, "Why?" but Dr. Stober, she increasingly felt, was unusually indifferent to the distress of others. This had not been obvious when she first rented the house to him, perhaps because he was younger then, and his wife had not yet died.

"I woke up this morning and she was gone. I thought she was in labor."

Dr. Stober received this news without expression or comment.

"I hope she's all right," Sonia said. "I can't understand where she would have gone."

"Perhaps to a friend's?" Dr. Stober said, and neatly turned the newspaper page. "She doesn't normally turn up here until nine."

Aldine never visited friends, but Sonia didn't see the point of telling this to Dr. Stober, who seemed impatient to continue reading the newspaper.

"Sorry to have bothered you," Sonia said, thinking for the twentieth time that Dr. Stober always managed to make it seem that he was the landlord and she was the tenant, rather than the other way around.

"I'm sure she'll be back any second," Dr. Stober said, eyes on the paper, and Sonia turned to open the door, expecting just before she heard it the little tinkling bell that warned Dr. Stober of arriving patients, a cheerful trembling of brass against brass that she thought for some patients must forever be associated with bad news badly delivered.

A square of paper lay in the stubbly grass, and Sonia bent to retrieve it merely to tidy up.

> *Dear Dr. Stober,*
> *I am borrowing your car to take a friend home. I'll bring*
> *it back as soon as possible. I hope you will not mind.*
> *Aldine McKenna*

Sonia was astonished at Aldine's misreading of Dr. Stober. He was exactly the sort of person who *would* mind, and mind terribly. Few people wouldn't. The midnight borrowing of an expensive car by a pregnant, penniless, unmarried girl? And how can taking without permission be called borrowing? The girl might call it borrowing and Sonia herself might not call it theft, but everyone else would. She had to concede—to herself, privately, if not to Dr. Stober—that the girl she had perceived as a young and less fortunate version of herself might actually be a reckless and foolish person who brought along trouble wherever she went.

Sonia didn't like walking back up the steps into Dr. Stober's office. She knew that he would be furious, and she supposed he would blame her for introducing Aldine into the house. She stopped to consider, briefly, the curled dead cottonwood leaves on the lawn and porch. She stopped to read the note again. She examined, as a calming exercise, the blue horizon, ribbed in the distance with bony clouds. Her mouth felt dry and her left shoe pinched. She put her hand to the heavy door and braced herself for the brass tinkling of the bell.

She was not wrong. He came to a boil fast.

"*Borrow* it?" he asked, incredulous. He bent over so he could peer through the lace curtains at the empty parking place on the street. He stared a long time. "This is inconceivable."

He said several times that he could not believe it, simply could not believe it, and then he asked her to tell him again how she'd come to know this foreign girl and why she thought it would be charitable to let her sleep under the same roof, work in his office, handle the files of his patients? "She's probably a gypsy!" he said. "A gypsy with a whole pack of other gypsies riding around in my car this very instant." He glanced again out the window. "You'll have to go with me to the police station."

"Why don't you wait and see? Give her time to bring it back?" Even to Sonia, it sounded crazy.

Dr. Stober gave a little explosive laugh. "Give her a big head start, you mean? Bigger than the one she already has?"

"I'm sure she means it," Sonia said, forcing herself to picture the sweet, honest face of the girl she liked, not the conniving gypsy of Dr. Stober's description. "She wouldn't steal," she insisted. "She could have taken it a long time ago, when she wasn't so near her confinement. Why didn't she go then?"

"Free medical care, I imagine," Dr. Stober said. He was gathering things up and setting them down, looking for something.

Sonia wasn't sure why she felt so defensive of Aldine, but she did. Perhaps it was her own judgment that she wanted to defend. "If she doesn't bring it back, I'll be responsible."

"What in the hell do you mean by that?" he asked. He'd found the papers he wanted and was stuffing them into a satchel.

"I mean that I'll pay."

Dr. Stober laughed incredulously. "For the car? Why would you do that?"

Sonia couldn't think how to formulate her reasons for Dr. Stober. She'd imagined her life taking a new turn with Aldine in it: a substitute daughter and grandchild, a late compensation for what had been denied her in marriage. If Aldine brought the car back, Aldine would come back, too, and Sonia wouldn't live alone in the back part of her childhood home as an increasingly frail and unwanted landlady. Dr. Stober surely suffered similar visions of his fate: no wife, no children, an empty house, year after year after year.

"She's like a daughter to me," Sonia said, not looking into Dr. Stober's face as she said it, fearing his laugh. "If she doesn't bring it back, I'll stop charging you rent."

"You've been hoodwinked," he said, not laughing this time, but his voice still contemptuous. "You've been fooled."

"Then let me be the one who pays."

Dr. Stober was quiet. When she forced herself to look at his face, he massaged his throat and said, "Wait for her to return it, huh? Like a library book?"

He set the satchel on his desk and looked up at the clock. "It's almost time for my first patient. Perhaps you should leave before I change my mind."

85

In the morning, the sun was almost too bright. Aldine felt dizzy looking at things in the room, which were exaggerated by the strong winter sun and her pure pleasure in being here. It was as if she were now living in a world dipped in ammonia and wiped clean: the skin of Ansel's hands, the hair on his arms, the blue cotton of the body-warmed quilt, the brass bed, the flecked mirror, the irises of Ansel's eyes when he opened them and saw her staring—it all shone, it all glittered. "Good morning," she managed to say.

He pulled the blanket higher and held her tighter. "Good morning," he said, warm, dry lips to her neck.

The cold air reminded them, in time, that they were hungry. Ellie had meant to leave nothing edible behind, but Ansel followed mouse droppings to a burlap bag of white beans tucked into a dark cupboard corner. Only a handful of beans remained. Ansel said they could be washed and cleaned, but it was barely a meal, and after soaking and boiling, tomorrow's meal at that. It was Aldine who thought of Sonia Odekirk's house. "She said no one was living there, not even her hired man," she told Ansel.

"But why would she have left food there?"

"They were too heavy, she said. All her jams and such. She meant to find someone who could fetch them."

Ansel opened the lower cupboards again, leaning his long body down to check the back of each one.

"We'll keep track of how many," she told Ansel. "Treat it like a loan."

The cupboard doors were gummy from the layers of paint and dust. They wouldn't quite close.

He didn't answer her, but pressed his arms against her and his face into the back of her neck.

"It's just until spring, anyway," she added. They had talked about the spring, when he would dig up the kitchen garden and they would plant the seeds that lay small and dry in their capped jars in the kitchen drawer.

They couldn't eat the sunshine, and they couldn't eat the air. He had to go. But how to get there, how to get back? They had passed few cars last night, it being so late, but in daylight neighbors would drive to town, do their business, note who was going where and doing what.

"I could drive the tractor," Ansel said. His fields met Sonia's eastern perimeter. The only house visible from Sonia's fields was the Tanners', and Sonia had told Aldine that Mrs. Tanner had taken her sad, over-grown boy and gone to live in Nebraska with a sister.

When he'd gone, Aldine stood blinking a few minutes in the kitchen, which was dustier than other parts of the house. She found a crack in the windowsill, a place where the outside air breathed in. She worked a ball of wax in her fingers until it softened, then pushed warm plugs of it into the crack. She thought of uncovering the radio and turning it on, but it seemed too much of Ellie, and she left the sheet draped as it was, a ghost in the corner, faceless and eyeless and yet some-how sentient. Aldine turned her back on it and swept up the mouse droppings; then she filled buckets with water and wiped the wooden counters and the black stove with wet rags, wringing and rinsing and dragging until it felt as if her body were a pump handle, and if she bent over one more time the baby would simply plunge out of her. The smell of wet dust was everywhere, and surfaces had a hazy gleam that she couldn't trust. Each time she wiped a thing, the wetness made it look clean, but as the water dried on the countertops or the red tin canister lids, a streaky whiteness revealed itself, one more invincible layer of dust, and then one more. Ellie and Charlotte had always gotten things clean, really clean, and she wondered what it meant that she could not. Twice while she was working, she glimpsed something moving along the floor and turned to see a mouse vanish under a door or around a corner. When she lay down on the sofa to rest, she heard a *scritch-scritching* from within the walls, and the ghost radio watched her in silence.

Ellie had not wanted Ansel anymore. She had not wanted this house anymore. That's what Aldine told herself. Ansel had told her a bit about the café, how happy Ellie was being in charge of it, like a different person entirely.

"What did you tell her about coming here?" Aldine asked.

"I said I was coming to check on the house. To see if things had changed at all."

Aldine was silent. She didn't ask, "Did you tell her about me?" but he answered, anyway. "She doesn't know about the baby," Ansel said. "I think she knows the rest."

Ellie was happy where she was, running the café. Ansel was happy here, on the farm. The weather would change and a normal spring would make it possible for her and Ansel and the baby to live here somehow. The exact manner—would a divorce happen, could it happen, could he marry her?—was too hard to figure out. For now, it would be as if the two of them had immigrated to a new and solitary country. The baby would bring them a fresh start and a fresh start was all they needed.

The view from the kitchen window was the same as it had been when she was a boarder: the brown ridge of the hogback, an empty corral, the tiny narrow house that was the bog, leaning a bit since they left, and the barn with its lone cottonwood tree. It was the same and not the same, because Ellie wasn't here resenting her, unless you counted the radio crouched under the dusty sheet.

With a sharp pang she wondered what Leenie looked out on when she did her dishes, and what she would do when she read Glynis's letter. Would she try to find Aldine? Would she feel about Ansel as Glynis did?

What have I done? she thought unwillingly when Krazy Kat appeared beside the cottonwood, stalking something in the dry grass.

Leenie would inquire, certainly, would start with Mrs. Gore and Glynis herself. The trail would lead to Sonia and Dr. Stober. To Dr. Stober's car, to this house, to the two of them hiding like criminals.

Dr. Stober's car needed to go back, that was the first thing.

Ansel must drive the car to Emporia at night when he was feeling well enough and park it right where they'd found it, then come back by train. Between now and then they would never add a single dent or mile. But when should he go? What if the baby started to come when she was all alone?

He couldn't leave her.

And yet the car must go back.

She was heating water for a bath when she heard the distant throb of the tractor. Oh, how she hoped Sonia Odekirk's pantry had been lined with red, green, and amber jars, a rich, gleaming mine of food. The clattering tractor noise rose, and the baby shifted inside her like a stone in a subterranean stream. She went to open the door eagerly, to welcome him home, to replace her terrible fears with his physical being. His back was to her, his colossal, comforting back, and she could see as he steered the tractor toward the barn door that boxes lay in the wagon he was pulling, and in those boxes were gold-lidded jars and plump sacks.

86

The Fallbrook *Enterprise* reported in the column "About You and Others" that Mr. Ansel Price had gone to his home state of Kansas on a business trip but was expected back for the nuptials of his eldest daughter, Charlotte, that the William Bartlett family had gone to Julian over the weekend to enjoy the snow sports, and that Clare Price had shattered his left thigh and was recovering nicely at home. "Visits, especially from local damsels," it noted, "would doubtless be appreciated."

Lavinia Gulden sat in a desk on Wednesday, November 8, and listened while Melanie Quail read aloud this old news (it had already spread through the grapevine) at the first after-school meeting of the Junior Red Cross League. Melanie, Myrtis French, and Candy Armstrong had only formed the league, Lavinia thought, so they could wear white nurse's caps and starched arm bands while making a big fuss about themselves, but Lavinia had joined because you had to belong to at least three clubs to make the dean's list.

"Well, *we're* damsels," Melanie said. "Maybe we should take young Clare Price his homework." The white hair on her arms, a fine blond airy meadow, stood up in the shaft of sunlight. If she had not been so pretty, people would have remarked more on the excess of hair. That was Lavinia's opinion.

"Maybe I could give him some oranges," Candy offered. Candy's father had a grove full of them, but it was late for Valencias and early for navels and, besides, the crops were so valuable now, after the hail and hard freeze, that Lavinia doubted very much that Candy would get away with free ones.

"I have to go right by there on my way home," Lavinia said. "I could take his books to him."

For a moment they all turned to her, as if surprised that she was still in the room.

"Well, I doubt he needs you to take his books," Candy said. Why did her trim rectangular teeth seem to make what she said irrefutable? "His sister's the home ec teacher," Candy added.

Lavinia lifted her chin and tried to stop blushing. "I thought Melanie just suggested we take his homework."

Candy, Melanie, and Myrtis regarded her, and she looked back as steadily as she could. They sometimes asked to borrow her Latin and English notes because they didn't pay attention in class, and they pretended to be nice to her when they bought things on credit in her father's IGA, but they didn't really like her.

"Are you sweet on him?" Candy asked, giving Lavinia a slow, condescending blink. "I think Lavinia's sweet on Clare, girls. I spy with my little eye a Clare-catcher."

Lavinia looked at Candy's rouged cheeks (or was that Candy's natural skin color, the color rouge aspired to be?) and shrugged.

"Why not let Lavinia take him her extra-tidy notes," Melanie said to Candy. "He's too Kansackian for us, anyhow."

Her way of saying, *Let's leave him for the sappy girl from Iowa.*

Myrtis said, "He's a demon in trig, though. And I heard he won a bet reciting 'Charge of the Light Brigade' beginning to end." And then when Candy and Melanie stared at her, Myrtis said, "It's probably not true, though."

Lavinia bet it was true, based on what she'd seen of Clare Price in Latin class, but didn't say so.

They talked about making centerpieces for Miss Price's wedding luncheon, which was going to be held at the Practice House, and about how to make some kind of present for each grammar school child (which even Lavinia had to admit was charitable) and when the meeting was at last over, Lavinia was free. She walked to the school office, then to Clare's homeroom desk, and then to the street.

Fallbrook was practically chartreuse when you squinted. The rain and hail had been followed by a sudden heat spell, which was normal in winter, but Lavinia still wasn't used to it. A rain would fall, cold and fitful, and then a dry Santa Ana wind would rattle the windows all night, sweeping every drop of moisture from the air and every foggy hollow from the ground. The Sleeping Indian would turn from brown to violet and the empty lots in town would fill with meadows of yellow sour grass. The sky became a vast blue kiln. Lavinia often had the feeling, as she walked slowly down Ivy Street, that she had moved to another country when they left Iowa three years before.

The road from the high school led to her father's store, where she worked every empty, sun-filled afternoon.

When she walked by the windows of the IGA, her reflection rippled and she thought of Clare Price lying in a bed with his shattered leg. She felt the weight of her books in the canvas bag, and the naked, smooth motion of her own unbroken body. As soon as she walked in the store, her mother stood up behind the counter and started to untie her apron. "Why didn't you tell me you'd be late? I have to mail something before the post office closes."

"I'm sorry," Lavinia said. "There was a meeting. Innyhoo . . . want me to mail it for you?"

Her mother didn't even consider it. "No, if I don't get a breath of fresh air, I'll scream."

Alone behind the cash register, behind the long wooden counter that she liked to stroke with her fingertips, Lavinia opened her Latin book, but thought about Clare Price instead. She liked in particular to think of him doing chin-ups in his gym uniform, lifting himself over and over. *Veni.* She had seen him doing that one day, on her way past the gymnasium, and she'd counted to forty before he stopped and turned. *Vidi.* Clare's brown hair combed neatly flat, his smooth, alert face, his light brown eyes, and his muscled arms distracted her in Latin and English. It was what she waited for, when she was in charge of the store: the tinkling of the bell at the door and the sight of his bare forearms, the possible brush of fingers as she handed him sugar or flour or coffee beans for the café. *Vici.*

She began to walk down the aisles, thinking of Candy's offer to take oranges to Clare. The store wasn't big, and the shelves were unevenly stocked because ranch people and even those with gardens in town were trying to live on their own canning. Bliss Coffee, Post Toasties, Blue Rose Rice, Cloverbloom Butter. She chose a box of White King granulated soap. There seemed to be a lot of that. Asparagus tips in a square tin because she had wanted to open it and see if they were lying in there like people in a bed. A box of powdered sugar because you could always use sugar in a café. Then she selected a package of Christmas candy that she had secretly hoped, but not expected, to find under their own tree. She hid the packages in her school bag and tucked them under the counter.

"The Red Cross League nominated me to visit Clare Price," Lavinia said when her mother returned and started dusting jars of jam. "I have to take him the lecture notes."

Her mother raised her eyebrows. "My Lavinia? The one who scorns all girls' clubs?"

"I still do. But I have to be in three clubs for the dean's list."

"So you joined a boy-visiting club. *Velly interesting.*" Her stupid Charlie Chan voice. But there were no customers and little to do, so she let Lavinia go.

The day's last light shone on the queen palm tree across the street. Through the window of the Sleeping Indian Café, she could see Mrs. Price serving coffee to Dr. Quigley. She stopped in front of the glass door and felt idiotic. She couldn't go into the room of a boy if he was alone, and he was going to be alone if his mother was serving coffee and his sister was still at school. The teachers always stayed late, it seemed like. Mrs. Price in her odd getup, black dress and white apron, saw Lavinia and waved, so there was no other choice: she had to go in.

"Hi, dear," Ellie said.

"Hi, Mrs. Price," Lavinia said. "How are you?"

"I'm fine," Ellie said. "Can I get you something?"

Lavinia felt Dr. Quigley watching her. Now what should she say? Lavinia never ate or drank anything in the café. She couldn't afford to. Though the lemon meringue pie on Dr. Quigley's plate looked wonderful.

"I was just wanting to ask about Clare," she stammered.

"Oh, how nice of you," Ellie said.

"He's going to be flat on his back for at least six weeks," Dr. Quigley said, smiling at Lavinia and then at Mrs. Price. "In boy time, that's roughly six years." For this, he received a sad smile from Mrs. Price, and then he took up another forkful of lemon pie.

"But he'll be all right," Ellie said. "That's the important thing." Actually, the important thing, Ellie thought, was trying not to picture the way the openings in Clare's leg oozed, the look of the nail disappearing in flesh. Clare actually moaned from the pain in his sleep at night. Days, though, he suppressed it. Dr. Quigley had shown her how to give him shots and she tried not to think of the bills. She tried not to think of Ansel's silence. She'd sent a cable to the farm days ago, and she hadn't heard a peep out of him.

"I have the lecture notes for him," Lavinia said, her face coloring. "From Latin and English. If he feels like it, but maybe he doesn't." If Mrs. Price told her to leave the notes in the café, what about the soap and tinned asparagus? What was she going to tell Mrs. Price about that?

"Maybe he'd like to see a friend," Mrs. Price said. "Charlotte's sitting with him."

That was a relief in one way, but—a small surprise—she also felt a little let down. She made her way, as directed, to the outdoor staircase, where Clare's little sister was sitting on the bottom step, waving a broom straw over a line of acorns. She was talking to them in a funny way, like she was reciting a poem:

> "Roll on, roll on, you noisy waves,
> Roll higher up the strand.
> How is it that you cannot pass
> That line of yellow sand?"

Then Neva knocked down the acorns with the straw and looked up at Lavinia.

"Hi," Lavinia said.

"Hi," Neva said, pushing back her hair with a grubby hand. "It's okay for me to be out here," she said. "I'm not sick now."

"No, I can see you're not," Lavinia said. "Besides, it's so warm out." She wasn't sure what Neva was talking about, but the girl looked perfectly healthy in spite of being one of those children whose arms and legs still looked bony inside her cardigan and puff-kneed woolen tights. If there was anything newcomers to Fallbrook had in common, it was a tendency to overdress their children on sunny winter days.

At the top of the stairs, Lavinia paused to compose herself. She could see bins of oranges outside the packinghouse, the queen palm tree, Mrs. Nuthall's dance studio, and the modest wood-frame houses that stood at odd intervals near Main Street. The El Real was by far the nicest building, so it seemed right that Clare Price should live there. The pink brick, the elaborate windows, and the Spanish roof belonged in some distant and important city, not a farm town. She and her parents lived in a house that had come in a kit that cost twenty-five dollars.

Lavinia stood on the landing and considered leaving the bag of groceries on the doorstep and going away. Miss Price had given her a B on the dress she was at that moment wearing because the stripes didn't match quite right in front. But of course Miss Price had heard Lavinia's feet on the stairs, and she opened the door.

"So," Miss Price said, "I guess you're here to make one of those damselly visits that would be appreciated."

"Yeah," Lavinia said, abashed. "Unless you think it's a stupid idea."

"Nah, come in, come in. The poor boy could stand some cheering up."

Lavinia stepped awkwardly into a dark hallway that connected a series of doors.

Charlotte led Lavinia into the nearest room, where suddenly—too suddenly, really—she found herself standing a few feet from Clare Price. One of his legs was much bigger than the other, a long lump in the bed. She tried not to stare at it, but to look at his face was difficult, too, because he was lying in a bed, and he didn't smile.

"Hi," Lavinia said. He was pale and obviously sick but to be near him was still to feel inferior. She wished she had been patient enough to make the stripes in her dress match. She felt suddenly overly warm; her slip was like an adhesive bandage.

"Hello," Clare said. He thought more remarks were probably called for but he couldn't think what they were. Right now the pain was gone but it was waiting for him. It always was. The sharp sting, the long shooting pain, or the ache. There were those three of them, lying quiet for a while, and then one of them would come.

"I have some wedding stuff to do," Charlotte said, touching Lavinia on the shoulder. "Will you stay with the invalid until I get back? My mom's right downstairs if you need her."

This unnerved Lavinia but she tried not to let on. She made a stiff smile and waited until Charlotte was gone to open up the heavy canvas bag.

"I brought you some things on behalf of the Red Cross League," she said. She was going for an ironic voice, but she could tell it just sounded twangy.

"The local chapter, anyway. The Melanie-Candy-Myrtis chapter."

His eyes shifted away. Because he felt like a charity case? Because of pain? She reached into her bag and brought out the asparagus tin, the powdered sugar, and the candy. Each in its own way felt absolutely wrong. She set them on his nightstand and in the ensuing silence her face grew hotter and hotter.

Finally she said, "I thought maybe your mom could use them. In the restaurant."

"That's swell," Clare said, afraid to speak too much or move his head. The pain had begun; he could feel it stirring.

"Except for the soap," Lavinia said.

"Nope. Can't cook with that." He hoped it would only be the sharp sting when the morphine faded. Not the long ache.

"And I have the lecture notes from English and Latin. So you won't miss what Miss Warren said in class." Lavinia held out her notebook but Clare just looked at her. It wasn't the stinging kind. It was the long ache. The ache was starting. It was weak but it would get stronger. He felt his jaw setting against the pain. "Just set it on the bed, okay."

Lavinia set it down, mortified. She never should have come.

"The phrase of the day's there," she blurted out. "*In omnia paratus.* That was today's."

Clare closed his eyes.

"It means, 'Ready for all things,'" Lavinia added. She knew he didn't care, but she couldn't help herself. "In case you wondered." She looked at the package of Christmas candy and wondered if he would even open it. "I guess I'll go now," she said.

His eyes slowly opened. "I'm sorry," he said. "I—the pain is coming back."

"Oh," Lavinia said, because, really, that changed everything. It wasn't her that made his face clench. It was the pain. "What should I do?"

"Just tell Charlotte," he said in a low voice.

"I think she left," Lavinia said. "Should I get your mother?"

He kept his eyes closed and teeth clenched as he nodded.

"Okay," Lavinia said, and nearly ran out of the room.

87

Aldine and Ansel drank juice Sonia Odekirk had made from black summer grapes and soup she'd made from summer vegetables. At night Ansel built a fire with wood he brought in from the barn, pieces of lumber and broken down furniture to which nails and cobwebs clung. At the hearth he broke the pieces down under his boot (a messy business Ellie would never have allowed) and fed the lengths into the stove until the air began to roast and the iron ticked around a belly of roiling flame. Krazy Kat slept in the armchair, curled into the nest of stuffing she had ripped free her first night indoors. Ansel had brought in the cat when Aldine had talked about seeing mice, and so her heart fell when she saw what the cat had done to the armchair, but Ansel just shook his head and said, "Well, I invited her in and she just felt at home."

They left the radio covered and Aldine felt it watching them in the dark when there was a moon and the sheet glowed dimly in the corner. Ansel brought out the fretted dulcimer and she sang in a soft voice while he played, trying to forget Dr. Stober's car and the letter her sister would receive soon and the impossible questions of the future. When he set the dulcimer aside, she leaned into his chest, feeling the animal nature of herself, momentarily blind to anything but her own warmth and hunger. She wanted to kiss him but he directed her kisses away from his mouth, saying "Doctor's orders."

"But you seem fine."

He nodded. This morning he had felt tingly and energetic, invincible. Sometimes he felt tired again and his lungs had the old crackle. "Still," he said, "just to be safe . . ."

She said, when his hand lay warm on her belly, "I want to call the baby Ansel."

"Naw, you hadn't ought to do that," he said. "Too confusing. What else do you like?"

"What was your father called then?"

"Lucian."

She shook her head decisively, as if finding the right name would make everything normal. "Unless you want to."

"Not especially." He seemed to feel it, too, the triviality of the name compared to their other problems. "And what if the baby's a girl? What then?"

She couldn't help thinking that if she were married to Ansel, she would name a girl after her sister. "I used to like the name Vivien," she said. Outside the cold deepened and the stars shone. It had been three nights now since they took Dr. Stober's car. She wished she could just decide to have the baby. To begin pushing and have that part over and then Ansel could drive the car back and park it in front of Sonia's house and go away from there without being seen.

"What if someone comes here?" she asked. "To see Ellie?"

Ansel was quiet for a moment. "Just say the truth. She's staying with her sister until Neva's better."

"And this?" Aldine asked, pointing to her belly.

"Say you got married in Emporia, and your husband is looking for work."

She looked doubtfully at the fire, seeing the spaces between flames, the crumbling red between crumbling white.

"No one's likely to come," he said, and she reminded herself that Sonia Odekirk had left the farm because the houses that had once been lit were all going dark. She tried to feel nothing but the warmth of the fire, the warmth of the quilt, and the warmth of Ansel's body that made a cave around her. Inside, the baby shifted but then lay quiet, as if he, too, was in no hurry to meet the future.

88

Charlotte placed a square of white satin under the metal form of the button, checked to see if it was centered, and pushed hard on the shank. The fabric crimped with a satisfying poof and then she held up a metal knob sheathed in satin, the fifteenth of the thirty-five buttons that would hold her dress primly closed during the ceremony (and would let it fall open afterward, which she knew Mister would like whether she did or not)—an excessive number of buttons, her mother said, but if Charlotte was doing all the work, what did it matter? Clare was sleeping, and Neva had gone outside to play with her friend Marchie, which meant she wouldn't keep asking if she could help.

Charlotte got up from the table and started downstairs to see if there was any more leftover applesauce cake, the yummy one with raisins, cloves, cinnamon, and brown sugar (she'd had the girls bake several of them in the Practice House, along with four lemon jelly cakes, and by offering them at the Elks Club bake sale collected a handsome sum for the school). Today, when she reached the bottom of the stairs and pushed open the door to the café, she was relieved to find the room deserted. Her mother frowned on her personal raids because the cakes and pies were for customers, but now that Clare was laid up, she was a little more generous, permitting Charlotte to cut a big piece of whatever Clare would eat, and keeping her peace when Charlotte cut a small slice for herself.

The day was blue-green and warm, like most days, and although the front door was propped open, the café was closed. It was Sunday, the day her mother used to restock and deep clean and make everything just so for the week to come. As she moved toward the covered cake stands on the counter, Charlotte could hear muted voices in the kitchen, her mother's and Aunt Ida's, along with the clink of the bucket and the shush of the mop. *Wedding.* She heard the word *wedding*, and stood perfectly still.

"Why not push it back a bit?" Ida was saying. "Give Clare time to get up and around, give Ansel time to get back." A sloshing sound—her mother kept mopping. Ida said, "You don't want to stand there in front of the whole town without your husband there, do you?"

The mopping stopped. Charlotte could imagine her mother straightening her back, taking a deep breath. "He knows the wedding is the day after Thanksgiving. If he doesn't come back for it, he might as well stay gone."

"You don't mean that."

"I do, Ida. I truly do."

The words closed over Charlotte's head like water. She waited for Ida to talk sense into her mother. She waited to hear bitterness or anger or hurt in her mother's voice. But her mother just said flatly, "I don't need him anymore. He's gone now, yes, but he'd been gone, even when he was here."

Neva's voice interrupted from the back door, and something clanked on the floor.

"Well, hi, Miss Marchie, hi, Neva!" Ida said in a loud, enthusiastic voice. "I thought you two were going to the creek!"

"We need provisions," Marchie said in her scratchy voice. "Cakes and things."

"Oh, you do, do you?" Ida said. "Well, let's see here," and Charlotte was afraid that Ida would see her standing there at the counter, so she hurried quietly back up the stairs while Ida's heels clopped across the linoleum.

Charlotte positioned another square of satin in the button press, picked up a shank, and tried to take pleasure in the poof. She didn't know what to make of her mother's eerie calm, but she definitely agreed with her on one point: the date was set. Mister was planning on it. She was planning on it. She would absolutely hate waiting one extra day, let alone a month, to move into her own house and reclaim Artemis, who was living with Ida and Hurd because there was no place to keep a dog in an apartment over a café. When Charlotte walked back into her classes on Monday, November 27, she intended to be wearing a genuine diamond ring. She wouldn't be the Big Cheese of Spic-and-Span; she would be Mrs. James McNamara. If they put off the wedding, then what? Pity—and, yes, smugness—in the eyes of girls barely three years younger than she was, and all of them wondering just where her father was, and what the real reason was that the wedding had been postponed.

Another thought, much worse, came to her as she popped out a button like a mushroom cap. If they waited, and her father stayed away, what would Mister begin to think of their family?

She'd thought the Aldine business was over. She knew she shouldn't have written that silly note, but Aldine had no reason to assume a married man wrote her a love note, for God's sake, and her father should not have held Aldine's foot in that pitiful besotted way, either.

As far as Charlotte knew, that's all that happened. But maybe her mother had seen something else. Maybe it would be like that Norma Shearer movie *The Divorcee*, and her mother, eyes lowered with vengeful lust, would teach her father a lesson by sleeping with Robert Montgomery, although of course there wasn't anyone in Fallbrook who looked remotely like Robert Montgomery. Dr. Quigley, maybe. Charlotte considered him briefly, his elegant chin and polished shoes, then wondered what made her think such thoughts.

No. Charlotte should marry Mister on the day they planned, while her family still had a chance of seeming normal. If her father came back to lead her up the aisle, she would hold his arm and believe him blameless. And if he didn't come back, well, then, Uncle Hurd could give her away.

89

When a week had passed without discovery, Aldine tried not to think of the car or Ellie. She would have the baby, and Ansel would return the car, and then everything else could be worked out. A light snow fell and Ansel spread out a broken-down carburetor on the dining room table so he could work near her instead of alone in the barn. Krazy Kat, locked in as she was, began to use for her relief the corner of the basement where remnants of coal had once been swept. This meant the cat made sooty tracks that were hard to clean in her state. The cat was a good mouser, but she often left behind a bloody head or tail, which Ansel disposed of, though again there was a stain left behind, and she couldn't always find the energy to mop and scrub.

"What did you say it's called?" she asked Ansel. "The Progress House?"

"What?" he asked. It was pleasant to work on the machine, a thing whose purpose and nature he understood, while she was sitting nearby, stroking the cat as he worked, especially now that everything outside the window was outlined with the finest, lightest, purest snow.

"The little cottage for teaching girls how to be housemaids."

"Practice, I think."

"I'm no good at it," Aldine said. "I'd be a poor pupil."

"I like it this way," he said. "You don't need any practice."

Later that day, when every bit of the snow had melted, Aldine was upstairs lying beneath layers of quilts, trying to keep warm, when she heard an approaching car.

Ansel was out working, but Aldine didn't know if he was in the barn or the field. She didn't know if he would hear the car. Aldine went to stand by the window, keeping herself out of sight, eyes fixed on the dried husks of the cottonwood leaves, a few of which clung stubbornly to high branches. She could see, too, the rusted edge of a white tin cup one of the children—Neva probably—had left in the rickety tree house. A black car pulled to a stop under the tree and a man got out. It wasn't a police car, Aldine was sure. But it wasn't a neighbor, either, at least not one that she had ever seen.

She froze beside the curtain, printed all over with open-mouthed flowers. The man's feet thudded and scraped on the porch, and she stiffened herself for the knock of his fist on the door.

Instead she heard Ansel's voice, and when she allowed herself to look through the window again he was striding across the yard, wiping his hands on a rag.

"Western Union," she heard, and Ansel's voice saying thank you, and a few other comments she took to be about the weather. She stayed where she was as the man got back into his car, as the car door shut, as the tires went once more over dirt and loose stones. She stayed where she was as Ansel opened the front door and walked in, as he stood, she was certain, to peel open the envelope and read whatever was inside. She waited in the stillness. The cottonwood branches scraped against the window, and the dead leaves made a whispering sound.

His boots shuffled and she waited for him to call her. "Aldine?" he said.

Still she couldn't move. "Up here," she called.

He was heavy sounding on the stairs, and the old excitement of hearing him approach, the skin response to his nearness, was still there beside the dread.

His irises were like glass. "It's about Clare," he said. In one hand he held the cable; the other he rested on the doorknob. "He crashed a truck the day I left."

She waited.

"Ellie says he broke his leg."

"Is he all right?"

"I don't know. They brought the cable out once before," he said, holding the paper up, "but no one was here."

She swallowed and took this in. "Why did they come back?"

"Someone mentioned seeing a light on."

They were both quiet. When the car had approached, she'd forgotten her swollen feet, but they were again making themselves felt. She needed to sit down, and she walked to the bed. She was aware again that she was cold and hungry, or cold and dizzy, she wasn't sure which. She sat on the smooth edge of the bed and made herself say it. "Will you go back now?"

Ansel shook his head. Ellie hadn't asked him to come back. Her telegram just said *horrible accident* and *broken leg nailed together*. But she would expect him to come back, he thought. That's why she sent the news.

"I'm in the middle of something in the barn," he said. "We can talk about it later."

She nodded. After he left the house, she went to the window and looked beyond the cottonwood to the barn, and beyond the barn to the field, and beyond the field to the thin brown line of road, a road on which she could see the black shape of a passing car, one in which the driver and passenger might turn their faces to look, to take note, to carry word.

90

The nearness of the wedding put Charlotte in a jangly mood. She was barely able to read the message Clare wrote back to Lavinia, the one he'd printed so elegantly in Lavinia's Latin notebook, the one she was supposed to return to his little Florence Nightingale. "So what's it mean?" she asked Lavinia on the front steps of the school.

Lavinia gave her a baffled look.

"*Quantum mutatus ab illo,*" Charlotte said, giving the words a flat, twangy sound to make it seem like she wasn't even trying for authentic pronunciation.

"How changed from what he once was," Lavinia translated. "Why?"

"Check your Latin notes," Charlotte said, handing over the book. "Clare's written you a little Roman apology. I think he's waiting for a High Latin reply."

If Lavinia had been smitten before by Clare's face and body, she now felt a torturous kinship, an almost fanatical desire to win him by irony and wit. She had his words in her book. His Latin words. She spent her lunch hour searching through her reader for something not too preachy or inspirational. At last, she decided on *semper eadem*— "always the same." She wrote it carefully in her most feminine cursive, swirling the last stroke of the *m* as if answering one of those riddles in a Greek play where you won a kingdom for the right answer. Then she carried the notebook back to Miss Price, who was cutting out what had to be her wedding dress on one of the long homemaking tables. "Here's today's work," Lavinia said shyly, wondering if Miss Price would read it. Probably she would. Of course she would!

Charlotte nodded without looking up from the creamy expanse of satin. The more she tried to weigh the fabric down and line it up for cutting, the more it slipped away from her like yards of milk. "I'll give your missive to the invalid."

"That's pretty fabric," Lavinia said. Sunlight poured into the home arts building and she could see a hawk circling in the blue sky framed by the window. A crow passed in the same arc, the two arguing in midair, as crows and hawks always argued, she never knew why, though it made her wonder. Wasn't one a scavenger and the other a predator? And wasn't there sky enough, and trees enough, and food enough for both of them?

"It's charmeuse," Charlotte said, her body tense with the effort of holding the fabric in place.

"You should come visit Clare again," she said. "He's going bats staying in bed all the time."

"I don't know," Lavinia said, fingering the chrome edge of the table. "Maybe he just wants the notes."

"Maybe," Charlotte said, "but maybe not." She pretended to study the grain line she was measuring until Lavinia had turned away and walked almost to the door. "He thinks you're clever," Charlotte said. "He told me." She smiled her warmest smile. What Clare had actually said was that Lavinia was a little too clever, but that was just the usual fear the male species had of being shown up in the Brain Department.

The door closed behind Lavinia, and Charlotte sighed. The charmeuse had half cascaded over the edge of the table, and she felt cranky and incompetent. What kind of bride—and domestic arts teacher!—was still sewing her dress four days before the vows? Last July she had described her curriculum as "vocational homemaking and related courses planned to help the girl of today not only to live as a member of her family group, but to live well."

Not only to live, but to live well. She had to laugh. What a stuffed goose she could be.

Charlotte was straightening the charmeuse when the door opened again and Mister stepped quietly in, a surprise because she didn't usually see him during the school day. It was awkward, his being both on the school board and her fiancé, but she gave him one of her lavish smiles as he approached, and he removed his hat. There was something apologetic about the way he walked toward her—something about the way he only half smiled—that made her wonder if something was wrong.

"How's my goddess of the hearth?" he said.

"Snipping this expensive cloth to ribbons," she said, giving it a rueful glance. "Should've used poplin, I guess."

He made a murmuring sound. "Well, maybe if you stop feeling the pressure of getting it done by Friday."

This immediately set off alarms. "What do you mean?" she asked.

His gaze moved from her to the window, then down to the hat he held in his hands. Something was going on—she could feel it. He usually eased close and leaned into her, letting hands slide where they could—those were his goatish ways—but today he sat there fiddling with his hat.

"I've been talking to Ida," he said slowly, as if reading the words from the inside brim of his hat, "and she thinks—we think—it would be better to put off the date. You shouldn't get married without your father here, and I feel a little selfish taking your whole family over to the church while Clare is an invalid."

"I don't want to put it off," Charlotte said at once, surprised at her own vehemence.

"I don't either," he said in a low voice. He tried now to lean against the table and bring her to him, but she stood fast and cold. "I don't want to wait," he whispered, running one hand down her arm and onto her backside, which stiffened her and made her glance at the doors and windows, afraid to see Candy or Myrtis looking in.

She eased free of him and said, "My uncle can give me away."

"He can, but I'm sure your father's trying to wrap up his business in Kansas and get back here for this. How will it look if we go ahead without him? I'm going to be in your family from now on, and I don't want to start by burning bridges."

"You don't know my father," Charlotte said, and at once wished she hadn't. What did she want? For her fiancé to think her father was off committing adultery? "I mean that he's not one to take offense. He's practical about things, and he'd want us to be practical, too."

He was quiet for a time; then he said quietly, "I just have a bad feeling about going ahead without him. Ida does, too."

Ida. Why doesn't Ida just go peddle her fish? Charlotte lifted the small metal disk she used to secure the fabric, and as she expected, the cut wedge of charmeuse poured off the table like a white waterfall. She didn't reach to pick it up but instead pressed the cold steel into her palm. Marrying McNamara would transform her. She would be a California society woman. She would have her dog again. She would have curtains that matched the sofa and she would have a whole wall full of books, more books than she had ever seen in one place at one time. With McNamara, she wasn't clumsy and catty but clever and desirable. She became what he saw, and what he saw was the person she'd always wanted to be. He did that to her, made true the mirror that all her life had been distorted.

She dropped her eyes. "You're not sure anymore," she murmured. "It's just an excuse."

He drew up the long triangle of silk and laid it back on the table. He shook his head slowly and tried to pull her into the long-limbed net of himself. She twisted away but he held on until she stopped, and pulled her to him, and this time she let her hips rest against his inner thighs, her chest against his chest, and it gave her a certain kind of reassuring pleasure to note the immediate effect she had on him. She looked over his shoulders and, strangely, without alarm, saw Lavinia Gulden staring through the window at them. Charlotte did something that surprised her: she gave the girl a wink and a small, knowing smile before pushing McNamara away from her.

When she glanced again at the window, Lavinia was gone.

"How about December ninth?" he said, his voice low and husky now. "It's just two more weeks. Believe me, it's harder for me to wait than you."

"And what if he doesn't come back? Would we postpone again?"

"Why wouldn't he?"

The smell that lingered from their embrace was from the Wrigley's fruit gum he carried in his pockets. "He didn't like giving up and coming here," Charlotte said. "He would have stuck it out if Neva hadn't been sick. Probably until we were all half starved."

"But he didn't say what he was doing?"

"He's checking the farm and he had something official to do with the bank." She let her eyes settle deeply on his. "I just think that it's going to be hard for him not to extend his visit, and he's not like a lot of people—he doesn't like big parties and big social events." This wasn't 100 percent true, so she added something that was. "When he married my mother, he said the wedding party could be as large as she wanted as long as it wasn't more than he could count on his toes."

"Well," he said, "where your parents live doesn't affect whether I'm going to marry you."

She noticed that he'd said "parents," that he assumed, as anyone would, that two parents would live in the same place.

There were footsteps outside, and the sound of scraping. "I'd better go," he said.

"But if he doesn't return, we won't postpone again?"

"No," he said. "We won't."

"Honor bright?"

He made a small laugh. "Honor bright."

As he neared the door, something occurred to her. "How am I going to tell the girls?" she asked. This, the smallest problem, now seemed the most galling.

"What girls?"

"The girls in my class. The ones who are making the centerpieces and all."

"Can't we just save them?"

"They're autumn-colored. Autumn and Christmas aren't the same color."

"They are in California," he said, and pushed through the heavy steel door with a dapper doff of his hat to the cluster of girls waiting to come in.

"He looked happy, Miss Price," one of them called out to Charlotte.

"He should," she laughed. "I just granted him a two-week reprieve."

They groaned as one. It was endearing, really, the way they took her wedding planning on as their own. "So my father can have time to get back," Charlotte said, then, glancing at the sprawling cloth, "and to give me time to finish this vexsome dress."

She laughed, and the girls did, too.

Later on, she did the job her mother gave her, and she wrote:

> *Dear Dad,*
> *Jim thinks it would be better if you were here for the wedding and Clare, too. We're going to have it on December 9th instead so please hurry back. Clare's using his leg to get all kinds of attention. Poor kid is pretty bad off, though.*

She wondered what would happen if she said Dr. Quigley sure seemed to be spending a lot of time at the lunch counter, but instead she just said,

> *We all wish you'd hurry back, and me especially.*
> *Love always,*
> *Charlotte*

91

There was a Bitler Feed Store calendar on the kitchen wall, but no clocks. One freezing night Ansel stood in front of the calendar and figured out, more or less, what day it was. He did it while Aldine was asleep because they tried not to talk about Clare, Charlotte's wedding, Ellie, or Neva. They tried not to talk about anything outside the little cocoonish world they'd made for themselves. Since the telegram delivery he'd listened so keenly for cars that even in his sleep he would think he was hearing the popping whir of tires and would bolt up in bed, listening until Aldine would stir and say, "What?" and he would say, "Nothing. Nothing at all."

Night was also when he walked to the end of the drive and pulled on the stiff metal lip of the mailbox, feeling around in the hollow box for letters. He'd done it four times and his hand had found nothing.

Counting up as best he could, he came to Thursday, November 23. He'd left Fallbrook on the fourth, so he and Aldine had been together a little over two weeks and no one had come to accuse them of stealing the car. Perhaps the baby would come that night or in the morning and he could take the doctor's car back to Emporia and explain. This was the concern above all others, the fear of being arrested and branded a thief. The other problems were there, though. They waited in the corner like Ellie's radio.

If today was Thanksgiving, Ellie's birthday was two days ago and Charlotte's wedding was tomorrow. He ran his finger along the tacky edge of the counter, and then let go. He was tired now, more tired than he let Aldine see. Sometimes when she thought he was working in the barn he lay down to sleep, hoping that sleep would make him stronger. He would have been glad to lie down in the house instead, to pull her close beside him and listen to her talk if she felt like talking, to let the elliptical vowels and tongue-licked *r*'s lull him into believing he could live in the mere sound of her.

One afternoon he had come indoors and suggested a nap, but then, when they were lying down, he said, "Maybe you would tell me one of your stories."

She told him how their family had gone on holiday to the Isle of Skye because their father was to play music there, and while their mother was in the village shopping, their father took them down to the firth to look around. The tide was low, which meant you could see the hairy underparts of the sea and the wreckage that people threw away but never really got rid of: a rusted iron chain with links the size of her own head, a safe, the gears of an old clock. Aldine loved the outing, she said, but her sister said it all smelled of death, and she kept complaining that the salt water would spoil her shoes. She wanted to be off to the shops, but that was when Aldine found the little egg case sticking to a rock.

Aldine gave out a small pleasant laugh that wrapped around Ansel like a flannel blanket. His eyes had fallen closed and he kept them so.

"I said, 'Come see! I found a mermaid's purse!' but Leenie thought I'd found some ugly old pocketbook that I was *pretending* was a mermaid's."

She fell silent and after a few moments, he opened his eyes.

"Thought I'd bored you to death," she said. "You came in to nap after all."

But he liked all the stories of her childhood, which she lingered over and made seem magical as fairy tales, so he coaxed her on. She told him how their father strode over to the rock, peered down, and began carrying on as if Aldine had found a giant pearl. "It was a shark's egg," she said, and because Ansel had never seen one she told him what it looked like: a flat hourglass ridged like a fingernail but translucent enough to reveal the tiny creature in its embryonic water. It was so small and helpless, Aldine said, as delicate as a human baby in the womb and yet there it was lying outside, stuck to a rock, with nobody to watch over it, amidst all the broken things people had thrown away.

"Then what?" he asked.

"Nothing. We went back to the town. We couldn't help it at all, my father said."

She fell silent again.

"I wanted to take it with me and put it in a jar so nothing would hurt it but Father wouldn't allow it. Said we shouldn't deny the living thing its sliver's chance to live." A moment passed and then Aldine said, "I never saw another one. I always looked after that, when I was near a firth."

Ansel listened with his eyes closed.

"A photograph would've been splendid," she said. "But we hadn't a camera."

Ansel said nothing.

"I don't have a photograph of you, you know."

"You don't need one. I'm here. I'll always be here."

He'd turned in the bed then so that she could snug close to his back, and soon they had fallen to sleep.

It was later that night that the wind started blowing again and what he thought had receded roared up in his head and ran its sharp fingers along his lungs, leaving behind a hardness that made him catch his breath, his whole chest percolating with what felt like chunks of swallowed fire, and it was the day after that, when he thought Charlotte's wedding had occurred without him, that he felt inside the darkened mailbox and found the letter that said they were still waiting for him.

He burned it so Aldine wouldn't know.

92

Leenie Cooper had been holding Henrietta by the kitchen sink, staring up at the whiteness of the mountain peaks and trying to decide if she should hang the diapers out on the clothesline first, while Henrietta toddled around in the wet but not frozen grass, or if she should nurse Henrietta and put her down for her nap and then hang out the diapers, which would use up precious minutes of the free-handed nap period but would save her the trouble of dressing Henrietta in a bunch of clothes she didn't like at just the time of day when she was likely to scream her foolish little head off about it.

Leenie turned away from these thoughts when she heard mail plop through the front door a full two hours before the usual time. She said to Henrietta, "Let's go read the mail then, shall we?"

She had been offended—outraged, really—when her three deeply felt letters to Aldine about this new stage of her life (including a darling picture of Henrietta in her pink bonnet) had not produced a reply of any sort, so when she looked down and saw the faint but legible Kansas postmark on the blue envelope lying there on the sunlit stripes of wood, she might have had a begrudging moment, but she did not. She thought at once, and glowingly, of Aldine.

She stared at the envelope, trying to make sense of it—it was a stranger's name in the return address, not Aldine's, and someone had scrawled *sorry—was addressed wrong!—D. Friggati* across the front of it. Mrs. Friggati was the next-door neighbor who hated Mormons. The letter was postmarked November 7, and today was December 4, which meant the Friggatis had held on to a piece of their mail for nearly a month! Why anyone would keep a misdelivered letter so long was a topic she intended to raise no matter how forbearing Will thought they should be. She whisked Henrietta to the sofa with a little cry, intending to hold her in one arm while she ripped open the envelope, but Leenie's sitting down made Henrietta drop into the nursing position, where she screamed and squirmed with thwarted rage the whole time that Leenie read:

> *Dear Mrs. Cooper,*
> *You don't know me but I'm a good friend of your sister Aldine. I met her when we were both working at the Emporia Kansas Harvey House. A man came here today looking for her, and I think he is the reason for her getting let go. She is expecting. That's why she hasn't answered your letters.*
> *Right now she is living with a nice woman named Odekirk on Neosho Street. I thought you should know.*
> *Cordially,*
> *Glynis S. Walsh*

Leenie read the letter three times, then did the routine unfastening and shirt arranging to nurse to quiet Henrietta's wild crying. She must think a minute, calm Henrietta down, then bundle her up and walk to the corner and catch a bus to William's office. He would know what to do, surely.

93

The second time someone came to the Price house, it was a whole family in a blue car. A man was sitting at the steering wheel and when he pulled to a stop, a woman in a turquoise coat stepped carefully out into the gusty wind. She bore a covered dish and from the way she was holding it, swathed in a checkered towel, the food was still hot. She was vaguely familiar, middle-aged and slightly plump, her hair tied with a white chiffon scarf that the wind picked at. She'd put on lipstick, too. Three children sat in the backseat, and Aldine, from her usual watching place, saw to her horror that the one at the window looking out was Emmeline Josephson. That was why the woman's face looked familiar.

Aldine drew back from the window and stood still when the woman knocked and called, "Ellie? Ansel?" A pause, then, "Anybody home?"

"Nobody answers," the woman said, apparently to the car. Aldine didn't dare look now.

"I'll see if he's out in the barn," the man said, and Aldine pictured Mr. Josephson on his way to the barn, self-important and annoyed, no doubt, at how long this charitable act was taking. Aldine's heart felt too big, and she leaned against the wall to steady herself. They would find Ansel, and maybe they would want to come in the house with the food.

They would have all sorts of questions. She might go into labor while the Josephsons were blethering on, and what would Ansel say to explain the noise she was making upstairs?

For several minutes, Aldine heard nothing but gusts of wind and the scudding of shoes, as if Mrs. Josephson were walking back and forth on the porch to look for something or to keep herself warm.

When someone spoke again, it was Mr. Josephson in a brusque tone. "Leave it there."

"Here?" Mrs. Josephson was incredulous. "On the porch?"

"Yes, on the porch, for chrissakes. Leave it and don't expect to get the dish back, either."

Aldine peered carefully out. Emmeline was stepping out of the car, followed by Berenice.

"Back in the car!" Mr. Josephson yelled at them. "Right now! We're leaving."

And in only a few moments more, they had all piled back into the blue car, and it was tearing away with the pop of spit-out gravel. Aldine sank to the floor until she had the breath to go downstairs.

The casserole dish lay just outside the front door, still wrapped in the checkered cloth, and the smell that came from it was heavenly. She carried the dish inside and sat down in the chair, unwilling to separate herself from its warmth and its savory scent, wondering what Mr. Josephson had seen or done or heard that put him in full retreat. She lifted the corner of the cloth and stared at the casserole with its perfect brown crust. For perhaps a full minute she sat holding the dish before Ansel emerged from the barn and joined her where she sat, holding it in her two warmed hands.

"Did they talk to you?" he asked.

She shook her head.

"See you?"

"No."

"Good," Ansel said, and then he said it again. "Good."

417

Aldine was ravenous, and she held the casserole in her hands. "What happened then? Why did they leave?"

He had heard the car, he said, and he had seen Josephson making his way to the barn. He had turned back to look at the doctor's Nash Phaeton in the corner of the barn. The tarps that they pulled over it did not quite cover the tires. Josephson would see it.

"So I went out," Ansel said. "I told him to keep his distance. I lied to him a little bit. Exaggerated, you might say. I told him I had TB and had come home to ride it out one way or the other." He smiled at Aldine. "Guess he believed me because he all but bolted for the car."

Aldine gave out with a light musical laugh, and he would've laughed, too, but he was afraid it would trigger the hacking cough. He'd let himself cough for Josephson's benefit. Let himself cough long and hard and when he'd spit onto the ground, they'd both stared at the blood-dark sputum. That was when Josephson beat his retreat.

Aldine pushed aside Ansel's tools to make space on the dining room table and they began to eat. Gulling Mr. Josephson made the good food better, in Aldine's opinion. Chicken and potatoes and gravy and carrots, all in a buttery brown crust—it seemed truly divine. For days they'd eaten meagerly on cornmeal cakes and stewed fruit and strange treacle-dark meat. Now they had home-cooked, hot-from-the-oven food. He ate, as he always did now, using his own spoon and bowl. She ate straight from the casserole dish. They ate and felt warmer, ate and ate on.

94

The first days of December had been hot and dry, as if summer had stolen into Fallbrook for a little visit, and when Lavinia climbed the stairs outside the café late Monday afternoon, she found Miss Price on the balcony, leaning on the brick wall with her eyes closed. If Miss Price had been smoking or hanging out laundry, it would've seemed more normal, but she was just leaning on the wall, eyes closed, wearing her red-and-black teaching dress with a pair of faded satin house slippers. Her hair was not fixed, and her complexion was very white. Lavinia didn't know whether to creep ahead or clear her throat. It didn't matter. A cat dropped from its perch on the railing, and Miss Price opened her eyes.

"Hi, Miss Price," Lavinia said. "Hot, isn't it? For December and all."

Miss Price touched a hair to put it into place, but her hands were stiff and jerky, and her eyes seemed almost evasive. She might recently have been crying. "Are you all right, Miss Price?"

Charlotte gave a little laugh, and felt something bubble at her nose, which she daubed with her sleeve. No, as a matter of fact, she wasn't all right. Nothing, not one little thing, was all right. "I'm fine," she said. "Kind of a tough day for Clare, though."

Lavinia's polite-girl expression fell away. "What do you mean?"

"Dr. Quigley took the nail out today. Clare's leg is up in a crane-thingy."

"The nail?" She didn't know there was a nail. Without wanting to, she thought of a fingernail being yanked out.

"I missed it," Miss Price said. "I was still at the school, but my mom had to help. She said Dr. Quigley held a match to the pointy end of the nail, which went all the way through his leg, and then he turned it around in there to see if he could free it up."

"God," Lavinia blurted.

"It wouldn't come free, and he was in such pain that my mom threw up, but Clare didn't yell or anything. Quigley couldn't get over that, how he didn't scream." She took a deep breath. "Anyhow, they had to put him under to tug and yank some more and it finally came out. Now his leg's all plastered up and hanging from the ceiling, and he says he's okay, but I don't know if he'll be up to much."

Lavinia glanced toward the door that would admit her to the hall-way. "Maybe I shouldn't go in."

Charlotte turned. "You should," she said. "You did your hair and all."

Lavinia shrank inside herself. She had curled every strand of her hair with rags, attempting something along the lines of Myrna Loy as the Countess Valentine, but what she saw in the mirror was more like Countess Valentine's crazy old uncle.

"You sure?" she asked.

"One hundred percent," Charlotte said.

Lavinia turned the knob and stepped into the dark hallway of the apartment. She'd been here nearly every day in the past few weeks and the rooms always smelled of whatever Mrs. Price was cooking down-stairs—pork today, and sauerkraut. Possibly a cake in there somewhere, though onions overpowered it. Lavinia sniffed her fingertips. No, that smell was her. They'd made another molded salad in home arts, and

Candy had told Lavinia to juice the onion because Candy had just painted her nails.

Lavinia rubbed her fingers on her skirt. Clare's door was ajar, and she wanted to go in and see him because seeing him was all she thought about night and day. She studied, through the gap between the door and the wall, the white plaster dirigible of Clare's leg. She couldn't see his face, but she decided that if he was asleep she could give herself the pleasure of looking at his face, then go away. She nudged open the door.

He was awake, and he looked so tired and gaunt that something luxurious and protective burst open and flowed through her.

"Hi," she said, whispering.

"Hi," he said, not whispering exactly, but in a low voice.

She straightened up and made herself speak normally. "Not so good, huh?"

"It's better now," he said, flicking his eyes at the suspended leg.

"It sounded pretty bad, the way your sister put it."

"Yeah, well." He produced a small ironic smile. "I didn't know today was the day, you know?"

"It's been exactly a month," she said.

This registered in his eyes. A surprise, but whether pleasant or unpleasant, she wasn't sure.

"Exactly a month," Clare repeated. "Dr. Quigley said the same thing." He issued a dry laugh. "I guess I should've been counting, too."

"Miss Price said Dr. Quigley couldn't believe you didn't scream or anything."

Clare made a small snorting sound. "Well, I was screaming inside, I can tell you. Inside I was screaming like a banshee."

She laughed. It was funny. He was funny. It was one more reason she craved his company. "Why didn't you just go ahead and scream then? That's what I would've done."

His eyes closed and opened in a long slow blink. "No, you wouldn't. Not if customers were eating in your mother's restaurant downstairs."

For a moment he seemed to be dozing. Then when he looked at her again, he nodded at the *Enterprise* in her hand. "How 'bout you read me something?"

She'd done this before. He liked the local gossip columns, especially About You and Others, which was townspeople news, and What's Buzzin', Cousin?, an earnest but inane account of high school events written by Myrtis French.

Lavinia sat down on the steamer trunk against the wall, crossed her ankles, and began to read aloud. She wondered if sitting on the trunk would activate the cologne she'd put on the backs of her knees, but all she smelled was the onion juice on her hands and the sauerkraut smell seeping up from the café.

"At-tention, Fallbrookites!" she read, trying to enliven her voice so he wouldn't fall asleep. *"Barney Patten and George Harris have both reported their Bourbon turkeys are laying, but we're kinda persnickety. We're holding out for some good Scotch!"*

Clare's eyes were closed, but his lips formed a small smile.

"I ate a turkey egg once," Lavinia said. "It was okay I guess." She tried not to touch her hair. "The yolk was really thick. I almost gagged on it."

Clare didn't speak, and Lavinia's skin suddenly glazed with sweat. Gagging on turkey eggs—this was something to talk about? She heard herself reading the next thing her eyes fell upon.

"La Rue Beauty Salon. Mar-o-Oil shampoo, seventy-five cents. Lash and brow dyeing, one dollar. Facials, one dollar. Artistic haircutting, fifty cents."

Why was she reading this to him? Lavinia felt sick in her stomach and chest.

Clare said, "Artistic haircutting. What would that be?"

"Why ask me?" she said in an irritated tone, and wondered at her own peevishness. She looked down at her lap, where her clipped, cleaned, buffed fingernails rested on her knees. She felt a yearning for him that was like the music her mother played over and over again on the gramophone, a recording of Artur Schnabel playing Beethoven's Sonata in G Minor on the piano. Each note longed for the next, but was trying to seem cheerful and unconcerned. In certain places, the music managed to be giddy, tripping along like a child. Then it was running headlong into grief.

"My sister's going to that place, I think," Clare said lazily, almost as if waking from a dream. "La Rue Beauty Salon. For the wedding."

He kept his eyes closed as he spoke. There was a mirror on the dresser opposite his bed, and she looked gravely at the kinks in her long hair, and at what she thought of as the Ursa Minor constellation of moles on her cheek. She always sat on his left side so he wouldn't see the moles so much. Her gaze shifted when he moved abruptly, his face tightening. She thought he might be feeling what he called the long dull ache.

"Are you all right?" she asked.

Long seconds passed and then he said, "I'm fine."

Just like Miss Price had said *I'm fine*.

"Why do you say you're fine when you're not?"

His eyes shot open and he squeezed his jaw. "Because that's what you *do*, Lavinia," he said in a low voice. "You say things are God-damned *fine* even when they are God-damned not."

They were both quiet a long while.

He'd never been mad at her before. Usually they would do their homework together, which wasn't difficult for him. At first, she was flabbergasted by his ability to read and recall but she'd begun not just to take it for granted but, very slightly, to resent it—why should remembering facts and dates and Latin declensions be so much easier for him?

He *had* won a bet reciting all of "Charge of the Light Brigade"—she had asked him about it—but it was a mistake, he said. "People don't really like their Kansas farm boys quoting Tennyson." He'd smiled at her. "Upsets their sense of order." She liked it when he recited poems for her. Usually he would close his eyes when he did this, as if the words could only be seen in some imaginary land. Once he recited lines and lines and lines of a poem by Shakespeare about Venus and Adonis, and though the density and complexity of the words made the language seem almost something other than English, she was carried along by his voice and the pure pleasure of the flowing, unfamiliar words, and then, abruptly, there was something about Venus kissing Adonis's cheek and chin and where she stopped she would begin again and exactly at the moment when her mind was catching on these words, and oddly awakened to their meaning, the voice stopped and his eyes clicked open, and he was staring at her in a way that she had never been stared at before. Before that, she'd wondered whether she was in love with Clare Price. After that, she stopped wondering; she felt it in her bones.

Thereafter, in addition to homework, they would talk.

Clare would tell Lavinia things, like how they'd burned all their dead hogs in Kansas after the hogs died of cholera, and how they'd once had a schoolteacher live in their house, Scottish or Irish, she couldn't remember which, but her name was Miss McKinnon and she had been like one of the family. He felt bad that they left her behind when they moved, and she never wrote back to him. Lavinia didn't like that story because she could tell that, though he didn't say it outright, this school-teacher was someone Clare had been smitten by, except there seemed to be something even worse than that. It seemed somehow as if Clare didn't mind—or perhaps even secretly enjoyed—Lavinia's knowing that there had been someone he'd loved in this way, which might be a way he would never love anyone else.

Now, quietly, Clare said, "I'm sorry. I'm sorry I talked like that. I know you didn't mean anything." A few moments passed. Then he said, "My mother says my father isn't coming back."

"But why not? Did the bank business go wrong?" She'd heard Clare and everyone else say that's what he was doing back there.

"That's what we thought," Clare said. "But he didn't answer my mother's cable, or Charlotte's letter. And instead of just checking on our old house, we think he's living in it. Some people we know, they've seen the lights on. And then a neighbor went over to visit, and found him there. He told the neighbor he was sick and was just riding it out, whatever it was."

A few seconds passed, and then Lavinia said, "What's your mom going to do?"

Clare shook his head. "I don't know. Charlotte started wailing about how McNamara would never marry her now, which I don't think is true, but maybe it is because my mother said not to tell him."

He turned his brown eyes to her. They reminded her of little dark pools in the Santa Margarita River, the shallows of which were flecked with gold sand. "You won't tell anyone, will you?" he asked, rubbing at the top part of his thigh like he wanted to get inside the plaster. "Like Candy and Myrtis or anyone."

Lavinia stiffened. "Candy and Myrtis? I don't talk to them about real things. I only talk about real things with you."

This registered with him, too, just like the fact that she knew the number of days since the accident, and he seemed to be trying to decide whether to speak further or not. "There's one more thing," he said finally. He twisted toward the nightstand and felt for a book inside the drawer. From the book he retrieved a folded sheet of paper, which he handed to her.

At the top, it said, *Rules to Be Observed for the Prevention of the Spread of Tuberculosis.*

"I don't understand," Lavinia said slowly as she read the rules. "Who's this for?"

"It was in my father's account book. Folded like this with a bill from Dr. Quigley. I remember that he went to the doctor before he went away because my mom thought he had bronchitis."

"Did you show this to your mom?"

"No."

"Well, what are you going to do?"

"I already did it."

Lavinia waited.

"When Dr. Quigley was here, before my mom came up, I asked him. He didn't want to tell me at first, but then he said he gave the paper to my dad. There have been cases of TB in people who'd lived in the Midwest on farms, so he gave my father the test. My father was supposed to wait for the results, but he left."

Lavinia looked down at her fingers. She didn't know whether to prompt him or to wait.

"The test was positive," Clare said.

"That means he has it, right?"

Clare nodded.

They both sat still, as if hiding from a large predatory animal that was sniffing for them in the woods.

"What about you?" Lavinia could barely croak out.

Clare shook his head. "He gave Neva the test when we first got here, and it was negative. He said that he took a sample of my spit when he operated on me that night after the accident. He said it was a public health issue. I don't have it."

Lavinia felt herself breathing again.

After a time, she said, "Maybe that's why your father isn't coming back or answering the door. So he won't infect anybody."

Clare pressed one side of his thigh. "I thought of that, but I don't see how he could even know."

"Did Dr. Quigley tell your mom?" Lavinia asked.

"I don't know."

Lavinia looked at the solid white plaster around Clare's leg, and then at his fine-boned, unbroken fingers, precise and honey colored against the sheet. "I'll bet that's why he left," she said softly. "He sensed it, and he went away so you'd all be safe."

Clare looked at her with what she took for doubt, and then he closed his eyes. "I don't think I can talk anymore, Vinnie," he said.

The nickname, used for the first time, found the nerves in her face and hands and made them feel more alive.

"Do you want me to go now?" she asked.

"No," he said. "Come closer, would you?"

She couldn't move the steamer trunk, so she went around to the other side and moved some clothes off a little wooden stool. Then she pulled the stool up to the side of the bed, and he opened his eyes to see where she was.

"Now give me your hand," he said.

She put her hand in his, and even after he fell asleep, she stayed there like that, letting go only when she realized that the *Rules to Be Observed* were still lying open on the trunk, so she refolded the paper and hid it in the account book, which she slid into the drawer, and then she sat down beside the bed and took his hand again.

95

Aldine was standing in the kitchen when the pain seized her, obliterated normal thought, and then let her go. It was like Krazy Kat taking a mouse in its teeth and then, at the height of terror, pretending to let it go. Aldine looked at the calendar. It was December 4. Since the Josephsons had come, she'd stopped crossing off the days and instead put next to each passing day a pencil mark so faint it could not be seen beyond close inspection. The pain again came and went. She walked upstairs to the bedroom, certain she would lie down and have a baby in a few minutes, but the awful clenching didn't return and she grew bored. The third time, she staggered to the barn to tell Ansel, but before she could open the heavy door, the tightness that made her stagger released her once again. She told him, "I thought it was coming," stood and watched him for a moment as he did something inside the tractor's unfathomable parts, trying not to look at the doctor's car. The barn was even colder than the house so she kissed him on the cheek and went back inside.

All morning, the gripping started hard and sharp, then tossed her aside to wait some more. It was exhausting, but she tried to keep herself busy. She washed a pan so she could bake a flat cornbread that needed no eggs, a recipe she'd found written on a yellowed piece of paper in the same drawer that held the vegetable seeds. She heated a jar of Sonia's stewed tomatoes. It looked as if it might snow, and by the time Ansel sat with her at the table, white bits had begun to swirl outside the window.

He asked if she'd had more pains.

"Six times," she said, and he neither nodded nor shook his head, but put his hand to her sleeved arm and said she should lie down after dinner.

Afternoon was silence, snowflakes that dissolved upon touching the ground, and increasingly frequent episodes of pain, which she waited for on the bed. Ansel had decided to work downstairs on some part of the tractor she could not identify. Seeing the greasy parts spread out on old newspaper on the dinner table made it almost seem as if the barn had come into the house, but she didn't mind. She liked the oily smell, in fact, and sometimes she had to laugh, thinking what Ellie or Charlotte would do if they saw tractor parts in the front room. Each time the hurting started she counted to keep from crying out, telling herself that she could get to a larger number than she had reached last time, and only if the pain was still fierce when she reached that number would she call him upstairs. What time it was when that happened, she didn't know because they never knew what time it was. The night had begun, and from then on he was either beside her in the bedroom, solid and still in the chair he had brought from downstairs, or he was preparing what he said he would need when the baby came; she looked up once to see him carrying a knife, another time, a stack of towels. He passed before her like a figure in a pantomime, the props suggestive of acts she could not foresee. She was mauled by the pain and abandoned, mauled and abandoned. Many hours passed in this way, the frequency of pains accelerating until there was hardly a break between them, and he looked at her and said he was going to see if he could feel the baby's head now. He said, yes, he could, but Aldine could only feel the huge-ness around which everything strained, an immensity that couldn't pass, despite the force of what felt like a river pushing it down. "Yes, now," he said, "it's coming now," and finally all the water in the river seemed to bear down at once and she felt the most wonderful shattering. "Look now," he said, and he held up a baby girl.

96

The day was cool but the sun was bright, a good day to see the Sleeping Indian and even the purplish gauze that was the ocean if you were on a hill, but Neva wasn't on a hill. She was in the alley behind the café. The trunk of the queen palm was rippled and hairy. Blond paint was peeling off the side of the café, where it said, *The Sleeping Indian Café—100% Clean*. Neva found a sunny place and sat down cross-legged. She fiddled with the black and yellow Bakelite bangles, rolling them around her wrist before using them to make a pedestal for the apple she was eating, one that would, for a while, anyway, keep the bitten part out of the dirt. Charlotte had said, "Why do you even want those ugly things?" but Charlotte probably just wanted them herself.

It was a green apple, her favorite, and she took another bite. She closed her eyes and willed her father to appear with Aldine. It was Friday, only one day more to Charlotte's wedding day, and Neva had asked Santa if he could grant an early request this year. She kept her eyes closed for an extra count to ten because she heard someone walking in the alley, a shuffling, heavy sort of walk, a man's walk, and her heartbeat quickened. But when she opened her eyes, it wasn't her handsome,

handsome father. It was Uncle Hurd. "Morning, Miss Geneva," he said. "The big day approaches."

She looked down at her apple. Maybe what her mother had said at dinner was true. Her father was going to live in their old house in Kansas, and they couldn't join him because of her. Because of her lungs. "When will he come back?" Neva had asked, and her mother wouldn't answer. She didn't like California if it was going to be like this. She slid her bracelets up and down on her wrist. They were sticky now from the apple.

When she looked up, Uncle Hurd was watching her so sadly that she put down the apple, stood up, and held out her arms. He lifted her up and she laid her head on his shoulder. He didn't say anything except, "That's better."

He held her and stared off toward the packing plant.

"You miss your dad, don't you?"

Neva pushed her head up and down.

"Well, we all do, don't we?" her uncle said and then she closed her eyes while he carried her around the café. She felt the warm cotton of his shirt against her face and legs, and then, when he pulled up a little and said, "Well, hello there, Boss," she opened her eyes and saw Mr. McNamara's big brown head and big white smile. Uncle Hurd's hand slipped a little when he set her down, and she felt the jolt of the pavement through her skin.

Mr. McNamara made a big show of holding open the door for Uncle Hurd and then he looked down at her. "What about you, girly? Would you like to come in?"

With the door open, the hot egg-and-sugar smell of custard seemed to brush up against her skin, and inside, behind the counter, her mother was talking to a customer and holding a spoon that shone in the long sideways sunlight.

"How about it?" Mr. McNamara said. "Could I buy you a root beer float?"

Neva turned away without a word. She didn't feel like having a root beer float that Mr. McNamara paid for and she didn't feel like watching men eat big mouthfuls of food and laugh big laughs. She didn't feel like playing jacks with Marchie and she never ever wanted to put on the flower-girl dress Aunt Ida had made for her, not if her father and Aldine weren't there. Maybe she would just stay home with Clare on Saturday. That was another reason there shouldn't be a wedding. Clare couldn't go, either. Charlotte should just wait some more until they were all back together again, was her opinion.

97

At dusk on December 8, Dr. Myron Stober was walking home through the streets of Emporia. It was cold. At first there were people here and there, but as he passed out of the commercial district, he became one of just two people on the street, himself and, ten yards or so before him, a small brown-haired woman in a green scarf. The woman kept glancing back with a worried look. He nodded and tried to smile, and he slowed down, but it aggrieved him that she kept throwing nervous looks over her shoulder. It was cold and he was losing light. He decided to cross the street, speed up, and get home.

But when he reached his own door and set the key to the lock, he heard footsteps, and there she was, standing on the sidewalk behind him: the woman in the green scarf.

"Good evening," the woman said, a little abashed. "I see we were going the same place after all!"

"My office is closed for the day," he said.

"It's okay. I was headed back there," she explained, pointing to where Sonia Odekirk lived.

He nodded without interest, but, instead of proceeding to Sonia Odekirk's, the girl lingered.

"You must be Dr. Stober," she said.

He nodded.

"I'm Glynis Walsh."

Again he nodded, then, pushing open his door, felt the first wave of warmth from within.

"I think my friend Aldine was working for you," the woman added. "I was just going to tell her good-bye."

Dr. Stober abruptly turned around. "Friend of hers, are you?" He stood facing her, and fingered the soft folds of the handkerchief that lay unused in his coat pocket. In the left pocket he kept the last handkerchief his wife, Lucy, had washed and ironed. In his right he kept the ones he actually used.

"Yes," she said, but she looked a little strange when she said it, as if he might try to disprove it. She stood still in the gray evening air, rubbing the dead grass with one shoe, each breath a small, shapeless cloud. "Do you know if she had her baby?"

"No," Dr. Stober said, and heard the coldness in his voice, so he added, "I'm afraid I don't." They were perhaps ten feet apart, and he wanted to learn whatever it was this girl could tell him about Aldine. In the days following the theft, the doctor had begun to feel that the arrangement he'd made with Mrs. Odekirk would never satisfy him. He could never enjoy the car that she'd promised to buy him (if in fact she could afford a Phaeton) and could never stop wondering what had happened to his own. He'd begun to think of himself as one of Dashiell Hammett's Continental Ops—Dick Foley, maybe, or Mickey Linehan. He gathered information. He waited. He trusted in the general weakness and corruption of others.

Dr. Stober took a step closer to the girl. He did his best to smile. "I've been worried about her, in fact. She was due a few days back, and I was supposed to deliver the baby, but she's run off."

Glynis looked genuinely surprised. "Run off?"

"I have a feeling the father showed up."

Glynis tugged at her scarf like it scratched her chin. He wished he could see her face better. It had grown darker and she stood beyond the illumination of the streetlamp. "I wanted to tell her I finally got transferred to La Castañeda," the girl said.

"I've been there," Dr. Stober said. In one of the Hammett books, *The Glass Key* or *The Dain Curse*, the Continental Op was talking gently to someone he wanted information from and the author used the word *crooned* to describe his way of speaking. Stober had liked that. It made him understand that the op's coaxing way of talking was like serenading. "La Castañeda," he said, doing his best, "it's quite grand, magnificent really, an absolute jewel."

"That's what I hear, too," the girl said. "And outdoor tubs with natural hot springs right next door."

"*Yes,*" the doctor said with luxurious emphasis, though he didn't remember any hot springs. He hadn't stepped foot in the hotel. Lucy had wanted to go in, but he'd been in no mood for it. "A tub of piping hot mineral water," he said to the girl, "now *that* would be the place to soak one's feet after a long day."

The girl laughed out loud. It was so easy, being pleasant; he wondered at the general veneration of it. "We'll tell Aldine of your good fortune when we see her," he said.

"Will you? Well, thank you very much."

"It might help . . ." He acted as if this was just occurring to him. "You wouldn't know who the father is, do you?"

"The baby's, you mean?"

"Yes, the baby's."

It was impossible to see Glynis's eyes clearly. Her face was so pale it seemed in the darkness almost white. He kept his hands in his pockets, rubbing his thumb back and forth on the soft, clean handkerchief, balling the dirty one with his other hand. "I'd like to know that she's safe," he said. "Mrs. Odekirk and I have been worried like you wouldn't believe."

Glynis, who had pressed the back of one hand to her lips for a long moment, took the hand away. "I think he did show up," she said. "He came into the restaurant looking for her."

He waited. Sometimes the Continental Op stopped asking and just waited.

"It was a name I'd never heard before. The man's name was Ansel."

Dr. Stober raised his chin slightly to show he was expecting a bit more.

"Price," she said. "Ansel Price."

He spelled it aloud and she said, "Yes, that's right. I saw it on his letters to her."

In Aldine's note she had said she was taking the car to help a friend. "This Ansel Price," he said, "did he come from around here?"

"Yes. Aldine lived with him and his family when she was a teacher in Dorland."

That was enough, Stober thought. More than enough. "Thank you, my girl," Stober said, his voice suddenly brusque. He stepped past the girl and strode toward the rear cottage.

"You'll tell Aldine, though, when you see her, where I'll be?" the girl called after him, but he didn't answer. He was already pounding on Sonia Odekirk's door.

98

Ellie had not expected her father to come to Charlotte's wedding. She'd even bet Ida five cents that he wouldn't. But here he was on the eve of the day, walking in while she and Ida put the finishing touches to the kitchen after a long day of baking. Herr Hoffman looked prosperous as ever, but smaller, his back no longer straight, his neck more deeply descended into the cavern of his chest. His blue eyes were as aloof as she remembered, though, when he presented himself in the door of the café, looked from Ellie to Ida, and said, "So this is California."

They both had their hair in rollers and scarves, which made hugging awkward. Tears ran down Ida's cheeks, as if she had missed him, but Ellie's eyes were dry as stones. For a fleeting moment she braced herself for the cold formality between her father and Ansel, but that dread was at once displaced with another: the fact that Ansel wasn't here for his daughter's wedding.

Her father was looking approvingly here and there in the kitchen. The pies stood in a neat row alongside the canisters of cookies, and everything gleamed in the kitchen. It was her mother who had taught her that, never to leave a kitchen with anything unclean or undone, but perhaps it had been her father who had demanded it. "Everything sparkling," he said, nodding to himself, and she was surprised how a compliment as mild as this could suffuse her with prideful pleasure.

And then in the next moment, her father said, "And where are your husbands?"

Ida cast a quick glance at Ellie, then told their father that Hurd was up at the house and why didn't she just go fetch him?

Ellie watched her go, then began folding the dishrag she was holding into small squares.

"And your Ansel?"

"He's in Kansas, Papi," she said, the old term of endearment out of her mouth before she could remember she was forty-one.

"Kansas?" he said, the coldness coming into his voice, but the back door opened, and there stood Neva, staring at them both, wearing those grating clacking bracelets of Aldine's. Ellie could tell her father wasn't sure who Neva was; he had probably not seen a photograph since Neva was a baby.

"That's my youngest, Geneva Louise. Neva, this is your Opa Hoffman."

Neva stared but didn't move.

"How old are you, *meine Liebste*?" her father asked, his voice a little too loud for the endearment to ring true.

Neva said she was eight. For once, Ellie didn't remind her to smile and to look adults in the face when she answered them.

"Do you want some coffee?" Ellie asked her father. "Then we have to get these pies into Hurd's car and over to the Practice House."

"The practice house?" her father said. "And what is this practice house?"

Ellie tried to explain, but the more she heard of her description, the less she liked it.

"So," her father said, "this is where good girls learn to become good wives?"

Ellie couldn't bring herself to say yes. "Something like that," she said.

Her father was nodding. "It is a good idea," he said. "We should have these practice houses all over the country."

"What can I do?" Neva asked. She came over and wrapped her arms around Ellie's legs. "I don't have anything to do."

"Go play Fat and Lean with Clare," she said. "And when Ida gets back, she'll help you try on your dress. I'll be upstairs soon."

Hurd had appeared, and he and Opa were soon discussing real estate over pie and coffee (*More dishes to clean*, Ellie thought). Her father asked one question after another about crop yield, abundance of water, cost per acre, hourly wages. She wondered if he even remembered that Clare was hurt. She'd written him about the accident but hadn't mentioned that Ansel wasn't here to help.

She began settling pies into cloth-lined baskets so they could be carried to the car and Hurd, seeing this, rose to help. He brought the car around to the back door and they took out all the pies except for the chocolate creams that were still cooling under wax paper.

"I'll bring those later," she said. She'd expected her father to ride to the Practice House with Hurd, but he didn't. He returned to the café and sat on a counter stool watching Ellie as she collected the cups and saucers he and Hurd had just dirtied.

"And why is your Ansel back in Kansas?"

She looked at him, then looked away. She wished Nevie hadn't gone upstairs. If she were still here, he wouldn't have dared to ask. Ellie scoured the dishes and silverware, rinsed them, dried them. Only then did her father say, "Eleanor?"

She hung the last cup from its cupboard hook, and turned around.

"He has TB," she said. She was surprised by the tremor in her voice. "He went there to keep it from us." She didn't like giving Ansel a noble reason for leaving her, but she preferred it to her own humiliation.

"And you know this without a question?"

She nodded. Dr. Quigley had told her. He had waited for a private moment. It wasn't just that his words were solicitous; it was his eyes, too, and his gaze seemed to slip in and slide through her body, a strange feeling to have while learning your husband is mortally sick.

"I think he went there to protect us," she said.

"And you and the children, none of you have it?"

She shook her head. "No."

"Good," her father said, nodding slightly. "That's good." It was a kind of declamation. The look on his face was the one she'd observed as a girl when he'd closed a ledger book containing satisfactory results and rose from his desk and said, *There*.

Footsteps on the stairs, then Neva pushed open the door and said, "Clare won't play Fat and Lean. He doesn't feel good."

Her father turned on the counter stool and faced Neva. "Your Opa needs a boutonniere," he told her. "Want to help him buy one?"

"I don't know what that is," Neva said.

"It's a flower. For proud *Großvaters* to wear."

"I'm going to be the flower girl," Neva said. "But I don't want to be."

"The flower girl will know what color I should buy," he said, "and where the flower shop is."

Neva shook her head. "There isn't a flower shop."

Her father made a low humming sound. It seemed almost as if the fact that the town had no flower shop was being added to his real estate computations.

"Ida's bringing roses from her garden," Ellie said. "We have flowers year-round here."

Her father seemed not to be looking at her but through her. Then he turned abruptly to Nevie. "And perhaps you could teach your Opa the Fat and Clean," he said.

99

The next morning, Dr. Stober posted a note on his office door saying that the office was closed for the day because of family business. He'd thought of writing *In order to reclaim stolen car* but decided against it; a shrewd investigator kept his intentions to himself. He walked to the shop of the man who formerly changed the oil in his car and said that the 1932 Nash Phaeton with carpeted floors that he had bought for his wife, Lucy, just before she died had been stolen, and that he now knew the name of the man who had stolen it.

"That's a nice car to have stole from you," the man said, sleepy eyed and sluggish. His name was Carlisle and he seemed too potbellied to slide himself under cars all day. There were no cars, at present, in the shop, and Carlisle had been warming himself beside a red-mouthed heater, laying out cards for solitaire. The air smelled of grease and cigarettes.

"I need you to drive me out where he lives. The man who took it."

"Where's that?"

Dr. Stober told Carlisle what Sonia Odekirk had told him the night before: "In Loam County, about seven miles due east of Dorland." The old woman had let things go downhill in her housekeeping—that was the first thing he'd noticed—and it had cost her what little respect he'd still had for her, but she was at least willing to confirm that she'd known someone named Ansel Price and that Aldine had lived with his family while she taught school.

"Loam County?" Carlisle asked and when Stober nodded, Carlisle said, "That's quite a drive." He placed the two of spades on an ace.

"I am aware," Stober said.

Carlisle flipped three more cards to a king he couldn't play, then whistled a single descending note to emphasize his displeasure with either the game or the plan. Dr. Stober wondered how frequently, if ever, Carlisle put a washcloth to his face.

"Five hours to get there," Carlisle said, flipping another set of three cards. "Five hours back. Minimum."

"Which makes it fortunate that I came at a slow time," Dr. Stober said.

"Might get a customer, though," Carlisle said. "Been known to happen."

"I'll pay for the gas, and I'll pay you by the hour," Dr. Stober said.

"Whether the car's there or not," Carlisle said, not as a question but as a contractual clarification.

"That's correct," Stober said. He wanted to say that he knew the car would be there, but it had occurred to him that if the Scottish girl and the runaway husband could steal a car, they could sell it, too. Or just keep driving it to destinations unknown.

"Alrighty then," Carlisle said, standing and leaving the cards where they lay.

100

Ansel held tight to the post in the center of the barn for the strength to keep upright. To cough as he coughed was like being made to turn himself inside out, lung by lung, and the liquid that was rising was not bile or water but blood, and more of it than he would have thought possible. But in time the bleeding stopped, and he was grateful, as he lay down on a horse blanket, that the blood was not bright red on the bedroom floor or on the sheets, like childbirth blood, because that would terrify Aldine. He would tell her what had happened later, after he had gathered strength to drive the tractor one more time to Sonia's house, for more provisions. He would tell her what they needed to do to keep her and the baby safe: separate this, separate that, he remembered. Separate forks, separate plates, separate beds.

101

Will Cooper stepped off the Santa Fe–Topeka in Emporia and wondered in which direction he should go to find his wife's sister, the one he had not saved. A porter provided directions to the police department office, where a sturdy middle-aged woman in a blue dress asked if she could help him in any way.

"I'm not sure," he said. "I've come here to look for my sister-in-law," and when he said her name was Aldine McKenna, he could tell that something serious was already known, that the name was familiar, the way her eyes flicked and she stood up and said, without smiling, "Just a minute, sir. Why don't you have a seat and I'll go have a word with the deputy."

102

Carlisle had just driven over the Loam County line and Dr. Stober was sucking on a clove-flavored Necco Wafer to keep himself awake when he saw, in the distance, a yellowish bank of clouds. They were driving straight toward it, so he guessed they'd be getting wet. Or maybe snowed upon. He didn't mind snow, especially if he was watching it from a warm quarter, could in fact be lulled by the hush of it falling. But he knew the dangers of a heavy snow, out driving in unfamiliar territory, down unmarked and unpaved roads. It was a curious color for a snow cloud, though, and the air didn't feel wet when Dr. Stober rolled down the window and stuck out a tentative hand.

"Jesus," Carlisle said. "It's one of them dust blizzards. Roll that window back up and hang on."

103

Aldine didn't see the growing bank of clouds because for once the baby had fallen asleep after nursing and she had fallen asleep, too, curled around her like the pod around a pea. She didn't wake up until Ansel stood in the bedroom at an unusual distance from the bed, his face stricken and strange, his manner odd.

"What is it?" she asked, talking low because Vivien was still asleep in her warm arms.

"I'm going now," he said.

"To Sonia's?"

"Yes."

"What's wrong? Don't you feel well?"

"A little fever's all. I'll rest when I get back."

"Maybe you shouldn't go. We still have cornmeal and coffee and syrup. You can go tomorrow."

"I think I should go now. The weather looks like it could get bad."

"Then you shouldn't go. Or you should take the car. You'd have no protection from the wind on the tractor."

"I can't drive the car until I take it back to Emporia. We decided that." His voice was strained and he sounded so tired.

"Give me a kiss then."

He didn't come any closer.

"Not even on the cheek?"

"I'd better not," he said, his voice almost a whisper. "I'll kiss you when I'm better."

"All right," she said. "When you're better. But take the car, please?"

He gave a little wave, then nodded and went down the stairs.

When she woke up again, the house was completely dark and she thought she must have slept the whole day, but then she heard the hurled grit of the wind, and when she looked out the windows, she knew what she would see. She tried to nurse Vivien in the darkness but Vivien howled; Aldine rocked and rocked her and tried to remember how long ago Ansel had left for Sonia's, and if that were long enough for him to be safe inside Sonia's house, where the walls would form a shelter against the wind.

104

Carlisle speeded up as if to get someplace before it hit. The clouds got higher and darker, and the few grasses that survived on either side of the road seemed to be trying to bury themselves. A bird swooped in front of their windshield so suddenly that Carlisle touched the brakes, and then they felt the thump of a rabbit under the wheels. Dr. Stober placed a smooth gray Necco Wafer on his tongue and checked the window again. It was tight. "Hang on," Carlisle said, and he pulled off the road and into a parking lot, where he snugged up close to the sheltered side of an abandoned building.

Like a living mountain the dust traveled toward them, and Dr. Stober was startled by the changing colors of the light within the car: pale yellow, then smoky gray, then no color at all: darkness in midafternoon, like an eclipse. The smell of the dust was overpowering and he coughed through the fingers he had instinctively used to cover his mouth and nose. It tasted like the dirt he'd eaten once when he was too small to know better, the same moldy, rusty taste and bony grit. He kept on breathing and swallowing. He took out the last handkerchief Lucy had ironed and wiped his tongue on it, and then touched its other side to his tearing eyes. He wondered calmly if he could suffocate in the car. He coughed, he cleaned his tongue, and he thought of Lucy.

It seemed longer, but by his pocket watch, it didn't last more than fifteen minutes. The blackness grayed, then browned, then turned a kind of brown-orange until the world was merely dingy. It was like opening your eyes in dirty water. He sat still in the car and waited to see what would happen. The dust remained in the air, but it was no longer buffeting the car. The wind had either died or moved on.

"You owe me extra for that," Carlisle said, pulling the car back onto the road.

Dr. Stober didn't answer, just touched his tongue to his sandpaper teeth, then wiped them with the handkerchief he found balled within his fist. This was the world we have made, he thought. Everything hammered and mortared and roofed and fenced had become as insubstantial as sand castles on dunes. When they reached Dorland a little while later, the light was still mauve. The queerest thing about the storm's aftermath was the absence of shadows; not even the buildings on the town's small Main Street could cast one.

105

The old leather belt was there, the one Ansel had used to keep himself attached to the tractor on long night rides, and Ansel considered tying himself on, but he wasn't sleepy. He could see Sonia's house in the distance: the frowsy brush of cottonwood trees, the bluish roof of the two-story house, the line of ash on the eastern side.

The house was still two hundred yards away when the storm began to take into itself the dirt through which he rode on the vibrating seat of the tractor. He had not hitched up the trailer this time, but still he could go no faster than seven, maybe eight, miles per hour. He pulled the handkerchief up over his mouth and nose, as he had always done, pushed his hat down farther on his head, and increased his speed slightly. The chugging became a whine, and he licked his lips under the handkerchief.

The wind, when it shoved him, was so fierce and skin piercing that he bent over to protect himself the way he had once protected Aldine, his arms and legs retracting into his rib cage as if remembering some primitive incarnation, when the body was part shell. He tried to take in breath, but dirt flew into his throat, and in his first coughing fit, he tipped backward and fell, striking the field with his shoulder and tumbling over. He had thought, when he climbed onto the tractor, that he would ask the doctor, when he saw him, if there was a treatment he could try. He would figure out a way to pay the man, over time, for the use of the car, and he would get through this bad time as he had gotten through others.

The tractor moved dumbly on, sightless, until it reached the road, on the other side of which was a fence erected by Horace Tanner. The nose of the tractor struck a well-buried post and chugged weakly for a while, then gave out when the front wheels of the tractor were buried several inches deep in powdery dirt.

106

It was four o'clock and the air was still orange-pink when Dr. Stober stepped out to urinate beside a tractor that had been parked haphazardly by the road. Empty houses, rusted cars, mailboxes with the doors hanging down like the tongues of dogs—he'd been seeing all these things since stepping inside the post office in Dorland and receiving directions to the Price farm. A roofless house, a pack of dogs, a wandering pig, he'd seen it all—but to just park a tractor midway into the road and leave it?

It was only when he put out his hand to steady himself and felt the warmth of the tractor's engine that it occurred to him to look in the direction from which the tractor had come. He saw a blue heap that was almost certainly human, small in the midst of the scudded soil and motionless, arm askew. He looked over at Carlisle in the driver's seat of the car, hunched over and fumbling with something, a cigarette, most likely.

Dr. Stober turned back toward the form. "Hello there!" he shouted. "Are you all right?"

The heap didn't stir.

"Hello?" he shouted again. Behind him, he heard Carlisle open the car door.

The doctor began by trotting, but the closer he came to the blue clothes and the stillness, the slower his pace. He walked the last few steps in dust that puffed up into his cuffs and shoes, and when he stood over the dead man's body he didn't know which bothered him more: that the ear canal was entirely filled with dirt, like a child's bucket, or that the soil by the man's mouth was as dark with blood as the bed in which Lucy died.

Carlisle drew up behind him, and stared down at the body. They both stood staring for a few moments. Carlisle stubbed out his cigarette and put it into his shirt pocket and said, "He's dead, in't he?"

"Yes," Dr. Stober said. "He's very dead."

107

It wasn't a long storm, not like the other one. Aldine stood up when the darkness browned bit by bit and she stood at the window with screaming Vivien, whose tiny nostrils were red from her anxious daubing. When she wiped her own nose, she expected the cloth to come away brown, but it didn't. Her nose was not dirty, and Vivien's nose was not black inside.

Aldine bobbed up and down fruitlessly, a little dance that she did when the baby cried, or when she didn't, as if a swayed baby wouldn't need to cry. She willed Ansel to drive out of the gloom. She could go out and walk to Sonia's house, she reasoned, but the air around the barn and the house was still fog-thick with dirt, and she knew Vivien shouldn't be breathing it. Look at Neva. Maybe the littlest had the weakest filters in their little pink throats.

Bobbing and humming, she tried again, desperately, to see if Vivien wanted to nurse, but the baby only tried for a few seconds, then opened her mouth to scream. "Oh," she said to her, "oh, please stop crying." She was tired of bobbing so she began to walk her, which sometimes worked, though it worked much better outside. Her breasts hurt and her arms hurt and her back hurt from holding the same weight in the same position for hours every day. Her neck hurt. She was hungry, too. She walked around the room and up the stairs, into and out of their bedroom and then into Clare's, where there was no furniture.

She kept walking but began now to jiggle the girl and sing the "Carol of the Birds." Perhaps it was the change of scene, or the song, but she stopped crying. Aldine dared not stop, circling the room, leaving footprints in the dust, and softly singing the same words, "*curoo, curoo, curoo.*" There was a folded piece of paper on the floor, the ink showing through the back like a cheap advertisement. She kicked at it once and knocked it closer to the wall. The green paint was cracked and dingy, and there was a crumbling hole in the wall with the biggest cracks, with bits of plaster dust dribbling out. She needed both arms to bobble Vivien and keep walking, but the temptation to poke at the hole made her stop, finally, after who knew how many laps or minutes, when to her relief the baby slept, and Aldine shifted her gently, oh so gently, against her chest and used one finger to probe at the hole in Clare's wall, still whispering, as if the words alone would maintain the spell, "*Curoo, curoo, curoo.*" The dust came out as she dug with her fingernail, and there was something pleasing about doing that, so she kept excavating, and then to her surprise a piece of metal tumbled out onto the floor. It was a ring or a bolt of some kind. She didn't dare to bend all the way over—that would surely wake the baby—but she eased herself down until she sat cross-legged with her back to the wall, hoping that Vivien would be too soundly asleep to notice that she was no longer moving. She almost always woke up when Aldine tried to unclasp her arms and leave the baby in the nest she'd made for her in the bed, but perhaps because she still held her, Vivien slept on.

Carefully, she reached out her hand for the ring and studied it. The gemstone had fallen out, she thought at first, but when she looked closer, she saw that what looked like scratches in a big lead-gray hole was actually the engraved signature of Tom Mix.

She slipped the ring on her index finger and listened hard for the sound of Ansel's tractor returning but she heard nothing, not even birds. She picked up the dirty piece of paper, laced at the edges by the nibbles of bugs and mice, and saw that it belonged with the ring. Above the white silhouette of a man in a cowboy hat (in other respects, the man appeared to be naked), the paper was labeled, *Tom Mix's Injuries.* All over the white silhouette were black capital letters and *X*'s, as if this were a pattern for counted cross-stitch. Then she saw that the letters corresponded to a list, which began:

> *Danger and difficulty have never daunted Tom Mix, nor broken bones stopped him. He has been blown up once, shot 12 times, and injured 47 times in movie stunting. The chart shows the location of some of Tom's injuries. (X marks fractures; circles, bullet wounds.)*

She had no photograph of Ansel and he had none of her. Why the silhouette of Tom Mix made her think of this, she didn't know. And now they had no photo of Vivien, which was worse, because her face was changing every day. But so, too, was Ansel's. So, too, probably, was hers. She looked again at the diagram in her hand. Tom Mix had certainly suffered. She would give him that. The *X* on his temple showed where his skull had been *fractured in accident.* The bullet wound where his privates would have been (these details had been omitted from the illustration) was where he'd been *shot by bad man while Oklahoma sheriff.* The letter *Y* indicated where his elbow had been *shot in real stagecoach holdup (1902).*

The note at the bottom said, *Scars from twenty-two knife wounds are not indicated, nor is it possible to show on the diagram the hole four inches square and many inches deep that was blown in Tom's back by a dynamite explosion.*

She would show this to Ansel when he got back. And the ring, too. Or maybe the ring would make him sad because it had belonged to Clare. She took the ring off and set it near her leg, and because Vivien was sleeping so peacefully, and because the injuries of Tom Mix, however fantastically exaggerated, had made their own perils seem smaller-scaled, she drifted off to sleep.

Some time later she awakened with a start. The noise downstairs, she hoped, was Ansel, but it might be the Josephsons again, so she didn't move. The noise came again and it was, she realized, someone pounding on the front door, not someone knocking his boots on the rug after opening it. Vivien woke up and began to cry.

They would hear the baby crying and this time they would not go away.

The knock came again, and then a man's voice.

"Mrs. Price?" said the deep voice. "Is that you?"

She didn't answer, just put Vivien to her breast, which the baby took this time. Aldine covered her and her front with the blanket and just sat there. The door wasn't locked. It was never locked.

"Mrs. Price?" the voice called. "It's the police."

Was it better to answer the police, or not to answer? She was numb with fear. Ansel wasn't back, or maybe he was back, and they had him. So many days had passed and they hadn't returned the car, so naturally Dr. Stober had called the police. The police had talked to Glynis. She and Ansel couldn't have been hard to find.

"Up here," she said, helplessly, her voice hoarse. She walked downstairs with Vivien clutched tightly to her.

One man wore a hat and a brown coat with a white shirt, not a farmer's sort of clothes. The other was Dr. Stober. Sick was what she felt. Sick all the way through.

"Do you know where Mrs. Price is?" the man in the suit coat asked. He held open a wallet that contained a badge, and she noticed that he was missing part of his pinkie.

Aldine didn't shake her head, and she didn't answer. She remembered that the dress she was wearing belonged to Mrs. Price. "She's in California," Aldine finally said. "Where they moved last spring."

The badge man nodded and Aldine followed his gaze around the room as he took in the greasy tractor parts and unwashed dishes on the table, the sheet-covered radio, the cat's nest in the armchair. Then he was looking again at her, in some new way now, as if she were not part of civilization, as if she had failed her time in the Practice House. He was the type with more skin than eye, great folds of it that made him look as sad as an elephant. He wasn't large, though. He weighed barely ten stone, she guessed. He didn't say his name, and she wasn't surprised. He didn't have to tell her anything.

"Do you know who this man is?" the policeman asked her, blinking his sad, wrinkled eyes and pointing at Dr. Stober, who had his hand tucked around his neck, as if he were disturbed by something.

She nodded.

"Do you know where his car is?"

She nodded again, parts of herself going cold and stiff, other parts wavy and sick. "We put it in the barn. We never drove it again after we got here. We were going to bring it back, like we said, but we had to wait for the baby to be born first. Ansel didn't want to leave me here before that in case . . ."

She spoke through the stiffening of her throat and face. "We were going to give it back."

The men didn't respond to this, only looked at each other and then back at her.

"Did ye already take him to jail then?"

"Who?" the policeman asked.

"Ansel," she said.

Dr. Stober kept his hand on his neck and looked away.

"You're going to have to go to Emporia," the sad-faced policeman said. "A relative of yours is waiting there."

"Who?"

"Man by the name of Cooper."

So Glynis had really sent the letter, and Leenie had sent Will. She kept her finger inside Vivien's fist, as if the baby could keep her from going. "But what about Ansel?"

The policeman blinked, and Dr. Stober kept his eyes averted. He felt bad, she could see that. For the first time in their acquaintance, he seemed human.

"Mr. Price got caught in the storm," the policeman said.

"Did ye take him to hospital then? Please let me go there first."

"That won't be possible," was how the policeman answered.

She thought it was because she didn't deserve it, and it seemed a long time since she'd deserved anything she wanted or received anything she deserved. "But later on?"

"I don't like to tell you this," the policeman said, and then he did tell her. She studied Vivien's ear and then said she just needed to get something upstairs, and the sad-faced policeman tramped right after her (she thought he suspected her of wanting to steal money, but later she guessed he was afraid she'd pitch herself out the window, baby and all). She didn't like to take her pinkie out of the baby's fist but she had to if she wanted the ring, which the policeman insisted on examining. He decided the ring was nothing, so she could have it. She put it on, and he handed her the paper, too, with a *suit yourself* kind of look, and then he followed her down the stairs. Dr. Stober had taken himself out of doors. He wasn't looking for his car, as she expected. He just stood with his back to the house, staring out at the horizon. Aldine found the dirty coffee cup that still lay on its side on the front porch and used it to prop open the front door so that Krazy Kat could get out. Then she settled into the backseat of the police car with her baby, who had begun crying again.

Seven years later, when she read that Tom Mix died, Aldine would fish the paper labeled *Tom Mix's Injuries* from the lining of her satchel and consider all the wounds and accidents that hadn't killed the man in light of the one that did: an afternoon of drinking in a roadhouse and then a car wreck at a washed-out bridge in the desert, doing eighty with a suitcase full of money.

108

It was ten thirty in the morning on December 9. For Charlotte, her wedding day had begun at 5:00 a.m. when she'd come into Clare's room and flipped on the lamp. Her eyes were red and her cheeks were wet. "Dad's living with Aldine, isn't he," she whispered to Clare. "He's left Mom for her and everyone knows. McNamara's going to jilt me. He won't want to be seen with the daughter of divorced adulterers."

Clare was squinting at the sudden light. "Who said he's living with Aldine?"

"Nobody. I just think it," Charlotte said, her voice thickening as she began to cry again. She pushed a handkerchief against her nose and saw her face in the mirror. "I look horrible. I look horrible and I'm going to be jilted."

Clare tried to raise his head up. "You'll look fine if you stop crying."

"It's Aldine's fault."

"McNamara doesn't know anything about it. Nobody does. Just stop crying or they'll ask what's wrong."

"I can't."

"Open the drawer there," Clare said. He laid his heavy head back down. Roosters were crowing in the Mexican camp near the packing-house, and a dog began to bark.

"Why?" Charlotte asked, not moving.

"Just open the drawer and then open the accounting book."

She went to the drawer and sniffled. She found the paper, unfolded it, and began by the lamplight to read the *Rules to Be Observed for the Prevention of the Spread of Tuberculosis.*

"Dad has it," Clare said. "Dr. Quigley told me. That's why he can't come back and we can't go there."

Charlotte kept reading, the handkerchief as small as a stone beneath her nose. When she'd finished reading, she didn't say anything. She folded the paper and put it back in the drawer.

Clare watched her compose herself around this new set of facts. He didn't tell her that their father didn't even know the result of the test. It had always been Charlotte who knew the dirty secrets, the bad stories, the things you didn't want to hear.

"I think he went there to protect us," he said.

It took Charlotte a few seconds to decide to believe it, and then she did.

"It's worse, but it's better," she said, and made a small unhappy smile. "I hate myself for saying it." She stood up and touched his hand, swaying slightly in her robe. She was big and soft in her curly hair and robe, and she seemed ready now to go ahead with this strange new part of her life. "I'll let you try to go back to sleep," she said.

He didn't sleep, though. He looked up at the ceiling and thought of Aldine's voice, the way it sounded and the way her mouth looked when she sang to Neva. He thought of her lying that night under the suit quilt in her nightclothes. Charlotte had turned off the lamp in his room, but not in the hall, so the edges of the dresser and the bed and his own feet stayed visible. He was awake when the sun rose and awake when Neva knocked on the door and brought in Opa Hoffman carrying a little paper box.

"Your little town has a doughnut shop," Opa Hoffman said. The old man liked him, Clare could tell. He'd been in the night before and after two seconds of looking at him had said, "You have the Hoffman eyes," and then when he asked about his scores at school, he said, "Yes. And the Hoffman brain."

Well, he was happy to eat a doughnut with the old man, if that's all it took to make him happy, but it wasn't long before his mother was there, ushering his grandfather out, beginning what she called the ablutions. He hated them, the embarrassing maneuvers, the washing Clare tried to do under the sheet. Neither of them spoke as they went about it all, his mother rushing because of the wedding, and he could hear Ida closing drawers and shuffling things next door. He could hear Ida telling Neva, patiently first and then crossly, to stop moving her head so much.

A while later, Neva stomped her way into the room, hair lacquered, chin jutting, eyes furious, red taffeta swishing. Behind her, Ida carried a red velvet headband wound with a small artificial poinsettia. "It pinches!" Neva said.

"It won't now," Ida said. "I wrapped the wire a little more."

"It *will*," Neva said.

"You look smashing," Clare said to Neva, who had given him a desperate look, as if he could tell the women to let Neva go bareheaded.

"I know! I'll hold your headband until we get to the church," Ida said in her happy-soldier voice, dropping the headband into her giant pocketbook. "And you can put it on right before you go up the aisle." Ida was dressed in taffeta, too, but hers was a pale green suit that she wore on all special occasions. She wore enormous pearly beads and pearly clip-on earrings and around her ringed hands pearly bracelets dripped. A green feather pointed out of her small green velvet hat, upon which perched a small black-and-green bird.

"We're going to be late," Charlotte said, striding into the now crowded room like a giant Easter lily in heels, one hand fluttering to her own headband, which was attached to a veil and threatened a backward slide. Her eyes filled with tears when she saw Clare, and she remembered a nickname from long ago, one he hated as much as she hated Lottie: "Oh, Dipsy. I'm sorry you can't be there."

"It's all right," Clare said. "Vinnie's coming with a new game her cousins sent from England. And chocolates. She said that specifically." The puffiness of crying was not quite gone from her face. "You look kind of ravishing," he said.

"Thank you, kind of," Charlotte said.

"Will you save me some of the chocolates?" Neva asked.

"Sure," Clare said.

He could hear his mother calling out to Hurd, and then coming up the stairs, and then each ornately dressed and perfumed woman was kissing him and adjusting some aspect of his bed. His mother's face looked tight. He figured this was because of his father not coming back, or maybe her own father arriving, or maybe both. She was wearing the pearls Opa had given her for Christmas and when Clare said they looked nice, she said, "They do, don't they?" She smiled and lowered her voice. "He asked me to wear them. I think he was afraid I'd pawned them or something." The whole party was clattering down the stairs when Neva ran back to give him a kiss on each ear, and then an Eskimo kiss, and then a kiss on his chin, which she called an Australian, as if each position on the face had a corresponding continent. "Bye," she said gravely. "Is Vinnie your girlfriend?"

He gave her an Australian and added a Polar, right on the crown of her wet-combed hair. "Vinnie?" he said. For a while now Lavinia had been visiting every day after school. He was grateful to her, and he thought she was probably the smartest girl he'd ever met, aside from Miss Warren, the Latin teacher. She'd gotten a new haircut, short and angular, so that she looked like a moll in a comic book, which sometimes he liked and sometimes he didn't. He felt a tug of something toward her, a need, maybe. He didn't know what it was. "No," Clare said.

"Marchie says she's your sweetheart," Neva said.

"Well, Marchie's wrong," Clare said.

It was then that Clare became aware of someone outside the open door to his room. "Neva," Lavinia said, poking her head in, "your mother told me to tell you they're all stifling in the car, and that your sister is going to have ten thousand kittens if you don't hurry."

Clare was pretty sure Lavinia had interjected the kittens part, but she didn't look saucy and amused. Her face was flushed and stricken, and he knew that she must have overheard.

"Okay, Neva," Clare said. "You'd better clear out. Wear the head-band for me, okay? And tell me all the good parts when you get back."

"I have a surprise," Neva said. "Wait'll you hear about that!"

Clare gave her his sternest look. "Don't do any surprises," he said. "Weddings aren't a good time for surprises."

"Bye-da-lie!" she called, which he was supposed to answer with "Bye-da-loo," but he was worried about the surprise and the strange way that Lavinia was now staring out the window at the baking-hot empty street.

When everyone else was gone, the hotel was suddenly quiet, but Lavinia said nothing. Her straight black hair gleamed where it came to a point beside her chin. She had applied fresh lipstick and he was pretty sure he'd never seen the dress before. It was red with white dots, and the collar came down over her breasts in folds of silky cloth that revealed a snowy triangle between her breasts. Normally, she wore long sleeves and high collars and heavy black skirts. He looked to see if she wore silk stockings and was surprised to see that she did. He wondered how much of this his mother had noticed.

"How do I look without the pulley?" he tried.

"Jake," she said, glancing without interest at his leg.

"I'm not supposed to stand up yet, though. The doctor wants me to do exercises in bed first." He intended this to be off-color because sometimes Lavinia was the kind of girl you could joke with, but she remained silent now, which depressed and annoyed him. He needed her to be encouraging. He had expected her to make a big fuss about it, to see the de-casting as a triumphant beginning to his triumphant recovery. She'd been saying all along that he'd walk across the stage on graduation day and give the valediction.

"That the new game?" he asked.

She had set the long rectangular box she was carrying on the chair. It said *Sorry!* in pink letters on the side. "Uh-huh."

"Can I see it?"

She handed it to him without comment.

"I see your motives now," he said, trying for a flirtatious tone. "It's a '*fast-paced game of pursuit.*'"

She shrugged and he saw that she was holding back tears.

"How about we play it then?" he said softly. "I feel pretty sorry already."

Lavinia didn't answer.

"Ah, come on, Vinnie," he said in a coaxing voice. He felt different. The tugging feeling was much stronger now that she was pulling away from him.

She sat down on the steamer trunk and looked out the window.

"Is that a new dress?"

She didn't say. She went on looking out the window and then she said, "I think it's time I stopped visiting."

"Why?"

"You know why."

"No, I don't."

"Well, I can't tell you then."

In the new, revealing clothes, Lavinia looked older and more sophisticated.

"You're all dressed up," Clare said truthfully. "You look pretty."

Lavinia glanced at him with what might have been gratitude, then looked back at the window, through which there was nothing to see, he thought, though in fact Bart Crandall was already limping toward the El Real with a night letter in his hand.

"Stockings, even," Clare said.

"Gift from the English cousins," Lavinia said. "The dress, too. They're kind of rich."

Clare was quiet for a moment, thinking about the procession that was about to happen at the church, with Hurd instead of their father taking Charlotte's arm. At the thought of his father he felt an icy panic, as if they were all moving forward in an ocean liner from which, in the darkness, their father had fallen, and if they didn't go back now, it would be too late. But he wasn't the person who could turn the ship around. He didn't even know if it could be turned. He sang softly to Lavinia:

> *"Bryan O'Linn had no stockings to wear,*
> *He bought him a rat's skin to make him a pair,*
> *He then drew them on and they fitted his shin,*
> *'Whoo, they're illegant wear,' says Bryan O'Linn."*

Lavinia looked down at her hands while he sang. Then she turned to him. Her eyes were black and large and her face was pale. "What's that?" she asked.

"Just a song I learned a long time ago."

"Do you know the rest?"

"Bits and pieces."

"Let's hear it," she said.

"No," he said. "Not if you're going to stay way over there and be mad at me." He felt such an insistent tugging now. He had to bring her back toward him, within reach.

Lavinia smiled a little and remained sitting with her knees together and her feet pointing inward. Her fingers were laced together and clenched on her knees. He could tell that she wanted to come closer, but in all their afternoon visits she had never done more than sit in a chair that touched the side of the bed. He had only once held her hand.

"Please sit beside me," Clare whispered. "We won't be wicked. We'll just be together."

Lavinia stood up uncertainly. She wasn't mad anymore, he could tell. "Well, how many verses are there?" she asked, smiling enough so that he could see she was forgiving him a little.

"Lots," he whispered. "At least eight."

She looked over at the bedroom door, which was still open, though of course the whole building was empty now, empty as a dead tree, and then she came over to the bed and eased herself onto the side of it. She kept her shoes on at first, then let them drop. She put her two feet up on the bed beside his, though she was on the outside of the blankets and he was inside. She stuck a pillow behind her back and head. "Well?" she asked.

"Should I start at the beginning?" he asked. He reached over for her hand and when he touched it, he felt her tremble. His own skin tingled at the contact, and he let each of his fingers find a place between each of hers. He wasn't sure that he could sing now. He cleared his throat and sang,

> *"Bryan O'Linn was a gentleman born*
> *He lived at a time when no clothes they were worn"*

He paused, hearing it differently now that Lavinia was so achingly close to him, now that what he wanted to do was stroke her naked arm. The tune still reminded him of Aldine but she felt far away, like an island that he could see but never reach.

"What a wicked song," Lavinia murmured.

"Wait'll you hear the part about the breeches," Clare said. It would shame him, later, to think of what he was doing the whole time his father was dead and he didn't know it. It would seem to Clare that he should have known, somehow, and in his memory, the courting of Lavinia took on a lurid cast that it shouldn't have had: he took his left hand and brought it across his body to her arm.

He ran his finger up the middle of her wrist to her elbow and she trembled. He was mostly upright in the bed, leaning on a mashed stack of pillows, and the silky folds of her dress touched his good leg. "Lavinia," he whispered and he was surprised at the beauty of her name when whispered like that. "Lavinia." When he turned his face toward her, she was close enough to kiss, and he stared into her eyes for what seemed a long time. She looked broken, in a way, as if his singing had done that to her. He kissed her once, then more and more, tenderly and hungrily by turns, gently tasting her jaw, cheeks, and ear, his hand in her sleek straight hair and on her neck. He couldn't twist on his hips to place himself closer to her, so he brought her toward him, and she shifted on the bed so that she leaned into him. The tugging in his chest was unrelenting, and it was entwined with his terror that he would be a cripple forever, that the most he could hope for was to move from the bed into a chair like the wheeled ones in Dr. Quigley's medical catalogues. Dr. Quigley was satisfied that the bones had grabbed on to one another again, that's what he said, but he wasn't sure if Clare should test the calcified joins with his weight, or risk snapping them in a fall. In a few weeks, maybe, Quigley had said. Clare shifted his weight, felt no warning pain, and kissed Lavinia as if she were the source of a potion that would transform him.

They didn't hear Bart Crandall outside the café door. They didn't see him reach out to open the glass door of the café, his face coated with sweat, his body tight with the importance of the cable he held, news that would spread from his hand like red wine on linen. With his hand on the knob he read the sign Ellie had written hastily before leaving:

Closed for family wedding. Open again Monday, Dec. 11.
Have a good day.

He stood in the sunlight and thought about which was worse: to leave a night letter in a place where nobody was, or to show up at a wedding with this news.

Regret to inform Ansel Price killed dust storm stop

Send instruct re burial to Emporia PD stop

Bart Crandall tucked the night letter in his pocket and stepped away from the glass door. He stared up Alvarado Street at the white wooden spire where the Price girl was getting married. The worst part was that his wife, Florrie, was looking forward to the reception. Maybe he'd just tell her to keep mum and he'd walk over at the end of the party and hand the letter to Mrs. Price. The date and time would be printed on there, but Ellie would understand, wouldn't she? Maybe she would even appreciate his conscientious delay?

"I'm afraid I'll bump your leg," Lavinia whispered, still letting Clare kiss her, still letting her hands do what his hands were doing, caressing his back, his neck, and face.

"It doesn't hurt," he whispered. His skin wanted only for the hunger to overtake him and lift him away from his legs and the painful clutch of the bed, the sheets, the pillows, and the unending sameness of the red wallpaper. The uneasiness was the question of whether he loved Lavinia, but later it felt like the foreknowledge of his father's death and the moment when Neva walked up the aisle of the church wearing not the red velvet headband (which she slipped off while Ida was fussing with her own hat) but a hand-knit cream-colored beret, about which a sobbing Neva would only say afterward, when Charlotte asked furiously what possessed her, that she just thought it would be nice to wear it in case Miss McKenna showed up.

He got it all much later: the story of the beret, the lingering of Bart Crandall at the door of the Practice House, so slow in leaving and so glum in the face that finally his mother walked over and asked if Florrie would like to take one of the centerpieces home, and that was when Bart took the cable out of his pocket and handed it over, "his eyes all teary," said Ida, who was standing nearby.

109

Aldine couldn't decide if she was glad or sorry about the deception everyone in Emporia, including Sonia Odekirk, agreed to practice: that the Price family would never be told about the baby or Aldine's presence in the house when he died. They knew Ansel died on the tractor, in a field, of a natural disaster. He was alone. He had tuberculosis. Nothing about these circumstances required her to be mentioned. She couldn't argue with it, really, as a means of causing less pain. But when Dr. Stober prepared a birth certificate for Vivien, he listed the father as Unknown. They buried Ansel in Kansas to bury the tuberculosis, and they wouldn't let her and Vivien leave until they were tested. For two weeks, they waited. The doctor thought she would surely have it, but she didn't.

After the train ride with Will, to whom she said nothing for hours and hours, she was kindly received in the Sugar House 4th Ward of the Church of Jesus Christ of Latter-day Saints (which met in a church made of solid pink stone) as the widowed sister of Leenie Cooper, a view they held of her without asking. She took her baby to church, as Leenie did, and the young girls of the ward liked to hold Vivien during the meetings. She took her baby to the park, as Leenie did, and watched her crawl on dry swards of grass.

It was the following August that Will drove them all to the Great Salt Lake, and she stood in the photo that was the last thing they sent to Aunt Sedgewick before she died, a photo in which you could not see the tin ring she wore on her index finger, inscribed with the name of Tom Mix, or smell the water ten times as dense with killing salt as the ocean. She stood by the water but she didn't wade into it. She did something she now did habitually. She smelled Vivien's soft, dry hair and neck. She wondered if someday her daughter would do as Leenie and Will did, like all the other Saints, and stand in the stone-white fountain in the stone-gray temple at the center of the wide, wide streets of Salt Lake City, and be baptized for the numberless dead, her head dipped back, her face full of hope. You could never tell who would be a believer, and who wouldn't. When Dr. O'Malley's will had finally been settled, bequeathing to Aldine a small amount of money, she'd sent it to Dr. Stober as compensation for his trouble, but he returned the bank check with a note saying he believed she'd paid quite enough already. He wished her Godspeed. He signed it *Sincerely*.

EPILOGUE

Fallbrook, California, 1957

Clare Price, the druggist, likes to eat at the counter of his sister's café. His legs, one of them lame, can slide into its shadows while his smooth-shaven face, trim haircut, and robust arms (at forty, he can still walk on his hands) absorb what little attention might come his way. He's eating what his sister calls the divorced man's dinner—French apple pie topped with Tillamook cheese—while he combs the back pages of the *Los Angeles Times* sports section in search of a score for the KU-Oklahoma basketball game. Things are looking up for the Jayhawks. They have a kid named Chamberlain.

Torkelsen had been sitting at the counter when Clare came in, but this is late afternoon, when people come to the café more for retreat than society, so he'd kept three stools between him and Torkelsen, the better to spread out his paper.

His sister Geneva, passing by with plates spread along each arm, says, "Another day in paradise."

She means this to be wry but he can't help saying: "It *is*, in its own way, isn't it?" Sometimes wanting to believe a sentiment like that was the best you could do, and was, besides, about the only thing standing between you and real gloom.

"You just missed your old flame," Torkelsen says.

This was not news. Geneva had telephoned the drugstore to warn Clare that Lavinia and one of her girls were at the café, and had called again when they left. "Coast is clear," she said, and hung up.

"So I heard," Clare says.

"That oldest girl of hers is going to law school," Torkelsen says.

Clare thinks of saying he'd heard that, too, but instead just murmurs and keeps to the paper. He's found the scoring line. KU by 20. Chamberlain with 41. 19 rebounds.

But Lavinia. Her girl going to Boalt School of Law and here to throw the news around, as if to say, *Look how well I've done without you*. It isn't the girl's success that's a disappointment to Clare. The truth is, he's less unhappy living alone, going about his routines, filling prescriptions, exchanging everyday pleasantries with everyday faces, watching *Jackie Gleason* and *Gunsmoke* on Saturday night.

He takes from the pocket of his shirt a ballpoint pen and a business card. On its back, he keeps Wilt's running totals in minute figures. With 41 points yesterday, that's—he does the math in his head—536 on the season. 339 rebounds. Clare is bent over the card entering these updated totals when the bell over the door jangles.

A young woman carrying a satchel has stepped in. Somebody lost on her way to somewhere else, Clare supposes, which might explain her off-balance manner, that and the fact that he, Torkelsen, and the other few customers are all staring at her. But she isn't lost. She says she's looking for Geneva Price.

"Come to the right place," Clare says, smiling.

The girl might be twenty or a little older—it's hard to tell, because she has dark hair coiled up severely and she's wearing a skirt and jacket like this is a business stop or she's looking for a job she fears she won't get. She's leaning awkwardly on one high heel when she says, "I understand her parents came out from Oklahoma during the dirty thirties."

Geneva has emerged, wiping her hands on a dish towel. "Kansas," she says. "Our parents came from Kansas." She glances at Clare. "That galoot is my big brother, Clare."

He gives a confirming nod. "Both our parents came out, but only our mother stayed."

The girl doesn't move. She says she's doing her dissertation on the economic effects of families migrating to California from the Plains states during the 1930s.

Clare grins past the girl toward Torkelsen and says, "That's a mouthful."

"I guess it is," the girl says, her face turning pink, and Clare feels a little ashamed of himself for making sport. "Anyway," she says, "that's why I'm here. I'd like to interview you and your sister, if I could. Your mother, too, if she's alive."

"Parents are both gone," Clare says.

The girl opens her satchel, and pulls out a narrow notebook with top spiral binding. Paper-clipped to the cover is a business card she hands to Clare. It says simply *Vivien Simmons, Teaching Asst., University of California, Los Angeles*. She must be older than twenty. She wears a wedding ring as small and modest as the one he gave Lavinia long ago.

The card goes from Clare to Geneva then back to the girl, who slides it again under the clip. She's a pretty girl, but that isn't it. She seems familiar in a way he can't put his finger on.

"Sure," Geneva says, "we can talk to you. Probably not right now, but maybe tonight—would that work?"

This is her normal laconic voice but Clare sees eagerness in her expression, which is both a surprise and an amusement. His sister is flattered by the prospect of being interviewed.

"Tonight around seven then?" the girl says, writing it down.

A car Clare has never seen before is parked in the palm shade across the street, a green DeSoto, '48 or '49. A woman sits on the passenger side wearing dark glasses and a sun hat tied down with a scarf. "That's a nice DeSoto," he says nodding toward the car. "That what you're driving?"

The girl acknowledges that it is.

"Forty-eight or forty-nine?"

"Forty-eight."

"It's got that *fluid drive*," Clare says, and the girl cracks a smile and says, "That's right. Fluid drive."

She's even prettier when she smiles, and even more familiar. "That a friend waiting for you there in the car?"

"My mother," the girl says. "She likes to ride along, but she doesn't like to come in."

Geneva asks if she'd like to take her out a Coke or a glass of iced water, but the girl says no.

"And photographs," the girl says, as if just remembering. "If you have any photographs of you and your parents . . ."

"Sure we do," Geneva says. "We have an album. You can't take them with you, but you can look at them. Our sister, Charlotte, took lots of pictures."

"Is she nearby?" the girl asks. "Maybe I could interview her, too?"

Clare and his sister exchange grins. "You might," Geneva says, "but Charlotte moved to La Jolla and keeps a pretty full dance card."

Clare says, "If you do go see her, we'll send along a picture so she'll remember what we look like."

This strikes the girl as funny, or maybe she just needs the relief of a laugh. A pleasant laugh, though. One he bets her husband likes.

She asks how she could see the album, and Geneva, peaches and cream, says it's right upstairs. Would Clare mind running up and getting it?

He slides from his stool. It's funny how mindful of his walk he suddenly is, crossing the linoleum floor. Everyone in town is used to the way his right leg swings out in a little arc, so he rarely gives it a thought, but now he feels the girl's eyes on him, taking it in. *Top-heavy.* Once, when they were out with another couple, a girlfriend in a laughing voice had called him top-heavy and then when she'd seen his fallen look, she added, "You know that's a compliment, don't you?" but he knew it wasn't. Stubby legs, one of them bad, and then the shoulders that compensated, the torso he was careful and some would say vain about. He's glad to go through the back door, close it behind him, and mount the stairs.

Clare finds the old leather album where it always is, in Geneva's living room on top of the TV console, and he carries it back down the staircase.

What happens next is disorienting. The girl has seated herself at the counter, and when Clare draws close and lays the album in front of her, he takes in a scent that makes him feel almost dizzy. It isn't perfume or shampoo, he's sure of that. It's the smell of her hair or skin. He leans back on the nearest stool to steady himself. He stares at her, but she seems not to notice. She sits perfectly still, staring down at the album, at the green coarse-grained leather cover, edged in gold, the word *Photographs* embossed diagonally above a silhouette of an Indian paddling a birch-skin canoe.

Geneva has marked all the photographs in her delicate hand. *The home place. Favorite layer Goosey. Our old tree house. Mom (Eleanor Hoffman Price) at Fair. Geneva & Clare, Spelling Bee. Ferris Wheel, Hutchinson.* The girl turns through these, and then, at the next page, she stiffens, and slowly leans forward. *Dad (Ansel Price) on the home place. Dad at packing plant. Dad when he was a cook at the Harvey House.* The largest photograph is of his father laughing about something in front of a pen of pigs. *A man & his pigs,* Geneva has written. The girl leans closer still and—this gives Clare a turn—runs her finger slowly around his father's face. It's like a blind person reading braille.

Clare touches the girl's arm and she jerks her hand away from the photograph. She looks at Clare, and her eyes are moist. She says, "I'm sorry. I'd better go."

"Who are you?" Clare whispers and when the girl starts to give the name she'd given before, he stops her and says, "No, who are you really?" and even before he's finished the question, he knows its answer. He gets up and walks out the door of the café and crosses the street to the green DeSoto parked in the shade of the palm with the woman waiting inside. He doesn't care how he walks. He doesn't care how he looks. He needs to hear the woman speak.

She watches him pass in front of the car but she doesn't turn to him when he comes to the door window.

"Hello?" he says to her.

For a moment she continues staring forward; then she turns her face to his. "Hello, Clarence."

He hears it as he'd always heard it. *Clay-dance.*

Later she would tell him that the first thing she thought was, *What a dead handsome man our Clare has become.*

He opens the door. He puts out his hand. When he feels her touch, it seems to go a long way into him and a long way back. *Seizeth. Breatheth.* He doesn't think these words exactly. He doesn't hear them. They have come as images, as he has seen them written. He opens his eyes. "Come inside," he says. "Neva will want to see you. You should come inside."

ACKNOWLEDGMENTS

I am humbly in debt to the following people: my husband, Tom, whose loyalty, encouragement, and love have given me everything I have ever wanted, including the time and means to write this book. The friends who had unwavering faith in this story, including Janet Reich Elsbach, Sorayya Khan, Lily King, and Jane Morris. My undaunted agent, Emily Forland, my insightful editor, Carmen Johnson, and my compassionately ruthless copyeditor, Rebecca Jaynes.

I could not have imagined these places or characters without the Fallbrook Historical Society; the Kansas Historical Society; Linda and Mike Kesselring of the High Plains Homestead near Crawford, Nebraska; my mother-in-law Barbara Hall McNeal Myers; and those who have kept Harvey Houses alive (or brought them back to life) throughout the western United States. Many texts provided historical details and inspiration, including the *Texas State Journal of Medicine*, *Annals of Surgery*; and the *Indianapolis Medical Journal*, *The White Death: A History of Tuberculosis* by Thomas Dormandy; *In the Shadow of the White Plague* by Elizabeth Mooney; *The Plague and I* by Betty MacDonald; *Living in the Shadow of Death: Tuberculosis and the Social Experience of Illness in American History* by Sheila M. Rothman; *Hard*

Times: An Oral History of the Great Depression by Studs Terkel; *Wage-Earning Women: Industrial Work and Family Life in the United States, 1900–1930* by Leslie Woodcock Tentler; *The Harvey Girls* by Lesley Poling-Kempes; *The Harvey House Cookbook* by George H. Foster and Peter C. Weiglin; *Model Ts, Pep Chapels, and a Wolf at the Door: Kansas Teenagers, 1900–1941*, edited by Marilyn Irvin Holt; *Farming the Dust Bowl: A First-Hand Account from Kansas* by Lawrence Svobida; and *Spatzies and Brass BBs: Life in a One-Room Country School* by Dr. Ken Ohm.

Lastly, I would like to remember the late Doris and Jack Reeder, who paid my rent every month in graduate school; my mother and my late father, who paid for my education and loved me uncritically; and the many Mormons who, like them, protected and inspired me with their faith when I was growing up.

ABOUT THE AUTHOR

Photo © Kel Casey

Laura Rhoton McNeal holds an MA in fiction writing from Syracuse University and is the author, with her husband, Tom, of four critically acclaimed young adult novels, including *Crooked* (winner of the California Book Award in Juvenile Literature) and *Zipped* (winner of the Pen Center USA Literary Award in Children's and Young Adult Literature). Laura's solo debut novel, *Dark Water*, was a finalist for the National Book Award. She lives with her family in Coronado, California.